UNCHARTED WATERS

ORCA COVE SERIES BOOK TWO

JEN FLANAGAN

SERENITY ENDEAVORS PRESS

Uncharted Waters

Copyright © 2024 by Jen Flanagan

First Edition: June 2024

This edition was first published in 2024.

Cover design: Haley Tenney

Editor: Monica Bogza

ISBN: 978-1-961501-03-4 (eBook)

ISBN: 978-1-961501-02-7 (Paperback)

Published by: Serenity Endeavors Press

jenflanaganbooks.com

Contents

Acknowledgements

If I hadn't found the love I have with my husband, this book would never have been possible. Thank you to my husband and my sister. You two have always and will always be my biggest fans.

My support group has grown! Thanks to all of you on Flanagan Fanatics! Your support has been the thing that keeps me going some days! You're the reason I write.

To my readers, thanks for joining me on this journey. I hope you're enjoying Orca Cove as much as I've enjoyed writing it. It is literally so much fun. I wrote the ending of this one, planning to take a break only to wake up the next morning itching to dig into book three! What a fun group of friends.

CHAPTER 1

"Whadya say?" The fisherman scratched his balding head, weathered brown from decades of sun and wind. He pulled a handkerchief from his back pocket, wiped his nose, and then returned it. Its worn, dark blue ends stuck out and waved in the crisp morning air. "It's a fair price."

Emiliano shrugged, his eyes scanning the geoducks stacked in two old milk crates. It was a large haul, white ones, no less. They were the tastiest. Tourists were starting to make their way to their little cove off the Hood Canal due to the warming spring and the fact that it was Friday. He'd probably sell them all by dinner.

But they were overpriced.

He checked the time. Seven fifteen a.m. "Throw in the bucket of oysters, and you've got a deal."

The older man's eyes squinted, elongating the crow's feet at his eyes with the motion. He leaned back on his heels, his fists firmly set on his narrow waist. "How do you know I have oysters?"

"Come on, Solomon. You've always got oysters. Let's get on with it." It was an old game. They would go back and forth before Solomon would offer up oysters or mussels, but it was getting late. He had to get the rest of the fish he'd purchased iced and ready for the day's sale. Especially if he was going to stop over at the café first. He ran a hand over his dark, closely cropped, wavy hair, feeling his heartbeat quicken in anticipation.

Solomon huffed. "You're in a mood today. I was going to give the oysters to Roy. Had to help me fight off the harbor seals for the geoducks, you know? He's earned a few."

Roy, he'd come to find out, was the fisherman's pet pelican. Emiliano bit back the sigh on his lips. He was being a jerk. It was just nerves; he should get over it. "How about this? I'll split the oysters with Roy for his service, and tomorrow morning, you give me first dibs on your haul."

Solomon narrowed his eyes. "I always give you first dibs."

"No, you don't."

"Yeah, I do. I don't go up the canal until after I stop here. Same's every morning."

Emiliano tilted his head. "I've seen you give that pelican the biggest, brightest fish in your net."

"Aw." He kicked at a pebble that had made its way onto the dock. "Roy's my partner. I've gotta give him his fair share."

He almost felt bad for the guy...but it was an animal. He'd seen the ungainly bird pick up old, discarded burritos in the park. It would eat anything resembling food, and unfortunately, the uptick in tourists left out quite a bit. "I bet you can set aside another large fish for him. But I get the biggest."

"Whatever the catch is?"

He nodded.

The fisherman leaned in conspiratorially. "I'll stash a few in the hold so he doesn't see them."

"Works for me." He didn't care about the fish, but he had to give him an out for the light bucket of oysters, or else the other fisherfolk would start shorting him on their hauls.

A pelican landed on a post a few yards down the dock and let out a hiss. Solomon jumped, his eyes wide, then let out a cackle of laughter. He slapped his knee. "You drive a hard bargain, Mr. Gil. It's a deal. I'll be back with your o ysters."

Turning, he made his way down the dock to his boat, his knees jutting out as he walked down the pier. He whistled, and the pelican flew after him. "Come on, Roy. You can pick out your half. Don't you worry. No, sir. He's not taking your fish."

Shaking his head, Emiliano hefted the containers of giant clams and headed through the back doors of Gil's Market and Marina. It was his dad's business and their second home, but he'd helped run it for as long as he could remember; a little boy standing on a stool to man the cash register. He'd been barely strong enough to press the lever on the old drawer. That feeling of pride, helping his pop with the store, was one of two things he knew with complete clarity.

This is what he was meant to do, provide for the townspeople of Orca Cove.

"Do you want me to set these out?" Tommy, one of their newest hires and the youngest on the crew, met him near the fish market. His apron was still clean, with no tears in the fabric, his name freshly embroidered in bright blue lettering.

"Not yet." Emiliano set the crate down and pushed it under the counter. "Nell's been wanting geoducks for her menu. I'm going to see how many she wants first. Throw some ice on them, though."

Tommy nodded, disappearing.

Wiping his hands on his own worn apron, Emiliano's eyes flashed to The Wild Café across the picnic area separating their businesses. He paused, lifting his hands, and headed to the bathroom.

What had he been thinking? He'd been handling fish all morning. No way was he showing up with fish scales and muck on them. Using the brush that sat in a wire basket on the counter, he scrubbed his nails. Rinsing them, he blew out the breath he'd been holding, letting the stainless-steel rim take his weight.

He looked in the mirror, searching his dark-brown eyes for the courage to say what he wanted to say.

Was it too soon? What would she think? His brow drew together in worry.

It was her birthday, and she'd probably be in a good mood. The fact gave him courage because it was another thing he knew without a doubt. He'd been in love with Nell Fitzgibbons since he could remember.

Humming, Nell swayed happily as she stirred a large stainless-steel bowl in her commercial kitchen at The Wild Café. The food was prepped for the day, and she had enough time to make a batch of cookies. She would put them on the dessert menu, and they'd sell well to the brunch crowd, but they were really for later, after the dinner crowd left and she opened the back deck for her f riends.

Her friends.

They were still in a strange place. Nearly inseparable, the six of them used to share everything, but things had changed when they'd lost one person and gained another. It still hurt.

Things were starting to feel more like old times, but in some ways, they would never be the same. Maybe they were finding a new normal. Either way, it was complicated, and this wasn't how she'd imagined spending the day.

And to top it off, she was worried about a customer who'd fallen ill after last night's meal. She'd always been fastidious about cleanliness, but now even more so. She'd scrubbed everything down in the kitchen with bleach, just in case.

It was all weighing on her mind, but she was trying to make the best of it. It was her birthday, after all, and cookies were hands down her favorite dessert. She'd made them just for herself.

Cake was fine, but it was fussy and not worth the extra effort today. *Flavor*, however, was *always* worth the time.

Flowers.

Her mind pinged through things yet to be done for the night's celebration, carefully avoiding anything business-related. Bills, marketing, and general office work had no place on a day like today.

She barely knew what she was doing in that realm, anyway. It made her feel lacking. No, she didn't need any more of that. Not today.

She'd ask Willa if she could gather some wild rhododendrons for the night's festivities. Her herbalist friend would be happy to wander the woods to find some. Maggie, her best waitress and friend, could put them in milk jugs for the table. Simple and pretty.

Her mind drifted to ingredients, eyes unfocusing as she created the recipe in her head. Black sesame paste. Setting her bowl down, she retrieved a jar from the cooler. After giving the bowl a playful spin, she drizzled the paste into the dough, watching it draw a spiral out from the center. Heat blossomed in her hand. It had been doing that. It was probably nerve damage from an old burn acting up. She'd certainly earned enough of them over the years.

"Are you playing with your food?"

Nell squealed, jumping in the air, and the bowl tipped, whirling haphazardly in wide circles. She fumbled the jar, finally catching it between both hands, but the dark paste spilled onto her fingers. A strong arm reached around her to steady the bowl, and a low chuckle rumbled within his chest.

"Emiliano! You scared the bejeezus out of me." She sat the jar down and wiped her hands on a nearby towel.

"Sorry, I didn't mean to startle you. You were zoned out." His eyes crinkled at the corners in amusement. "Again."

"I was tasting through the flavors." She lifted her shoulders as though that explained it all.

"In your head?"

She nodded, then stopped, realizing how it sounded. "That's weird, isn't it?"

"Not at all." His head gave a sharp shake. "That's what makes you an amazing chef. We're lucky to have you in town. You bring in half our returning tourists."

"Aw, thanks, Emiliano." The sentiment seeped into her heart, warming it. "Although it's most likely the weather, the view, the amenities, and possibly even the o rcas."

Visitors had the unusual perk of viewing the graceful marine animals in their little cove off the fjord nearly year-round. It added a little magic to the air.

Then again, it wasn't the only thing that did.

"Oh, them, they're just an attraction. You're the main course."

A laugh bubbled up and out of her unexpectedly. She lifted a hand to cover it. The younger man wasn't typically this playful. And she'd known him since he was a toddler.

"You know it." She smirked and did a little jazzy wiggle, playing along. "Eat your heart out, Jamie Oliver."

He leaned against the countertop in a relaxed pose, watching her.

"What brings you in this morning?" she went on, wiping up the spilled paste.

"Just got a crate of white geoducks. Want any?"

The perfect addition to her birthday meal. Her eyes opened wide. "I love geoducks."

"I remember. How many do you want?"

"I'll take ten to twelve. The weather is bringing in the tourists. I'll throw them on the menu tonight." She'd leave some as sashimi; the rest would be sautéed and added to a pasta dish with fresh chanterelles.

"You got it."

"Just give me a little while to finish up here, figure out what else I'll need, and I'll be over to pick them up."

Even though she had regular deliveries from Seattle, most of her local produce and meats were from Gil's Market and Marina.

He nodded, then pointed to the bowl. "What is it?"

"Cookies." She lifted her head proudly.

"Birthday cookies?"

She nodded. "How'd you know it was my birthday?"

"Good memory." He tapped his temple. "What's in them? No way they're just regular ol' chocolate."

"It's not chocolate at all; it's rye flour. Half rye, half wheat."

"No chocolate?" His eyebrows went up. "No way."

"Well, of course, there's going to be chocolate." She rolled her eyes. "I'm adding dark-chocolate chunks later."

"What's that?" He reached out a finger towards the spilled paste. "It looks like chocolate sauce."

"Black sesame paste. I'll sprinkle on black sesame seeds just before I bake them."

"That sounds interesting." Reaching out, he took a tasting spoon from the container on her counter and hovered over the bowl. "May I?"

She nodded.

After running the tip through the dough and unmixed black paste, Emiliano lifted it to his mouth and closed his lips over it. His eyes closed as well, his unfairly long eyelashes lying against his perfect skin, and his brows drew together in thought.

Nell knew exactly what it would taste like. It would be rich from the eggs and butter, the rye would impart a spicy, earthy note, and the black tahini paste would pack a mellow, nutty punch with an exotic element. She could see his mouth working over the food, tasting all the ingredients with fervor.

Without meaning to, she leaned forward as though a magnet was pulling her towards the man so fully appreciating her cooking. A stirring she hadn't felt in a while bloomed within her.

That was new.

She hadn't noticed how close he was until that moment, and heat spread across her cheeks.

"That's delicious," he said, opening his eyes wide with admiration.

Nell's gaze met his, ratcheting the rising emotions even higher when he flicked his tongue out to capture dough from his lower lip.

"And." Her eyes unfocused again. "Nori. Shredded, dried nori sprinkled on at the end to balance the sweetness. Instead of flake salt."

"Seaweed on cookies?" He narrowed his eyes in thought. The dark pupils were still connected with hers, and he bent forward, shortening the space between them. When her breath caught in her throat and her heart raced, he asked, "Are you sure?"

Metal clinked against metal, jarring her out of her stupor, and her head whipped to see he had disposed of his spoon into the used-tasting-spoon container on her counter. She glanced back up at him and took an unsteady step back.

"No." She shook her head. "I mean, yes. I won't use too much. It'll be good. Trust me."

The words came out in a rush alongside her emotions. By the time she had composed herself, he was standing at the door.

"I always have." His hand rested against the doorjamb. "Thanks for the taste."

"No problem," she breathed out. What was wrong with her? Was it because she'd had a yearlong dry spell? She'd better get a hold of herself. "See you later."

He inclined his head and turned to go, but stopped short.

"Happy birthday, Nell." His words were soft, like peach fuzz.

"Thanks." She tried to smile, but her thoughts were still unfocused.

After he left, she grabbed her towel and scrubbed her face, trying to wipe the fog away.

It was all in her head. Emiliano hadn't been coming on to her. Heat bloomed across her again, but this time, it was out of embarrassment. He didn't need her swooning over him. He was a sweet kid, giving her a compliment. Well, technically, a man now. Barely so.

When had that happened?

She sighed dramatically. Here she was, newly thirty-five, and he was only twenty-eight.

Seven years. It was a large gap.

She still remembered him in middle school, when she was dating Gary. She shuddered. Yeah, no. What did she think she was, some sort of creepy cougar? They had enough of them in the mountain side of town—the four-legged kind. She shook her head. Not gonna happen.

It had just been a while. Too long. She'd get herself together and shake it off.

Throwing the towel in the laundry bin, she picked up the bowl and stirred the black paste into the batter. Smooth, sure strokes to barely blend it in. It would be streaky and leave a chewy bite of oily nut butter.

Yes, this was better. Her brain was back on cooking.

Standing on tiptoe, she reached the Ghirardelli dark-chocolate chunks with one hand and a pinch of sea salt in the other. Shaking a generous amount of the rich bits into the bowl and releasing the spice, the burning sensation in her palm returned. She flexed her hand to ease the feeling, pausing to taste the dough. Perfect. Exactly as she had imagined. She smiled, watching her spoon clink in the jar next to Emiliano's. It wasn't crazy that she was reacting to a man. Maybe she was ready to start thinking about dating again.

Her hand stopped as Gary's face popped back, so fresh, into her mind. Younger Gary, the one she'd fallen in love with in middle school. Tears sprung to her eyes.

She'd loved him since he told her that her backpack was unzipped, spilling pencils, erasers, and snacks all over the sidewalk in front of Orca Cove Middle School. He had knelt and helped her gather her things when the other kids giggled at her misfortune.

She smiled at the memory, then at the million more that zipped through her mind. The two of them opening the shop together, just a booth on the beach before they had enough money to buy the old storefront. And later, when they got married out on the beach and then again when they renovated and made the space above the shop their permanent home.

It didn't seem so permanent now.

Bittersweet. The word was true on all fronts. Bitter and sweet on the tongue and the heart. Bitter from the pain and lost dreams. Sweet from the beauty that had thrived within those dreams. She didn't regret any of it, but still...it stung like a freshly wounded sore, seeping and throbbing.

Nell kept her hands busy, finding her large cookie scoop and sheet pans. With a practiced hand, she scooped ball after ball of beautifully hued dough onto the oiled stainless steel.

Her plans for the future had been demolished. Was she allowed to think about another path now? Could she ever find love again? Did she even deserve it? She'd had better than most. And it had come so easily. Part of it, anyway.

Nell reached for the black sesame seeds, scattering them over the beautiful, rich mahogany-black streaked mounds.

Next was the nori, as her hands lightly crushed the bright green shredded strands.

Oddly enough, it was the camaraderie she missed the most. Someone to run through the daily plans and problems with. A partner to share her life. Her friends were helping, but it wasn't the same.

And she missed the look from a man. The one that stirred her deep inside. So much so that she was manufacturing it from the shop kid next door. The thought lurched in her stomach.

Maybe it wasn't the end of love for her. She was only thirty-five, after all. It wasn't ancient. Ignoring the spikes of burning that now sprang into her palms, she scattered slivers of nori across the top of the cookies. The green and black were vibrant against the varying chestnut shades.

Perfect.

She glanced up at the clock. It was still early. She'd have time to take a small box of them over to Emiliano when she went to pick up the geoducks. They'd be to thank him for thinking of her and remembering her birthday. Nothing more, she told herself.

He'd agree the nori was a good touch.

Smiling in satisfaction and hope for the future, she finished garnishing the cookies and slid them into the oven to bake.

CHAPTER 2

"Emil," his dad said loudly, garnering his attention as soon as he pushed through the rear marina doors into the shop. The responsibilities of the store resumed their normal position as a mantle on his shoulders.

"Morning, Pops." As Emiliano walked past the chilled fresh-meat cases and toward the dry goods, his eyes drifted from shelf to shelf, noting items that needed restocking before the day's business kicked into high gear.

Hugo Gil, his dad and the owner of the store, held up a paper ledger. "This can't be right. It's not adding up."

"Pops." He forced his feet to a stop when he reached the older man, although he wanted to continue his list. "Why are you still copying everything manually? It's all logged in the online ledger."

"You know I don't trust computers."

Didn't trust *him*, was more like it. He'd been in charge of the books in high school, but only if he did it his dad's way. "Computers have less manual error."

"And you could lose it all in an instant." His dad snapped his fingers.

"I back it up every night on the external hard drive."

"And if that goes down?" Hugo's jaw set.

"The backup is on a second server. It syncs the data across both environments, so if one goes down, we can still recover it from the other." He'd explained it a million times before.

"Huh." Hugo tapped the notebook on a shelf. "I'm still not sure I trust it. If it's online, can't someone hack i t?"

It'd been online for over a year now, but...

"It's a secured server. Encrypts the data." He'd ensured it. In fact, he'd added the firewall himself. It was the least he could do with his computer science degree. He'd ended up back at his dad's shop, but he still loved playing around with technology.

"Either way, I can't make the numbers on there match mine."

It was Emiliano's responsibility, and yet his dad wanted him to do it the same way he'd been doing it for years. Emiliano bit back the sigh that had started to make its way up and held out a hand, casting a look over his shoulder to see customers making their way in. "I'll take a look at it. Just give me a few minutes to restock for the day, and I'll update your numbers."

"That's my boy." Hugo clapped him on the shoulder. "Don't forget I'm making my grandmother's famous paella on Monday night. Don't make plans."

With whom? He didn't exactly have anyone to make plans with.

"I won't forget. I've been looking forward to it." It was true. The dish took most of the day to make, so he didn't get it often.

"I thought you might. You've been working so much lately. I felt you deserved something special for your efforts." His dad beamed at him proudly. "I finished the inventory last night as well. We should sit down later and decide what to order for the next month. Your estimates panned out well. We sold most of what we ordered."

"Sounds good." He'd use a new algorithm he wrote to predict sales based on past year-over-year usage. Of course, he wasn't going to tell his technology-adverse father that tidbit. Raising a hand to the couple making their way over, he tucked the ledger under an arm.

"Morning, Emiliano," the man said, carrying a crate full of burlap-wrapped items.

"Morning, Nick." He smiled at his friend and the wild-haired sunshine at his side. "Morning, Willa. Did you bring more boards to sell?"

"He has something new." Willa leaned forward, her green eyes wide in excitement.

"If you're interested." Nick raised his shoulders, his emotions locked down tight. "No sweat if you're not."

The new woodworker was an early retired cop from Seattle and had helped remove a threat from their quiet little town a couple of months ago. He was a natural talent but still didn't have a lot of faith in himself. "Of course we are. Everything you make sells well."

"It's a little different." He chewed his bottom lip, set the box on the ground, and removed a larger item. Unwrapping it, he revealed an intricately designed jewelry box. The box itself was a tiger-striped wood. The single drawer and lid were made from darker, streaked wood. The same darker wood was embedded into the corners in thin horizontal sl ashes.

Emiliano lifted the lid to see it was lined in black velvet. A mirror was attached into the top of the lid with copper fittings, matching the copper hinges and latch. He let out a whistle. "It's beautiful."

"It's okay."

"What do you want for it?"

Nick scratched his neatly trimmed shadow of a beard. "Whatever you think it's worth."

He made it too easy. Some of the local craftspeople had to be gently nudged to sellable prices. Chucking, he lowered the lid. "I'll look up some comparable items online and get it labeled. You know, with work like this, if I made an online store, it'd sell for twice what I could get out of it locally. I'm surprised you didn't put it up on your online makers store."

"I thought about it, but it's so much easier, selling things through you. Much less work than trying to create a social media presence and keep all that mess up. I just want to make things and let you sell them."

"But I take a cut."

"So does the makers site."

"It has to be a larger cut than a commercial site like that."

"It's worth not having the hassle. I haven't posted anything new with them in months. In that time, I've made more products and worked on bigger projects."

"If I do create an online store, you'd be able to reach more people." It was something he'd wanted to do for years, but he hadn't had enough revolving stock yet. He'd talked a couple of local shop owners into the idea, and a few of the other local craftspeople said they'd be interested and could keep up with the additional demand, but he felt he needed more than that.

"What's that about an online store?" His dad took note of their conversation and moseyed over. "I thought we nixed that idea last year."

Emiliano felt his nostrils flare. After the morning's flop with Nell and his inability to tell her how he felt about her, the additional failure was more disheartening than normal. Why would his dad care if he did all the extra work? "I think it would be a smart expansion. And makes online shopping available to our locals. We could have their items ready for pickup or hire an extra hand to do deliveries."

"I bet Mary would take advantage of that," Willa added helpfully. "Even though her hips haven't bothered her as much lately, she still doesn't like to get out of the house unless it's for her garden."

He'd heard the herbalist's salve did wonders on the older woman's rheumatoid arthritis. She was still as cranky as ever, but at least she got around easier.

"If she doesn't come in, how will we check in on her?" Hugo asked.

Willa went on. "I actually think several of the aging community would like it. And it would make it more accessible to the surrounding towns as well."

"Would you finally toss your hat in the ring and sell some of your salves and soaps online?" Emiliano had offered her a full endcap in the shop if she ever wanted them to stock her products, but she preferred a hands-on approach with her customers.

"Um." Willa paused, her eyes darting to Nick's. "I'm not sure. I focus on the locals. I want to stay small scale."

"I could set it so it's only available for local pickup or delivery, no shipping options available." He had already figured out how to configure the site. "It'd be based on their zip code and preferred method for delivery."

"I'm not sure it's a good idea," Hugo said flatly. "We'd have to discuss it again. The last time we talked about it, we decided against it."

His dad had decided against it. Emiliano still thought it was a good idea.

He'd have to continue to build a solid case before his dad would even consider it. "We can review the pros-and-cons list when we look at this month's orders."

"Sure." His father waved a hand, moving off to talk to another customer.

Breathing a sigh, he caught a look of pity from his friend.

Nick clapped him on the shoulder. "Keep at it. You'll wear him down."

"Thanks." He shook it off. Focusing on something he could accomplish at the moment, he bent over the box and flipped open a few of the burlap edges to reveal freshly oiled wood. "How many'd you bring?"

"Ten new ones. Five charcuterie and five cutting boards. Plus the box." Nick shifted on his feet. "Is it too many?"

"Not at all. The last ones sold fast. I think we only have one cutting board left. With all the tourists in town, those'll go quickly."

"I'm amazed the charcuterie boards went as quick as they did. I wouldn't think hunters and fisherfolk would be interested in a meat-and-cheese presentation."

Emiliano's mouth bent up in a coy side smile. "I paired them with the wine bottles and set fake food on them. They sold like hotcakes."

"Nice! You were born to do this," Willa piped in cheerfully.

"I was raised doing it. Same thing." Feeling better about the morning, he lifted the crate. "I'll get these labeled and out later today. I just have a few bookkeeping things to do first."

With a wave, the couple wandered over to the produce section, and he made his way to the storeroom in the back.

It was always the same thing. Emiliano dropped his head into his hands. His pen lay forgotten on his dad's ledger between his elbows.

Was it even worth doing it online if he still had to duplicate every one of his efforts? The right way, as his dad would call it. The numbers trailed out in neat little rows directly under his nose. They had a beautiful simplicity. He understood why his dad liked to see them laid out like this. Maybe if he printed out a report that mirrored this format, his father would be able to see it the way he wanted to. Maybe it was just an issue of understanding.

He sighed. No. It was an issue of change.

Maybe if he had the courage to push back more on his dad...but he knew he never would. He just didn't have that kind of bravery.

He was a coward. He couldn't share his feelings with the woman he loved, and he couldn't stand up to his dad.

Sure, he'd gone off to school and had his own friends outside the shop, but when push came to shove, he retreated back here, where things were comfortable, working long hours to keep his dad happy and meet the customer's needs in Orca Cove.

His eyes fell on the picture of his dad and him hanging on the wall between their desks. It was his graduation, and his father's arm was wrapped proudly around his youthful shoulders. One of the few times his dad had been entirely, exuberantly happy.

Nearly his whole life, it had been just the two of them. Emiliano had earned his degree just to come back and work at the shop. He was fine with that. He loved Gil's. Besides, he owed it to his dad.

He could make it work. He *would* make it work.

And if he could sneak in a few improvements over the years, he'd do it. He wouldn't give up hope.

Now, if only he could convince himself the same about *her*. Absently, he picked his pen back up and tapped it against the wooden desk, *her* face floating through his mind's eye. Her light-brown hair, pulled back into a pony-tail, wasn't curly like Willa's wild mane. It was more like a pin-up girl's hair with soft, undulating waves. And when she let it down...it was tough to think straight.

Nell Fitzgibbons. Wilder, he corrected himself, putting a name to the face in his head. That failure was more diffi-cult to ignore.

If he didn't make a move soon, someone else would. He might lose the only chance he ever had.

He thought he'd have the courage today, but then she'd flashed her million-dollar smile at him with that mischie-vous light in her eyes, and he'd been a goner, thrown back to the flustered youth, unsure of himself.

And what if he pushed her too far too soon? What if she didn't feel the same way?

Today had given him hope. It seemed as though she'd been flirting back with him. As though she was seeing him as something other than the kid from the store, years younger in school.

Back then, it had been so much more difficult. Her late husband was such a good guy. Gary had been with Nell since they were in middle school. Emiliano had been so conflicted about his feelings for her, but that didn't stop how he felt about the sweet, resourceful girl—now woman.

She understood better than anyone what it was like to serve the townspeople. They were in the same business, just offering different parts of the same wheel. And right next door to each other, to boot.

He procured the produce and meats. She cooked them and served them up. To take it further, he served some of her sandwiches and salads in his cold cases and she was always quick to tell customers where they could get more of a particular produce or cheese they liked. They were like melted butter and Dungeness crab, a perfect match.

At least, it felt that way to him. Fate had other plans, it would seem.

"Isn't it a little early for a nap?"

It was a female voice.

Emiliano bolted to his feet. The woman of his dreams stood at his office door, a smile illuminating her perfect face, along with what had to be sesame paste streaked adorably across her forehead. He had to force his heartbeat to still. She was here for the geoducks. He cleared his throat. "Did you, uh, get your clams?"

"Tommy's topping my cooler with extra ice." She indicated with her head. "Which is silly. I'm just walking across the grass with them."

Good kid. He'd told him to always ice fresh catch, regardless of where they were traveling. You never knew when someone took a detour...or how long Nell would stand here and chat. His fingers crossed behind his back, not wanting to jinx himself. "It's just policy."

"Anyway." She held up a bakery box he'd only now noticed she was carrying. His heart resumed its pounding. She'd brought something special for him? "I thought I'd prove my point."

The cookies. It had to be.

Steadying his nerves, he crossed over to her and took the box. Edging the lid open, he saw six perfectly symmetrical cookies, rich in color, swirled and speckled with dark brown and finished with bright green flecks. The scent of chocolate hit his nose. They were almost too pretty to eat. Almost.

As he selected the closest one, he noticed her watching him, her eyes wide in anticipation. She was excited to see his reaction. Maybe he had a shot, after all. Hell, he wasn't going to waste it. He'd make sure she saw every single taste he experienced. Every bit of appreciation.

He took a bite, his eyes mirroring hers in surprise. Wow. He'd expected them to be good—Nell was the best—but he wasn't expecting the layers upon layers of nuanced flavor she'd imparted in them. "Spicy from the rye, chewy from the sesame paste. And you used very dark chocolate."

"80 percent," she announced, her chin lifted.

"It's almost bitter." He let his eyes drift shut, chewing the cookie. "Warm sweetness. Brown sugar?"

"Yes."

"And the salt." He opened his eyes to find hers trained on his mouth. Humor left his mind as warmth spiked low in his stomach. Parts of his body felt like they were on fire. Hot, burning fire. "Hot damn, Nell. Those are incredible."

"I told you so." Her voice was almost breathless. "I told you the salt from the nori would work like flake salt."

"You were right. It shouldn't surprise me. I've never tasted anything you've made that was bad." It was true.

"You're very good at identifying flavor."

He raised his shoulders in a shrug. "I taste everything we sell. I'm not going to put out bad products."

"You always have the best produce. Perfectly ripe." Her eyes were still trained on his mouth.

He nodded. "I try."

"It's why I'm so successful. A cook has to have good ingredients."

"A chef does," he corrected her. "And you could make peanut butter and jelly taste fancy. It's all you."

"Thanks."

He took a step closer, reaching a hand to her face. Her eyes followed the movement, then flashed to his in question with a little hesitancy. He swept a thumb over her forehead. "Black sesame paste."

She blushed. "I should go."

No.

"Nell," he blurted out.

She stopped, her eyes a little less wary.

"I hope you have a good birthday party tonight."

Crap. Come on, Emiliano. Be courageous.

A ghost of a smile passed over her face. "How'd you know I was having a party?"

"You always make dinner for your friends to celebrate your birthday." He softened his gaze. He knew her.

"Thanks." She turned to go.

"Also." The words stumbled out. He could do it. Thought fled his brain like water draining through the docks, leaving his mind and mouth dry like the aged boards. "Pops is making paella Monday night. He's using those canned tomatoes you brought over last season. I thought...I thought you might want to join us."

"Um." Her hands came together in front of her, searching for the apron she no longer wore.

She'd taken it off to come over. Was that a good sign? Had she cleaned up as he had done before visiting? Or was he simply searching for signs where there were none?

"He hasn't made it in years. It's an old recipe of his grandma's, on the Spanish side. I thought you'd be interested." He spread his fingers wide as if that was the only reason.

She exhaled softly, the smile returning to her face. "That would be amazing. I love paella."

He gave her a friendly nod, and she was out of his office. His hands pressed into the wall next to the door she'd left through, his head falling in concert with his heart.

She was relieved it was just about food. It wasn't about him. He'd been a fool to think otherwise.

CHAPTER 3

Nell spun into her office, shutting the door to muffle the lively chattering from the early morning crowd. As her forehead fell onto the cold wood, she pinched her eyes shut and tried to quiet her heart.

What was she doing?

She needed to get a hold of her emotions before she threw herself at the poor kid—young man, she corrected herself. Whatever. She'd seen how other girls looked at him. He was gorgeous, with his dark eyes, perfectly pouted lips, and shirt strained across his biceps, rounded from carrying crates around all day.

Maybe she had made a mistake in agreeing to dinner. She didn't want to ruin their working relationship.

Pushing from the wall, she took her apron from the hook behind the door where she'd hung it and slid it over her head. Her hands ran down over her stomach, softened over the years. She was no longer in her prime. Why would he be interested in her? Her mouth twisted down, disliking the taste of the thought. She pulled the ties around her waist, knotting them more aggressively than necessary.

Was she all washed up? It was possible. Somewhere between building a business and losing a husband, it might have happened. She was practically approaching middle a ge.

"Nell." Her door opened, and Maggie, her waitress, bounded in. The blonde woman's cheeks were pink from exertion. "I unpacked the geoducks for you. Do you want me to keep them on ice for dinner?"

She was already falling behind. Hadn't she only taken a few minutes? "That's okay. I'm going to slice some for sashimi."

"That sounds great," Maggie said excitedly. "Do you need any help?"

Did she look like she needed help?

No, she wasn't going to go down that road again. After losing Gary, she'd distanced herself, thinking everyone just felt sorry for her. Instead of accepting help, she shut herself a way.

"Aren't you busy with the breakfast crowd?" Nell looked towards the dining room. It sounded busy out there.

"Yeah." Maggie didn't move, but her head swiveled back toward the door. "I just wanted to make sure you were okay."

Ah, it had been shut. Typically, she left it open so she could keep a pulse on things. She'd closed it frequently after Gary passed. Any time she broke down, drowning in her own sorrow.

Gathering Maggie's shoulders between her hands, she leveled her eyes with her friend, the person who had been with her since basically the beginning of the café. Who had helped her get through the grief. "I'm fine, Maggie. I promise."

Her friend's eyebrows tilted in concern. "I'm sorry, Nell. When I saw the door, I just panicked. And with today being your birthday..."

"I know." She closed her eyes against another wave of emotion before it bubbled up to the surface. "I just needed a breather. I'm good."

Maggie's shoulders sagged in relief. "Good."

"But I *am* pissed."

"Because?"

"Nobody told me I had sesame paste on my forehead." She threw her hands up in the air, making a dramatic show about it.

Maggie stifled a laugh. "I thought you knew."

"And I was wearing it as a fashion statement? Why would I walk around like that, let alone go to Gil's like that?"

"You walk around with some sort of flour smear nearly every day. When did you start caring if you have food on you?" Maggie teased her.

Nell sidestepped in discomfort. "I don't know what you're talking about."

"Sure, you don't." Her friend winked.

"Anyway, I'm fine. Okay?" She changed the subject back to something safer.

"Okay." Maggie hugged her tightly, then broke away, her gaze trailing past the door. "Cause I gotta go."

The waitress disappeared as quickly as she'd entered.

At that moment, Barnaby walked by, stopping to take note of her appearance. "You have a little something on your face. It's not a good look."

"Where were you earlier?" she asked her bartender.

He raised his hands in question. "Doing what you pay me for, making incredible mimosas for the brunch crowd."

"Fine," she said exasperatedly. "I guess doing your job is a good excuse for not letting me know I had literal food on my face."

Placing a hand on a jutted-out hip, he asked, "And just who were you trying to impress?"

"No one!" she tried to argue, but it came out high-pitched. Good grief, she sounded like a school kid.

His eyebrows went up.

"Never mind." She shooed him out of her doorway. "Go make mimosas."

"I came by for a reason."

"Oh." She stopped. "What's up?"

Snorting, he executed a perfect eye roll. The motion was practically made for Barnaby. If it hadn't been, then he'd perfected it. "That kid came by again. He wants to know if he and his band can play here, on the back patio."

"What was his name?" She searched through her memory. "JT?"

"JD."

"His band was something weird, like Attack of the Killer Tomatoes."

The snort came louder this time. "How old are you? Uprising of the Dung Beetle."

"Ew." Her mouth turned down. "At a restaurant?""They're grunge," he said as if that explained it all. It did. "You've never had live music before. Is it something you're interested in doing?"

She'd avoided answering the kid—JD, she reminded herself—when he came by to ask the first time. Her initial instinct was to get Gary's advice. And then she remembered she couldn't, and she'd spiraled. Not as bad as before, but it had sent her into her kitchen for a good three hours.

They had tiramisu on the menu the next day, complete with homemade ladyfingers. And she had researched how to make her own mascarpone cheese, to boot.

"I don't know. What do you think?" She wasn't sure how to make a decision like this on her own.

"It's not a bad idea. Lots of bars have live music. I've worked at several."

"Do you think it would change the atmosphere?"

"Definitely."

She wrinkled her nose. "Is that a bad thing?"

"That's up to you, boss."

She hated that. She didn't feel like a boss anywhere but in the kitchen.

It wasn't a bad idea, though. She supposed she could try it out. "Did you hear them play?"

"Just a little bit. The kid was pretty pushy about it." A smile cracked over Barnaby's dark-brown skin.

"Old or new music?"

"A mix of both."

"Are they any good?"

"Not bad. I didn't hate it."

"Okay." She said it on an exhale, terrified she was making a bad decision. "One night. Next Saturday. Well after the dinner crowd starts to die down. They don't go on until eight p.m. After that, we'll see."

"You got it." He tapped the doorframe once and was off before she could go back on her decision.

She regretted it the minute he left. Could she stop him? Crap.

The place would turn into a tourist trap, and she'd piss off all the locals. When winter hit, it'd be lights out.

She screwed her face up in frustration and attempted to calm her irrational thoughts. It'd be okay. A trial was barely a decision.

She could get her friend Shelby's opinion before making any long-term choice. Shelby was a *real* businesswoman.

Nell headed towards her kitchen, where everything she did always turned out right. She could work through whatever was happening to her libido and forget about being in charge of a business.

After she sliced the sashimi, maybe she'd make some fresh pasta to go with the geoduck and chanterelles. Washing her hands, she felt the now-familiar burn along her palm and scrubbed against the towel to dry it. She considered making a doctor's appointment later in the day. Then again, maybe it was muscle tension. Shaking it out, she flexed her hand and grabbed a bowl.

"Are you coming?" Maggie's face appeared at her door.

Nell looked up, having just finished the plate of thinly sliced raw geoducks with a sprinkling of basil microgreens she'd picked up fresh from Gil's Market that morning.

"Yes, just…" She wanted to add the beurre-blanc sauce she had made. Swirling her wrist, she drizzled it with a flourish, then set small dipping dishes of wasabi and soy sauce to the tray. After wiping the edge with a clean towel—no paste on it, this time—she brandished it high in the air. It was perfect.

It had taken her a while to summon the courage to be excited about tonight, but she was finally getting there.

For many years, she had felt like she and Gary were in a second, private group all on their own, apart from their found little family of friends. And now that he was gone, she knew what it was like being on the outside.

"Everyone's here," Maggie said, leading her out of her kitchen.

Her friends had been building a new family without her. Who did she have? Her business? Her memories? They paled in comparison.

Luckily, she'd had the rest of the afternoon to work through her emotions in front of her stove.

Gary, their sixth member, had been replaced by Nick, Willa's boyfriend. Not that Nick could ever replace Gary. And even though she was happy for Willa—all of them, really—she was still angry.

Angry at the loss of Gary. Angry at the changes. Angry with everything.

Maggie and Willa had tried to keep her connected, but it wasn't the same. She hadn't helped anything, blocking them out with the pain.

Setting her face, she followed Maggie through the kitchen's swinging door, platter in hands. Her arrival on the back deck heralded birthday cheers.

She'd leave her anger in the kitchen and celebrate with her friends. It'd all work out.

See? It wasn't so bad. They were here to celebrate her.

Willa and Maggie had set flowers on the large table pulled together in the center of the deck. The Edison bulb lights that were strung over the tables illuminated the glassware. Duke, briefly their only male in the crew, held up two bottles of mysteriously labeled red wine. They looked ancient. And expensive. Probably payment for some shipment he'd carried on his courier ship.

Nick stood behind Willa, his arms wrapped around hers, which were covered by the light cardigan she wore to beat the light evening chill. No, she wasn't going to dwell on missing a supporting arm around her.

Nell's eyes found Shelby, the strong, powerhouse female. Her dark, straight hair was tucked aggressively behind an ear. She could be like Shelby.

At that moment, her friend held up her fingers, wiggling them in the air. "Those are really fresh. I can still feel the water in them."

Maybe not.

She paused halfway to the crowd. Her tough friend had gained a secret weapon, like the rest of her group. A raging thunderstorm that had rolled through on Gary's last birthday bestowed each of them a different power from the ocean.

Each of them except her.

Nell woke to a pounding on her door.

Eyes wide in panic, she swung her legs out of her bed. Squinting at her phone, she read the time as five a.m. and noticed several notifications of missed calls. Snatching it up, she pulled her robe on and headed down the stairs to find out what couldn't wait 'til morning. She briefly considered stopping by the kitchen to grab her butcher knife, but when she made it to the landing of her restaurant, she saw Willa's face on the back deck.

Memories from the night before ramrodded her with an emotional fist. They'd all fought.

She'd accused them of forgetting Gary and bringing an outsider in to replace him. Her mouth pulled back in self-disgust, remembering the hurt in Nick's eyes.

She paused. Did she want to talk to Willa just now?

Oddly, her friend didn't look angry, staring back through the large wall of windows. Before she crossed the wood planks between them, she looked at the phone in her hand. Two missed calls and a text from Willa. She read her friend's words.

I know what happened! It's good news!

What in the world did that mean?

Hand pressed to her stomach, she tried to calm the tension. Nell went to Willa and unlocked the door, then held up the phone.

"What happened?" Nell asked.

Willa pushed past her, pulling her around in a circle as her hands gripped Nell's robe. The woman's hair was even wilder than normal. It looked like she had just rolled out of bed.

More and more memories poked holes in Nell's psyche. It hadn't been just her. They had all released pent-up frustration.

It had all started when Shelby said Willa was lazy, too trusting, and unreliable. Willa had told Shelby she was too focused on monetary worth, that she was cold and didn't let anyone in. It was entirely unlike their peace-loving friend.

Then Duke said Nell had monopolized Gary's free time. He'd accused her of taking any remaining time from him and his best friend. It was obvious he resented her for that.

That's when Nell hit back. She'd let all her pain and anger loose.

Eventually, Nick had even joined the blaming party, claiming there was no way Gary had been that perfect. He couldn't fill those shoes. He'd been set up for failure before he was even brought into their fold.

"I'm so sorry." The words fell, cold, from her shocked lips.

"It's not your fault," Willa said, bouncing on the balls of her feet. "I came over as soon as I woke up and realized what happened. Well, I tried calling, but then I just came on over. But, most importantly, it's not your fault!"

"Of course it is." She tried to pull away. "Even if I didn't start it. I didn't have to let loose on everyone like I did."

She had gone on about every one of them.

"No, you don't understand." Willa shook her. "You weren't skipped! You got a power, too."

"What do you mean?" The herbalist was normally fair and forgiving, but she was being unusually naive.

"Your power." Her eyes lit up. "It's in your food."

"My food? What do you mean?"

"You know how, these past few months, we've been hanging out again and having a lot of fun? And the patrons have been saying how they're having such a great time at Wild's?"

"Yes?"

"Yesterday was your birthday." Willa gripped her biceps. "What were you feeling when you cooked?"

Nell glanced at her feet. She didn't want to revisit that.

"There's no way you weren't thinking about Gary," Willa said.

"Of course I was." Nell's eyes flashed in annoyance. Had Willa woken her up to rob her of her last thirty minutes of sleep just to get back at her?

"What did you feel? Sadness?"

"Of course." It seemed like they were going to play this game. But if that's what her friend needed to repay her for her outburst, she'd pay it. She felt horrible.

"What else?"

"And anger."

"That's it!" She released her hold on Nell and raised her hands excitedly.

"I'm so sorry, Willa. I should never have said those things."

"I don't care about that. You didn't mean it." She wrinkled her tiny nose. "Well, you did, but it's not personal. You're dealing with a lot right now."

It was her turn to take her friend's arms in hand. "Willa, what is going on?"

"That's your power!" she exclaimed again. "Your emotions are passed through your cooking. You're like a reverse empath."

"I don't even know what that means." She shook her head.

"When we all started hanging out again, finally coming back together after all that time apart, you were cooking with happiness and joy. It passed through your food, and everyone was having fun. That's probably why we had those nights where it was like we were drunk, but Duke had only brought two bottles of wine and we'd only drunk one. Remember that?"

She did. It hadn't made any sense. The first night Nick joined them, they had gotten giggly, stumbling around and singing. She'd wondered if Duke brought fortified wine or something, but logic told her that her palate would have noticed. She'd even asked Maggie if she wanted to stay over. Something fuzzy in her brain started to follow what Willa was saying, but it didn't feel comfortable.

"What does that have to do with empathy?"

"Empathy is when you are sensitive to others' feelings. I think you're, like, reverse empathic and can make others sensitive to your feelings."

"That's crazy." She sat down heavily in a nearby chair in the rear part of the café.

"You were angry while cooking yesterday. You haven't been that angry in a while. We all fought."

"So, it *is* my fault." It was all she could put together at the moment.

"Yes." Her friend shook her head. "No. Not like that. You didn't know you were doing it."

"Wait." Nell stood back up. "Are you telling me my livelihood is dependent on me being in a good mood?"

"Well." Willa stopped for a moment. "I hadn't thought about it like that. I'm sure you can get the hang of it. I can show you how to meditate."

It couldn't be real. If that was her gift, it was a nightmare of one. A curse, really. Frantically, she thought back over the past few months, after the lightning had struck the water in the cove, with all of them in it. They'd worked out that something magical lived beneath the waves. The orcas had confirmed it. The orcas, they'd come to find out, were shape-shifters of sorts, if orca-shifter was a thing or even the right term. At least, the one they'd found out about was called Percy, but there were possibly others.

It was odd.

No. It was completely crazy and absolutely unbelievable. But surprisingly enough, it was true.

Shelby was able to feel water directionally; it's how she'd known the geoducks were fresh. Willa could use it to heal people, amping up her herbalism practice, but she kept it local. Duke could move water, and Maggie's was the coolest of all.

She could make it rain. Nell had seen her float water droplets with her own eyes. It was real.

And the reverse-empathy-cooking thing made sense, as ridiculous as that sounded. She recalled a couple of depressing days when the entire restaurant moved slowly. It was quiet, and everyone went home early. It was probably good they'd closed before their normal time. Who knows who she could have hurt.

"I'm going to have to find another profession." The words sounded emotionless and flat in her ears.

"What are you talking about?"

"I could hurt people, messing around with their emotions like that. What if someone was clinically depressed?"

"What if you helped them?" Willa looked at her hopefully.

She let her friend lead her to a booth at the back. Too many thoughts were going through her mind to object.

"Wait!" Nell took hold of Willa's arms. "Joe got sick last night after he left here. That was probably my fault, from this weird empathy thing."

"Were you feeling sick last night?"

"Not really, but I didn't feel great." She ran her hands through her hair, the long strands hanging and knotted from another sleepless night.

"Was he the only one who fell ill?"

"As far as I know."

"Then, you're probably fine. If you were feeling something, odds are better that more than one person was impacted. You cooked nearly all the food yourself."

It was true, but it didn't make her feel better.

"We don't really know how this thing works yet."

"Do you want me to call Maggie to come in and help open?" Willa held her hand.

Nell just shook her head. "I'm not opening. Can you put a sign on the door for me? There's no way I can cook for anyone until I know what's going on. Until then, The Wild Café is closed."

CHAPTER 4

There was a closed sign on the café's door.

The place never closed.

Emiliano stood at the window of Gil's Market and Marina as though the sign would magically disappear and the world would go back to normal again.

Neither of them closed, except on Mondays, which was why his dad had picked it for paella night. During the week, Pops and he took turns cooking, but his dad never made anything fancier than a one-pot meal unless it was their day off.

Mondays were for relaxing and old recipes.

It wasn't as though they worked around the clock for the other six days, but well, some weeks they did.

Shoving through the market door, he walked across their shared lot to read the cardboard note. The sign had hastily erased remnants of words, but he couldn't read what had been written and removed. All that remained was "Closed."

It did nothing to calm the rising concern in his chest. Stepping back, he peered up to the second floor, imagining Nell up there. Something wasn't right.

Snorting, he backed away. He didn't need to look like a creep, staring into her bedroom windows. So he went back into the market, flexing his hands in frustration.

Hopefully, she was okay. Did he have a reason to message her?

"You alright, man?" A customer casually dressed in jeans and an old flannel over a white T-shirt strolled over to him. He raised a hand and pulled his too-long hair back from his face, tucking it behind an ear on one side.

"Yeah." It was Duke, one of Nell's friends. Maybe he knew what was going on. And if not, he'd check on her. "Nell is closed. I walked over to see for how long, but it doesn't say. I hope she's okay."

A shadow passed over Duke's face, but it disappeared so quickly Emiliano wondered if he'd imagined it. "I'm sure she just needed a day off."

"Have you checked in on her?" They all had over the past year.

"We saw her yesterday, yeah." He scratched the new growth of whiskers barely visible on his chin. "She was okay. A bit stressed, but okay. I'm sure that's it."

Emiliano nodded. "Maybe you should check on her, just the same."

Duke nodded, his eyes sharpening with interest. "I'll do that."

The man was a cargo courier, moving shipments by water, likely to avoid customs. He dealt in expensive goods, so he didn't miss much.

"Can't have our best customer getting sick." The chuckle he pushed out sounded fake even in his own ears. He fought against the grimace. "Anyway, it's still good to check."

"Sure thing, man." Duke gave him a hardy clap on his shoulder. "By the way, do you have any of those geoducks left? I thought I'd snag one for dinner."

"Let me check." Emiliano went to the iced-fish section. "Quite a few tourists came by yesterday and cleared us out pretty good. We might have gotten some new ones in while I was running errands."

"I meant from yesterday's catch specifically," Duke said, making him pause.

Why would he want older fish?

"Nell said it was some of the best geoducks she's ever had. That woman is particular about her food," Duke went on.

"But wouldn't a fresh one be even better?"

Duke shrugged. "I just thought I'd see what the fuss was about. Besides, it'd be cheaper, right?"

If they hadn't sold it all, it wouldn't still be on ice; it'd be packaged in the cooler. Emiliano changed directions. He scanned the shelves of the cold room. The man drove a hard bargain on anything he bought from him, but he also had an expensive taste in food and wine.

"It's your lucky day," he said, procuring a cellophane-wrapped geoduck from the cooler and handing it over to the man. "The very last one."

"Awesome." Duke held it up in thanks. Giving him a friendly tilt of his head, he went directly to the check-out lines.

Very, very strange.

At least, Duke was going to check in on Nell.

The urge to text her rose again, but they hadn't texted much socially. It was mainly the occasional work-related message. Not that he hadn't slipped in a funny text in there once or twice in an attempt to get a smile out of her.

No. He'd let Duke handle it. They were friends and had a long history. She'd be okay.

Selfishly, he was also worried she wouldn't make Monday-night dinner.

Emiliano pushed the sleeves of his cream-colored Henley up his forearms. The bathroom mirror in his studio apartment over his pop's workshop clearly reflected the panic in his eyes. He rechecked his close-cropped hair, still wet from the shower.

It wasn't going anywhere, yet he checked it again, patting the wavy do.

He debated another spritz of cologne, but stalled his hand. The one was enough. This wasn't a date. Not even close.

He swallowed the lump in his throat.

Walking out of the damp bathroom, he leaned over the coffee table where he'd left his phone. She hadn't texted to cancel. That was a good sign.

Especially since he hadn't seen any glimpse of her the entire day before. He couldn't remember a Sunday when The Wild Café had ever closed.

Even after Gary had passed, Nell only closed a few days during the week. They'd been back in business by the weekend. Somber, and with only a light menu of stews and casseroles with rustic bread, but they'd been open. No one minded. They just wanted to be with Nell, to help shoulder her grief.

And she had disappeared into her inner sanctum, her kitchen and office. Few words were shared during that time. It had taken months before he could get her to crack even a single smile.

Only recently, after gangsters had followed ex-cop Nick Ryan from Seattle to plague their peaceful little seaside town, had he seen her come back together with her crew, her little clique from high school.

They were several years older—Duke being the oldest—but they had always been tight. He'd wished he could be part of it.

The threat must have brought them back together. Or it might have been because Willa finally had a boyfriend and she needed help navigating it. Either way, they'd bonded together and gotten the bad guys in jail and shipped back to Seattle.

He was glad they were patching things back up. Nell seemed happier.

And she would be here within the hour.

The pastry box she'd brought him, with the delicious-as-sin cookies, sat on his dresser. There was only one left. Lifting it from the container, he slid it into his mouth, biting into the onslaught of flavors. Alone in his place, he swayed in pleasure.

After closing the little box, he left it on his dresser. He'd recycle it eventually but wanted to hang onto the reminder of the gift a little longer.

Once he laced up his boots, he thumped down the wooden stairs to the gravel driveway, finding his dad hunched over the large paella dish set up over a fire in their yard.

His nose lifted. The signature spices ignited memories in his mind. "Smells great, Pops."

It was a labor of love. The prep work for the family recipe took longer than the actual cooking time. Even so, his dad liked to stoke the fire to just the right temperature before placing the food over the open flame.

"It's going to be a good batch," his dad promised, poking a vegetable back under the steaming surface of the liquid. He lifted his head. "When's Nell coming?"

"She should be here any minute." Emiliano checked his watch. He couldn't see around the garage to the restaurant, but he tilted his head as though willing the corner of the building to slide over and give him a view of her approach.

He wiped his palms down the sides of his pants.

"Open the wine." His dad pointed at the bottle of Tempranillo on the patio table. "Let it breathe until she gets here."

"Will do." Inspecting the bottle, he noticed it was one from their cellar. "You went all out tonight."

"Seemed right, having company. You don't bring many people over."

It was true. He'd never considered it. But before he could say anything, she was there, in their driveway, radiant in jeans and a T-shirt, a cardigan in hand. And good Lord Almighty, she had her hair down.

"Am I too early?"

Early? He'd been waiting for her his whole life.

Emiliano swallowed.

"I'm glad you could make it." He broke through his nerves and gestured toward the wine waiting on the table. "Can I pour you a glass?"

"Sounds good." The waves of her hair swayed with each step she took closer. The streaks of colorful sunlight filtering through the canopy of trees over them didn't hold a candle to the various shades in her hair. The strands of copper, the soft glow of warm cocoa, and the darker streaks of chocolate mixed with her thick, deep chestnut-colored wa ves.

"I was worried you wouldn't be able to make it." He masked the hurt in his eyes. He'd hoped she would reach out to him. They did have—not exactly a date, maybe, but definitely plans. And they were friends.

"And miss Hugo's grandmother's old recipe?" She smiled beatifically at his father. "Not a chance."

"I'm glad you're feeling well." Hugo stood from the bubbling liquid. "I assumed you were ill."

Emiliano stopped pouring wine to listen. He hadn't wanted to pry, but he was curious.

"A little." She paused. "I think I just need some time off."

"You're opening tomorrow, though, right?" his dad asked, a little too sternly. He didn't believe in taking vacation.

"I, uh, haven't decided. Maybe."

"There's nothing wrong with taking time off," Emiliano cut in, handing out glasses of wine. "We're just glad you could make it."

"Thanks," she said, accepting the drink. Although it wasn't clear if she was showing gratitude for the wine or for the save. Maybe both.

He made a mental note to overstock the deli meat and canned soups. If Wild's was really going to remain closed a while longer, people would be looking for quick meals.

The townspeople were used to stopping into the café a few times a week. It was the central hub of the town.

Thankfully, his dad had turned his attention back to the soup.

"I heard your geoducks were outstanding." Emiliano gestured to a set of chairs around the fire, and the two of them sat down. "Not that I was surprised."

"They were a great batch." Her face lit up. "You get the freshest catch."

"I get up early." He raised his glass.

"They all sell to you first. You do good business with the fisherfolk."

"It's all part of the job. You know what that's like."

"Not really." She studied the wine in her glass. "I'm not really great with the business stuff."

Ah. Gary had handled the work relationships.

"You know what? I'm not sure I agree with that." He shook his head. "I see how you talk to the locals. They love you."

"They love Maggie."

"Well, that too. It'd be impossible not to." He laughed. The woman had a heart of gold. "But I've seen you make decisions on ingredients when we can't source what you w ant."

"That's about food, not business." Her eyes turned to the fire, but even the reflection of the light couldn't disguise the sadness hiding within them.

"You've driven me down in cost more than once." He couldn't help but push. He needed her to know how special she was.

"You're easy to work with. Easy to talk to."

"Not everyone would say that."

"You're fair, but also friendly."

"I try to be."

"It seems so easy for you."

"Nell, the people in town don't just come to you because you're an excellent cook. You are, for the record, one of the best cooks in the state, but that's not the only reason they come." He noticed her attention turn and focus on him. "You always have something on your menu for those who can't afford much. It's still delicious and interesting enough that they don't feel embarrassed to order it."

"I'm not having anything on my menu they could simply toss together from the store. What would the point be in that? Anyone can do that."

"Even so, you don't have to do it. You choose to, so people aren't left out, and they know it. You give out free desserts for birthdays and even discount Mary's birthday steak every year. It's the only reason she orders it."

It was one of the few occasions their resident hermit left her property. "I don't remember their birthdays, though. Maggie does."

"It doesn't matter. You decided to put the policy in place."

She shrugged her shoulder.

"You care, and they know it," he insisted.

The corner of her mouth kicked up in half acceptance. "Maybe."

"There's no maybe about it. You may not always know what to do in the business world, but you care about your customers. That's half the battle."

He wasn't sure if she fully believed him, but the sadness didn't linger as heavily in her eyes.

She lifted her nose and her lids drifted shut. "Is that bay leaf? And thyme?"

Spinning in her seat, she found Hugo watching her. "You've got a great nose. Good timing too. The sauce is ready for the meat."

"You want me to get it?" Emiliano asked. At his father's nod, he stood to head to the kitchen.

"Need a hand?" Nell asked. "I'm not used to not helping with food."

"That's why you're going to sit and be waited on." Emiliano pointed at the seat she had started to stand from and disappeared into the house. But by the time he returned to the back patio, she had settled in next to Hugo, her face in the steam coming from the bubbling red liquid.

"This is going to be amazing." Her eyes were half hooded in pleasure. When they landed on the pan he took from Emiliano, however, they lit with interest. "Clams, shrimp, and is that...chorizo?"

"Yes." Hugo gently added the meat to the sauce.

"There's something else in there too."

"Chicken. Paella is really just a stew. Traditionally, it would be a mixture of whatever you had on hand. Rabbit and chicken are more traditional, but so is chicken and chorizo, like this one. There are a lot of people who say you can't add seafood to true paella, but, really, that was because it was expensive in Spain, even on the coast. I prefer to follow the heart of the recipe, not the exact i ngredients."

"I like that." She gave him one of her rare full-bodied smiles.

After stirring the stew, Hugo lifted the spoon to taste it, and his mouth flattened. "It's good, but it's not quite like Grandma made it."

"Did she make it with seafood?" Nell asked. "They're going to add flavor."

"Sometimes. That's not it." He took another taste, then pointed to Nell. "You taste it."

Emiliano watched her take the old wooden spoon. She was meticulously careful about sharing food instruments in her kitchen, and he was worried that would carry over outside of it. But she leaned over without hesitation and tasted the soup. Her eyes drifted shut.

"That's delicious." She lifted a hand to her mouth before opening her eyes. "I've had paella before, but the sofrito in this one is so rich. It's layered really well. This must have taken you hours."

Hugo's chest puffed out. "I started it around lunchtime. I used smoked paprika, saffron, turmeric, thyme, and bay, like she did. But something is missing. I was too young to remember all the ingredients."

"Did your mom ever find any recipes sitting around?"

Emiliano sat down to listen to their exchange. Everyone knew Hugo's grandma died when he was young. Then he lost his dad when he was barely out of high school. It was Hugo and his mom, much like it had been Emiliano and his dad. Hugo had opened the fish market as soon as he'd been able to invest in it. The shop was what it was today because of his dedication to the town.

The older man's shoulders slumped. "Most of the recipes were just notes. They were missing a lot of steps and ingredients. She never thought to learn them. We never expect our loved ones to leave us as quickly as they do."

"Recipes are just notes. Mine change all the time." Nell smiled. "You got the most important part down. Cooking a slow sofrito gives it its signature taste."

"I just miss Grandma's paella." He gave her a soft smile.

"What did it taste like?" She looked at his dad with an intelligent curiosity, listening closely.

His face furrowed in thought. "It had a richness to it. It's tough to explain. Like a little earthy note that was pungent, but not overpowering."

Emiliano could see Nell's mind searching for the taste. "Could I try something?"

"Of course."

She stood up and hurried into their house, reemerging with a few bowls, spoons, and spices. After setting each bowl out on the patio table, she froze, her hands hovering over each. He could see the tension in her fingers as her eyes found Emiliano's, and a coy smile seeped into them. "You said I wasn't to cook tonight. Can you help me?"

God, she was cute. Excitement overshadowed any concern he had. He hurried to her side. "Of course. What do I do?"

"The spices have to be crushed, but only a pinch." She set jars in front of each bowl. "One in each."

Scooping out a bit of each, he crushed it between his fingers and scattered it in the bowls.

"Shake out the big pieces. You only want the little bit at the bottom, or it'll be too strong. Then add a few tablespoons of broth to each." She directed Hugo to add the stew after Emiliano removed a little of the larger bits, then she stood back, her hands clasped tightly to her midsection. "Give it a little stir. Ideally, it would simmer together, but it should give you an idea of the flavor."

Mixing each of the little bowls, Hugo sniffed them curiously. At Nell's urging, he began tasting them. The first one earned a curious expression and a short head shake.

The second one, disgust. The final bowl, though, had him pause, spoon hovering over the remainder of the liquid. His eyes opened wide, and he whispered, his voice heavy with emotion, "That's it."

"Rosemary," she said, beaming. "It's not as common, but sometimes, it's found in paella."

"What's that one?" He nodded curiously to the first bowl.

"Aleppo pepper. You've got a great spice cabinet." She grinned. "It's not traditional, but I thought it might taste good."

"It really does." He tasted it again. "But it wasn't the flavor I was looking for."

Going back to the bowl with rosemary, he took another spoonful, savoring it longer in his mouth. "It's just a touch, but it makes the difference. It tastes like home."

Tears welled in the older man's eyes, and Emiliano laid a hand on his shoulder. "Can I taste it?"

"Yes, after it's simmered in the stew." He rushed to sprinkle a decent pinch of the spice into his hand. Using his other palm, he crushed it over the pot and stirred it in. "Not long, though. The shrimp is cooked, and it won't do to have it overcook."

After a few more slow, measured stirs, he stopped and retasted. The quiet happiness on his face declared it ready, and he ladled it into larger bowls, waiting on the patio t able.

Hugo was lost in his own memories, so the two of them followed suit, unsure of what to say. In silence, they all sat at the table and enjoyed the simple pleasure of a hearty s tew.

If Emiliano hadn't been in love with Nell before, he certainly would be now.

After dinner, he'd find a way to ask her on a real date. He was done waiting.

"Thank you so much for sharing your grandmother's paella with me," Nell said, smiling up at Hugo. She allowed Emiliano to take her bowl. It wasn't often she was waited on so thoroughly. It had felt uncomfortable and necessary, given her newly discovered affliction.

She'd nearly slipped up earlier, ready to mix the spices into the bowls. It wasn't until the familiar burning lanced across her palm that she remembered her curse. She still refused to call it a gift.

With Willa's and Maggie's help, she'd figured out that the burning, itching sensation in her palm was the power's signature. She still didn't know the full extent of it. Was it safe to cook if there was no burning?

She wasn't going to risk the people of Orca Cove. She'd find some way to experiment, but she wasn't cooking for anyone at the café until then.

"It was my pleasure, my dear." Hugo bowed playfully, then gathered the large cooking pan of leftovers and carried it inside.

He'd been quiet but happily eating his stew. It made her feel good to be able to help him taste his grandmother's recipe. That kind of nostalgia was one of the pleasures of cooking for others. Also the care; people loved being cooked for. She'd always thought it was like going back to childhood. Growing up, your parents or loved ones cooked for you. It was a reminder of childhood security, an instant bond between her and her patrons. At least it was for her.

Which is why this curse was so directly life-shattering. It was taking away the one thing she loved, the one thing she had left.

"Are you okay?" Emiliano paused, hands full of their used bowls as concern tightened the corners of his eyes when they searched hers.

"Yes." She forced a smile. "Of course. Thanks again for dinner."

He smiled in return and disappeared after his father.

Nell picked up her wineglass and toyed with the stem. At least she could enjoy tonight. There was one sip left, and she tipped it back, enjoying the delicious flavor of the Tempranillo.

Emiliano came back out to join her. "Would you like some more?"

"I should be helping you clean up." She moved to stand.

"I told you. You're not lifting a finger tonight." He raised the bottle, peering through the dark glass to see the line, and Nell watched the fabric of his Henley strain against his biceps and chest. "We can split what's left," he said.

"None for me." Hugo pushed through the kitchen door with the last of his things. "You two enjoy it. I'm going to wash Grandma's pan and sit in my chair."

"I can help you clean up, Pops." Emiliano set the bottle down and looked at Nell. "I'll just be a few minutes. You can sit by the fire and warm up. It's getting chilly."

"Not a chance. I wash that pan myself. No way for you to scratch it!" He winked at his son.

Nell couldn't imagine Emiliano damaging his father's precious pan, but he nodded with a small smile directed at his dad.

And they were alone.

It felt odd, but also nice. They'd been friends for a long time. Sort of. More like business partners. Either way, they knew each other well. And she felt comfortable with him, even if her libido was in overdrive.

"You want to split it?" At her nod, he tipped the remainder into their two glasses. It was almost a full second pour. Handing her wine to her, he moved to the chairs around the fire pit. "Would you like me to get you a blanket?"

She blushed at all the attention. She was used to waiting on others, not the other way around. "I brought a cardigan. I think I'll be fine."

"Are you sure?" He narrowed his eyes. "I'll get one just in case."

He disappeared into the house while she settled into the chair next to his, staring into the fire. It was a lovely night. She could see the outline of the mountains in the distance and the cove, with their two shops, across the street. It was a beautiful place to live.

"Here you go." Emiliano joined her, handing her a soft, fluffy, chocolate-colored blanket while keeping a navy one for himself. "I was getting a little chilly too."

He smiled at her, settling into his chair. The firelight played in his eyes lined by long, dark lashes as he took a long sip, his full lips closing over the rim of the glass. It wasn't just his youth; the man was startlingly beautiful.

Blinking back to reality, Nell took a long sip of her drink. Good Lord, she needed to get a grip on herself. "The wine is good."

He nodded, holding his glass up to look at the scarlet liquid. "Pops always insists on Spanish wine with Spanish meals, but it really is a good match."

"Definitely."

He turned a little in his chair so he could face her better. "I'm glad you joined us tonight. We don't often have dinner guests."

"I'm flattered, then." It was a nice reprieve from her current situation, even if just for a little bit. "Hugo's grandma's recipe is really something. I wasn't just being nice. All his time and efforts really showed."

She let the pleasure of the food be visible on her face, sighing at the memory.

"I know." The corner of his mouth ticked up, and his eyes softened. "You're genuinely a nice person."

Heat bloomed on her chest, moving up her neck, and it wasn't just the wine. "I try to be."

"No, you don't just try, Nell." His eyes were intent on her. "I see how you care for the people of Orca Cove, not just your friends."

"I'm a cook." She shrugged. "I'm just serving my community.""Not everyone goes the extra mile." He shook his head. "You're basically the only full-service restaurant on the cove. You could get away with much less."

"Well, I wouldn't be satisfied with myself if I didn't. Besides, I love to cook. It's what I was meant to do. It's nothing you don't do. I've seen you make sure you highlight Nick's woodworking and offer top dollar to Solomon's fish."

"Nick's an artist." Emiliano nodded firmly. "And Solomon gets the best fish. Somehow, he just knows where to find them."

"See?" she said with a laugh.

"They need us." He shrugged.

"They do."

"Maybe we're just both good people."

"I'll agree to that. We both try, at least."

"That, we do."

She smiled at him. He did get her.

His gaze softened again, and he worried his lower lip as he looked directly at her. Her insides went gooey like barely baked brownies.

"Nell, tonight was great."

"It was."

"Would you consider doing it again?"

"I mean, if Hugo has other recipes he wants to cook for me, who am I to say no?" She giggled, trying to lighten the mood.

"That's not what I meant." A slight wrinkle briefly formed between his brows, and he shook his head. "Would you consider going to dinner with me? As a date?"

Her heart stopped, and she could no longer hear the crackle of the burning wood. Her eyes flicked around until the world righted itself. "A date?"

Had he considered *this* a date? Maybe it was attraction she had registered from him, after all.

Could she? Should she?

She gulped loudly. "I'm not sure what to say. I had no idea."

He glanced down at his wine, then back up to her. "You don't have to answer now. You can think about it. When you're ready."

When she was ready... Hadn't she just considered dating? It still felt so soon, so raw. Then again, she wasn't sure the pain of losing Gary would ever *not* feel raw.

"Thank you." The words were all she could muster as she let herself consider it for a moment. Thin ribbons of hope unfurled inside her, followed by the warmth of desire.

He dipped his head in a short, satisfied nod and looked back at the fire. "Tonight, I finished the cookies you gave me. I'm embarrassed to say I didn't share even one. They were probably the best cookies I'd ever had."

Desire was replaced by fear, clawing up her insides with sharp, icy hot talons. Nell felt the blood drain from her face. When she had considered dating again, she was baking those very cookies.

He wasn't interested in her. She'd spelled him into attraction.

"Maybe you're wrong." Maggie tried to take Nell's hands, but she broke away, spinning around the room. Willa stood off to the side, her own hands tightly wound around each other.

They were all there. Unfortunately. To witness her most spectacularly embarrassing moment.

She'd left the Gils' house hastily and incredibly rudely. Unsure how she'd ever explain her exit to Emiliano, she'd stumbled out of there, making excuses immediately after realizing what had happened. How would she ever face him again? She'd tried to make something up about forgetting a late meetup with Maggie to talk about the menu, but the look on his face said it all.

He knew it was because of what he'd shared, and he looked shattered.

It was all her fault.

She was in such a state when she got back to the café that she hadn't even noticed Maggie was still there.

Of course, she'd texted the entire crew. All of which were now gathered around her in her dining room, witnessing her losing her very last sliver of control.

A rational portion of her brain tried to tell her she should be appreciative of their support, but she couldn't muster the courage to push past her discomfort. They all knew what she'd done. Mortified was a better word for it.

"I'm not wrong." She swallowed the bile rising in her throat. "I was thinking about... Well, it was just a weak moment. Obviously, I'm not ready."

"There's nothing wrong with being ready." Willa laid a hand on her shoulder. "You're a human being. It's normal to want connection."

"But it's barely been a year." Nell searched her friend's eyes for something. Acceptance, maybe.

"It's been over a year. And only you will know when you'll be ready or what's in your heart. It's your decision to make."

That was the problem. Her heart would always be broken.

"I can't even imagine what Gary would think." Her late husband's face popped up in her mind, laughing like he'd so often done, and she slumped into a seat at a table in the back.

"Gary would want you to be happy." Duke spoke quietly from a few feet behind the rest, and everyone turned to look at him. "You know that, Nell. That's all he ever wanted." Tightness constricted around her heart. It was true. Then the tears came, hot and raw, flooding over her cheeks. How on earth could she think of another man? No one measured up to Gary.

And no one ever would.

"Maybe it wasn't Nell Friday night." Maggie stood at her elbow, twisting one hand in the other. "It could have been the geoducks."

"It's not the geoducks," Duke said calmly.

"How do you know?" Maggie insisted. "Lots of strange things happen in the water from the cove."

It was true. Maybe it wasn't her, after all. Nell listened to the two discussing her whole future as tendrils of hope rose up within her.

"I went back to Gil's and got another geoduck."

"Maybe it was from another batch," Maggie said helpfully.

"It's not," Duke said with finality, giving Maggie a stern look. "I made sure."

And just like that, Nell's heart sank.

"Come on." Shelby stood in front of her, reaching out. "Let's get moving."

Nell stared at the offered hand. "What are you talking about?"

"Come on." She insisted, pulling her up and out of the chair and marching them into her kitchen. "You're done wallowing. It's time to figure this out."

Everyone else filed after them, finding a spot along the counters and blocking the door. Apparently, they agreed.

"Figure what out?"

Duke picked up an apple and an onion from her baskets as Shelby rolled her eyes before grabbing the container of dried nori. "I don't know what to do with these, but pick something."

"For what?" It was getting ridiculous now.

"We have to figure out your powers."

It was like pouring lemon juice over raw wounds. Nell winced. "I can't cook."

"Oh, you will." Taking the apple from Duke's hands, she shoved it and the nori at her. "Go on."

She stared at the food now in her hands. "But what if I hurt someone?"

"You won't. We're in a safe environment." Shelby pushed her towards her stove. "'Sides, Willa's here if you screw us up too badly."

Horrified, Nell spun around only to find Shelby giving her a side grin. One hand was perched on a hip, and an eyebrow was raised. She'd been messing with her. "But I could..."

"But you won't," Shelby insisted. "It's temporary, and we trust you."

"But what if it's not temporary?" "We're all fine today, with no lasting anger. We all had those drunk nights that didn't last long." She did finger quotes around the word *drunk*. "I wasn't angry by the time I went to bed. My best guess is it only lasts a few hours, four to five at most."

Still long enough for Emiliano's love spell, Nell thought sadly.

"Okay, then." Duke appeared at her elbow. "What's first?"

"Um." Nell looked at the apple. "I could make a spiced, sautéed apple pretty quickly."

Duke pulled something from the shelves under her counters.

"Uh, no." Nell took the pan from his hands. It was a saucepan. What was he thinking? "Don't touch my cookware."

Smothering a grin, Duke backed away, hands in the air. He tucked a too-long edge of his hair behind his ear and leaned against her refrigerator to watch. "It's your kitchen, b oss."

"I'm not your boss." Nell grinned, already pulling her apron over her head and tying the straps around her waist. She quickly washed her hands and began cutting and slicing. Butter went into the skillet, along with brown sugar and cinnamon. A little cardamom. Once they were sizzling, she slid in the apple slices, stirring slowly.

"You can do it." Maggie patted her back in encouragement.

"My goodness, that smells good." Willa stepped in closer. "Do you have enough for all of us?"

Nell spun around, her spatula held tightly in hand. "This is only to test. I'm making a few different things, a few different ways."

"Just make whatever I get smell that good."

"Done," Nell said, not looking away from the dish. She swirled the spatula, gathering sauce from the bottom of the pan to drizzle up and over the apples. After a few minutes, she turned the burner off. Taking a small bowl from a shelf, she poured half the apples into the dish.

It needed something. Limoncello. She drizzled the tiniest amount over the apples, then turned to grab the vanilla ice cream from the freezer and scooped a small amount out, folding it over into a nice dollop and laying it atop the apples. Frowning, she found a container of nutmeg in her pantry and grated a little on top of the ice cream.

Stepping back, she wiped her hands on her apron. "Who's going to try it?"

"Willa, you might as well," Shelby said. "I don't think it will have any effect."

"Why not?" Maggie cocked her head, curious.

"The rest of us have to use something from the ocean. Yours is probably the same."

"Then, why'd you have me try the apple?" Nell asked.

Shelby raised her shoulder, pushing away to pick up the container of nori. "Because we had to rule it out."

"You also didn't have any burning," Duke said, standing over the remaining apples. "Try adding the nori to that, but don't think on it very much. See if you can feel neutral. It's possible you could learn to control it."

"What were you feeling when you made this?" Willa asked around a mouthful of sautéed apples. "These are the best apples I've ever had, by the way."

"Thanks," Nell said, pleased. She hadn't cooked since her birthday. It felt like a balm to her wounds. "Happy, actually. It felt good to make something for someone, even if it was to test how far my curse goes."

"It's not a curse, Nell," Maggie said. "You'll see."

"How do you feel?" Nell ignored her words. "Happy?"

"Sure, but no more than before," Willa answered.

"Are you sure?" They had to be certain.

"Definitely." Willa set the bowl in the sink. "I was worried about you, too, and still am. That didn't go away. Saturday night, I got angry, and things felt unfair. My own feelings and emotions were overwhelmed by that for a while. I think you're good."

"Thank goodness." Nell sank against her countertop. Then she stilled. That meant she couldn't cook seafood anymore. It was still a life sentence. She owned a restaurant on the water.

"Try the nori." Duke gestured.

"To apples?" Nell shook her head firmly. "No way."

"It's just to test it out. It doesn't have to be the most amazing apples I've ever had."

"Those were." Willa pointed at her dish.

"I should have offered to taste the first one," Shelby said dryly.

"Yes, you should have." Willa gave a sweet, wide smile.

"You guys are impossible." Nell took her container of baking ingredients from a shelf and set some Baker's chocolate on the counter. Making quick work of it, she chopped some up, then melted it in a saucepan with a drizzle of olive oil over low heat. Olive oil instead of butter. It would add a green element that would taste good with the nori. Incorporating raw sugar, she stirred the bottom, careful not to burn it.

On impulse, she drizzled in some of the tahini butter she'd used in the cookies and took it off the heat.

Getting another bowl out, she added a larger scoop of vanilla ice cream. After pouring over a good amount of the sauce, she picked up the nori.

"Any burning?" Duke asked.

"Not yet." Nell shook her head. She unscrewed the lid, peering at the potentially harmful ingredient. There was only one way to know. Breathing out slowly, she thought of a clean sink of dishes. Nothing to do. Everything sorted and put away. Calmly, she picked a pinch of the nori and blew out, sprinkling it over the ice c ream.

No burning, no itching. Taking another pinch, she crumbled it in her fingers and calmed her mind, letting just the dust hit the sauce.

"Still nothing?" Duke asked.

"Nothing."

"Good job!" Willa clapped her hands.

"We don't know yet." Nell stared at the bowl in front of her. Worry swirled in her belly. A hot line ran across her palm, and she shook her hands out, backing away from the counter. "It's burning now, but I don't know if it can affect it if I'm not touching it."

"One way to find out." Duke snatched up the bowl, scooping up a large spoonful that contained half of what Nell had portioned out. It disappeared into his mouth, and he moaned.

Willa's mouth hung open. "Is it that good?"

"Oh, yeah," Duke said, talking over the dessert as she had. He swallowed. "That's amazing."

Shelby crossed her arms over her chest. "You had to take the chocolate sauce."

"Hey, I'm risking my life." Duke winked at the stern brunette and wolfed down the other half as well.

"Hey." Nell snatched the bowl out of his hands.

"It was a joke!" Duke laughed, backing away.

"And?" Maggie pushed in. "Do you feel anything?"

"No. Not yet, anyway."

"One more." Shelby pushed her back toward the stove. "This time, I want you to intentionally try to spike your emotions. Think of something, anything strong."

"Are you sure about this?" Maggie grabbed Shelby's arm. "Maybe we should try something light and easy. Something in the middle.""We proved she could use it without changing people's emotions if she's neutral. It's time to test out the opposite."

"We don't know for sure," Nell argued. "It could be that I was passing neutral emotions on."

"What's the difference?" Shelby shrugged.

"I won't have to worry about my emotions if I know I'm not passing them along. I could just relax."

"Well, try a happy one, then, if it makes you feel better," Shelby said.

That sounded less scary, so Nell found a slab of haddock in her cooler and heated another skillet, adding butter and garlic.

Music blared behind her. Twisting around, she saw Maggie had turned on the radio. When she flipped through the stations, Season of the Witch started playing. They all paused, then burst out laughing.

"Witchy song for witchy purposes." Maggie circled her wrists, doing a wiggly side shuffle around the room.

"We're not witches." Willa laughed.

"We're not far off!" Maggie giggled, pulling droplets of water from the kitchen sink. She grabbed Willa's hand and swung her around in a circle.

It was impossible not to laugh at the two giggling women. Shelby rolled her eyes halfheartedly before adding a sway to her hips and nudging Duke, who took off in a slide across the floor. He spread his arms dramatically, then took off the other way.

She knew it was for her benefit, and it was ridiculous, but she still loved it. Her palm started burning, and she held it up. "It's burning again."

"Mine tingles. We all feel it differently." Willa took Nell's hand to look at it. "Where?"

Nell pointed. "It's reducing now."

"Go back to cooking," Shelby commanded, still swaying from side to side. "Don't be afraid, at least not this time. Just smile and have joy."

Taking the wooden spatula back in hand, Nell flipped the fish in the garlic-butter sauce. She would ignore the worry. She was cooking, and damn, did she love doing that. Taking small dance steps, she skipped over to the white wine and poured a little into one corner of the pan, letting it bubble up and cook into the butter solution.

She should have added it earlier, but she hadn't thought of it.

Using a spoon, she basted the fish. Her hand still burned, but it had died down to a simmering warmth.

Turning off the flame. She slid the fish onto a plate. A handful of pistachios, and they'd be done. She chopped them finely on her cutting board, along with a little parsley that she sprinkled over and handed the dish to Shelby.

Shelby stepped back, shaking her head. "That one goes to Maggie."

"But she's already happy." Willa laughed.

Sure enough, Maggie still had a wide smile on her face.

Shelby glanced at Duke. He shut off the music, and she pinched Maggie's shoulder.

"Ow!" Maggie cried, her chin crunched up. "Why'd you do that?"

"To get rid of the happy," Shelby said blandly.

"Fine." Maggie snatched the plate and picked up the fork. "Nell's haddock is the best. Your loss."

"No doubt."

It only took a few bites before a slow smile spread over the short blonde's face. If it hadn't reached her eyes, it would have been creepy.

"How do you feel?" Duke asked.

"Great." Maggie giggled. "That's better than two glasses of wine."

"We should save the leftovers." Shelby eyed the rest of the fish.

"We should sell the leftovers." Duke edged in closer.

"Not on your life." Maggie forked the last of it into her mouth and dance-hopped to the sink. "I'll do dishes."

"You might as well wait until we're done." Shelby turned to Nell. "One more. You know what to do."

Nell's hand stilled. She knew what was left.

"You sure about this?" Duke asked.

Shelby nodded tensely, crossing her arms.

It would change things, knowing for sure. But Nell had to know. Wordlessly, she pulled scallops out of the fridge. They were quicker. Using the same pan to hopefully reduce the pain, she heated more butter and garlic.

The scallops cooked in seconds, but the burning had already started. Leaning into it, she thought about her loss. Her heart cracked open, and there it was. Stabbing fire raced across her palm in a long line.

It was enough.

Flicking off the burner a final time, she slid the scallops onto a small plate. This time, she didn't bother to garnish it. It would do its job fast enough. For some reason, she was sure.

Shelby hesitated only for a moment, then her teeth set and she pushed off from her place near the counter to take the offering. Forking up a large bite, she breathed out. Then she walked to the sink and popped the rest of the scallop into her mouth.

When she turned back, she was nodding. Already, silent pain shone on her face.

"That's it."

And she walked out.

CHAPTER 6

He'd messed up. He'd messed up so badly.

Emiliano sat on the side of his bed, his head heavy in his hands. He shouldn't have brought it up. He had pushed her. He'd promised himself he wouldn't do t hat.

It was just that things had gone so well. Nell seemed to have enjoyed dinner. She'd been radiant with excitement while helping his dad find the missing ingredient in his grandmother's recipe. Something important to his pops. He hadn't thought he could care more for her than he already did, but it had warmed his heart to see the man open up like that.

And they'd talked, Nell and he, *really* talked. They'd laughed and chatted about things other than work for once.

She had looked so lovely, illuminated by the firelight and relaxed in the chair, sipping her wine. He hadn't been able to help himself. It seemed so natural and had come out easily, asking her on a real date. It had felt right.

The funny thing was, at first, she hadn't seemed to object to the idea. Had he just projected on her? Was she just being nice? He was at war with himself.

And his hands scraped through his short curls in frustration.

No, he hadn't been wrong; she'd been interested. He'd doubted himself a lot regarding her, but it had felt too real. I t *had* to have been real.

She'd been interested.

If that was true, what had gone wrong?

Standing, he paced his bedroom. After two laps, he left his room to stalk through his living room, his legs unable to stop moving. Maybe she'd just gotten scared. Maybe her feelings had overwhelmed her.

That sort of made sense. Maybe she just needed time to get used to the idea.

Needing more space, he continued onto the balcony over his dad's garage and down the wooden steps. As he walked, he took in a deep breath of the fir-scented air.

The moon lighting up the night sky, was nearly full tonight and hung clear over the market. The sound of the waves crashing called to him, and he found his way down to the pebble beach, the small rocks shifting underfoot. Far in the distance, he spotted an orca's fin in the moonlight reflected on the ocean behind the market, and the peaceful sight calmed his mind as always.

The lights at the back of the café were on. His feet stilled, the pebbles ceasing their shifting crunch. He wasn't trying to spy on Nell. He should go.

Turning to leave, he saw figures in the café. Concerned, he watched for a moment until he recognized them. Her cr ew.

No danger, he decided, and resumed his walk, away from the market and café.

She'd gotten nervous and called her friends.

They were close. But what did that mean? Did she want their opinion on the situation?

Shoving his hands into his pants pockets, he pushed his feet at a comfortable pace. First, she'd shut down the café the day after her birthday, and tonight, after their dinner and his date proposal, she'd called in her friends. Maybe she was still struggling more than he'd realized. Maybe she needed more time.

Feeling like he had found a reasonable understanding of what was going on with the mysterious Nell, his footsteps lightened.

The other option, the one that always haunted him, was that, for some reason, women never stayed in his life because he wasn't enough. That was unthinkable. Not with her, the only woman who'd ever been a constant in his life.

He would be patient. She was worth all the time it took.

"Son, did you place that Seattle order?" Hugo stopped at the office doorway, one hand pressing against the doorjamb.

Emiliano snapped his laptop shut, his mind blanking on the order. "Uh, yeah. Canned goods and pasta, mainly."

His dad's face screwed up in a frown. "We'll have to place another one, then. Soon."

Emiliano stood, trying to look casual. He'd been working on the new website for Gil's Market and Marina all morning, adding the new online-sales portion, with an e-commerce module to order items for pick-up or delivery. Slowly, he calmed his rising panic. His dad hadn't seen.

The entitlements were turning out to be trickier than he'd imagined. He needed to include a flag for each merchant, like Willa, who didn't want their products to be available for shipping. She wanted to stay local, and he respected that.

His fingers itched to dive back in. He was so close to figuring it out.

"Is there something else we need?" he asked.

"Yeah." His dad glanced back out toward the floor and took a couple of steps inside their shared office space. "Conrad's worried about hikers or something on his property."

"Someone's messing around on Brooks Farms?" It was where they got some of their produce.

"Yeah, hikers or hunters, likely some tourists in town. It'll blow over, but he wants some game cameras, and we're out."

"We can make an extra order." Emiliano jotted a note down on his notepad. "Or if it's important, I'm sure Duke could pick something up for us the next time he's in Seattle."

"Nah." Hugo's nose wrinkled. "He was hot and bothered about it today, but let's see if it holds. It coulda just been some crazy kids or even a bear. If he mentions it again, we'll figure something out. Otherwise, let's stock a couple extra at the beginning of the tourist season."

"Sounds good." He nodded. Even though Conrad wasn't one to overreact, they could wait. His dad had talked to the man, and he kept his hand on the pulse of the townspeople. He had likely judged his concern correctly. Still, he'd check in on Conrad at his next produce delivery. Just to be sure.

"Also, you hear that Joe got sick last week?"

"No, is he okay?"

"Yeah, he felt ill after dining at the café."

"That's weird." It was also strange he hadn't heard anything about it. News traveled fast around here. "He the only one?"

"Seems like."

"Probably not the café, then."

"Doubtful, but best to keep an eye on expiration dates. Nell gets most of her ingredients here."

"Good idea. I'll get Tommy's help."

"Sounds good."

Hugo motioned to the closed laptop like it was the proverbial elephant in the room that it was. "Everything good there?"

So, he had noticed.

"Just off a few pennies on the online ledger. You know how frustrating that can be." He hated lying to his dad, but he had to get the website working properly before he could tell him about it. His pops wouldn't want him to waste time on it, and if he saw him struggling, he'd try to convince him it was impossible. Change was hard. "You know how it is. It's more difficult to find an entry error of a few pennies than a large one."

"That's because you're using the computer." Hugo wagged a finger. "That machine does all sorts of crazy stuff. You'll probably figure it out in the paper ledger."

Where there's room for all sorts of manual errors, like with additions and subtractions, on top of entry errors. Not to mention, he couldn't search and find specific numbers like he could on the web application. Emiliano gritted his teeth and flattened his lips. "I'm sure I'll figure it out."

"I'm sure you will, son." Hugo absently patted him on the back and headed out.

Of course, he expected him to fill in the manual ledger as well. He'd probably look for it later.

His head dropped into the palm of his hand propped on the desk. Maybe he'd been at the computer too long. Pushing away, he returned to the floor.

Tuesdays were always busy. Even though they were open six days a week, the one they took off always meant an influx the following day. His eyes scanned the shelves for holes, making his mental list of things to do when traffic died down between lunch and rush hour.

Speaking of lunch, his attention drifted over to The Wild Café and the people walking in and out the door. His pulse picked up. Nell had opened.

That had to be a good sign, right? She must be feeling better.

His stomach growled, letting him know it had noticed the time as well. He itched to go over, grab lunch, and check on her. But after the way things had ended last night, he thought it better to wait a day or two.

Instead, he inspected the fresh fish at the back of the market, near the marina and registers. All the chests were newly iced.

Tommy shot by.

"Nice job, bud." He motioned to the younger man, still in his teens but only just, and pointed to the fish.

"Thanks, boss." The teen paused, looking around nervously.

He brushed past the formal title. It still sounded strange to him. He'd told the kid to call him Emiliano a million times. "Everything okay?"

Red crept up Tommy's neck. "Yeah, boss."

Frowning, he followed the youth's eyes, which shifted from him to a young lady a couple of aisles away. Ah. Young love. He remembered what that was like. He might still be in love with the same female, but it had changed. It was no longer tinged with the fairy-tale dreams and lustful nature of the young. Still, he recognized it.

"Is she the one?" He smiled gently.

"Uh." Tommy's eyes tore away from the blonde, widening in panic. "What do you mean?"

The young man's voice came out in a squeak, his tone pitched high.

"We've all been there, Tommy, my man."

"That's for sure." Duke surprised them both, and Tommy physically jumped an inch from the ground. "Sorry. I wasn't intentionally eavesdropping."

The smirk on his face disagreed with the apology, as Duke shifted a small shopping basket half full of items to his other arm.

"Is it that obvious?" Tommy's body was tight.

"Only if you have eyes." Duke chuckled.

"Only if you're paying attention." Emiliano gave Duke a pointed look, then turned more understanding eyes to the smitten young man. "You're not normally this distracted."

"Oh." He looked over at the girl once more, then cast his eyes down.

"It'll be okay. I promise." He clapped Tommy on the back in a friendly fashion.

"You've felt like this before?" Tommy looked up at him.

"Oh, yeah. Definitely."

"What do you do about it?"

"Well, it depends."

"Generally, you find out if she feels the same way," Duke offered.

"It's not always that easy." Emiliano bit back a wince. He didn't want to build up the kid's expectations if it didn't work out. Unrequited love was a tough one. "Sometimes there are variables."

"At that age?" Duke's lips flattened, and he raised both eyebrows.

So Emiliano glanced at the girl. She looked of similar age to Tommy and was a local. Maybe he was projecting onto the kid. He sighed. "Duke's right. You should find out how she feels."

"What if she doesn't like me?" The kid turned to look up at the two men, and his eyes were full of hope.

Emiliano had nothing to say. He'd never figured out how to deal with that. His eyes involuntarily shifted to Duke, whose smile faltered.

"If she doesn't like you, then that's that." The older man took charge of the situation. "You'll have tried. You can try again with the next person who strikes your fancy. It's no big deal."

"No big deal! Not everyone is perfect like her." Tommy lifted his chest. "And if she doesn't like me back, I may never find anyone else."

"Of course you will."

"Not necessarily." Tommy's voice drifted to a whisper. "Maybe she doesn't like me because of me.""If she doesn't like you, it doesn't mean anything but that you aren't the right person for her, at least not right now." Duke's eyes stayed locked on Emiliano's as he struggled to keep his emotions in check. "Things change, you know? You never know where life will take you. Just be open about it and do what you can. That's all we can ever do."

The lump in Emiliano's throat was growing, and he struggled to swallow. Tommy looked from Duke to him. To get his validation of the man's thoughts.

He'd never dealt well with rejection. It always felt ex-pected.

His mom hadn't stayed. Of course, *they* wouldn't stay. He wasn't holding it against the women. It just wasn't something he'd seen in his life, with him. Like there was something wrong with him.

The only thing that had given him any hope was that they weren't "the one." Nell was. Always had been. It didn't make a difference if it was returned or not.

"That's right." Emiliano struggled to nod his head. "It's better to try. If you don't try, you'll never know. It's all you can do."

Duke gave a single short, crisp nod. Then he held up a fist to Tommy. "Now, go get over there and say hi."

"Can I, boss?" Tommy looked to Emiliano for allowance.

"Of course. You've gotta check on the customers. Just don't take all day."

Tommy hopped up almost vertically on his toes before he caught himself. He coughed, straightened his apron, and made a beeline for the young blonde woman.

The two men watched the encounter. Twenty feet away, the young people shifted uncomfortably on their feet.

"He'll be just fine," Duke said, leaning on an ice chest containing fish. His eyes were still trained on the couple.

"Yeah, it looks like it."

"I mean, even if she's not the right one, after all. He'll still be fine."

"I hope so."

"You will, too, you know?" Duke's eyes were still trained on the couple.

"What do you..." He let his voice trail off. Duke had always known how to read people. He wasn't even going to argue with the perceptive man. "But she's the one. I've tried with others."

"Maybe they weren't the right people. Maybe she's still out there."

"Maybe. But maybe it's just her. Maybe it's always been her."

"Always?"

"Always."

"Shit." Duke finally looked at him, eyes searching him as a man, several years younger, but as an equal. "I'm sorry, man. That had to suck."

He laughed out loud when the humor of the situation struck him. "Yeah."

They stood there a while in silence before Duke spoke again. "Well, shit."

"It's okay." Emiliano lifted his shoulders and let them drop. "It is what it is. It doesn't change anything."

Duke's mouth pursed. "You've got to be careful with her. She's special."

It was Emiliano's turn to raise an eyebrow.

"I know you know that," Duke went on. "Just don't rush her. I'm not questioning your feelings for her, but if you push her, it won't end well for either of you."

"Look, it's okay. I'm not some crazy stalker."

"I know that."

"I'm not going to try to make her love me."

"I know that, too."

"Then, what are you worried about?"

"I've known you a long time." Duke paused, checking in on the two kids who had progressed to a private conversation. "You don't have to wait around for her. If she's not ready, that is."

"I appreciate your concern, Duke. I really do." The boy still living inside Emiliano was flattered at Duke's attention. As a kid, it would have been a dream come true. Duke was always the wild card, fun but a little unhinged. He'd grown since then. "And please don't worry about Nell. I've made my feelings known, as you're probably aware. And no matter what she decides, I'll respect it. But it won't change how I feel. I've learned to live with them."

It looked like Duke wanted to say more, but after a moment, he nodded. "The geoduck was delicious, by the way."

"Yeah?" Emiliano almost choked on the words, so relieved by the change in conversation. "I still think you should have gotten a fresh one."

"I don't mind taking what some would consider a second choice." His eyes glimmered with intention.

"I guess I'm not good at that. I'd rather skip it and wait for the best."

"Choices like that can leave you lonely...and hungry."

"True. That's okay. For me, at least." Emiliano let it hang between them. "Are you okay with that?"

He didn't need the man's blessing, but it had been Duke's best friend who was married to Nell. He'd lost Gary, too, and could see Emiliano as a poor second choice for one of his closest friends.

"Yeah, I'd say so. Not that it's my choice." Duke stretched out a hand between them. "Alright, man. Best of luck to you, then."

The extension of friendship meant more to Emiliano than he could ever express.

He shook his hand and walked away in search of lunch and something to calm his completely exposed nerves.

CHAPTER 7

"**A**re you sure this is going to be alright?" Nell stood nervously in the doorway that separated the kitchen from the dining rooms. They'd convinced her to open today. Maggie was helping with the cooking, and Nell herself had barely stirred anything.

It was torture.

Willa had texted later the night before after checking in on Shelby. She was okay. Duke reassured her that they tested it all out, and there was no reason to believe that what they'd learned wouldn't apply on a larger scale. It seemed localized to seafood, and her hand burning signaled they were in the danger zone.

In theory, it would be okay. But was that safe enough for her customers?

Maggie promised to follow all her orders to a T, and Willa recommended she try meditating to better control her emotions while cooking. Not that she was ready to trust testing the waters on her control, but meditating seemed a little out of her reach. At least right now. That was more up Willa's alley.

They hadn't heard from Shelby after she'd left the night before. Nell had texted her, and she'd eventually replied that she was fine and to give her the evening. She'd touch base with them the following day. She hadn't yet, though, and it made her nervous. Willa had promised to stop by Siren's Song cabin rental, which Shelby owned and operated, to check in on her.

"Of course, it's going to be alright." Maggie patted her on the shoulder and wiped her hands on her apron.

It was messy. Nell glanced down at her own, well-loved one, and her hands pressed the front of it against her legs. She felt like a sham. She hadn't cooked any of that food, not really.

"Thank you." Nell's voice was soft.

"Hey, it's going to be alright." Maggie grinned at her. Her sweet, round face lit with kindness.

They'd made large batches of prepped dishes: a rich, hearty elk stew and vegan lentil sloppy joes. They were due for a few rainy days and cooler temperatures, so it worked. Carlos came that morning to help prep, as usual, so they had salads and a couple of easy dessert options. Luckily, he didn't ask why Nell had asked him to do more than normal.

The only concession she'd been willing to make was the bread. She had reluctantly agreed to Duke's offer to pick baguettes and buns up to serve with the meals. It was a limited menu. She felt bad about it, but she excused herself by telling her staff that she was working on new menu items. The same lie she had told Emiliano at her hasty exit. No one complained.

Yet.

"I'd better go check on the tables." Maggie took a couple of steps backward. "You gonna be okay for a little while?"

"Of course I will." She didn't need a babysitter. Catching herself, she let out the tension she'd been holding. "Thank you."

It wasn't Maggie's fault she was limited. She didn't need to take it out on her.

Nell watched her friend stop at the tables. The petite woman listened to everyone, placing a hand on a shoulder or leaning in to share a laugh. Nell didn't know what she'd do without her.

Even though they were deep in the middle of lunch hour, the skies had turned gray and the first drops of rain were beginning to fall. Across the parking lot, she could see Gil's Market standing under the heavy, water-filled clouds.

Sadness clenched her heart like the ties of her apron knotted at her waist, and she loosened them to get a deeper breath.

She'd been tempted to cross over and get the bread herself. She could have reinforced her story from last night and told Emiliano what they were considering adding to the menu. Coincidentally, her lie had served a double duty for her. It didn't sit any better in her stomach, though.

The visit would have only been to make herself feel better. She was certain he had seen through the excuse and it would just make him feel worse.

Nell just really wanted to see him. That was the truth of it, but it was better to give him a few days and let them get back to normal, simply colleagues. He'd appreciate the break after his heartfelt ask and realization, the morning after, what an idiot he'd been.

It was settled; she would put some distance between them. It had been nice to dream for a little while, and she still remembered the mesmerizing look in his eyes, lined with thick lashes, as he gazed into hers.

She'd get over it. She'd gotten over much harder things.

"We have two more orders for the elk stew and a large chef's salad." Maggie bustled back to her, sticking her pen behind an ear. Blonde tufts of hair stuck out from where they had been displaced by the pen.

"Let's get to it." She turned to lead the way, directing Maggie around the kitchen like that animated children's movie with the rat. It was still her restaurant, after all. Garnishes and perfectly toasted baguettes, sliced on the edge, would still be served.

"Nell." Barnaby banged into the kitchen.

Both women froze.

"Yes?" Nell plastered a bored expression on her face as she stood at Maggie's shoulder.

"I don't think I've ever seen you let anyone use those knives." He gestured with his chin.

It had torn her up inside to let anyone touch them. They were one of the first expensive purchases they'd made. Gary had bought them for her when they cleared their first thousand in the black. Every knife slip and nick on the cutting board had made her cringe. But it was necessary.

"Maggie's learning a few things so she can help out more often." Nell tried to pass it off.

The warm smile Maggie sent Barnaby was more believable. "I've been wanting to do this for a long time."

Hers didn't sound untrue. Either that, or she was much better at lying.

"I just wanted to let you know that the band is scheduled for Saturday night. After the dinner crowd, as requested."

Crap. She'd forgotten about that. It would draw people, wouldn't it? Wasn't she supposed to advertise something like that? Should she?

"Thanks." She barely registered Barnaby's exit.

Her head swam. She couldn't think about it today. Maybe tomorrow.

The need to cook something simmered feverishly in Nell. Taking a small bowl off a shelf, she cracked an egg over it, carefully separating the white and discarding the yellow in another bowl for later. Then she repeated the process with another egg. While whipping the whites into frothy points, she added sugar, a touch of cinnamon, salt, and vanilla. Finally, she folded walnuts in and poured them out onto a pan to bake. She'd add the candied nuts to Carlos' pre-mixed salad, along with dried cranberries and a little blue cheese.

Stretching her neck, she caught Maggie's raised eyebrow.

"It's not seafood." She raised her spatula in surrender. She had argued with them about precautions, even though they thought it was safe, and here she was, throwing caution to the wind. Well, maybe not caution. Tested and well-thought-out odds, she supposed, but it felt reckless.

"I'm not arguing." Maggie set down her knives. "You probably want these back."

"More than you can imagine." Nell looked up at the ceiling. "Fine. There's no seafood. I'm all good here. Class dismissed. You can get back out to the floor."

"You've got this." Maggie gave her a wink and be-bopped out to the floor.

A couple of hours later, Nell emerged from her kitchen to see what was going on in the dining room. She'd filled the rest of the lunch orders on autopilot and escaped into her own little world. Once the rush died down, she'd relaxed even more, alone in her kitchen, expanding the menu for dinner. She even started a batch of bread that would be ready for the evening rush.

It had stopped raining, and she felt better than she had in days.

Suddenly, a familiar figure coming in through the back patio door caught her attention. Not Emiliano, but her friend Duke.

"It looks like you got a handle on things," Duke said, approaching.

Grabbing her hands behind her back, she stretched deeply, easing the strain in her shoulders. "Maybe a little. It's easier when I can cook."

"Makes sense." He leaned against the varnished wood planks lining the restaurant's interior, giving it its warm, inviting feel. "Any burning today?"

"None."

"That's good. You're doing better than me when I first realized."

"What did you do?" She stepped in closer, curious how someone like Duke would fare after learning he could control the movement of water.

The right side of his mouth ticked up, and his eyes glistened with mischief. "Let's just say no one moved as quickly as The Aurelia that day. I got out of hand, though, at one point. I'm glad she held up. She's a tough old girl."

The pride in his boat was evident on his face.

When he was younger, he'd go off for days, following a job, but no one ever knew what it was. Gary had said he was working as a hand on a cargo ship at one time.

After a longer-than-usual disappearance, he'd sailed into Orca Cove's marina on her, his new pride and joy and, more importantly, new home. He moved out of the place he'd shared with her and Gary, and had been living on the fishing vessel ever since.

That was a good day. Their little apartment over the café wasn't large enough for the three of them, with one bedroom and a fold-out couch.

"That she is. I'm glad she made it through unscathed," Duke said with a smile.

Not particularly beautiful, The Aurelia was an old steel shipping vessel, but she had a mysterious air about her. She looked mighty fine at the end of the marina, knocking back and forth in the waves.

They always looked forward to seeing Duke come back into the cove. It meant dinners with the crew and fun stories. At least for a while.

"I was lucky. And I'm glad you're figuring your power out as well."

"Thanks, Duke." He hadn't always been this easy to lean on. That had been Gary's role in the crew. Ever since his passing, Duke had stepped up for them all. Nell thought it was good for him. He benefited from having a place.

"I'm assuming you don't need any more bread for the late crowd?"

"No. I've got it covered."

"Good."

"Have you heard from Shelby or Willa?"

Duke pushed off the wall, tucking a chunk of hair behind an ear. "Not yet. I was going to head over to the yoga studio and see if I could catch Willa."

"Okay. Let me know how she's doing." Nell still felt bad about Shelby taking the brunt of her emotions, even if she had signed up for it.

Duke nodded but didn't move away.

"What is it?"

"Have you thought about what to do about Emiliano?" He asked it so casually, rocking back on his heels.

Embarrassment reared up in the flush that grew on Nell's cheeks. "Not yet. I mean, I'm not sure what to do. Maybe I'll give it a few days and see if he's freaking out over what he said."

"Ever consider it wasn't the cookie?"

Nell paused, almost too busy in her self-loathing to understand what he was suggesting. "That's crazy."

"Is it?"

"Yeah." She stalled mid sentence. "Well, of course it is. Emiliano's like a kid."

"Is he?"

She was getting tired of the questions, and she couldn't handle the up-and-down emotions, thinking like that. It would be too much. "Yes, it had to have been the cookie. There's no way he'd be interested in someone like me."

Nell gripped the edges of her apron tightly, as though it was armor protecting her against the truth. She needed to keep those thoughts at bay. She was better off without them.

"If you say so, Nell." Duke let his head fall an inch, then looked back up at her. "Either way, you'll have to face him eventually. You do work together. Better to work through it than let it fester."

"Cause you're so good at that." She let the words loose before she could stop herself. He'd always been aloof and ran off at the first sign of difficulty. Unless he dealt with it with his fists, that was. At least, in the past, he had.

Duke let the words fall, soaking in them for a minute before nodding slowly. "And look how well it's worked for me."

"I'm sorry, Duke." Nell raised a hand to him, but he took a half step away.

"It's okay. You're right. I ran when things got tough. At times, it was the best I could do. I'm trying to grow from it, trying to do better now. Maybe we can both learn from i t."

Well, damn. Maybe he had grown up.

All the years Duke had been Gary's best friend, Nell was around to see the bad and good of it. She'd not always approved of their friendship, but Gary loved fiercely and always believed in the carefree man.

"I wish Gary could see you now." A tear slipped out of her eye. It wasn't a sad one, though. Well, it sort of was, but it was in that space of tender evocation, the sweeter side of g rief.

Duke took a slow breath, stepping back farther. "Thanks, Nell. I would have liked to grow with him, though."

"I'm just glad we got what time we did with him. We're all better for it."

"That's the truth."

She didn't stop him when he turned to leave. They both needed a moment with their memories.

"We're serving short ribs with polenta tonight?" Carlos looked up from the board where Nell was finishing writing the menu on the back deck the next morning. He was just coming in. "The special for the past two days has been beef. It's good, but where's the fish?"

Nell's mind went blank. It was a valid question since the little café stood on the cove's shoreline and was known for its seafood. "I'm still tweaking a few new recipes. It's just the limited menu right now."

"But I heard Gil's got a load of mussels. Wouldn't that be easy while you're busy with the other stuff?"

Steamed mussels in a garlicky white-wine sauce sprang to Nell's mind, and her fingers itched to start a sauce base she could pull from to steam batches of mussels per order. Angel-hair pasta to serve with it. Sourdough garlic-bread points. A radicchio salad with mustard greens and a light vinegar dressing with pomegranate seeds. And she'd started a new batch of sourdough, now that she wasn't scared to make more.

Wait. She couldn't make mussels.

"It's a possibility." Maggie appeared magically at her elbow, eyes wide in suggestion. "It would be pretty easy and let you work on other stuff."

Nell bit her lip. It sounded risky.

"Mussels sound good," Shelby said, taking the back-deck steps two at a time. She had her running gear on. "If you're having mussels, I'm stopping by at lunch."

Nell smiled thinly at her friend, hoping she wasn't mad at her, but the woman didn't seem to be harboring anything against her.

"Do you want me to pick mussels up, or are you going to pick them out yourself?" Carlos asked, already gathering buckets from behind the bar.

"Uh." Nell hesitated. She typically picked out her own, but she wasn't sure what to say to Emiliano. "Can you grab them? I need to get the sauce started."

"Sure thing, boss." Carlos yanked his apron off over his head. "Are two buckets good enough?"

"Yes, that'll work." Nell nodded, distracted by the decision that had taken place without her full agreement. It wouldn't be like her to hesitate over fresh mussels. They'd just have to take extra precautions.

The sound of beating wings overhead jerked Nell's attention upward as a large white pelican grunted, rising upward and away from them after a near dive onto their patio.

"That was close." Shelby frowned, following the pelican's departure. "What the hell was he doing dive-bombing the deck? There's no food out."

They watched the pelican drop from a thermal current and then pick up another before reaching the small fishing boat bobbing in the middle of the cove.

"I think that's Roy, Solomon's pelican," Willa said, entranced by the bird's landing on the rail next to the old fisherman.

"What, he couldn't get a parrot?" Shelby laughed at her own joke. "Is it because he feeds it so much? I've never seen a pelican follow someone that closely before."

"I have no idea." Nell tilted her head, watching the odd duo. "He talks to it like it's his friend."

"Weird," Shelby said.

Yep, her friend was back to her normal self.

"Maybe." Willa frowned.

"What?" Nell asked her.

"When those Seattle gangsters came after Solomon and me under the bridge, Roy dive-bombed them. Not like the fly-by he did here, but really dive-bombed them. He squawked and hissed and put up a fight to protect Solomon. Then, later, Percy, the orca-shifter, said someone told him where to find me. I'm guessing Solomon asked Roy to find help."

"You really believe that?" Shelby squinted at her open-minded friend.

"I do."

"Well, shit." Shelby propped her fists against her waist in a superwoman pose. "What do you think that's about? Do you think it's the water? Is it spelled? Is it making more magical people and animals, er, birds?"

"I don't know." Nell walked closer to the deck railing to watch the aging fisherman laugh at the bird. "It's possible Solomon was out there that night. Maybe he's just able to talk to animals."

"The night of the storm?" Willa walked over to join her. "That would make sense. But is he ever out that late? Fisherfolk get out early, especially Solomon."

"Not often, but I've seen him on the water in the evening, setting traps."

Shelby snorted. "We seem to keep growing. There looks to be six of us now."

"Maybe," Nell said, not entirely convinced.

She had thought there were only four. Even though the powers she'd gained still didn't feel like such, it was nice to know she hadn't been skipped for some weird reason. She had felt left out, no matter what she said.

"They're pretty smart, aren't they?" Willa watched the pelican hop up onto Solomon's shoulder like an obscure, overgrown parrot. "Pelicans, I mean. He really seems to be communicating with Solomon. And it appears he's fond of him. Does that mean he can talk to other sea-related animals? Assuming his powers are limited to the sea, like ours are."

"Probably." It made Nell think of shellfish and other sea creatures they've often served on the menu, and she grimaced. "If they can communicate, I feel bad about serving them in the restaurant."

"Mussels can't be smart, can they?" Shelby shuddered. "Please tell me they're not. They just open and shut their shells."

Her hands moved like clams opening and shutting.

"Probably not." Nell raised a hand to her chin, tapping a finger against her upper lip. "But I don't think I'll serve octopus anymore."

"Good idea." Shelby and Willa said in unison, still watching the boat.

CHAPTER 8

"Good morning!" An older woman raised a knobby hand to greet Emiliano.

"Good morning, Loris." He raised his hand in return, walking down an aisle in the market. "How're you doing this fine day?" He didn't fight the smile appearing on his face when he saw her bedecked in neon-blue leggings and a hand-painted, mandala-patterned, multi-colored tunic top. A matching purple headband completed the outfit. She might have been getting up there in age, but you'd never know it. The woman was light on her feet. "You look younger every time I see you. How is that possible?"

"Oh, hush." She waved off the compliment and blushed deeply, although the smile on her face ran from one ear to the other. "It's that salve of Willa's, you know? She's got my knees feeling like I'm twenty again!"

Loris pumped up and down on her knees a few times to illustrate it. She pulled her slim arms to her sides, bent at the elbow, her hands in tight fists.

"There are mornings when even I can't do that."

"Before long, you'll be needing her salve too!"

"I suppose we all have to age. It's part of life." He leaned on the corner of a crate of fresh zucchini to talk to her.

"You sound like it's so easy. You're young. But eventually, it's not going to seem so far away."

"I'm sure you're right, Loris." He hadn't thought about it in regard to himself, but he sure did with his dad. He was starting to show his age. It hit him in his core to see the only family he'd ever known lose his strength and vitality.

At one point, Hugo Gil would have been just like him, full of hopes and dreams. And love. But he'd fallen for the wrong person. Emiliano's mother hadn't been the kind to stay.

Emiliano might be in love with someone who didn't share his feelings, but at least his heart was with someone deserving.

"I'm just glad to see you doing so well." He inclined his head.

"I'm doing pretty good, aren't I?" She perked up, pleased with herself. "I go to yoga almost every day. That must account for something."

"And your hikes."

"That's right! I walk nearly every day. I love to watch the orcas."

Orca sightings had increased to an almost year-round occurrence. Their hometown was named correctly, after all. The pod had taken up residence in their little cove.

"I do too," he said. "They're so peaceful, aren't they?"

"They really are. Makes me feel warm inside to look at them." Her gaze got lost, focused on the window behind them, which was leading off to the water. "Maybe we should try to get Bernie outside. It might make him feel better too."

"What's wrong with Bernie?" He hadn't heard he was sick. He was a truck driver who lived on the outskirts of town.

Loris laid a hand on Emiliano's shoulder. "Oh, he got terribly ill last night. They're wondering if it's food poisoning."

"Food poisoning?" The man wasn't much of a cook, traveling so much. When he was in town, he ate at the café or grabbed something to go from the market. "Where do they think he got it?"

"Who knows? He travels so much; he could have picked up something anywhere."

"True. So why are people wondering if it's food poisoning?"

"Well." Loris leaned in closer and lowered her voice. "After Joe got sick, they're wondering if it's something at the café."

Emiliano frowned, shocked. He'd heard Joe wasn't feeling well but would never have guessed it was because of Nell's cooking. No one had ever gotten sick from it. Like, no one. Nell was one of the most careful cooks he'd ever seen. She kept a spotless kitchen. "I can't imagine anyone getting sick from the café."

"I know! It would be unheard of. But you know how people talk."

He did, unfortunately.

"It could be so many things." He shook his head. "Does Nell know?"

He couldn't help but look through the window at The Wild Café. The beautiful log-sided building looked so homey and inviting. Nell would take something like this personally. It would be a huge blow. She cared about the residents as much as he did.

"No idea."

"Maybe it's best to keep it under wraps for now." The outgoing woman never met a stranger. Loris wouldn't mean to gossip, but she shared a lot with a lot of people. "May be best not to mention the food-poisoning idea. You know how people talk."

Loris nodded sagely. "Good point. My lips are sealed."

He doubted that but hoped she'd be a little more careful with her conversations.

Once she'd made her way down the aisle to resume her shopping, he considered letting Nell know what was going on. He didn't want her to worry, but if she heard it from a customer, it would be worse.

He crossed his arms, still indecisive. She hadn't visited the market the last two mornings. Carlos had come instead for mussels yesterday and again today for crab. It was unusual. It had to be because of their night.

He had expected her to be aloof, unsure of how to approach him after he'd showed an interest. Thank the gods he hadn't declared his love. A feeling of dread spread through his chest.

She probably thought he was just a young kid, full of crazy fancies.

He'd let her think that, then. And give her time to see if any interest was returned. If not, he'd try to move on. He'd do his best, anyway.

He'd give it another day. She was bound to come in at some point.

Three days.

Emiliano had waited three long days to even see Nell. She was avoiding him. What did that mean?

She was either entirely embarrassed *slash* offended by his feelings, or maybe, possibly, could it be because she was embarrassed *slash* shocked by her own feelings? He had little hope, but it was there.

He had spent most of the morning tweaking the user interface for the new online-ordering system he'd built. He still had some work to do on entitlements and account creation, but it was getting there.

"Did you hear about Bernie?" His dad walked through their office space, dropping a folder on the counter. "And now Mary.""Mary's sick?" He sat up straight in his chair, dropping his pencil onto the notepad he'd been making lists on. Mary, Mary, Quite Contrary, the kids used to call the grouchy elderly septuagenarian. She might be difficult at times, but she was one of theirs. "I heard about Bernie, but not Mary. Is she okay?"

Hugo nodded. "She's refusing to go to the hospital, but she's been throwing up."

"That's not good. Is someone with her?"

"Tommy checked on her this afternoon after doing her lawn. He said she's doing okay but doesn't look well."

Tommy was Loris' grandson, so it stood to reason she would be checking in on her as well. Not that Mary would like that. She didn't like small talk. Loris loved it and the elderly woman. He wondered if anyone had told Willa. She might have some herbal remedy that would make Mary feel b etter.

"I bet Nell will make her some chicken soup or bone broth," he said.

"Might not be a good idea just yet." Hugo slid into a chair across from his son's. At Emiliano's raised eyebrow, he added, "Mary had food delivered last night. Talk is that something's spreading from the café. The rumor is new. It's not made the rounds."

Yet. That was the word he'd left hanging in the air.

It wouldn't take long until it did. The few isolated cases might be nothing, but it was better to deal with things like this head-on.

He needed to talk to Nell.

After closing for the day and cleaning up in the bathroom, Emiliano took a moment to give himself a testing sniff. It had been a long day. Deciding he was presentable enough, he looped his finger around the keys hanging by the office door and headed out. His dad had opened this morning, so it was his turn to close. Turning his key in the lock, he looked across the parking lot to the café.

It sat quietly under a full moon as the waves lapped against the shore just beyond. People sat at the outdoor tables, and the bar was half full. Edison bulb lights were strung over the space, creating a vibe. It was a good place, full of warmth and laughter.

Nell would have already closed the kitchen, but he didn't see a light upstairs yet. She was probably still putting things away.

Attempting not to overthink it, he pocketed his keys and headed over, taking the outdoor steps up. Barnaby looked up at his approach, raising his head in acknowledgment as he crossed to the bar.

"Good day?" The man asked, polishing a crystal tumbler.

"Not bad." He took a seat. A little liquid courage might not be a bad idea before facing the woman who'd rejected him three days prior. "Glenfiddich?"

Nodding, the darker-skinned man turned, selected a bottle from the shelf behind him, and poured him a hefty two fingers. He looked up. "Neat?"

"Yes, thanks."

The barman slid the drink across the bar, and Emiliano grabbed it. He couldn't list more than a couple of handfuls of times when he'd sat on this back deck for a drink. It wasn't that he didn't want to patron her business; Nell's food was superb, but he'd always felt a little out of place. These were her people. Her friends. It almost felt presumptuous.

He set money on the bar and took a sip. The warm, spicy-sweet liquid slid into his mouth, and notes of caramel and toffee spilled over his tongue. A sigh slipped past his lips.

"Looks like you needed that." A sparkle lit the bartender's eye.

"Maybe a little. It's been a while."

"We don't see much of you over here." There was a friendly, scolding tone in his voice. "Unless you're doing business with the boss."

"I should rectify that." He took another sip, feeling a little better about things already. The worn wood bar top under his hands felt good. Supportive, even.

"You should. We're glad to have you." Barnaby picked up another glass from the rack and began to hand-dry it. "What are you up to this evening?"

"Not much. I have to open tomorrow, so it won't be a late night." Man, he sounded lame. Twenty-eight years old, and he was going to bed early.

The bartender only nodded. He didn't judge.

"I, uh, was going to say hi to Nell, though, if she's still up." He glanced at the French doors behind him, which separated the outside deck from the interior dining room and kitchens. Suddenly, he felt as nervous as a kid. If he'd been here on business, he wouldn't have hesitated, but he sounded like he was asking permission to go backstage and see someone he didn't know.

Barnaby's eyes narrowed slightly, and he gave Emiliano a calculating stare. Then, after a beat, he nodded sharply. "Just make sure you call out when you get back there. Don't want to give her a scare."

Emiliano's heart pounded. The bartender had just given him permission. It was now or never. Standing from the barstool, he lifted his glass. "Can I take this?"

"Just leave it on the bar on your way out." The bartender turned to help another customer, dismissing him for his visit.

Swallowing his nerves, Emiliano put a hand on the door and pushed. The overhead lights were off, but the outside lights were enough to illuminate the dining room. It was easy to see the kitchen door in the center hall, where it separated the back and rear dining areas. The door to Nell' s office was across from it, along with the door to her upstairs apartment.

The two dining areas helped keep the noise down in the café. At the moment, the only sound was a light murmur of voices from the deck and muted music playing over the outdoor speakers.

Would she be in her kitchen or her office? Hesitating only for a moment, he turned to the kitchen door and took a deep breath. Speaking clearly, he raised his voice so it would be heard over the music. "Nell?"

Pausing the space of a few beats of his wild heart, he rapped on the door and spoke again before pushing it open an inch. "Nell? It's Emiliano."

Nell stood with her back to the stove. A dish towel was knotted in her hands, and her eyes were wide.

"Sorry if I scared you." He tried to make it sound casual, hoping the drink in his hand would make it look impromptu, but now, he felt like it was in the way. "I wondered if you'd have a few minutes to talk—about the restaurant, I mean."

He'd attempted to reassure her he wasn't here to ask her out again, but it made him sound pathetic. He bit his tongue.

"Oh." Her mouth formed a perfect O, but she didn't move. After she recovered, she hurried forward to the small table in the center of her kitchen, where he'd found her making notes on recipes and setting menus for the day in the early morning. "Please sit."

She pulled out a chair and sat herself, the towel twisting tighter in her hands.

He knew it was uncomfortable after how they'd left things, but he would repair that. Hooking a foot around the leg of a chair, he slid it out and sat in a relaxed pose, raising his glass appreciatively. "You've got a nice bourbon selection."

"Thanks." She blushed. "Barnaby keeps it stocked."

"Hiring him was a smart move."

"Gary did that. It was his idea to open the bar. He always knew what to do." She glanced down and wiped a strand of hair from her face. "I have no idea how to make all these decisions."

"You're too tough on yourself. I think you're doing a great job."

"Hey, I still feel bad about the other night." The words spilled out of her mouth. "I totally forgot about the Willa thing, and I feel so bad, running off like that. It was rude."

"Hey, no sweat." He shrugged it off.

"I probably could have called her and not freaked out like I did. I just felt bad."

"It was still a nice night. I'm glad you were able to join us."

Keep it cool.

"Me too." She gave him a brief smile. "I'm still dreaming about that paella."

"Pops won't stop talking about it, too." He rolled his eyes playfully. "I hear nothing but how you saved the dinner and reclaimed his grandmother's recipe."

"Oh, that's silly! Hugo's paella was incredible already. The rosemary just put it over the edge. His grandmother knew what she was doing."

"So do you." He gave her a smile, but she glanced away again. *Easy,* he reminded himself.

"Thanks."

"Anyway." He cleared his throat. "Nell, I wanted to stop by and let you know Mary's sick."

"Oh, no. Is she okay?"

"Yes. Well, I think she is. I haven't seen her. Tommy checked in on her earlier today."

"So, Loris knows." Nell nodded, relieved.

"I was thinking of letting Willa know too."

"Did you want me to tell Willa?" She let the question hang in the air.

She probably thought that was why he'd come to visit.

"That'd be great, but I wanted to let you know because she had food delivered last night from the café. After Joe and Bernie got sick, I heard someone mention it might be food poisoning."

"Oh, no," she repeated, the blood draining from her face.

"I'm sure it's nothing." He couldn't help himself. He reached across the table to cover her tight hands with one of his. "But you know how talk is. I thought it'd be better if you heard about it from someone other than the rumor mill."

Nell nodded slowly, her gaze fixed onto something in the distance. "What if I made them sick?"

Emiliano squeezed her hands encouragingly. "Nell, I've never seen a cleaner kitchen. I can't imagine you did anything wrong."

"That's why we didn't get as many people today. Maybe I should close tomorrow." Her eyes searched the room for answers. "I should scour the place from top to bottom."

"I'm sure an extra cleaning would suffice." She really was adorable.

"What will I do, though?" She looked up at him expectantly, openly asking for help, concern etched on her face.

It broke his heart to see her worried like that. There was nothing he wouldn't do to help her. "Do you want help cleaning?"

"No. I've got help. I meant with the café." She slumped over the table.

"Are you not getting enough business?" He hadn't noticed a lack of diners.

"We're doing okay. But when we expanded, Gary had all these plans to reach farther into the community and bring in people from neighboring towns. Even if I figure out this food thing, I might have already lost customers."

"This will blow over." Releasing her hand, he leaned back in his seat and sipped his bourbon. "You'll do an extra cleaning tomorrow, just in case, and people will have forgotten by Saturday."

"But I need to bring in *more* business. And—" She stopped short, covering her mouth with her hands. "Saturday night, the band is playing!"

"You've got a band lined up?" He was impressed. "That's a great idea! What are you doing to market it?"

"Market?" The words squeaked out of her mouth. She was spiraling. "I don't even know."

He had to do something.

"Okay." He set the glass down with a resolute thud. "We'll put up fliers at the post office and outside the restrooms at the market. You can ask the band if they have any promotional pictures. They might even make fliers. Find out their social media accounts so you can link them on a post. You'll want to make one."

"A post?" She blinked.

"You have social media, I'm sure of it. I know I saw some posts a while back." He might have screenshot one of the photos of Nell in her kitchen.

"Yes, Maggie created some for the café. She's taken some pictures of dishes and a few of us here and there."

"That's perfect. She can even share the menu specials."

"That's a great idea!" She perked up. "That should spread the word."

There she was.

He could see the spark of her passion for the café reclaiming itself.

"If you get the word out tomorrow and Saturday, I don't think you'll have any problems getting a full house for the gig."

"But what if people don't like them?"

"Then, you can try another band. I'm sure others in the area would love the opportunity."

"What if it was a bad idea and people don't like having a live band play?"

"I think you're overthinking this. Most people love live music. If it doesn't go well, you don't have to continue."

"You're right." She blew out a breath, then looked up at him with warmth. "Thanks."

Heat flooded his body, and he adjusted his position in the chair, suddenly uncomfortable under the full weight of her smile. "Anytime."

Before he could say anything else, she was out of her seat and whirling around her kitchen, gathering her phone and notepads. Scribbling down notes, she flicked through her phone and paused. "But how do I create a post?" Laughing, he stood from the table and went to help her out.

CHAPTER 9

Walking down the sidewalk to Willa's yoga studio, Nell couldn't help but smile. The early morning air was crisp, but the sun was out, warming her face and shoulders under her light jacket. Even though she hadn't been able to post anything to The Wild Café's social media pages because Maggie had the passwords, she and Emiliano had a fun time, laughing over her lack of technical abilities. It hadn't come as any surprise to her that he, however, was as savvy as they came.

Of course he was. All the young people were.

He hadn't made fun of her, and she hadn't felt old about the fact, at least. That was nice.

The best part was that things seemed like they had gotten back to normal between them. Maybe a little more like friends than they had been, but that was nice too. Emiliano had grown into such a nice young man, and with their businesses right next to each other, it made sense they would be friends. It made it even more fun to work together.

He'd talked her down from what could have been a full-blown downward spiral of emotions, too. With the news of people getting sick, she'd nearly given the whole thing up. And abandoning the only pleasure she had left would have been the end of everything she knew and held d ear.

No, he'd convinced her it was isolated enough that it was probably random and unrelated. That made more sense. Besides, she'd been so very careful, and after testing it all out, she felt even more confident thinking of it as an illness passing around town.

Approaching the glass door of Willa's studio, she smiled at her reflection in the window. She didn't look half bad today. Finally getting a bit of sleep must have helped.

"Morning, Willa," she called out as she entered the little studio, and the bell over the door rang with a happy chime. The scent of patchouli and lavender wafted through the air from a diffuser in the corner.

"Good morning to you." Willa stood from where she was setting out yoga mats on the freshly mopped floor.

It looked like she'd timed it right, catching her between sessions.

Willa propped her hands on her hips and lifted a bare foot to rest her heel against her other ankle in a kickstand. "And what are you doing out of your kitchen at this time of the morning?"

"Well, Carlos is helping prep, and Maggie has taken more duties in the kitchen."

"How's that going?"

"Terribly." Nell sagged, sliding onto a bench near the door. "Not the help. I mean, I hate needing it, but it's nice not being so busy from early morning to late at night."

"Right. Then, what's the problem?"

"Maggie is a terrible baker." She winced.

"She is?" Willa's long, slim legs folded neatly underneath her as she sat down in a cross-legged position on the floor in front of Nell. "But she's around you all the time. Surely, some of it would have rubbed off."

"You would think." Nell scratched the side of her head. "I mean, I'm grateful, don't get me wrong, but if I'm not walking her through every part of the process, it falls apart. She doesn't have the patience for all the extra steps to make the right texture and crumb, depending on the technique."

"It took you a while, too, if I recall."

"It did, but I really wanted to learn."

"I think she wants to." Willa glanced nervously toward the door. "A couple of months ago, I stopped by her place and found her trying to learn by herself, to help take the load off you."

"Crap." Well, that didn't make her feel any better.

"She's terrible at everything?"

"Not at cooking. Her clam chowder is actually quite good, and her salmon chowder is nearly on par with my own."

"Really? I can't imagine that..." Willa's voice dripped with sarcasm.

But Nell waved her off. She'd given up being humble about her cooking. It was the one thing she excelled at. She wasn't going to pretend she didn't think it was good. If she did, why would anyone eat at her restaurant?

"*That* crisis is nearly averted. I'm doing the baking now. There's no seafood in it. As long as I stay away from nori cookies, we should be safe."

"But they were so good." Willa nearly whined in displeasure.

"And Maggie still wants to learn. I don't understand it."

"She's trying to help you out."

"She is by taking care of the seafood dishes."

"Under your constant supervision."

"Mostly." Nell lifted a shoulder in a half shrug.

Willa raised an eyebrow in response.

"It's my restaurant. My livelihood."

Her friend snorted.

"I'm gabbing." Nell spread her hands out and stood from the bench. "But that's not what I'm here for."

"Oh, right." Willa tilted her head. "The other crisis. What is it?"

"People are getting sick in town. Did you know?"

"Only about Mary." Willa sat up straighter. "Who else?"

"Joe, Bernie, Mary. In that order." Nell ticked them off, not liking the number. "I heard there was talk that they'd all eaten food from the Wild Café. You already knew about Mary?"

"Of course. Tommy told Loris, and she headed right over to my place to let me know."

That sounded like Loris.

"Emiliano told me last night."

At that moment, the bell over the door chimed again, and Loris sailed in. "Mary's feeling better today."

"That's good to hear." Willa smiled at the older woman, then turned back to Nell. "Now, what's going on with the other two?"

Nell shrugged. "General sickness? I haven't heard what symptoms they have."

"Well, it's unlikely it's because of anything from the café." Willa's eyes shifted to Loris and back to Nell, indicating more than just the food.

"I've been careful." Nell nodded, casting a quick look at Loris as well. She was busy setting up a mat and didn't catch on to their underlying conversation.

"I have no doubt."

"But I thought it would still be good to look into it. I'd appreciate it if you checked in on them."

"Of course I will." Willa unfolded herself, standing straight up, and crossed over to hug Nell. "I'm sure it's nothing but a little sickness passing through town. Mary had common flu symptoms and is already recovering."

"Thanks." Nell returned her hug, relieved to have the herbalist looking out for her.

"Don't worry. Willa will mix up some witchy stuff for them, too, if she needs to!" Loris wiggled her outstretched fingers and grinned maniacally.

Willa's eyes fully rounded. "It's not witchcraft!" Her voice came out in a high-pitched squeak.

"She's such a talented *herbalist*." Nell grabbed Loris, steering her away from her friend's panicked look. "You can't deny talent like that."

"Oh, don't be silly. I was just playing around." Loris laughed. "Honestly, you two."

Nell caught Willa's eyes over Loris's head. That was close. They didn't know if it was witchcraft or not, but it *was* magical. It depended on the definition of witchcraft. They knew so little about it.

Either way, they weren't exactly sharing that they had magic with the town, and they didn't need the town gossip, sweet though she was, spreading rumors like that.

"You need something, boss?" Maggie said as she pushed through the kitchen doors.

"Yes." Nell looked up from her phone. She needed to get the ad posted to social media before they got busy for the lunch rush. "Can you give me the password for The Wild Café's account?"

Maggie looked curiously over her shoulder. "Sure, boss. But do you know what you're doing there?"

"Yes. At least, I think so." Nell looked up to see Maggie's face turn down. "What's wrong?"

She glanced back at the picture she'd cropped from the Dung Beetle's website.

"Oh." She'd cut their heads off. "That's not good."

"And how'd you put the text on that photo?" Maggie leaned in closer to inspect it.

"The edit tool on my camera?" Nell's voice rose an octave. It did look a little immature, but she couldn't figure out how to do it otherwise.

"If you use the one on the media site, it formats it better."

"It does?"

"Also, it's the Uprising of the Dung Beetles." "That's not better."

"No, it's not. But it could be worse." Maggie sat next to her.

"Could it be? For a restaurant?"

"Oh, definitely." Her friend's eyes widened.

"I don't even want to know."

"Want me to help?" Maggie offered sweetly, her trademark smile turned up to full power onto her.

"Yes. Please." This time, there was no hesitation. She honestly didn't want to have to learn another format. "Hey, what if I give you a little extra and you be our social media expert, too."

"Really?" Maggie lit up even more than before. "That would be amazing."

Nell handed her phone over. It was another business decision she'd made by herself, and it felt right.

How about that?

"I called JD and got his account to tag." Nell tapped the notepad on the table with her pen.

"I found it." Maggie was already typing, but she had her phone in her hands, not Nell's.

"How'd you find it?"

"I looked them up." Maggie glanced up from her screen to see Nell's expression, and she paused. "Oh, is it okay if I use my own cell to post it? It's just easier that w ay."

"Sure." Apparently, she'd made a good choice with Maggie. She already knew more than Nell did after talking to Emiliano for an hour the night before. Not that she hadn't enjoyed the chat. He was smart about that stuff.

"We could even post the seasonal menus and nightly specials." Maggie glanced up, excitement evident in her voice.

"That's exactly what Emiliano suggested."

"Emiliano?" Maggie snapped her head back. "You guys talked?""Oh, just a little."

"This morning?"

"Um. He stopped by last night." She suddenly felt uncomfortable about it. That was silly. She didn't have any reason to.

"So, things are okay between you two again?"

"Yes. Everything is fine."

"Oh, good." Maggie blew out the side of her mouth. "What?"

"Nothing." She went back to flicking through her cell.

"What is it?" Nell blocked Maggie's phone with a hand to get her attention.

"It's just that you were so depressed after that night with the dinner at his house. And I've seen the way he looks at you. I think he really likes you."

Nell frowned. She thought they'd been over that one already. "It was just those cookies."

"Okay," Maggie said blandly.

"Really. It was a close call."

"If you say so, Nell."

"Yeah, he's too young for me, anyway. Honestly, what in the world would he see in me?"

"You're amazing." Maggie punched her lightly in the arm. "Don't sell yourself short."

"Thanks." She shook her head to clear it. "Anyway, when I got their account info, I asked the band if they had any pictures for a flier. They went ahead and made some and are dropping them by around lunch."

"Great idea!"

"It was another of Emiliano's, actually. He's apparently better at marketing than I am.""You're learning." Maggie raised her phone. "You hired a social media expert."

"True. And we're going to put up posters later this afternoon, between the rush hours."

"You and JD?"

"No."

"Oh." She sat back in her seat, a wide grin spreading across her face. "You and Emiliano."

"Oh, stop it." Nell pushed her chair back, making a loud scraping noise in the little kitchen, and got busy prepping for lunch. "You're probably needed in the dining room."

Maggie's face and hands were scrunched tightly in joy and amusement. She practically squeaked as she danced out of the kitchen.

"He's here." Maggie's face poked through her door.

Hurrying to the doorway, she put her best boss face on and hissed. "Shh."

Maggie's giggle tinkled, and she hopped away. Her boss face needed some work.

"How's the day going?" Emiliano asked as he pushed through the door and cast a curious expression behind him, likely toward her elated waitress.

"Good. You?" She'd have to talk to Maggie about that. She didn't want rumors to spread. It would make her sound pathetic. Nell nearly shivered with disgust.

"Pretty good." He strolled in, his hands tucked into his jeans pockets. Jeans that fit so nicely around a perfectly round butt.

"That's good." She tore her eyes away and back to his face.

"These are good." He picked up the stack of fliers JD and his friend Austin had dropped off an hour earlier.

"Yeah, the band made them. I wouldn't have done nearly as well."

"You'd have figured it out."

"I did make one good business decision today."

"You did?" He set the papers down and gave her his full attention.

"I hired Maggie to be my social media expert." Nell lifted her chin. "Well, really, I'm just paying her extra to do i t."

"Great idea! She'll excel at that." He raised a hand to give her a high five.

She swelled with pride; It was nice sharing personal achievements with someone.

"You ready to get outta here? Or do you need to finish anything up first?"

"I'm ready." Nell grabbed the stack, and they headed out of the kitchen.

When they passed Maggie, she was standing next to Barnaby and they were leaned in closely, talking low. Maggie's eyes were still bright and sparkly.

Nell cleared her throat loudly, capturing Emiliano's attention away from them. "Where should we go first?"

Thankfully, he didn't seem to have noticed what they were talking about.

"We can start at the post office and head back this way, ending at the market. If we start at the market, I'm worried I'll get caught up in work."

"Makes sense." She liked his dedication. Not everyone understood how much it took to bring a dream like this to fruition.

But was it his dream, too? Or just Hugo's? His dedication indicated he felt that way too, but they'd never talked about it.

"What are your plans with Gil's?" she blurted out before she could even consider censoring her thoughts. "Long term, I mean. Do you love it? Are you going to work there forever? I can't imagine you doing anything different, but surely, you have dreams too."

She was rambling again.

The smile he gave her put her at ease. Even his dimple was on display. "You know, no one ever asks me that."

She blushed. She *had* to get her libido under control. "I know what it's like to run a business. You have to really want it. It's a commitment."

"It is." He nodded, then looked up at the cloudless sky as he took his time to form words. "When I went off to college, I wasn't sure whether I would come back to work at the market or not. I know my dad thought I would. He wasn't a fan of my computer science minor. But after I got my degree, it felt like the right thing to do
."

"I bet it was strange being away for so long." She remembered how different the store felt during those years. He'd come back during the summers and on breaks, but it wasn't as lively without him.

Emiliano's steps slowed. "It was tough seeing my dad struggle while I was away."

Nell stopped walking. "Is that why you came back?"

"Partly."

"That may not be enough, Emiliano." She put a hand on his arm. "Not long term. If you're not passionate about it, the hours and the pressure of responsibility will overwhelm you."

He gazed gently down at her, covering her hand in his. The action made her pulse hop like water in a hot skillet.

"Gil's is home. I was raised there. And this town"—his head rose as he surveyed their little downtown strip, with the neighborhood to the south and up the mountainside and the cove to the north—"is home. It's in my DNA to serve the people of Orca Cove."

"But computer science. It's very different from what you're doing today. I mean, I couldn't do something I wasn't interested in. I was meant to cook."

"Damn straight, you were." He released her hand and headed back up the hill toward the post office.

"Thanks." She blushed again, then brushed off his comment. "But there has to be something. Don't you have other passions? Techy interests?"

"I do." He leaned in as he said it, as though it was a secret. "And I'm working on incorporating them into the business."

"Ah. If you make some changes, you'll be doing more of what you love, and you'll make the store more yours. That's a brilliant idea."

"I like to think so." A small line appeared between his brows. But he caught her look, and it disappeared.

"What's the problem with that?" She hoped he didn't mind the probing.

"I have to convince Pops. That's all."

"Hugo doesn't like anything to change." He wouldn't even consider modifying his beloved grandmother's paella recipe. She couldn't imagine the difficulties Emiliano would face trying to talk his dad into his ideas for the market. He'd poured his life into it.

"That's correct."

"So, what are you going to do about it?"

"I don't really know yet." He gave her a sad smile as they reached the door of the post office. He entered, dropping the conversation.

By the time they had finished putting posters up downtown and got to the market, Hugo greeted them at the entrance.

"Son, I'm glad you're back." He pushed a folder into Emiliano's hands. "I need to pay some bills; can you update the ledger?"

Emiliano's shoulders sagged a perceivable inch. "Pops. The program is up to date. And I reconciled it with the bank account last night. The balance is accurate."

"Oh, you know I don't trust that machine's numbers." He waved it off.

The younger man's jaw set. "They're my numbers, not the machine's. I checked them. They're correct."

"It doesn't make sense to me. You understand."

"Then, why don't I give you the balance? Or I can pay the bills."

Tension rose between the two men, and Nell was starting to feel uncomfortable. She shifted from foot to foot, trying to decide if she should back out quietly.

"I need to be involved in the finances of my own shop. Wouldn't you think?" Hugo's bottom lip and chin rose in argument.

Emiliano didn't reply. Nell could see the emotion pass across his face as he struggled to find the right words. "Aren't we in this together?"

"Of course we are, son. And you help out a lot here, but it's still my responsibility, my livelihood."

"You don't think it's my livelihood, too?"

"Built it from the ground up."

"Yes. I'm just trying to make my mark."

"Your mark? I know you're young, but it's already working. Why change that?"

"Why, indeed?" Emiliano threw a quick, tight look at Nell. "Sorry to cut things short, but I have some work I need to do for my dad."

For his dad. The words hung heavily in the warm afternoon air.

"Thank you, Emiliano," she called out after him as he headed towards the offices in the back.

"Sorry about that, Nell." Hugo shook his head, his eyes still on the back of his retreating son. "Kids today."

"Kids?" It wasn't her argument, but she wasn't about to just agree with him.

He shrugged. "Well, seems like it sometimes. You know what it's like."

"What?"

"That place is your dream. You wouldn't let anyone come in and tell you what to do." He gestured across the lot to her café.

"Actually, I was planning on talking to Shelby about that. I'd like some advice now that it's only me. I'd like another person's perspective." She didn't add that she didn't even like making those decisions on her own. She did, however, realize she wouldn't want to take advice in a direction she was completely against. "And Emiliano's helped me already with some things. That's why we're out today. He had some great ideas on marketing."

Hugo huffed. "I don't like change."

Nell watched the father walk off in such a similar manner as his son that it would have made her chuckle if not for the angst between them.

Instead, she bit her lip.

There was nothing she could do. She'd check in with Emiliano in the morning when she bought fish. Besides, he knew how his dad was. This wasn't new for him.

When she got back to the café, Shelby was lounging backward on an outdoor patio bench with her legs stretched out in front of her and her elbows on the tabletop behind her. Her eyes were shut, enjoying the unusually sunny day.

"Speak of the devil," Nell announced.

Shelby's lips curled into a grin before she opened her eyes. "Oh, don't you know it?"

The dark-haired woman sat up and spun, setting her feet under the table and propping her head on her hands to get a better look at her friend.

"What'd I do now?"

"Nothing yet."

Shelby cocked her head. "What do you *want* me to do?"

"You could try earning some of those free baked goods with marketing advice." Nell tried to girl-boss it like Shelby so often did, but even she thought it felt like an empty threat. They both knew she was going to continue to throw extra cookies and slices of quick bread in with her lunch order.

"Works for me. What do you need?"

That was easier than she thought it'd be. Maybe her boss face wasn't that bad.

"I'm having a band play here tomorrow night."

"Good idea." Shelby picked at the half-eaten sandwich in front of her. "Two words. Social media."

"On it. Or rather, Maggie is. I hired her as my social media guru."

"Expert." Maggie's voice piped up from the other end of the deck, where she was folding purple napkins for the dinner crowd.

"That's right. Social media expert."

"Great idea." Shelby took a bite of her pickle wedge. "Then, what do you need me for?"

"I want to do more." Nell sat down across from Shelby and spread her hands out on the table in front of her. "We built this place to accommodate more people, but never did anything to bring them in. I need to do that."

"Social media will help get the word out. Make sure you tag local companies with the products you use." She raised a finger to Maggie, who nodded, taking the note. "Like Brooks Farms Berkshire pork."

"Wait, that's it." Nell got excited. The perfect idea formed in her mind. "That's brilliant."

"I know." Shelby closed her eyes and tilted her head back to enjoy the sun again.

"No, silly." Nell swatted at her arm, causing the other woman to jerk her eyes open. "I use lots of local foods, but I've been trying to spread the love, if you will."

"You've been hanging out with Willa too much."

Nell ignored her. "I need to partner with them, instead."

"Don't you already exclusively use Brooks Farms' pork?"

"Not exclusively. Gil's orders meat from lots of local farms. I get a discount since I buy so much. I'm helping them and getting a better price than if I bought from them directly."

"But if you used them exclusively and advertised for them?"

"I don't think I'd gain a lot there, and I wouldn't want to short Gil's any." They didn't need that kind of stress right now. "But I'm thinking elsewhere."

"Like?" Shelby waved a hand, waiting for her to explain.

"Little things, like Lavender Farms jams."

"You like to make your own." "But their huckleberry is some of the best, and I love the lemon zest they add to their marionberry jam. It's very similar to mine. I could bend on that one item."

"It's a good idea, and people will like it, but I'm not sure you're going to see a huge uptick of customers from Liberty or other neighboring towns just to support Lavender Farms. You'd probably get Jan and Hank more often, some of their family, and die-hard supporters. But it's not likely to amount to much."

"That was an example. I could partner with several local companies like that. Like honey from Hills Apiary." The ideas were forming together faster than she could speak. "I could get a discount, and they'd get the name recognition. Maggie could post about it and tag them. Their customers would come to get their products in dishes, and our customers would go visit them to get more of it. It'd be like a tourist advertisement as well, a way to try the local flavor.""It's a good idea." Shelby nodded. "But I think you still need more than a few products."

"Wine." The idea hit her like another bolt of lightning. But this zap didn't come with special gifts. Or curses. However, a warm, elated feeling settled down on her as she fleshed out the idea. It felt like coming up with a new, perfectly balanced baked dessert. "I need to go visit Mt. Olympus Vineyards."

"Okay." Shelby pursed her lips and stared out over the ocean. "But people are picky. You wouldn't be able to carry them exclusively. You'd need to have some California wines too. And some international ones."

"Agreed."

"Keep track of your sales, and once you've shown success with Mt. Olympus, you can go to Napa or Sonoma to do the same with them."

"Or Russian River wines," Maggie piped up from where she worked.

"Or Oregon wines," Nell added. California seemed so far away.

"I wouldn't extend it too far, or it won't feel as special." Shelby's lips pursed as she considered the idea. "What about Yakima Valley? Keep it local with Washington wines."

"I could do it with a local craft beer, too, and a local distillery." Nell stood to look at what labels they had on hand.

"It's a good idea." Barnaby propped his hands on his slim hips. He'd been listening as he set up for the day. "We still need the classics and some specialties, but a local option to feature in seasonal cocktails would be a great idea."

Why had she never considered using her friends and the crew for marketing advice before? This was amazing.

"This is going to be so cool!" Maggie clapped her hands together in excitement.

"And you're going to be doing a little traveling," Shelby said, as though it wasn't a big deal.

It was like cold water from the cove had splashed up over the railing and doused her. She was only playing at being a businesswoman; she had no real skill at negotiation.

"Can you come with me, Shelby? Please? I'll give you free cookies for life."

"Free cookies?" Shelby tapped a finger on her teeth. "I supposed I could do that. As long as it works in my schedule. I do have a business to run, too."

"Sold. I'll work around your calendar." Nell stuck out a hand to shake on it with the resident badass boss lady. She could take notes and work on her boss face.

She needed to do something quickly. She'd already noticed a small decline over the last few days. Word of mouth spread quickly. Even though most people trusted her, some wouldn't want to risk whatever sickness was passing through town.

CHAPTER 10

Despite ripping off his light jacket, Emiliano couldn't relieve the heat radiating off him. It wasn't just normal warmth; it was anger. Full-on rage, if he was being honest. His father didn't even think of him as an equal in their own business. Had he been kidding himself this whole time? His whole life? It was like he was still a little kid, running around, taking orders, and thinking he was making a difference.

"How adorable," he would hear people say. *"He's helping his dad out."* *"No,"* he'd correct them. *"He was an owner, too. Gil's was his, too."* They would smile and pat him on the head. But he knew. Or he had thought he did.

They had been right all along.

And the worst part was that it had all happened in front of Nell. He might not be able to get his dad to see him as a man, but he needed her to. And she was starting to. Wasn't she?

She was coming to him for advice and letting him help. He loved being a bigger part of her life. She got where he was coming from. It was like she understood him. Even with the frustrations with his dad and her hasty exit at dinner, this last week had been like a gift.

He sat down heavily in his office chair, his elbows propped onto the sturdy wood desk and his head dropped into his hands. Again.

What should he do now? His fingertips dug into his scalp. Had his entire career been a joke?

Seven years.

For seven years, he'd been working for his dad, thinking he was making a difference in the lives of the people at Orca Cove. Dammit, he *had* been making a difference. The problem was his dad didn't see it that way.

He'd rejected offers from several large companies in Seattle to pursue system development and writing code. Even one as a data scientist. Right now, he was kicking himself for not taking that one. Analytics was even more interesting.

Maybe he should see if they still wanted him. He would have to take a few classes to get up to speed on some of the newer stuff, but he'd kept his skills up.

Turning his computer on, Emiliano tore open the blasted paper ledger. Even if he decided to find another career path, he wouldn't leave his pops in a lurch. It was his dad, after all.

Some fathers didn't even want their kids.

His fingers clicked on the keyboard as he signed in and pulled up the electronic ledger he'd painstakingly built. Scanning down his dad's notes, he checked off entries and added others, keeping the two as consistent as possible. Luckily, nothing had been entered incorrectly, and he didn't spend hours finding an error.

Finishing the work, his fingers hovered over the keyboard. Maybe he should just delete the program.

It was senseless to spend this long maintaining something useless. If his dad was going to insist on keeping the paper ledger, he was wasting his time.

Using his mouse, he navigated to the other program he'd been working on. It had been a waste of the last few months. How many hours had he spent on it? It, too, had been a waste of time. Selecting the program, he dragged it over to the recycle bin. He hovered over it, considering, then stopped, moving it back to the desktop.

Maybe he could use this as a building block for something else, somewhere else. But for now, he had to get back on the floor and see if anyone else needed anything.

Powering off his computer, he shut the ledger and set it down on his dad's desk at the other end of the office, where he saw a picture of the two of them at his WSU graduation. Both wearing the bright purple colors of the university.

His dad had been proud of him that day. Emiliano's fingers hovered over the frame. Had it only been because he told him he'd be coming home to the cove to help out? Was that when it all went wrong?

His mind full of unwelcome thoughts, he left the office and went to find something more physical to do.

"No, but I can put a special order in for you if you need it quickly." His dad's voice greeted him when he made it out to the market. He was talking to Conrad Brooks, who didn't look very happy.

"Everything okay, Conrad?" Emiliano asked, approaching the two.

"No." Conrad spun around, his shoulders tight. "Something's going on at the farm, and I need to find out what it is. Hugo didn't even order the game cam I asked for."

"Conrad." His dad held his hands up to calm the taller, beefier farmer. "I'm sure it's an elk or a bear or something."

"A bear could be attacking my livestock. Elk and deer eat crops. That's not good for my farm, either." His fisted hands were pulled tight to his sides. "If you'd have ordered it when I asked for it, I might know what's going on."

"What makes you think something's going on?" Emiliano asked.

"Twice, I've found crops trampled in the corner of the field." Conrad looked up to the ceiling. "I just know something's not right, okay?"

"I believe you." Emiliano's hand went to Conrad's shoulder. "It's your farm. You probably know that place like the back of your hand, like we do with this store. You've gotta trust your gut."

"Exactly."

"I'll put in the order myself today." Hugo placed a hand across his chest.

"Let me see what I can do about getting it here faster," Emiliano offered. If he could find someone heading out to Seattle, he might be able to get it in the next day or two.

"Thanks, Emiliano." Conrad's shoulders dropped a half inch.

"Of course."

"I'm sorry I didn't get it ordered faster." Hugo tried to step in closer.

"You didn't order it at all." Conrad's tight mouth made it clear he still wasn't happy with him.

Emiliano watched his dad hesitate, unsure what to do. "We're really sorry about the delay. I'm sure Pops didn't realize it was so important."

"I really didn't. I thought it was likely a bear passing through. I didn't want you to have to pay extra shipping and the bear to not come back through again."

"Even if it is a bear, I have no idea how it's getting on the property. The whole area is fenced off. I need to find out how it's getting in."

"I didn't realize." Hugo's head dropped.

"We should have asked, Conrad. We're very sorry." Emiliano did what he could to appease the man.

"We'll do better next time," Hugo said quietly.

Conrad nodded his head, his mouth relaxing a little.

"I'm sure we can get it in the next day or two. We'll do what we can."

"Thanks, Emiliano." Conrad turned and walked away.

Silence settled down between the two remaining men.

"You handled that way better than I did." His dad's voice was still soft.

"Conrad's not one to exaggerate."

"I know." His father's shoulders slumped. "I should have given it more weight."

"You will next time," he reassured his dad. He might still be mad and frustrated as hell, but he'd made his own share of mistakes at the store. His dad had been pretty forgiving most of the time. He'd always ensured he understood the gravity of the situation, but then he let up on it, and they moved on.

"I will." Hugo picked up the clipboard he carried and took a step toward the back offices. "I'll go get that order in right away with expedited delivery."

"Why don't you give me a half hour first? Let me see if I can get it here faster."

"What are you going to do?""I'm going to see if one of the fisherfolk is heading to Seattle."

"That might take all day.""Still faster than the two-day delivery." Emiliano rubbed his chin. "You know what? It'd be better yet if you went ahead and ordered it. If I get it here faster, we can just stock the extra one, so we'll have one on hand or in case Conrad needs a second one."

"That's a good idea." Hugo nodded. "You've gotten good at putting the customer's needs first."

It was the closest to an apology he was going to get.

"I learned from the best." He accepted it and headed outside.

***"Duke?" Emiliano called out as he approached the fishing vessel the man used as a cargo ship. He'd thought of the courier as soon as he set foot on the docks and saw the waves splashing against the ships' steel sides. It was a lot cleaner than one typically used for bringing in a haul. He'd taken a lot of time to turn it into a home.

"Are you here, Duke?"

The afternoon had brought light rain. The mist settled onto Emiliano's head. He could taste the salt in the wet air and where it landed on his upper lip.

Across the large bow, the bridge door opened, and Duke raised a hand in greeting. He looked surprised to see him. "Emiliano. Everything okay?"

"Yes, at least for the most part." He tried for a friendly smile. "Do you have a few minutes?"

"Of course." Duke strolled barefoot across the wood slats of the foredeck. "Come on aboard."

"Thanks." Emiliano swung a leg over the rope at the entryway and took the few steps leading down to the deck.

He'd never been invited on board before, but he'd seen it from the dock many times over the years. Benches lined each side of the 15-yard deck, and a picnic table was set up in the center. It looked more like a backyard deck than one on a ship.

Duke met him halfway.

"Any chance you're heading to Seattle today or tomorrow?" Emiliano asked.

"I have a run early tomorrow. What's up?" The wind had picked up, and the moisture in the air dropped the temperature by a few degrees. Duke pulled the sides of his flannel shirt and buttoned up a few of the lower buttons.

"Conrad needs a game cam." He wouldn't normally disclose people's purchases, but in a town as small as Orca Cove, everyone knew what was going on with everyone. Hell, their conversation with Conrad was probably already known by a few people. And likely, his earlier argument with his dad as well.

"Is it an emergency?" Duke cocked his head.

"Not sure. He's worried something's getting over his fence."

"That's not good."

"No, and we didn't get it ordered, thinking it was just a bear passing through."

"We?" Duke raised an eyebrow.

"I didn't follow up on it, either," Emiliano said honestly. "Conrad's concerned, so I told him I'd see if anyone was traveling to Seattle and could pick one up. There's a shop just off the Port of Seattle's marina that sells supplies."

"I know the place."

"If you could bring it back with you, I'd pay you extra for your time."

"No problem." Duke nodded.

Check. Emiliano felt that rewarding assuredness that he'd helped another resident. Relief eased his tight muscles. "I really appreciate it."

"It's honestly no sweat, man. I got you." Duke clapped him on his shoulder.

Once again, the feeling of being accepted by someone whom his younger self would have considered the "cool kid" struck him deeply.

Duke wandered over to the railing and peered over the water. "There might be a storm coming in."

He hadn't noticed anything earlier, but following the man almost a decade older than him, he saw the waves kick up and their tips crest with white. "The wind is picking up."

Duke shook his head.

"It's not just that. It's shifted. Look." He pointed out over the water. Across the cove, farther out, the waves died down. They sat calmly in areas before picking up into larger swells, but it seemed to be heading this way. Duke leaned over the railing and smiled back at him. "The fish too."

Sure enough, swarms of them were swimming toward shore. They didn't like the temperature, turbulence, and pressure changes that came with a storm and would either swim deeper or take shelter under a fishing boat. If one was brave enough to fish in this weather, they stood to get a good haul.

Emiliano noticed the orcas farther out in the cove. "They are still around. I would have figured they'd come in, too."

"They aren't as easy to scare off, I'd say." Duke leaned against the railing, one bare foot propped up to cross at the ankle. "They're brave souls."

"Not a lot higher on the food chain than them. I'm surprised they're not going in for the feast."

"I'm sure they will. Maybe they're just checking it out first." The corner of his mouth ticked up, and he tucked the ends of his hair behind an ear where they had been waving around in the wind.

The clouds over them were getting darker, heavy with water. They looked ready to spill out.

"Good thing you weren't planning on a trip today."

"Eh." Duke raised his shoulder. "It wouldn't have been too bad. I've made it through worse."

"Still. It looks like it's really going to come down."

"It does." His gaze focused on something on the shore. "That's interesting."

"What?" Emiliano spun to see what he was watching and noticed Maggie bustling across the deck, pulling the umbrellas from the tables. But instead of looking like her normal, cheerful self, or even worried about the storm, her motions were jerky. "I don't think I've ever seen Maggie a ngry."

"It doesn't happen often." He tucked his hands into his jeans pockets. "I'd better check on her."

"I can if you'd like," Emiliano offered, neither of them taking their eyes off the short woman storming across the deck.

Duke turned to him and assessed him. "Will you let me know if it seems important? Particularly with Maggie. She's...well, it takes a lot to make her angry."

"Of course." He pulled his cell from his back pocket and unlocked it to add his number.

"Here." The ship's captain flicked a finger, asking for the device. Once he had it, he punched in his number and handed it back. "Thanks."

"I'll text you either way." He pocketed his phone. "Thanks for the run tomorrow. Let me know what I owe you when you get back."

"Will do."

Emiliano exited the boat, letting the long wooden dock lead him back ashore. The waves were kicking up even higher, splashing saltwater across his boots, and the ground underneath him pitched back and forth. It was a good thing he was used to it, having been on those docks as early as he could walk. He may not be a fisherman, but he had sea legs as good as any.

As he neared the Wild Café, he saw two male customers talking to the still-fuming Maggie. Concerned, he took the back stairs and approached them. "Everything alright?"

Maggie shot him a glance, then turned her attention back on who had to be tourists. He'd never seen them before.

"Yeah. We're having a storm, and these two gentlemen need to go home." The tiny woman with the short, pixie blonde hair propped up the umbrella in front of her, her arm going rigid, the lines of her muscles sharpening under the pressure.

"Aww. We don't want to go home. We'll go inside," the taller one with curly, orange hair said. "Carl was just playing."

"Yeah. I didn't mean anything by it." The other man held his hands up, his eyes glazing over, the surface spinning like the waves beyond him.

Emiliano stepped behind her. "Sounds like you two were heading out."

"Yes, they are." Maggie stamped the end of the umbrella against the deck.

"But it's early," Carl whined.

Nell pushed through the back doors of the café. Catching sight of the situation, she propped her fists against her waist and raised her voice. "Do we have a problem out here?"

"No problem, ma'am," Carrot Top said. "We were just coming inside. It's storming out here."

Nell's eyes flicked between the two, then noticed Maggie. Her hands were winding around each other.

"We need to shut the place down for an hour before we can reopen for dinner." Nell flicked the towel from her shoulder and waved it in the air, indicating the stairs. "Everybody out so we can clean."

"It's probably a good thing, anyway," Carl said. "This place's a dump. I'm surprised the health inspector hasn't shut them down."

"Sorry, ma'am." Carrot Top pulled at his friend. "Come o n."

"They should be nicer to their customers. If they're not careful, someone's gonna call them and report the place." Carl waved the fork in his hand, stumbling on his feet.

They hustled to the end of the deck, Nell hot on their heels, and Emiliano hot on hers. She had it under control, but damned if he wasn't going to be there to back her up if she needed it.

The men took the stairs, the red-haired one leading the other to a car farther out in the lot.

"Thanks, Emiliano." Nell glanced up at him, a small smile ghosting her lips.

"I didn't do anything. I was just making sure they decided not to be stupid."

"Your presence probably helped them with that decision."

"I'm glad I was here."

"Me too." She blinked. "Everything okay?"

She was talking about his dad. Embarrassment about his reactions and subsequent anger shot through him.

"Yeah, I was walking by." He toed the deck, then swung a thumb at Maggie. "I noticed Little Miss Sunshine over here all spun up in a fury."

Maggie ran a hand into her pixie-cut hair, her eyes shifting to the ground. His attempt at humor fell flat as they picked up on her nervous body language.

"You okay?" Emiliano asked.

The short woman nodded, tugging on the strands. "I'm good." She shot him a weak smile, and her breath blew out in a short burst. "Freaking jerks."

Nell pulled her into a tight hug, patting the younger woman on her back, but the tension had left Maggie's body.

Feeling better now that he knew the two friends were okay, Emiliano raised a hand. "I'll see you later. I have to get back."

Nell broke from her friend and put a hand on his arm as her eyebrows tilted inward in concern. "Seriously. You okay?"

He leaned his head closer a notch and softly smiled. "Yeah, I'm good. Thanks."

She nodded and pushed off, heading back to Maggie. Slinging an arm around her, she guided her back into the café, closing the door behind them.

Warmth from her touch traveled up Emiliano's arm and into his heart. It circled inside him, radiating comfort.

Taking the steps back down the deck, he paused to look back towards The Aurelia. He held up his hand to shield his eyes. The sky had cleared, and the sun was shining.

That was weird.

CHAPTER 11

"**I**'m going to go check on my tables." Maggie pulled away from her.

Nell's fingers wrapped around her friend's arm, tugging her back.

Maggie turned, eyebrows drawn together in confusion. "You sure you're okay?"

The blonde's face lifted, and her lips drifted up into her normal sweet smile. "Yeah, thanks. They were just being drunk jerks. It's not like it hasn't happened before."

"You shouldn't have to put up with that. We don't have to tolerate things like that here, do we?" They ran a tight ship at Wild's. If people got out of hand, they got tossed out. She'd call Sheriff Warren or Nick if she had to

.

"No. The last time someone got lippy with me, Barnaby heard and sent him packing."

"I bet that was fun." She'd been inside the kitchen at the time and only heard about it afterwards. The bartender didn't hesitate to speak his mind. He had probably let him have it.

"You have no idea." Maggie's nose scrunched up like a kid getting into mischief. "But I'm all good, and I need to make sure my guests are."

"Okay. Let me know if you need help out there."

"Sure thing, boss." Maggie tossed a hand up in the air and disappeared into the dining room.

Nell tugged her apron off over her head and spun to go back into the kitchen. The sun was shining on the back deck. It looked like the clouds had dispersed quickly.

They had looked large and heavy. She'd been certain it would be a downpour. It looked like the little waitress's emotions were triggering her power.

After tossing the apron in the laundry basket near the door, she grabbed a spare. She hadn't had time to take the other one off before running straight out onto the back deck, and she wasn't risking potential germs with her guests.

She needed to plan some new recipes for the warmer weather and coming summer.

Tying the clean apron around her and in a knot, a mischievous smile spread across her face. New recipes could wait. She had an idea. But first, she texted the crew, telling them to come by tonight after closing for a new kind of taste test.

And they needed to talk about that storm.

Nell washed her hands and got to work. The dinner rush would be hitting them soon, and she needed to get the ovens heated and the sauces started on the stove.

It didn't take long for her to get swept up in the steam and activity of the evening meal. And when that settled down, she was able to start her second project of the night: a special dinner meant only for her friends, at least for now.

Stopping to wash her hands a final time, she checked the clock. It wasn't quite eight, but in her text to her crew, she'd asked Maggie to post that they were closing a little early. She preferred not to do it on a Friday night, but they hadn't hit their busiest time of year yet. The few tourists they had could wrap up early.

Everyone had confirmed they would be there. Propping her fists on her waist, she glanced toward the door. Like clockwork, Shelby burst through it, a glass of wine in hand, singing a popular song about the start of the weekend. She gave a mighty fist pump along with a heartfelt rendition.

Shelby was always early for free food.

"Bad week?" Nell tilted her head.

"Nah, just ready for Friday." Shelby took a sip.

"You own your own business like me. The weekend doesn't mean free time."

"Don't I know it." She slumped against the wall behind her. "But don't kill my jam. I'm pretending."

"Pretend away." Nell picked up the tray in front of her, filled with special goodies for the evening. She nodded toward a second one loaded with bowls of small dishes put together from the leftover prepped food. "Get that one, will you?"

"Sure thing." Shelby set her glass on it and started to lift it, but it tilted and sloshed over one side.

With a practiced hand, Nell propped her tray against a hip and snagged the glass, adding it to her load instead.

"Oops." Shelby grimaced.

"No sweat. You have to compensate for the weight."

"Who knew waitressing could be so challenging?"

"Everyone." Nell laughed at her own joke. She backed out of the swinging kitchen door, holding it for her friend.

Out front, she saw Maggie locking up after Conrad and his wife. A trio of tourists stood in front of the restaurant, looking around. She almost felt bad, kicking them out early. They probably would have purchased another r ound.

"They're not leaving town until Sunday," Maggie said, wiping her hands on her own apron. "I sold them a case of beer so they could go back to their cabins and have another."

"Good thinking." Nell saw them make their way to their truck.

"Don't worry, they only had one a piece. They'll be fine driving."

"What would I do without you?"

"Hire another waitress?" Maggie shrugged, but she had a smile on her face. She knew how much Nell appreciated her.

"Come on. I'd lose half my guests."

"Nah. You're the only restaurant in town," Shelby tossed behind her, dancing sassily through the rear doors and out onto the back patio.

Maggie shook her head. "That's not true. Everyone is crazy about your food."

"Are you sure you want dinner? You could pick something up from the gas station down the road," Nell teased her friend back, setting her platter on the bar instead of at the table they normally sat at.

"Nah," Shelby repeated, waving her suggestion off. "I'm already here. Might as well stay."

Rolling her eyes, Nell poured the wine the other woman had opened and left on the bar. "Did Duke bring this?"

"No, I brought it." Shelby snagged a glass off Nell's platter.

"You did?"

Shelby shrugged. "I can't always mooch off you."

"Since when?"

"Hey." She tried to look offended, then abandoned the act and pointed to the tray on the counter. "What's this over here for? Are we eating at the bar?"

"No, this isn't dinner."

"It's certainly food." Shelby eyed the dishes curiously. "What is it if it's not dinner?"

"I'll explain when everyone gets here.""They'd better hurry up." Shelby pouted, poking at the spoons in the bowls at the table. "It smells good."

"Whadya mean? We're right here." Duke pushed open the gate at the entrance to the outside deck, holding it open for Willa and Nick, who had just walked up the stairs holding hands.

It warmed Nell's heart to see the two of them so obviously in love. They'd had a rocky start, but she was glad Nick had worked through his fears. Maybe it was time she did too.

Smiling, she swept out a hand. "I have something for you to try."

Like sharks circling their prey, the six of them gathered around the table. They had been six before they lost Gary. Now, they were six again. She was glad Nick had joined them and that he and Willa made such a great couple.

She just missed having someone at her side as well. It had been a challenging year.

At least she had them, her found family.

"Try?" Duke asked. "Something new?"

"She's not letting us try it yet." Shelby leaned in. Her finger pointed to the second tray on the bar. "She's being very vague about it. It must be important."

Nell's plate was at the head of the table. Naturally. It was her restaurant. And she wanted to see their reactions.

"But first, please enjoy dinner." She sat down melodramatically, ignoring Shelby, as her arms swept out to display the bowls of seafood pasta, rice pilaf, strips of tri-tip steak, brussels sprouts, and kale and apple salad. She'd added the last one because it was getting warmer, and if she had any hopes of wearing a T-shirt and shorts this summer, she needed to cut back on the desserts.

Which was not easy to do when you were a chef, but she did like a good salad. It seemed more were in her future.

Her friends paused, watching her warily.

"Oh, for goodness' sake." She grabbed the seafood pasta since it was the closest. She'd fill her plate with salad after a taste of this. And maybe just a little of the pilaf. She'd put saffron in it, and it smelled heavenly.

"You don't have to tell me twice." Duke spooned a large helping of rice on his plate, then reached for the pasta she'd set down.

They all dug in silently, except for requests for passing dishes and the wine Shelby had likely convinced Barnaby to open for them.

"I did have one more conversation topic for tonight." Nell broke the silence. "Did anyone notice the storm earlier?"

"Yeah." Duke frowned. "It came and went, as mercurial as the ocean."

"It probably came from it," Willa added.

"The ocean shifts, sure, but this felt like something else. I couldn't put my finger on it."

"I think it might be one of us." Nell looked at Maggie, knowing the sweet waitress had no idea of her power.

"Not me!" She bound her hands in front of her. "I didn't do it."

"I think you might have," Nell offered gently. She felt bad bringing it up in front of the crew, but they were all in this together, and they all needed to be there to support each other. She was starting to realize that. "Unknowingly, of course. Those drunk asshats were causing problems. You can make it rain."

It was pretty obvious, really.

Maggie slumped in her chair. "I'm so sorry."

"Why are you sorry?" Duke asked. "You were being challenged, and you used what you had."

"But I didn't realize it."

"We're all still getting the hang of our powers." Willa motioned towards Nell.

"Speak for yourself." Duke brushed imaginary lint from his flannel sleeve.

"I could have caused problems in the cove." Maggie looked out over the now-calm water. "I could have been the reason for a flood or a boat crash."

Nell could see the struggle on Duke's face to control his expression. It wasn't funny to Maggie, no matter how cute the petite woman was. "Sweetheart, that's where I come in. If the waves get outta hand. I've got i t."

Maggie nodded, still curled inward. "I had no idea."

"Now, you do, and we know what to do if you have trouble again." Nell inclined her head. "Duke's got your back on this one."

"Damn straight," he replied, snagging the last mussel from the pasta and plopping it into his mouth.

Maggie seemed eased by the news. When was she going to realize how valuable she was to the rest of them?

It didn't take long for all the bowls to empty and all five faces to turn to Nell.

She bit back a smile. This was going to be fun.

"We have another taste test tonight." She stood, gathered the empty bowls, and carried them to the counter. She returned with the second tray and put it in the other's place.

"A new menu?" Maggie asked.

"No." Nick tilted his head. "You're testing your magic again."

"I am." She finally smiled. "I'm taking a lesson from Willa, though."

Willa's eyes rounded, and she clasped her hands in front of her. "You're using it to help people?"

"I'm trying."

"Then, you see it's not a curse!"

"I'm exploring the possibility." Nell sat down, picked up her wineglass, and took her final sip.

"We need another bottle." Shelby rose from her seat.

"You might want to wait on that." Nell waved her down. She lifted the cover from the tray and presented the food.

"What does it do?" Willa asked, peering at the little plates.

"You intentionally magicked the food?" Maggie said curiously.

"I did." Nell nodded. "Willa uses hers freely. All of you do, but only hers and mine affect other people. She's not afraid to use hers."

"I'm careful." Willa raised her hand.

"I know you are, but you wouldn't let fear keep you from helping people."

"No. We were given these gifts for a reason."

"We don't know that," Shelby piped up. "Lightning struck. It could have easily been a coincidence."

"Either way. I'm not wasting it," the curly-haired herbalist said.

"I'm trying to take a leap of faith." Nell picked up the first plate and held it out in front of her. "Who wants to try Happy Halibut?"

Willa's eyebrows disappeared under her bangs. "Really?"

She nodded, excited by the prospect. She'd only had to think of her friends to conjure up the happiness to make them.

"I'll try them." Willa reached out a hand, but Shelby caught the plate before she did. Her fork stabbed a small square of fish and popped it into her mouth.

"My turn for the happy one. 'Sides, it'd be wasted on you. You're already happy all the time. How would we know if it was working on you?"

Willa's lips flattened, and the others laughed. The sound was music to Nell's ears after the distance they'd had post Gary's passing. Most of that was her fault, being unable to face the rest of them without her partner. It had all felt so wr ong.

Although the danger that had followed Nick was scary, it had brought them back together. She was grateful for that. She needed them more than she'd realized.

"Don't worry." Nell picked up another plate. "I have one for you. Relaxed Rockfish."

"I should have had that one." Shelby's mouth twisted. "I'm always stressed."

"I guess you shouldn't be greedy." Willa used her fork to take a piece and ate it. She savored the bite. "So good."

"That's okay. I already don't mind." Shelby's mouth turned up in pleasure. She sat on her hands and rocked forward, watching the rest of them with delight.

"Bliss bars." Nell picked up another plate. "Smoked seaweed on brownies."

"I really want to try that one." Nick's eyes widened. "May I?"

"Since you're being so polite, absolutely." Happily, she presented him with the plate, and he immediately popped one in his mouth.

"How is bliss different than happy?" Duke asked, watching the rest of the crew carefully.

"It gets rid of stress, like the relaxing one, but everything is right in the world." It reminded her of that first night she'd accidentally enhanced their mood. It felt a little like a light buzz, but with a deep contentment. She'd had to dig deep to find that feeling, even for the moment it took to sprinkle the seaweed on the bars.

"Delicious." Nick spoke around the gooey chocolate.

"These are awesome." Willa slid back into her seat, settling in comfortably.

"Are you tired?" Maggie asked Willa, eyeing the remaining piece of rockfish.

"No, just completely relaxed and calm."

"That sounds amazing."

"There's one final plate." Duke reached out a hand. "What'll I be having?"

His face was set, his eyes not rising from the food to meet hers. Nell realized after their last taste test that he probably expected her to have put her grief into one of them again.

He was nervous. As nervous as Duke got, anyway.

"I didn't make anything bad, Duke," Nell said. "I'm not doing that again."

His gaze rose to meet hers. Tension eased from his shoulders, and he popped the slice of geoduck in his mouth. "Well, then. What can I expect?"

She was going to warn them first, but when he swallowed, Nell raised her hand to cover her mouth. She hadn't expected anyone to grab that one so haphazardly.

Duke's eyebrows rose, and his hands covered his mouth to match hers. A bubble of laughter spilled out of his mouth like a gurgle of water moving down the stream. He clamped down on his mouth and shot to his feet.

"Giggle Geoduck." Nell was finally able to get it out without laughing in return.

"Best day ever." Shelby leaned back in her chair, her own laughter rising as Duke finally gave in to the biggest set of giggles she'd witnessed outside of girls' night.

Willa just smiled as she reclined in her seat, completely at ease.

"Ooh, you should make"—Shelby's eyes squinted—"Success Shrimp."

"I'm not sure how I'd do that," Nell replied. "I don't know if I can recreate success.""You make successful bread all the time," Maggie pointed out.

"Thanks, but that's through practice and knowledge. Besides, I think it's about emotion and frame of mind."

"How about Confident Cod?" Maggie asked.

"I could probably do that," Nell considered. Everyone seemed to be enjoying the name game and the fun-inducing fare.

"That'd be awesome." Maggie's eyes lit up.

"What'll we have, then?" Nell asked her diminutive friend. She'd made three of everything. It had taken her quite a while to get all the emotions right. The giggle had been the most work. She'd resorted to dancing around the kitchen with exceptionally bad dance moves all by herself to produce that sort of laughter.

It had also been pretty fun.

"Maybe the Relaxed Rockfish." Maggie's eyes cut to Willa. "That looks awesome."

"I'm going for the Bliss Bars." Nell reached for the brownies. "I do love chocolate."

Taking a bite, she settled into her seat, knowing the feeling of rightness would soon settle over her. She'd need to make more of these.

It seemed like she'd finally figured out how to use her strange ability as a gift. And it felt really awesome.

CHAPTER 12

"Emiliano."

He jerked out of his trance.

He'd been stocking cans of tomatoes. To be fair, he'd been looking out across the parking lot. Nell was out on the back deck of her café and seemed happier than she'd been in a while. There was a looseness to her movements. It delighted him to see her smiling and at ease.

"Yes?" He turned to see Duke pause between two shoppers before walking up to him, box in hand.

"Here you go. One game camera. As promised." Duke plunked it on top of the cart full of cans he'd been hauling around the store during the afternoon restocking. The tourists had cleaned them out quicker than normal today.

"That was quick." Emiliano picked up the box to examine it. It was a standard game cam, just as Conrad Brooks had ordered. He hoped it would set the farmer at ease and he could learn what was going on at his property.

"I'm pretty amazing. Just ask me." Duke buffed his nails on his blue flannel shirt.

Emiliano snorted, shaking his head. "You're something. That's for sure."

"Come on. I delivered."

"You most definitely did. I am in your debt."

"That's more like it." Duke had a satisfied, smug look on his face.

"Thanks, man." Emiliano clapped him on the shoulder.

"Sure thing." Duke picked up a lemon from the basket on his cart and tossed it in the air. "I'd better pick up some groceries while I'm here. I'm nearly out."

"We got fresh rockfish this morning."

"That's one of my favorites."

"I know." Emiliano brushed fake lint from his Henley-clad shoulder. "I'm pretty amazing."

Duke laughed heartily. "That, you are."

Emiliano grinned at their easy banter.

"Hey, man," Duke turned to him. "Let me know how things go at Conrad's place if anything is going on there more than some adventurous wildlife."

"It's probably nothing, but sure thing."

"Thanks, man." Duke clapped him on the shoulder as well and made his way to the fish counter, lemon in hand.

Emiliano finished stocking the cans and fresh fruit he'd brought to the floor. Then, wiping his hands on his jeans, he pushed the flatbed cart to the back. He'd take the camera to Conrad immediately. The farmer had already waited too many days.

It was a short drive west to Brooks Farms, about halfway to the neighboring town of Liberty. Pulling into the gravel drive, Emiliano spotted the man coming out of one of the machine sheds dotting the property.

"Conrad." He raised his hand in greeting.

"Emiliano." The man hefted the large bag he'd been carrying on his shoulder to the ground and crossed over to him. He wiped his gloved hands over his canvas work jeans. "What can I do for you this afternoon?"

He held up the box. "The game cam, as promised."

Conrad's eyebrow went up. "That was fast."

"We found someone who was making a trip to pick it up."

"You mean *you* did."

"Well." Emiliano shifted his feet. His pops had always been there for him. He was the only one who had been. It felt right to do the same for him. "I did, yes. It was an oversight, and I found a solution. I'm sorry it happened."

"I appreciate you stepping up to help out."

"I'm sure it wasn't intentional."

"I don't doubt that."

"Still. It wasn't taken seriously, and I apologize for that."

Conrad nodded, then clapped out a hand to shake Emiliano's. "Accepted. You made it right."

"So, what's going on out here?" He turned to examine the field that lay beyond them. Nothing looked out of place to him.

"That's what I'm trying to find out." The farmer rocked back on his heels, his arms crossed. "Something's off. That field has had some damage. And I'm pretty sure that was up last night."

He gestured up to a ladder that lay next to the closest barn.

"Do you think a bear would do that?"

"A bear could have been prowling around and knocked it over, sure." Conrad's mouth twisted. "But it would have left tracks."

"There aren't any?"

"There are a few smudged tracks farther back, but nothing identifiable. Mainly, out in the field, near the fence line."

After the wet winter, they hadn't had nearly as much rain as usual. Tracks would be difficult to capture in an area like this.

"And nothing disturbed the pigs," Conrad went on, indicating the shelter where he kept his animals. "So, probably not a cougar, either."

"Thank goodness for that." They'd had enough predator problems a few years ago. Emiliano could see areas of the field that looked broken or trampled on, but farther out, there was a large section of produce that was brown. "Maybe it's an elk."

The Roosevelt elk lived throughout the Olympic National Forest. Brooks Farm sat in a valley just east of the woods, with a fence along the produce runs.

"I've not seen elk get over fencing like that. If anything, they'd be mangling the fence to get in."

It was true. He'd seen elk go to war with anything that kept them out of the land they were used to grazing on. When they thought an area was theirs, they'd fight over it

.

"I can see why you wanted the camera. I hope you let us know what you find out."

Conrad bent down to the bag of feed at his feet and hoisted it up to his shoulder. "Will do. Can you put that on my truck bed on your way out? I need to feed the piglets before they eat the wooden railings."

"We wouldn't want that." He lifted a hand in acknowledgment and deposited the box safely on Conrad's tailgate before returning to Orca Cove.

Stepping out on the marina at the rear of Gil's Market, Emiliano could see the band setting up on the Wild Café's back deck. He'd been trying not to spy on Nell the rest of the afternoon; he didn't want to be creepy, but it was so nice to see her happy. Now that the band had arrived, he noticed her nerves had returned.

Nell spun back out the rear door, pointing to the young adults setting up their equipment and stopping to speak to the patrons sitting nearby. She'd cleared a few tables at one corner of the deck for them to set up. It looked like she was still worried about bothering her guests.

But the outdoor tables were nearly full, and the café had gained a good turnout.

He'd puttered around the market after dinner, taking note of a few inventory items, trying to determine the right time to head over. He wanted to be there for support. It wouldn't be weird, he told himself. He'd helped her put out fliers, for goodness' sake. He could call them fr iends.

Hopefully, it wasn't the dreaded friend zone.

It was why he'd made a point to let his feelings be known. He felt better putting himself out there. He didn't care if he looked like a fool, but he wasn't taking the risk of her not knowing how he felt. The ball was in her court. She could either leave their relationship as it was or take the next step.

Running his hands down his front, he checked for anything he might have missed earlier. He was wearing a relatively clean navy Henley and tan slacks. He took a long breath to calm his nerves, just like he did every time he went to see her, and crunched across the lot to the café.

The night had cooled, but it was still warm enough to be out without a jacket. It was the best time of year. The cove was calm, and the gentle lapping of the water on the docks helped to further settle his nerves. If it was meant to be with Nell, it would happen. He couldn't change t hat.

Out of the corner of his eye, he noticed an orca poking its blunt nose above the surface. He paused, fascinated by the large creature as it bobbed, shifting as though observing the lively café deck and then the man walking across the asphalt. What was probably only moments felt like minutes as the two connected in a near-silent moment.

The orca moved first, dipping under a wave and reappearing a meter farther out. Emiliano watched its fin as it glided an s-shaped path to the far edge of the cove.

Blinking through the fog of the moment, he reached the bottom step of the wooden deck stairs and looked up at the strung bulbs illuminating the outdoor dining area. He smiled, for once feeling better about the evening.

"Bourbon?" Barnaby asked from behind an open space at the bar.

Emiliano hadn't seen the bartender approach, but grateful to have found a seat, he immediately took it, sliding onto the tall barstool. "That'd be great, thanks."

"It looks like your marketing plans paid off." The bartender indicated the crowd.

"That was Nell. I just gave her a few ideas."

Barnaby just watched him, pouring the liquor into a clean glass and sliding it over.

"Thanks." He lifted his drink, uneasy under the older man's gaze. "Nell made the call on everything herself."

The sea of people parted, and Nell broke through. She had taken her apron off but still had a towel draped over one shoulder.

"Hey." She paused by his stool.

"Hey, yourself. Good turnout."

"Yeah." She looked around the deck. Her cheeks were rosy and she was a little out of breath, but her eyes were bright with happiness. "I just hope the band is good."

"They'll do fine," Barnaby spoke.

"What do they play?" Emiliano asked.

"Seattle sound," Barnaby answered, already pouring another drink.

"I should have guessed that." He'd seen the band on the fliers they passed out. Uprising of the Dung Beetle couldn't have been anything other than grunge. Paying the young musicians closer attention, he recognized one of them. "Is that JD?"

Nell looked at him strangely. "You know him?" "I knew his older sister, Star. He was a few years younger than me in school." He'd dated Star for the second half of sophomore year until summer rolled around. She'd left him for some tourist who was a half head taller with a six-pack.

Another one who hadn't stuck around.

"A few years younger? He seems so young." She turned to look at Emiliano, their age gap laid bare between them, and her eyes cut to the people pushing to the bar to get drinks.

"Great idea to have live music," a man commented loudly over the crowd. It was Eddie Jones, and he looked like he'd already had a few, but he was still smiling.

"Thanks."

"Yeah, Nell." Patty from the post office raised her drink high in exhilaration. "Just what we need for a Saturday night. Why didn't you do this earlier?"

Nell laughed, her eyes finding Emiliano's again in the crowd. "I should go."

"Of course." He dipped his head. "Do your thing."

Before she hurried off, she leaned in closer so he could hear her over the rising noise of the band checking their equipment. Her hand landed on his forearm. "Thanks again for your help."

"I didn't do much."

"You helped plenty." She shot him a blindingly happy grin and pushed off, disappearing in the throng of people.

Warmth ran from his arm straight to his chest and pumped him up to feel like he'd given her at least a little bit of what she needed.

When he took a sip of his bourbon, the spicy drink warmed his chest even further, and he noticed the ever-present bartender had been watching their exchange, his eyebrows raised as though saying, "See?"

He lifted his shoulder in reply. He had no response. Barnaby disappeared, and he settled in to hear JD's guitar strum a Nirvana song. The sounds of his youth reverberated on the deck. Well, maybe not his youth, but it was still something he'd held on to. He couldn't imagine many kids being unable to connect to music about being outsiders, struggling to find their place in the world. It was the music of the young and a sound that still felt powerful for him.

Maybe he should invite Nell to dinner again. He didn't want to seem pushy, but they were friends now, right? He'd visited her after hours. She'd come to dinner with him and Pops. Why not?

"Fancy seeing you here." A voice at his elbow had him turn. Nick and Willa stood at the bar, behind him.

"Hey. How's it going?" Emiliano slid from his barstool to offer it to Willa.

"No, thanks. We have a table in the corner." She nodded behind her at Duke and Shelby, who sat, deep in conversation.

"You traveled far to support our friend," Nick said gravely.

"Yeah, it was quite the journey, making it across the parking lot in this terrible weather." Emiliano sighed loudly. "But I made it."

Nick clapped him on his shoulder. "I hear you helped out with the marketing plan."

Glancing self-consciously at the bartender, who was, of course, paying attention, he exhaled. "Not really. I just offered some ideas and help."

"It was nice of you."

"Yeah, Shelby offered some advice too, but she's getting free cookies for life out of it," Willa added.

"She obviously knows what she's doing better than me." Emiliano chuckled. "I missed the boat on that one."

They laughed.

Nick peered around, watching the crowd. "Everyone seems happy."

"Yeah." Willa's eyes narrowed in thought. "Are they happier than normal?"

"I would hope so. This is the first live music we've had in Orca Cove since we had that folk music band play at the farmers market two summers ago," Emiliano said.

Willa blinked and shook her head, then smiled broadly at him. "Of course."

"Any progress on the website?" Nick asked.

"Not really." Emiliano wanted to tell him there wasn't a chance in hell for it to happen. That is, unless he did it without his dad, and he didn't think he could compete with Hugo. That didn't sit well with him.

"I thought the site was coming along well. Did you run into problems?"

"Sort of." He debated telling him he was having trouble figuring out the delivery-billing portion of the site, but the town had likely heard about his argument with his dad. It was only a matter of time until everyone knew. "Pops isn't keen on the idea."

"Would it help if he knew folks were interested in posting our products for online sale?" Nick asked. "I'd be able to stop selling on the one I'm using. There's no way Gil's could support that much additional product."

"I know." Emiliano's head dropped a notch. Boy, did he know. That was the problem. "He's not a fan of change."

Nick stilled for a moment, taking in his body language, then held up his drink. "To change."

The solidarity of the gesture lightened his mood. Lifting his glass, he clinked it to Nick's and repeated the words.

"We'd better take our seats before someone steals them." Willa tugged at Nick's hand, indicating two male tourists trying to cozy up to Shelby. With her straight dark hair and almond-shaped eyes, she commanded attention.

Not for Emiliano, though. Shelby wasn't his type. Finding Nell near the doors, watching the crowd, her hands entwined in front of her, he smiled, unable to help himself.

Yeah, that was his type.

"Gotta run," Nick said. "Let me know if there's any-thing I can do to help."

"I appreciate it," Emiliano said, meaning it.

If only it was that easy.

Letting the bathroom door swing shut behind him, Emil-iano stifled a yawn. It looked like the band was finishing up outside. He checked his watch and realized he should take off before it got any later.

But first, he wanted to say a quick goodbye to Nell. His face tensed with indecision. When he'd caught sight of her earlier, she was busy with another group of regulars excited to tell her how much they were enjoying the music. She'd done a great job with everything.

No, he'd give her a wave across the deck if he could catch her attention on his way out.

But before he could make it back outside, the patio door swung open and Nell, a broad smile plastered on her face, slid through it.

"Emiliano!" The words soared from her, as light as air.

His face echoed the joyful curve hers wore as she came to a stop in front of him.

"You pulled it off." His head tipped forward. "It's not surprising. You're a fantastic cook. Probably even the best in the area."

"Probably?" she challenged him, her grin turning sassy and playful.

Was she flirting with him?

"Well, I'd have to do a more thorough comparison. That restaurant in Liberty is pretty good, and I've heard their pizza is stellar."

"Better than mine?"

"You don't make pizza all the time." He shook his head sadly. "You can't blame yourself."

Nell acted like she was shocked. "Well, I guess I'll have to change that."

"If you ever decide to up your game"—he laid a hand over his heart—"I'm willing to help you taste test."

"You'd do that for me?" She kept the game up, much to his delight.

"You know what they say; practice makes perfect." He dug into the role, pressing his lips together. "You see,

Nell. I'm a giver. It's what I do." Then, feeling daring, he w inked.

Nell couldn't keep her face straight anymore, and tinkling laughter lifted from her throat. "You're too much, Emiliano Gil."

"Nah, I'm willing to do anything to talk you into pizza more often."

"For helping me out, you got it," she said with finality.

Damn, he didn't want her to feel like she owed him. "I honestly didn't do much. You put it all together and made it a success, not that I had any doubts."

"You never doubted me. Thank you for that."

"I believed in you, Nell. You should do the same. You're a capable woman."

Her eyes softened at the corners, and the way she looked up at him... Hell, it was like every dream he'd ever had.

He was a goner.

Without even realizing it, his hand drifted to her cheek, cupping it with reverence. He wanted to remember this moment and the way she was looking at him for the rest of his life.

She tilted forward in response, and Emiliano's heart beat like maracas against his chest. He was certain she could hear it. But before he even dared consider leaning in to meet her halfway, she jerked back, as though coming out of a fog.

Her wide, doe-like eyes darted to the man coming in the back door and back to him. Then she barked a nervous laugh, tucked an invisible strand of hair behind an ear, and danced away. "I should get back out there."

"Yeah, it sounded like they were nearly done," Emiliano blathered. What was he saying? Of course, she would know that. She had just come in.

"Yep." Her voice was pitched higher, a fake smile on her face, as she watched the man make a beeline for the restroom. "Thanks for coming, Emiliano."

"Of course," he said with as little emotion as possible, following her back out to the deck.

Having already paid his tab, he wove through the thinning crowd and didn't take a breath until he thundered down the wooden steps and faced the ocean. Its dark surface reflected the crescent moon hanging overhead.

Inhaling as deeply as possible, he tried to tamp down the sadness creeping up his chest. He was pretty certain she was attracted to him, but it seemed like she didn't think she should be.

Great, another person thinking he wasn't good enough.

CHAPTER 13

The stainless-steel meat tenderizer made a satisfying bang against the wood edge-grain cutting board Nick had gifted Nell. She was pounding out pork cutlets with a little more aggression than necessary and oscillating between the exhilaration at the achievement of a large turnout at their live music the night before and embarrassment at practically throwing herself at Hugo's son.

Images of a young Emiliano flew through her mind, pulling up a stool to check out her and her girlfriends' purchases of soda and Push Pops. Her insides shriveled up at the cringeworthy memory.

For a moment, she'd had the crazy thought that maybe he might actually have feelings for her, but... Whack, her mallet hit the poor, unsuspecting pork, and she came to her senses in time.

Their earlier interaction by his firepit and mention of a date was a fluke.

Whack. She pounded another cutlet flat. It was satisfying, taking her frustrations out on the perfect cut of pork. At least, she'd had a successful night and a solid check in her new marketing plan.

They'd had people who weren't tourists. Actual locals from an expanded radius than they'd ever brought in before. Not a lot, naturally, but it was a step. That part felt like a real win. One she'd really needed since doing this thing all on her own. It was kinda scary.

And Shelby would be going with her to visit Mt. Olympus Vineyards soon. It would be the first of many local products she hoped to use to support other businesses and bring in a larger customer base.

Gary would be proud of her.

Her mallet paused, hovering over the next cutlet.

Would he?

They'd talked a lot about plans and the future after he was diagnosed with leukemia. He wanted her to continue the business and to thrive. She thought he would be proud of her, and she hoped he somehow knew of her accomplishments. Maybe not see all the trials and tribulations she'd faced, but her current victory at least.

It only felt right. They'd started The Wild Café together, a play on his last name, "Wilder." Keeping this place afloat and flourishing felt like an honor to his legacy. She couldn't let it fail.

After dipping the tenderized pork in a milk-and-egg solution, she dredged it in well-seasoned sourdough breadcrumbs and layered on wire racks for that evening's dinner's special.

She'd prepare mushroom gravy with blue oyster mushrooms if Gil's had enough fresh ones. Nell made a mental note to pick some up when she had a break. Stretching to ease the tension in her shoulders, she rose on her toes to pull down a stainless-steel bowl from a shelf over her counter. Her eyes shut, and her hand hovered over the flour as she decided what to make.

Flavors of lemon and lavender floated through her mind. A little salt and butter. Shortbread cookies. Shelby liked those.

And she had to ensure the savvy businesswoman wouldn't change her mind on going with her to the vineyard. She needed her help. Shelby had been making deals since they were in middle school, and had two small businesses by the time she made it to high school. It was selling extra school supplies to forgetful kids and organizing shopping days in Seattle with young adults who had licenses, but still, she was making money at a young age and investing it in herself. The parents were okay with the trips because they technically had older chaperones. Shelby'd always known how to make a good deal for everyone involved.

And the woman was fond of shortbread.

Maybe Nell would take some cookies over to Emiliano as a thank you for helping out with the fliers and talking her off the ledge about the live music.

Remembering their conversation, she frowned. It had been news to her that Emiliano was so fond of pizza. How had she missed that?

While zesting lemons, Nell considered having some on the following Saturday night's special. The band had agreed to come back after her customers asked for an encore. They hadn't gotten enough of the nineties, alternative grunge music.

And she had enjoyed the blast from the past as well, but it would have been better if they had a more food-friendly name than Uprising of the Dung Beetle. Nell shuddered again at the thought. Dung and food didn't go together.

Unless you were a dung beetle, she supposed.

Squeezing the lemon juice from the zested lemons, she considered the pizza for Emiliano. They were friends. He'd had her over for dinner at his house. For paella, which was more than just dinner; it was a celebration of traditional foods with a family recipe. It was quite an honor.

She bit her lip. Would it be weird if she invited him over for pizza? Tomorrow was Monday, their day off, and she could try a few different pizza recipes on him to get his opinion.

She had to prove she was better than that restaurant in Liberty, after all.

Chuckling at their inside joke, she considered if it was really a good idea. She could deliver them as a thank you and still get his feedback. Would it be weird to invite him one-on-one? Should she invite Hugo? It was Emiliano who had helped her out, been her friend and sounding board. He could probably use some space from his dad. They were working through an awkward stage.

They were turning into friends, right? And friends sometimes hung out. Cooking dinner was something she did as easily as breathing. Food was her love language.

With friends, she corrected her inner dialogue. She hadn't meant it like that.

Making food for people was how she showed them she appreciated and cared about them. *That they were friends*, she corrected herself again.

Would it be so wrong to care for the guy, though? He'd been there for her. She'd known him practically for as long as she could remember. That wasn't weird.

She just liked him so much. They talked the same language, taking care of the townspeople of Orca Cove. But it was no sweat; they could be friends. And if she appreciated his physique? So what? She'd noticed Nick was a good-looking man, protective and kind, but she'd never thought about him that way.

She was getting all twisted up because she had doubted herself so much this past year. And when he told her to have faith in herself and called her capable, she'd nearly melted. It was exactly what she needed to hear. And with the night's success, it had hit deep. That was a ll.

Convinced, she gently folded the lemon zest and lavender buds into the crumbly shortbread dough. She'd bring it up when she stopped by for mushrooms and saw how he reacted. If he acted weird, she'd suggest dropping them off and be done with it.

"Knock knock." Nell stood at Emiliano's door, putting on her best casual expression.

"Nell." He looked up from a ledger he was working on, his shoulders hunched and tight. It seemed he'd been there a while.

"Everything okay?"

"Yeah." He dropped his pen and stood, looking her up and down, his eyes landing on the sage-green box in her hand.

Nell's stomach somersaulted. She reached out to the doorjamb to ground herself from its fluttering.

"I came over for blue oysters, and since I made cookies, I thought I'd drop you off some." She handed them to him. "As a thank you for your help. I really appreciate it."

"It was nothing." He took the box and studied it.

"Not to me. I needed the support. I've been a little unsure about how to do things since Gary passed." She brushed a strand of hair back into its ponytail. "But I'm getting there."

"You are." The corner of his mouth ticked up.

"Anyway." Nell crossed her arms. "I think I have a reputation to protect."

"Your reputation?" He looked at her curiously.

"In pizza-making." She nodded sagely. "You mentioned I could use some practice. Well, I'm ready to prove you wrong."

"You are, huh?" He sat on the edge of his desk, setting the box down beside him. "What did you have in mind?"

"Well, I think I need to do it right. To settle it once and for all, I'll prepare several pizzas to showcase my talent and see if I can make your taste buds explode."

Emiliano's eyes widened, and he coughed, then cleared his throat. "Sorry about that. My taste buds, huh? That sounds dangerous."

Nell's stomach dropped farther, realizing her faux pas. She hadn't meant to sound suggestive.

"The explosion part? Yeah. I agree. It can be." She shrugged, trying to play it off. "If you're not up for it, I understand. It's pretty risky."

Dang it, she'd done it again! Bearing down to keep her face even, she checked to see if he'd caught it. Yep, he was grinning like a fool.

"I think I'm up for the task."

"Great." The words tumbled out of her mouth. She was dying to get out of here. "How about tomorrow at six?"

She realized she hadn't waited to feel him out on having dinner with her. Her eyes flashed to read his reaction.

"At your place?" His eyebrows went up.

"Yeah." The words were drawn out more than she'd meant them to be. "Or I can drop them off if you're busy."

He could back out if he wanted to. No harm, no foul.

"That sounds good." He nodded casually. "I'm free tomorrow."

"I figured."

"Thankfully, my backpacking trip got canceled."

"Backpacking?"

"Just kidding. I'm not cool enough to have plans. I thought I'd try not to sound lame."

"I never have plans on Mondays." She always tried to rest and recharge.

"Except paella night."

"Except paella night," she agreed.

Her friends had never cooked for her. Not that she minded. She was the chef. Still, it had been nice to be catered to.

Paella night hadn't ended so well.

She wouldn't be drugging him this time, so they had a shot of it being good fun between friends. Absently, she remembered she'd delivered cookies that day too. There wasn't a chance that she'd inadvertently spelled them again, was there?

Her mind raced through their ingredients.

No, she was safe. Besides, she'd made a habit of playing calming or happy music while cooking now. It helped maintain her mood. She was good to go.

"It's settled, then." She stepped back into the hall, anxious to leave and get back to her mushroom gravy. She also needed to jot down notes for tomorrow's pizza d ate.

Night! It was a pizza night, for sure. Not a date.

Flustered, she leaped when Emiliano spoke again.

"Can I bring anything?" His voice had a velvety quality that pleasantly slid down her spine. It was like the texture of rich chocolate sauce; soft and warm.

"No. I think we're good." Her voice squeaked, and she coughed to cover it.

"I'll see you at six, then. Looking forward to seeing what you come up with."

"See you!" She plastered on a wildly happy face to cover her emotions and hightailed it out of there.

Almost all the way across the lot, she realized she'd forgotten the mushrooms and spun to double back.

"What's up, Nell?" said a voice, breaking her already frayed focus.

"Huh?" She froze, spotting Willa and Maggie sitting on the outdoor deck of the café, watching her emotional spiral.

"You okay?" Willa sat down the bowl she was holding and stood up to come closer to the stairs.

"Yeah." Nell laughed at how silly she had to look, and her hand went to her head. "I got turned around and forgot to get the blue oyster mushrooms."

Maggie's eyebrow shot up as she set down the silverware she was wrapping for the brunch crowd. "Did you get caught up in a conversation with Emiliano?"

Nell could feel her face flush.

"Yes, but." She paused. "I took him cookies."

"You took him cookies?" Willa asked. "That was sweet."

"It was a large batch." She played it off, suddenly uncomfortable about the thought of flirting with Emiliano. She didn't want them to think it was anything. "He helped with the plans for the live music. We're friends."

"Friends," Maggie repeated.

"Yeah." She frowned. She was allowed to have friends. "We work right next to each other. It makes sense."

Willa came to her aid. "It definitely does."

"I'm glad you're friends." Maggie smiled broadly.

Looking around the parking lot, Nell jumped up the back steps to meet them. What if someone was hearing them discuss her friendship with Emiliano? What would they think?

"You don't have to make a big deal about it," she mumbled. "But I've got to go back and get mushrooms for dinner."

"Solomon's over there," Willa said suddenly, her eyes on the fisherman walking up the dock. His pelican was flying around in the sky overhead. "We should talk to him ."

"Good idea." Maggie leapt up. "We can find out about the oyster thing."

"Oyster thing?" Willa asked.

"Shelby and Nell were worried about eating fish and shellfish if he can talk to them."

"Oh, I hadn't thought about that." Willa winced.

Maggie's apron whipped off her and landed, perfectly folded, on the table. She brushed past Nell on the stairs, looking excitedly over her shoulder. "Come on!"

Unsure what they were going to say, Nell hurried after her friend. She could hear Willa following.

"Good morning, Solomon!" Maggie approached the older man, her soft, round face beaming at his weathered one.

"Well, good morning, miss." Solomon reached up to pull off the light skullcap he'd been wearing. "How're you doin' this fine day?"

"Good, thanks." Maggie waited for her friends to catch up. "How're you healing up?"

"Oh, fine." He passed the hat back and forth between his hands. "I'm fit as a fiddle now, thanks to Willa."

He had been caught in the crosshairs when the criminals came to Orca Cove after evidence Nick had to lock their boss up for good. Luckily, Willa had been there and healed him with some plantain amped up with saltwater from the cove. The emergency personnel were shocked when they arrived and the wound was already healing.

The whole thing was written off as a graze.

"Glad to hear that."

"Hang on there, Roy." Solomon turned and waved at the pelican circling them. It landed several feet behind them on a railing. "I'll get your fish in a little bit."

"Hello, Roy." Willa smiled warmly at the bird. "Aren't you a beautiful pelican?"

Solomon chortled. "He likes you."

"I like him." She moved a little closer, still giving the bird some space. "I think I owe you thanks."

"What's that?" Solomon asked.

"I believe he did me a favor that day on the beach when we were attacked."

"He chased them off, for sure." Solomon nodded energetically. Then he froze, turning to the bird. "What's that, Roy? Oh, well, why'd ya keep that to yourself?"

He cackled in laughter.

"Did he say who he told where I was?" Willa asked, prodding to see what Solomon knew.

Percy, the orca-person—they still weren't sure how to refer to them—had found her on a tiny island in the Hood Canal.

"He says he told the orca, who brought you here."

Nell and Willa exchanged looks.

"The orca saved her." Nell watched his expression. "He brought her to shore."

Solomon bobbed his head. "Good job, Roy. You get an extra fish tonight!"

"I'll bring him some leftovers from tonight's dinner," Nell offered. "He deserves it if he helped my friend."

"Well, isn't that somethin'?" Solomon said to the pelican. "Did you hear that? Nell's gonna bring you gourmet food. Fixed just for you."

She knew she'd said leftovers, but she let it go. Let Roy think it was made for him. He'd earned it. She might even throw in some extra oysters if she had them.

"Tomorrow morning, on the dock?"

"Four o'clock?" Solomon asked.

"Uh, can we do a little later?" It was her only morning to sleep in.

"Sure. Let's try six."

"O-kay." The word drew out. She could make it work. Maybe.

"Have you talked to the orca?" Willa asked. "I'd like to thank him as well."

"No, I didn't see him." Solomon's attention went back to Roy for a moment. "Roy says he was here last night."

"Ah, so one from our usual pod."

"I guess." He shrugged. "I don't know which one he is."

"Solomon." Nell cleared her throat. "Have you ever talked to the orcas?"

"No, I don't think so." He shook his head.

"Have you ever talked to the fish you catch?" Willa asked.

"Not really," he replied.

Maggie rejoined the conversation from where she was studying the pelican next to Willa. "Because they don't talk to you or because you're catching them?"

"They're fish, ya know?" Solomon's face scrunched up. "They don't make much sense."

"What do they sound like? I don't get to hear them." Willa's eyes lit up.

"Ah, well, let me see." He propped one hand on a hip and scratched his head with the other. "Kinda like birds chirping, but underwater, with a gurgling sound. I've only caught a word here and there. Fish. Food. Swim. That's about it. I think, anyway. It's hard to tell. I could be putting words in their mouth, if you will."

Solomon bent over, laughing at his own joke.

Nell exhaled in relief. It sounded like they weren't very intelligent. She didn't feel as badly about using them as meat. "What about mussels? Can you talk to them? Or the geoduck?"

"That would be silly." He waved off. "They're just shellfish. Now, the otters, they're downright chatterboxes."

"Really?" Willa's eyes lit up with excitement. "I'd love to talk to an otter."

"You wouldn't really understand them much," Solomon said.

"I don't have your gift," Willa said. "It's a beautiful one."

"It is!" Then he frowned. "But some people get weird about it. Like I'm putting them on."

"I can imagine." Willa's eyes flashed to the two of them. "I have a little gift with plants, particularly from the ocean."

He slapped his knee. "I knew all that healin' wasn't normal. I told the EMT, but they didn't believe me."

"That's okay. I'm trying to keep it quiet. People don't understand."

"That's not a bad idea." Solomon considered her words. "But I can't ignore Roy. He's my friend and business partner."

"I understand." Willa touched his shoulder. "Could you keep my gift to yourself, please?"

"Of course. It's not mine to share. 'Sides, I don't talk to so many people."

"Thank you." She beamed at him.

"Can you talk to everything from the ocean?" Nell decided it was okay to go in for the question they all wanted to ask.

"Maybe I shouldn't say so, but pretty much." Solomon shuffled his feet, his tall waterproof boots squeaking against the dock's wooden planks. "'Cept those that don't really talk."

"Like shellfish?" Nell asked for clarity. "I can imagine squid and octopus are pretty smart."

"Oh, those octopi." He shook his head. "They're crazy smart!"

They had the giant Pacific octopus in the Hood Canal, but they weren't good for eating, anyway. Still, she wanted to be sure where to draw the line.

"Honestly, I want to know because I serve them on the menu." She laid it out to him. "I felt bad when I considered you might be talking to ocean creatures. I didn't figure they could talk."

"Ah, I understand. Don't you worry, dear." Solomon leaned in. "Stick to fish and shellfish, and your conscience is clean. At least, that's what Roy says. The sea lions aren't that particular. They'll eat a squid if they get a chance."

It was a relief to know she could resume adding fish on her menu. She'd been hesitating.

"Did talking to Roy begin a few months ago?" Maggie asked.

"Hmm. That sounds about right."

"That's when mine started too." Willa smiled at him.

"And we're keeping that one zipped." He mimed zipping his mouth.

Her smile grew wider.

Nell wanted to tell him about hers, but she felt a little uncomfortable about it yet. She was starting to feel like it wasn't a life sentence, but she didn't feel ready to discuss it with the fisherman. Even though she'd known him nearly all her life, she had never known him that well.

"Thanks for the help, Solomon." She bobbed her head. "I'll see you in the morning."

And even though it felt silly, she turned and waved at the white pelican hovering on the railing. He hissed in reply and bobbed his head.

Nell hopped away two feet, and Solomon laughed so thoroughly, he had to prop himself on his knees.

"He was just saying goodbye." He wiped a tear from his eye. "I tell ya."

Shocked by what they had discovered, they made their way back up to the deck.

"Well, that settles it," Maggie said. "It was all six of us on the same night.""It was the storm." Willa's focus drifted over to the edge of the cove, where she had seen something flashy in a cave under the water when she and Duke went snorkeling. "It had to be the mermaid."

"We don't know it's a mermaid," Nell said, trying to keep them focused on the facts.

"It's something down there," Maggie said. "Something magical."

She couldn't argue with that.

"Oh, crap." Nell's head dropped back, and she exhaled loudly.

"What's wrong?" Maggie asked.

"I still forgot the mushrooms."

CHAPTER 14

It was getting harder and harder for Emiliano to hold himself back from peeping like a stalker at Nell, but he forced himself away from the window to talk to a customer asking for fresh herbs.

The woman he was over the moon with and two of her friends had just run across the lot to the marina to talk to Solomon. Willa and Maggie inspected his strange pelican, and then they all left, waving at his pet bird.

The whole encounter looked...odd. Very odd.

He was getting curious and trying not to be.

The door of Gil's Market opened, and Nell rushed back inside, making a beeline for the mushrooms. Grabbing one of their larger baskets, she filled it and headed to the check-out counter. Seeing him watching her, she turned red and pointed at the blue oyster mushrooms, then shrugged.

She must have forgotten them on her way out. He raised his hand in reply and went back to checking the aisles. Nell didn't need him following her around the store like a puppy.

He'd talk to her the following night, anyway. They had a pizza date.

It wasn't a date, he corrected himself. It was a smorgasbord of pizza she was making to showcase her talents and earn her standing of best pizza in the peninsula.

Just for him.

The thought filled him with hope. And other warm, squiggly feelings.

At least that was the story they'd made up in their...flirting? Friendly teasing? It was getting more difficult to tell. The lines were blurring. It felt like a good sign.

Head full of too many dreams and ideas, Emiliano stepped out the back of the market, where the building transitioned to the marina. Duke stood at the entry to the dock, talking to a tall, well-muscled man with very dark skin. He'd seen him around town a few times, but he didn't know his name. He was dressed lightly for the spring weather, in cut-off sleeves and board shorts, but his most remarkable feature was the thick scar that ran from the corner of his eye down his face and neck before disappearing beneath his shirt.

A stranger was just a friend you hadn't made yet. At least, that's what his dad used to say to him.

"Morning, Duke." Emiliano walked toward the men. Rays of light hit his eyes, and he glared up at them. "The sun's decided to make an appearance."

"Sure did." Duke opened his stance, including him in the conversation. He shot a quick glance towards his friend, though. "It's been a while since we saw much of it."

"Morning." The scarred man nodded. He looked friendly in a cautious sort of way. His smile was polite, but it didn't reach his eyes.

"No news from Conrad?" Duke asked.

"Not yet." Emiliano had texted him the evening before and let him know it had made it to the Brooks Farm and that he had signs of trampled crops.

"No tracks. That's just weird." Duke turned to the stranger. "A friend of ours is having a visitor on their farm."

"No tracks?" the man repeated.

"He's being vigilant. I'm sure he'll get to the bottom of it." Emiliano didn't feel comfortable sharing that Conrad had a game cam set up on his property with the stranger.

"Knock it off, Roy. Nell said she'd be here tomorrow." Solomon's voice preceded him as he made his way up the pier, his knobby knees kicking out with each step.

"Morning, Solomon," Emiliano said, acknowledging the interesting fisherman.

"Morning," he replied, pulling a skullcap over his head and tugging it into place before turning his face toward the sky. His wild eyebrows furrowed. "The sun's out."

"Most people are happy to see it." Emiliano rocked back on his heels.

"It's not a friend if you're on a boat all day." Solomon gave one last huff towards the clear sky and finally saw the new person in their party. "As you well know."

"Ah, you're a fisherman too?" Emiliano asked Duke's friend.

"Sort of." He looked curiously at Solomon and the pelican hopping around a couple of yards away. "I spend a lot of time on the water."

"Emiliano." He extended his arm to welcome the man. "I've seen you around."

"Percy," he said, shaking his hand with a firm grip. "Nice to meet you. You own this place, right?"

That was a sore subject.

"My dad does." He settled with. "I help out."

The slightest of frowns flashed over Percy's face, but he recovered quickly. "That's nice of you."

"It's in the blood." Emiliano raised his shoulders, shifting away from the crew. He wasn't trying to horn in their conversation. "Let me know if you need anything."

"I need rope," Solomon announced.

"Sure thing. We've got a few thicknesses, depending on what you need it for. Let me show you."

"Thanks." Solomon followed him to the double doors. "Stay, Roy. I'll be back."

Emiliano inclined his head to the men on the dock, but he caught an odd expression from Percy again. He was still watching Solomon like he was trying to figure him out.

He'd let Duke explain Solomon's pet pelican. It added to the fisherman's charm. This was the Pacific Northwest, not the Caribbean. The pelican fit.

"Stop it," Emiliano commanded his stomach aloud. Butterflies had taken residence in his lower abdomen, and he was starting to feel like a schoolboy, nervous about his first date. It wasn't his first, first date, but it was his first date with the love of his life.

No.

His brain kept trying to tell him it wasn't a date, but his heart wasn't listening. Nell Fitzgibbons—*Wilder*, he corrected himself—had invited him to dinner at her place, just the two of them, after he'd playfully suggested she needed to up her pizza game.

He stilled. Could she seriously be offended by his comments and be trying to prove her worth? He shook it off. He was second-guessing himself. She'd been flirting back. At least playful, if not flirting. They were good.

And she'd brought him the most delicious cookies he ever tasted. Just for him. He'd let Tommy and his pops have one each, then squirreled the rest away like he'd done with the dark rye-and-tahini cookies. Honestly, he was at a loss to decide which ones were better. The herbaceous rosemary was a savory combination with the tart cranberries and warm vanilla-butter combo. He'd never had anything like them.

It was just like her to come up with something that creative. He'd never met anything like her, either.

Emiliano snagged his canvas jacket and the bottle of wine he'd bought, then took the steps down to the street. Breathing in the cool air, he followed the short path to the café.

To Nell's house.

Figuring the back deck would be a better choice than the front door, he hopped up the wooden steps and approached the glass door. There was no doorbell, so he gave it a firm knock, then ran a hand nervously over his closely cropped hair and straightened when he saw Nell emerge from the kitchen beyond.

She unlocked the door and let him in, casting a soft smile behind her as she headed back to the kitchen. "I hope you brought your appetite."

"I skipped lunch in preparation." He patted his stomach, gave her a quick, friendly wink, and handed her the bottle of wine when she paused to open her kitchen door. "I made sure I had plenty of room."

"Thanks." She read the label. "Good choice. On both accounts."

Stepping aside so he could enter, Nell waved a hand over the countertop in her kitchen with an exaggerated flourish. It was entirely loaded with pizza—ten small pies, to be exact. They looked more like street tacos than pizzas, but each was perfectly topped with puffy, charred crusts and cut into fours.

Emiliano blinked. "Who's joining us? I'm not sure I can eat five pizzas by myself."

The giggle that tickled its way up Nell's throat stole his heart. She covered her mouth with both of her hands.

"They're only six inches across," she said, her voice light and joyful.

"That's still more tacos than I've ever eaten in one sitting." He could hear the awe in his voice.

"Really?" She squinted. "Ever?"

Emiliano searched his mind. "That's probably not true. I was a high-school boy once."

"That's what I thought." She untied her apron and hung it on the back of her door, wiping her clean hands on the towel that graced her shoulder before propping her hands on her hips. "I think you've got it in you."

"Oh, I'll give it my best."

Emiliano wandered over to the pizzas, studying each one in succession. Nell didn't do anything simple when it came to food. Even if it was a simple dish with simple ingredients, they were the best-quality ingredients, chosen to highlight flavor. She celebrated food.

"Walk me through these masterpieces," Emiliano asked, finding her watching carefully for his reaction.

She cared what he thought. The realization zapped through him like lightning, landing with a weighty buzz in his fingertips and toes. When had that happened?

"Of course." Nell walked to the left edge of the long counter and held her arm out to the first pizza. "Margherita, a classic with buffalo mozzarella, a simple marinara, with basil and garlic." She moved on to the next one. "Italian sausage with sautéed onions and green bell peppers." Then she pointed. "White pizza, a creamy béchamel base with roasted garlic, smoked Gouda, and topped with sautéed morels and smoked mussels. Pepperoni, another classic. I didn't mess with that at all, but I sliced the pepperoni thinly so it cupped. It's a thing." She shrugged.

"BBQ chicken. I'll admit I don't really think this counts, but it's actually crazy good, so I had to. I made a smoky bourbon barbeque sauce as the base, with chicken and sha rp cheddar cheese."

She paused for a moment to throw him a look before moving to the next dish.

"Marco's pizza. This is a new one I've been hearing about in Chicago. It's a green pizza with a pesto base, chunks of goat cheese, walnuts, and sautéed mushrooms. I made a second green pizza with my own spin. It has the pesto base, but then buffalo mozzarella, tomato slices, basil, and a balsamic vinegar drizzle. I'm really excited about that one. Salami pizza, with a garlic-and-herb-flavored butter base, salami, pepperoncini, and Parmigiano-Reggiano." She gave him a smile. "Popper pizza, with a garlic cream-cheese base, crumbled bacon, and thick slices of jalapeño. And finally, for dessert, ricotta cheese base with broiled peaches, basil, sea salt, and a bals amic drizzle."

Nell took a huge breath and stood back, clasping her hands behind her.

"I don't..." Emiliano was at a loss for words. "I don't know what to say. This is beyond incredible."

Red crept up her neck, and she ran her hand up, tucking a loose hair behind her ear. "It's just pizza."

"It's not. This is a showcase of your talents as a chef."

"It's pizza. Pizza isn't a big deal." She lifted her shoulder.

"It's sourdough, isn't it?" Of course it would be.

"Yeah."

"And you made all the sauces yourself."

"I didn't pickle the pepperoncini's or make the ricotta or buffalo mozzarella."

"The horror." He mock gasped.

"Nor did I make the salami, bacon, or Italian sausage."

"Why am I even here?" He placed a hand on his chest, his eyes casting skyward as he shook his head sadly.

Nell giggled, and he was done for. Check the box.

"Don't keep me in suspense. They're hot, for goodness' sake!" Nell finally burst out of her shell. Waving a hand, she picked up a small, square, sage-green plate and shoved it into his waiting hands. "Get to it!"

Doing as told, Emiliano selected four quarters to start with. He went with the classic margherita, the Marco, the white pizza with morels, and the popper pizza. He loved everything jalapeño.

Nell, having uncorked the Barbera wine he'd brought, sat down a glass in front of him and handed him a rich-plum linen napkin.

"Thank you." He laid the fabric over his jean-clad knee and paused over the uneaten food. It was almost too pretty to touch. Besides, knowing Nell had made it just for him gave it a kind of ethereal value.

Across the small table in her kitchen, Nell plunked down with her own small plate filled with quarters. She glanced up. "Go on."

Grinning like a fool, he scooped up the Marco pizza and took a bite. Pesto and garlic flooded his senses, and he spoke around the hot bite. "Holy cow."

"It's pretty good, huh?" She smiled back at him coyly.

"How do you know? You haven't tried it yet." It was still sitting on her plate, untouched.

"I made a couple of the more suspicious ones first to ensure the flavors worked." She glanced down, not meeting his gaze.

Humbled and excited to try the rest, he took a second bite of the Marco and then dug into the next one. "Chicago knows what they're doing."

"It started with this one kid. I guess his dad has family connections, if you know what I mean." She laid a finger across her nose.

"Really? And he's in pizza, instead, huh?"

"So, it would seem. The kid knows flavors. This is really something." She raised her own Marco pizza.

"All of it is incredible." He finished tasting all the slices on his plate. Each was just as satisfying as the last.

"Did I save my reputation?" she finally said, watching him consume food in a manner that must have resembled a starved man.

"What? Oh, yeah." He sighed loudly. "Liberty's got nothing on you."

Nell gave a satisfied smirk, settling down in her chair. "You've got to try the rest."

"Oh, don't you worry. I wouldn't think of stopping now." His chair scraped when he rose to refill his plate. He didn't want to look like a glutton, but it wasn't every day that he got one of Nell's pizzas. Let alone ten different, fully thought-out ones.

"How're things going with Hugo?" she asked, delicately munching on the green pizza in her hand.

The happy hormones gifted to him from the carbs and the attention from the love of his life dipped. He wasn't sure he was ready to talk about his dad. But then again, if he wasn't willing to share with her, who could he share with?

"Honestly, it's been draining." He sat back down, another full plate in front of him. "He's so set in his ways."

"It can't be easy."

"It's really not."

"Do you think he'll come around?"

"I hate to say it"—he toyed with another slice—"but I don't think so."

She nodded silently, staring at her food. "What will you do?"

"I haven't decided yet. Part of me isn't done trying."

"Good for you." She raised her glass to clink with his. "I think you've got this. If anyone can do it, it's you."

"I don't know about that." He tapped her glass gently with his. He was probably the last person who would get Hugo to bend. He'd do anything for the people of Orca Cove and had raised his son to do the same. They were for service, his dad would say.

"I have faith in you."

She meant it. He'd never seen her lie bald-faced, like that. She was good at skirting issues, sure, but never outright, unprovoked.

Since he was starting to feel a bit uncomfortable, he changed the subject, "Is it strange not having your family nearby? I can't imagine being that far away from Pops."

Nell's parents had moved to California when she got engaged at eighteen.

She wiped her hands on her napkin. "I had Gary when they left. I see them every couple of years or so."

"That's nice."

"And I still have Gary's dad. I don't see him that often, either, though."

Emiliano remembered he'd moved to Seattle to be closer to his brother after Charlotte, his wife, passed away a few years ago.

"How's he doing?" Losing his son a couple of years after his wife had to have been awful.

"He's doing okay. This past year was hard on him."

"I can't even imagine."

Nell studied a jalapeño on her plate, slowly chewing a bite, and he instantly regretted bringing up the memory of her loss.

"Well," he said, picking up another slice of pizza and keeping his face straight. "At least you have Mary."

Nell nearly spit out her mouthful as laughter spilled out. The older woman was a cousin, or something, of Gary's mom. She was the most crotchety, grumpy woman he'd ever met, but every once in a while, he thought he saw through it. He wasn't sure what had made her a grouch, but he believed there was a kind person underneath it all. That was probably true for most people.

"To Mary." Nell lifted her glass. "May we all live to the ripe old age of saying anything you want."

"Hear, hear." He lifted his in reply. The mood had been successfully improved. "So, I heard you had an early start this morning."

"A little bird tell you that?"

"Either that or a large pelican."

She smirked at him. "I had some extra fish lying around."

"Not something you hear from most women."

"I'm not most women."

"I'll second that." Emiliano pushed away from the table to get another few pieces.

"Still have room for more?"

"I can't stop until I've tried them all." His eyes widened very seriously. "That's not how you taste test."

"I love your dedication, but I think I'm done."

"You can't stop until you taste the peach one. It's dessert."

"Split the slice with me, then." She slid her knife across the table.

"No way! This one's mine." He protected his plate. "Just kidding. I can get another."

Taking the knife, he cut the small wedge into two miniature slices of pizza. They were impossibly cute. Carefully, he wiped the extra balsamic sauce on one piece, slid the knife underneath it, and set it on her plate.

"Thanks."

After a second glass of wine and an intense scrutiny of the ten pizza options, some of which required a second taste, Nell raised an eyebrow. "So?"

"Totally full now, thanks."

"No. What're your top three? I'll add them to the rotating menu."

"My taste buds aren't as sophisticated as yours."

"Doesn't matter. Everyone likes something different. Hit me with them."

She smiled at him with such a brightness it nearly stole his breath.

"The Marco was good, but you were spot on with that pesto and balsamic combo. Wow. The Italian sauce, the white one with the morels, and I'm not embarrassed to say it, but the popper one. Can I also add the peach one as a special mention? It's amazing."

"That's five!"

"When you give me an unreasonable request, I'll give you an unreasonable answer!"

Laughing, he stood to help her clean up.

"You don't have to do that. You can leave it."

"I'm not." He took the plates from her hands and went to the sink to load the restaurant dishwasher and turn it on to wash.

"How do you know how to do that?"

"We had a businessman try to convince Pops to open a café on the marina. He showed us all sorts of appliances that we'd need for it."

"Really? Before I had my stand?"

"Yes, just a little bit before."

"I'm amazed you still remember."

"It's pretty straightforward once you've seen it."

She frowned. "But why didn't he do it? Orca Cove needed a food option like the café."

Emiliano breathed out heavily. "He doesn't like change."

"Well, I can't say I'm not glad he didn't. I probably wouldn't have been able to open my little sandwich shop."

"Nah, you'd have found a place to do it. You're born to cook."

Nell smiled at him, putting the last of the food away and wiping down the surfaces. "The only thing that'd make those pizzas better would be a wood-fired oven."

"Are you going to get one?"

"Maybe, if people love the pizza as much as you do."

"They will. Hey, you could ask Nick to build you one. I'm sure he could figure it out."

"You think? I'd hate to impose on him. It's not like the normal stuff he makes."

"I think he'd love doing it for you."

She considered it. "I'll think about asking him."

It was probably time to leave. It was late, and they both had work the following day.

"I had fun tonight." He wiped his hands on a nearby kitchen towel and leaned against the counter.

"Me too." She smiled at him in a completely relaxed manner. "We should do this again sometime."

"My turn to feed you next."

"No one ever cooks for me...except for Hugo," she added after thinking. "That would be really cool."

"Done. I'll think of something incredible."

"Honestly, I'm okay with anything."

"I would not serve you just anything, but don't you worry. I won't be stealing your best-chef title."

"Best chef. Hmm." She made a soft, satisfied sound and laid a hand over her heart as they walked to the back deck. The clouds had parted, and the star-filled sky was bright overhead. "Sometimes, I'm amazed we get to live here."

"I know." He scanned the water, absently searching for a dorsal fin. The waves were lapping gently against the pebble beach, and the boats in the marina bobbed rhythmically. "Thanks for including me."

"Of course." She turned to him, her gaze drifting up his chest to find his eyes. Her pupils dilated in response to their closeness. "It was a good night."

The welcoming smell of toasted bread and the spicy scent of marinara wafted from her clothes over to him. She smelled like heaven, of all things, warm and comforting. Without realizing it, his hand drifted up to her cheek again, but this time, he touched it gently.

Doubt filled his mind. The last time they got this close—hell, the last two times—she'd pulled away and ran. The last time it had happened, just two nights ago, it was because someone had interrupted them, and she'd put six feet between them.

She represented everything he'd ever wanted in a partner. Someone reliable and kind. Someone who might possibly stay.

Unless she was embarrassed of him. She was obviously attracted to him, but she didn't want anyone seeing them together.

Nell leaned forward and laid a hand on his chest. It felt like acceptance.

They should talk before things go too far.

Far?

Wasn't it already too late for him?

"Nell." His voice came out in a whisper. He had the woman of his dreams in his arms, and his brain struggled to keep its perspective. She wasn't in the same place as he was. It'd be impossible for her to be.

He was losing his resolve and slowly leaned over to close the gap between them. His lips brushed hers softly, then he found home and melted into her. Just before he lost his mind altogether, he pulled himself together.

Woman of his dreams or not, he wasn't sure he could handle rejection from her, of all people. But what if he was just a rebound for her? She deserved to know how he felt about her before they went down this path.

With every ounce of control at his disposal, he pulled away and focused on their shoes instead of her swollen lips. "I should go."

Before he could change his mind—or at least, change it again—he made a beeline for the stairs.

CHAPTER 15

*W*hat had just happened? Nell walked back inside the café like a dazed woman.

Emiliano had pulled away. Had she actually thrown herself at him? The thought curdled in her stomach like spoiled milk.

When he'd asked her out, he was spelled, influenced. And she might possibly have influenced him again with the mussel-and-morel pizza to be a little carefree. *Geez.* It must have made him a little uninhibited in combination with the wine. Would she ever stop taking advantage of the man?

And not just any man, but a young man. He *was* a man, not the kid she remembered, but she'd admit to herself that she was shocked to hear he knew the band members from the other night. It made the age difference even more evident.

She locked the door, her head spinning, and escaped to the security of her upstairs apartment. But not before she stopped by the kitchen for a square of the leftover Bliss Brownie bars she'd carefully sealed and stored at the back of her fridge.

Stripping down, she stepped into her shower and cleaned off the day.

She did care about him. Hell, if she was being honest with herself—and here, in her shower, with the steam separating herself from the real world, she could be—she'd admit she liked him, genuinely liked him.

She dunked her head into the water when she realized she had feelings for the beautiful man he'd grown into.

The shame and embarrassment didn't hit as deeply this time. It was probably the work of the Bliss bar. She still didn't like the thought of throwing herself at him, but the feeling wasn't as overwhelming. Logic was helping her see through it; if she could still think through the bliss, maybe he could think through any stress-free influence she had baked into the pizza.

Sure, she'd pressed herself against him and lifted her mouth to his, but he'd closed the gap.

And she wasn't going to be so naive to say men can't control their emotions. He'd absolutely kissed her. He'd kissed the hell out of her. The memory erased her shame and melted into her stomach like the warm, gooey brownie would have been had she taken the time to warm it.

Then, why had he pulled away?

Did he think it was a bad decision?

That made sense. It probably was. Oddly enough, the idea didn't bother her much. Probably another side effect of the bliss. Emiliano may not even decide to stay in the area.

Less overwhelmed, Nell dried off and went to bed. She'd need to get up early in the morning to start bread.

"What's going on with you?" Shelby asked, looking up from the breakfast burrito she was currently consuming on the back deck of the café. She had stopped by on her morning run, and her hair was pulled back in a short, dark ponytail.

Nell looked up from the silverware she was helping Maggie roll into dark purple linens, and blinked. "I'm trying to decide on the menu for the week."

"Sure." Shelby plunked down on a chair across from them, crossing one leg over the other. "You haven't obsessed about the business once."

Nell froze. "I do that?"

"Of course you do."

"I'm sorry." She meant it. She didn't want to overwhelm her friends with her problems. "I shouldn't."

"Shut up." Shelby rolled her eyes. "It's what friends do. I'm a business owner. It makes sense that you ask m e."

"So is Willa," Nell said.

Shelby only raised an eyebrow. "Willa would rather give all her services away for free to those who need it. You came to me for a reason."

"But I'm obsessing, so it's unhealthy." Nell struggled to understand what she was getting at.

"Hell, no. I obsess all the time, especially about business. I just mean, you're not obsessing, so that's new. What's going on? You haven't once asked about your next steps. You should be working on it."

"Okay... so I need to be thinking about what to do next?"

"I would."

"Okay." Nell snuck a glance over to Maggie, who was, as usual, watching quietly. "I was going to ask you to go with me to the winery."

"Good idea." Shelby nodded. "When?"

"Well, next Monday is a week away, but we could go then."

"Wineries aren't always open on Mondays."

"I could close for you," Maggie finally spoke.

"I couldn't ask you to do that." Nell shook her head. "I had hoped I could schedule a special meeting on Monday."

"You didn't ask me. I offered." Maggie set the last few rolls of silverware she'd finished into the bucket and retrieved a fresh stack of linens from the other side of the table. "I'm more than capable."

"I know that, but still."

"It's a good idea," Shelby said. "I have my receptionists do all sorts of administrative duties for me. Cleo is better than Terri, but delegation is important if you're going to be successful. You can only do so much as a single person."

"But." Nell's hand froze over the silverware she was stacking. It didn't feel right to have anyone take over her duties. Or was it that she didn't trust anyone to do them? Didn't she trust Maggie?

"But what?" Duke came up the outside stairs.

"Nell was just trying to say why Maggie can't close for her so we can go to the winery this week."

Duke studied the three women. "Maybe I should come back."

"Come on, you know that's not true." Nell leaned over the table, her palms flat on the wood. "I trust Maggie completely. I just feel like it's my responsibility."

"I honestly don't mind," Maggie said.

"Then, what day do you want to go?" Shelby asked, pushing her.

"Wednesday or Thursday would work," Nell said, relenting.

"I'm busy Wednesday. We'll go Thursday." Shelby wiped her hands on a napkin and stood.

"What are you doing Wednesday?" Nell asked. Wednesdays were quieter than Thursdays, with the tourist influx amping up for the weekend.

"I have a business meeting in Olympia." Shelby helped herself to the orange-juice dispenser on the bar and stretched, getting ready to resume her jog.

"I've never seen anyone eat and run," Duke broke in. "Isn't that supposed to make you sick or something?"

"Iron stomach. And I get hungry." Shelby patted her flat belly. "What else?"

Shelby looked back over to Nell.

"Well, the band is scheduled to play every Saturday for the rest of the month and all of June. And Maggie has it posted on social media."

"I added some tags for live music and local music to match those they're using in Seattle," Maggie said. "And I made an events page on our website so people can see the schedule."

"Beautiful." Shelby nodded appreciatively.

Maggie blushed.

"She's doing a great job." Nell nudged her with her elbow, as a hissing sound scared them all out of their conversation.

Jumping, she found a white pelican perched on the deck railing behind her. He grunted.

"Oh, no, you don't!" She started towards the pelican, then stopped. If Roy hadn't helped Willa, she might not be with them today. But she couldn't have him coming by, begging for food every day. The guests wouldn't like it.

Propping her fists on her hips, she considered what to do. It felt weird, but lately, her life was strange, so she went with the idea that formed in her mind and addressed the bird.

"Roy. I'm happy to give you some special leftovers in the morning, but you can't come up on the deck here. I have guests who don't understand how amazing you are. Their loss, but still, I could lose my business license."

The bird cocked its head to the side, its beady eye blinking from a lower lid. After a moment, Roy opened his large yellow beak, then snapped it shut.

"If you go down to the parking lot, I'll bring you something special." She pointed to the stairs and beyond, between The Wild Café and Gil's Market and Marina. "Over there."

Roy hopped up and down, snapping his bill again, then it lifted into the air, its large wings flapping fast enough to direct a back draft into her face. Turning to see her friends staring at her, she saw Shelby's mouth hanging halfway open.

Nell hurried upstairs to her personal kitchen, grabbed a container of leftover mussel pasta she'd stashed there, and bounded down the stairs. She couldn't keep anything for over a day in the commercial kitchen for health-code reasons, but she could in her personal one.

Pulling to a halt at the top of the deck stairs, she saw the pelican sitting patiently on a parking block. Approaching him cautiously, she dumped the contents on the pavement and backed away. The bird hopped over to it, grunting loudly, and scraped his beak sideways over the pasta, collecting nearly all the food in one single scoopful. Then he lifted from the ground in a giant leap and flew away, banking towards Soloman's boat docked in the marina.

"I hope that was Roy." Nell exhaled loudly, leaning on the bottom-stair railing.

"Extra fish lying around?" The voice startled her.

Searching the lot, she saw Emiliano in the doorway to the market.

He looked beautiful in a charcoal Henley and his duck canvas jeans. But the best part was the smile on his face.

Even though her stomach flip-flopped, it looked like they were still friends. She breathed out. "Morning. I mean, yes. Leftover pasta with mussels."

"Expensive pelican food."

She turned her hand over, her palm facing up. "At least it didn't go to waste."

He laughed aloud. "Morning." Then after a pause, he lifted his head. "Thanks again for the pizza last night. It was incredible. Remember, next time, it's my turn."

Then he dipped his head and disappeared into the market.

Face burning, Nell made her way up the steps to find her friends still staring at her, waiting for an explanation.

"I'm pretty sure that was Roy." She pushed past them and resumed stacking silverware onto a napkin and rolling it up. "I met Solomon yesterday morning and gave Roy a thank you for helping Willa out. Apparently, he thought that gave him direct access to free food. Hopefully, I corrected that."

"You still gave him free food," Shelby pointed out, ever the pragmatic one.

"But on my terms, in a way that won't scare my customers or cost me my license."

"Fair." Shelby turned her head, looking back towards the market, then trained on Nell. "Now, what was that about?"

"I told you; I was paying Roy back." Nell brushed her hair behind her ear and chuckled self-consciously. "I sure hope that was really Roy, or I'm going to feel sillier than I thought I already looked."

"No. The shopkeeper's son." Shelby wagged her eyebrows.

The title didn't sit well with her new resolve at his man status, and Nell loudly dropped a stack of eight wrapped utensils into the container. "We're friends now."

"Who's friends now?" Willa said, joining them on the deck, Nick coming closely behind.

It appeared they were having an impromptu party.

"What's this about?" Nell looked at the rest of them in question.

Shelby picked up her phone. "I figured if we were nearly all here, we should *all* be here. Of course, that was before the fun new gossip."

"What gossip?" Nick asked.

Willa tried and failed to control her smirk at Nick's interest. She took a seat at the table.

"You're just delaying your run." Nell narrowed her eyes at the savvy businesswoman. "And trying to get more cookies."

Shelby pursed her lips. "I'm not embarrassed by it. What about you?"

"I. uh." She nervously looked around the deck. "Aren't there customers we should see to? Food to make?"

"I checked on the two couples while you were feeding Roy. No one new yet." Maggie expertly rolled another set of silverware. "Shelby filled me in."

Of course she was on top of the diners.

Nell cleared her throat. "Um, Emiliano and I are friends now."

"She made him pizza last night," Shelby added. "And he's cooking for her next. *As planned.*"

Nell shot her a glare. "It's not a big deal. We're friends, right?"

"Friends are always a good thing." Willa laid a hand on her arm, offering her a supportive smile that said she had no issues with the friendship, whatever it was.

"This is all just new to me." Nell wrung her hands. "I don't know how to navigate these uncharted waters."

"Argh." Shelby made a one eyed, playful growl.

Nell looked at Duke for his reaction.

"I already told you I didn't have a problem with it." He shrugged and tucked his hands into his pockets. He didn't look very comfortable with the conversation.

"Then, what's the big deal?" Nell looked up to the sky for answers.

"We didn't get invited to pizza night, guys. We're not okay with that, right?" Shelby spread her arms out, looking to the rest of them for support.

"I'd agree with that," Nick spoke up, pressing his lips together in a tight line. "That's not okay. I mean...I like pizza."

"Good point, man." Duke nodded, finally getting into the conversation. "Pizza is good. Especially Nell's pizza."

"She uses the sourdough." Maggie sighed, her eyes going glazed. "With the most perfectly crisp crust and chewy center."

"What kind of pizza did you make?" Willa asked dreamily.

"I, uh, made ten different kinds," Nell said softly.

"Ten?" Shelby said louder than necessary, sitting up straight. "Do you have leftovers? You better not have given them to the bird."

"I didn't give them to Roy," Nell laughed. "They were small, six-inch pizzas. Emiliano ate half easily."

Shelby lifted a finger. It danced in the air like she was writing a note. "Then, there's what? Three six-inch pizzas left? On average? Maybe more?"

Nell frowned, her head shooting back. "How'd you know that?"

"You don't eat much in any given sitting."

"I taste the food a lot."

"Exactly. So, there're leftovers. Where are they?" She stood.

"How do you know I didn't send them home with him?" Nell sighed, relinquishing the rest of the pizza to Shelby and her friends. She could and would make more. "In my fridge upstairs."

"You're not a fan of leftovers." Shelby disappeared into the café, on her way to pilfer her personal fridge.

"Are you adding pizza to the menu?" Maggie asked.

"Not this week, but more frequently, yes." Nell's friends knew her well. This much attention to food meant she was playing with recipes.

"Yes!" Nick rubbed his hands together excitedly.

It was as good an opening as she'd get. "You wouldn't happen to know how to make a wood-fired pizza oven, would you?"

A seriousness fell over Nick's face, and he zoned off onto an unknown place in the distance. Nell found Willa's gaze, who was full-on smirking at her boyfriend. No longer hiding it at this point.

"That means he's building it," Willa said from behind a raised hand to shield Nick from her commentary.

"He'll build it?" Nell asked.

"No, he's actually building it as we speak," Willa clarified. "In his head."

"I need to plan a trip to Seattle." Nick stood. "I need some supplies."

"Don't you need to know the design?" Nell asked. If she was commissioning a pizza oven for the café, she wanted some say in the matter.

"I'll give you a few options," Nick shot over his shoulder. Then he stopped and turned. "Do you mind if I take off, sweetheart?"

"Not at all, babe." Willa lifted her head to meet his kiss. "See you when you come in later tonight."

"Thanks." Nick muttered a few other things and disappeared down the back steps.

"What? How much will that cost?" Nell's voice constricted. She wasn't sure she could afford it.

"Don't worry. He won't charge half the market rate," Willa said, waving a hand. "But I'll warn you; he's not good at making custom orders. He'll make something beautiful, but it'll need to be something he loves. That's why he has his online shop and sells at Gil's. Custom orders just end up forgotten in a corner of his shop. It takes away his creativity."

Nell could understand that. She hated it when people substituted too many ingredients. If they asked for an item to be removed, that was no problem, but wildly destroying how she curated a dish? Why bother coming to a restaurant?

"Fine." She nodded decisively. "I like his work, particularly if I get at least some say."

"All the options he gives you will be ones he likes. But a word to the wise: if you ask for his favorite and decide on that one, it'll be completed in half the time." Willa winked at them. "He gets very excited about building things he loves."

"Noted."

Shelby reappeared, doing a little skip dance across the deck while carrying a container full of her leftover pizza.

"You shouldn't eat it out here. It's not on the menu or particularly fresh."

Shelby raised her shoulder, shoving a slice of cold pizza into her mouth. "Who cares?"

"My business license does." Nell crossed her arms. She peered behind her to the nonexistent customers and food inspectors. "It *is* pretty quiet right now."

"Then, eat quickly, my friends." Shelby prodded the Pyrex dish toward Willa and Maggie. Duke pushed away from the railing he was leaning against and snagged two small slices.

"See?" Shelby said around a mouthful of pizza. "It's almost gone."

Nell frowned, snatched up the final slice of pepperoni, and resealed the empty glass container.

"Are you going to put the Relaxed Rockfish on the menu, too?" Maggie asked.

"Or are you spiking all the seafood dishes now?" Shelby asked.

"The customers do seem happier than normal," Maggie said.

"I'm going for a general good mood, nothing over the top," Nell explained, then turned to Maggie. "I was thinking about it. Maybe not the Giggle Geoducks, though. We probably shouldn't advertise our gifts that much."

"If we worked together, I could help you identify some herbs that are known for happiness or relaxation. It would make it more natural and less obvious," Willa offered. "I have some lemon balm that I've been watering with distilled seawater to help with depression. It's very uplifting."

"Then I could add it to cookies or baked goods. It would be easier to serve than seafood dishes or working seaweed into sweets." Nell was already recreating enhanced meals in her head. Absently, she realized it was a lot like what Nick had done.

She was feeling better about her future pizza oven.

"Woah, now," Duke warned. "Both of you touching it? We don't want someone to have a manic episode."

"Oh, good point," Shelby said, talking around her last bite of crust. "God, this is delicious."

"You should have tried it fresh," Nell said. "It was one of my best."

"I wasn't invited." Shelby gave her a cross look.

Oh, right.

"I'll make them again when I try out the pizza oven. You can see what flavors we're going to feature."

"I bet Emiliano got to help decide that." Shelby wrinkled her nose.

"I'll make all ten flavors again." Nell rolled her eyes. "You can all be a part of the final decision."

"That's more like it." Shelby pulled a purple linen from Maggie's clean pile and wiped her fingers on it. "We're your official taste testers."

It was true. They'd always done that for her. Nell felt a loyalty to her friends who'd been with her and Gary from the beginning.

"Doesn't all that food kind of negate the benefits of running?" Duke narrowed his eyes to poke at Shelby.

"At least I'm exercising," she threw back at him. "You just steer your boat."

He raised his eyebrows, looking down at his tall, lean, and lightly muscled physique.

"Oh, shut up." Shelby stood. Reaching back, she tightened her mini ponytail and headed towards the stairs.

"It's more than I do." Nell ran a self-conscious hand over her softly rounded stomach. It wasn't huge or anything, but well, she was a cook. She made good food, and she enjoyed it. "Maybe I should try it."

"You look amazing the way you are." Willa reached across the table to cover Nell's hand with her longer, more delicate fingers.

"Laters!" Shelby raised a hand.

"I'll see you on Thursday!" Nell said loudly. "Don't forget."

"You'll see me before then! A girl needs to eat," Shelby replied just as loudly, disappearing down the steps. "And don't forget to call the winery to get the appointment. We can do a tasting before or after, but we don't want a wasted t rip."

Nell's stomach churned at the thought.

She just needed to be like Shelby and put on her boss face. She could do it. Hopefully…

"And what's this about paying Roy back?" Duke finally brought the conversation back around.

"Oh, yeah," Maggie piped up. "We think Solomon can talk to fish."

CHAPTER 16

E miliano folded the cardboard boxes he'd just broken down and stuffed them into the recycle bin behind the market. Flipping the lid shut, he turned to go back inside, but the woman pacing across the parking lot stole his attention.

"Everything okay?" he dusted his hands off and approached an obviously distressed Nell Wilder.

"What? Yes." she wrung her hands, looked at the café, and then back at the parking lot.

"What's going on?" He tilted his head. It wasn't often he saw her this upset.

"It's nothing." She wheeled around again. "It's just..."

He waited patiently.

"Maggie is all prepared. It would seem like I don't trust her. But I do." Nell tugged at the navy canvas jacket she was wearing despite the warm afternoon.

"I know you do."

"Well, she'll think I don't."

"Why would she think that?" Emiliano attempted to keep up with the conversation.

"She's been planning for tonight for days now. She's made lists and prepped food. Carlos is here to cover the extra tables."

"She's helping out with your duties? So you can take a day off?" It still didn't quite make sense, but she was stressed out, so he was here for it.

"Yes, well, no." Nell ran a hand over her hair, brushed and free of its ponytail. The sun chose that moment to peek out from the cloud it was currently taking shelter behind and shined down on her long, wavy locks, highlighting golden-and-cinnamon colors in her rich brown hair. "I'm supposed to go talk to Fran at the winery."

"The winery? Mt. Olympus?" That made more sense. It must be the business deal she'd been gearing up for. "Did Fran cancel on you?"

"No." She shook her head. "Shelby did."

"Ah. Everything okay with Shelby?"

"Yeah. Broken water pipes." She waved it away, then froze, her eyes widened. "Not that it's not a big deal. She's pretty stressed about it. If she doesn't get it fixed, she'll have to pay for hotel rooms for her guests."

"Did she call Mike?" Emiliano asked. Mike was the best plumber in the area.

"You know Shelby. She's trying to fix it on her own, but she'll call him if she can't get it handled in the next hour or two. At least, that's what she said."

He nodded, wanting to be there for her, but not quite understanding why she looked so indecisive. Maybe he should try a different tactic. "What time do you have to leave?"

"I can't!" Nell threw her hands up in the air. "I mean, what am I supposed to do?"

"Aren't you meeting Fran?" He didn't know who Fran was, but apparently, they had an appointment.

"But...but...how am I supposed to do this?" Nell finally stopped pacing. He could see tears form in her eyes. "I don't know what I'm doing!"

Suddenly, it all made sense. She didn't want to go by herself. She was worried about doing things on her own.

He'd been so impressed by how she took charge; he'd nearly forgotten.

"Oh, you've got this." He exhaled quickly and shrugged his shoulders. "You already know what you want to say and what you want to accomplish. That's half the battle."

Her eyes found his, and he could see her attempt to rally at the situation in front of her. Even when stressed, she didn't want to take away Maggie's win. This, from a woman who'd never trusted anyone to run her kitchen before.

Mentally, he tried to remember who was working at the market that day. Tommy was on the afternoon shift, and his dad was closing.

"I know you're completely capable of handling this meeting," he went on. "But I do love Mt. Olympus wines. If you'd like some company, I'd be happy to join you."

Nell grabbed his forearm, latching on like to a lifeline. "Would you really do that?"

"Not that you need it, but of course." His heart swelled at the opportunity to do something for her. "Like I said, I like their wine."

It was true. It was also true he'd travel to hell and back if she needed him to. No matter the reason.

She melted into him, and a tear slipped from her eye to travel down her cheek.

"Hey, this is going to be fine." He pulled her closer, tucking her under his arm. She felt so perfect there.

"Thank you." She looked up at him, and he could see her gathering herself back together. "I'm going to be okay."

"Damn straight, you are." He touched her chin. "With or without me."

"Yeah. You're right. I can do this." She nodded, then looked up at him shyly. "But could you come with me just the same?"

"Done."

Nell let out a long breath. It was deeper, softer, and steadier than the ones before. She'd be okay.

"I just need to run inside and let them know."

"You weren't supposed to close tonight, were you?" Creases formed between her brows, and it made her look more charming.

"Nope. It's my evening off." It wouldn't have mattered if he was; he'd have gotten someone to cover him. "I'm just going to make sure they know I'm taking off. Where are we on time?"

"We have a bit of room. I'm not scheduled to meet her until four."

"Perfect." Reluctantly, Emiliano lifted her hand from his arm and pulled away from her. "I'll only take five minutes. Meet you here."

Nell nodded, her hands clasping in front of her, as she looked over her shoulder at the café as though she was going to book back inside and whip her apron back over her head. He could practically see her fight the instinct to get back to where it was comfortable.

Ripping his eyes from her, he left to find Tommy near the cash registers. "Would you mind covering for me for a couple of hours? I need to take off early.""S ure thing!" Tommy hooked his thumbs into his apron. "Anything you need me to do?"

"Just check in on Pops in about an hour and again before you leave. Make sure he doesn't need anything."

"Will do."

Emiliano's foot scraped as he slowed in front of their combined office to see his dad look up from Emiliano's computer, open and bright, with his new website for Gil's Market & Marina. "What is all of this?"

He gripped the doorway to keep from snatching his computer from his dad. "I'm working on something."

"This looks like a new website." Hugo's face was stony. Not an ounce of kindness or patience was present. "Did you think you could just change things without asking me?"

His stomach plummeted. "No, of course not, Pops. I was planning on showing it to you."

"Before or after you changed everything?" Hugo closed his laptop with a snap and crossed his arms. "Once everyone sees all the changes and gets excited about something they think will make their life easier, but in the end, will just drain their happiness?"

"Woah, what are you talking about? Why wouldn't we want to make people's lives easier? Wouldn't it be nice for Mary to order her groceries online and have them delivered to her door? It might help her get a good dinner even when she's not feeling well!"

"And then, if she gets really sick and can't make it to the phone, no one will know because they're not used to seeing her."

"How would that happen? Everyone in town checks in on folks like Mary."

"Not if they assumed she was getting things delivered." Hugo dug his heels in, his jaw jutted out. "Not happening on my watch. You can forget about it."

"Forget about what?" Emiliano crossed his arms even though he realized he now mirrored his stubborn dad. He had reason to be pissed.

"About the online store and delivery service! It's not happening." Hugo's hand came down heavy on top of his laptop, and Emiliano thought he heard a crack. "I should have stopped you when you started talking that nonsense about the online ledger."

"You never even gave it a chance."

"If I knew that's what you were wasting time on these past few months..."

"Wasting time?" Emiliano flared with anger. "I'm good at that, Pops. I went to school for it, if you recall."

"Another waste of time and money. You should have focused on business classes. That would have been more helpful."

"Really?" His eyebrows went up at his dad's statement. "So I could be helpful in the family business? Oh, wait. It's not a family business; it's *your* business, and I'm just an employee. What good would business classes do?"

He had better things to do than to stand around and argue with his dad, who didn't even believe in him.

The woman of his dreams was waiting for him, and they had a kiss to talk about.

Shoving away from the doorway, he slammed the door shut as he stormed out. He knew it was childish, but he had so much pent-up anger. It had seemed like the least destructive thing to do.

When he got to the glass door separating him from Nell, he laid his hands on the cool pane, ready to bust through it as well, but he paused. She didn't deserve his anger. So he breathed in, counting to four, like Willa had instructed during her yoga classes, and breathed out. He'd only taken a couple of them as a teenager, but he remembered that one. It had come in handy over the years.

He was still pissed, but at least he wasn't seeing red. It would do.

"All good." Emiliano rejoined Nell. "Do you want to take my car? I can drive."

"Oh, it's a business thing. I should probably..." She looked back to her little Toyota Camry sitting at the back of the lot. It looked like it hadn't moved in a while. It probably hadn't.

"If we take mine, you can go over whatever you want to say."

"Good idea. If you really don't mind."

"Not at all. I like to drive." He led them to his place behind the market and pressed the code to open the garage door and reveal his dark-gray Subaru Forester.

"Is this new?" She ran a hand over the hood.

"Not at all." He chuckled. "It just doesn't get used a lot. I bought it after I graduated college."

"College?" Her eyes enlarged, and then she darted a look at him. "I guess that wasn't that long ago, was it?"

He shrugged and opened the passenger door for her. "Five years isn't exactly recent."

She gave him a soft smile and slid into the seat. "Sometimes, I forget you're so much younger than me."

And there it was. It was the perfect lead-in to a conversation they needed to have.

After getting in the driver's seat, Emiliano buckled his seat belt, started the car, and slowly pulled out onto the street toward Highway 101. "I wouldn't say it's so much, but there is an age gap. Does that bother you?"

He glanced over to see her fingers fidget together in her lap and her face redden across her cheeks. "Um."

Despite his clenched stomach, he searched for the right thing to say. "What about it bothers you?"

"There's nothing wrong with your age." She shoved her hair behind her ear, but her eyes continued to stare into her lap. "There shouldn't be anything wrong with having friends of all ages."

Friends? They were back to that?

"Nell." It probably wasn't a good idea to push her, but he needed to know where they stood, especially after being let down by his dad. "We kissed."

He could hear her sharp intake of breath. "We did."

"Do you regret that?" He glanced at her. She was sitting as stiffly as humanly possible. He hated making her uncomfortable, but he needed to know.

"I, uh. Not really. Should I?"

"Should you regret kissing me?"

"If I recall, you kissed me." Her voice raised an octave.

"You're correct. I did. But I thought you wanted it too." She'd been in his arms, staring up at him. What was a guy to do?

"I did." Her voice was soft and breathy now.

"Do you think it was wrong?" *Please say no.*

"Not exactly wrong." Her hands twisted again. "It's just that you're so much younger than me."

"Seven years. It's not exactly a huge gap."

"But you're young and in the prime of your life. And..." She waved a hand in his general direction. "Very in shape."

He humphed loudly and smiled at her to find her looking at him in surprise. She wasn't joining him in the humor.

"Wait, you're serious?"

"Well, of course. You're like some young Adonis, and I'm a soft, middle-aged widow."

There it was. She thought she was undesirable?

"Thank you for that, but you must not have any idea how attractive you are to me. I think you're just absolutely"—he risked another glance at her—"incredible."

She ran a hand over her curls.

"And don't get me started with your hair."

"My hair?" She squeaked. "It's so boring. It's brown."

"It's rich and glorious," he corrected her. "And it's perfectly wavy."

"It's not curly. It's not straight. It's just this crazy..." She lifted a chunk to inspect it.

"Beach waves." He finished for her. "Some people pay big bucks for hair like yours. We sell all sorts of products for it. And you have it naturally."

"It's probably the salt in the air."

"Either way, it's beautiful."

"You really think so?"

He raised an eyebrow at her. "I'm not playing games with you. If this works between us, it's going to be because it's honest and real."

"Do you want that?" Her voice was soft again.

"If you want it. If you're ready. I wasn't sure when you would be."

"I think I am."

"Then, what's the problem?"

"Well, like I said, you're...that. I'm worried it's wrong."

"For who? The age thing, then. You think of me as a child?"

"Definitely not." She laughed. "I did at first, and well, you were. But definitely not now."

That made him smile. At least he hadn't completely lost his ability to sense attraction.

"So...you're not embarrassed of me?" He stared blankly through the windshield, trying to focus on driving.

"Embarrassed of you? Why would I be?"

"When we were together in the hall, the night of the live music, we were close, and someone walked in. You jumped away as though you didn't want anyone to see us together."

"Oh, that." She dipped her head. "I didn't want you to be embarrassed to be seen like that with me. Especially if it looked like I was some old lady trying to throw myself at y ou."

"You were embarrassed *for* me?"

"Sort of?"

"Nell." He reached across the seats to take her hand in his. "Please don't ever be embarrassed for me. I'm the little boy who worked the cash register instead of hanging out with all the cool kids. I've never fit in like that. People will have their opinions. I don't worry about what others th ink."

"Are you sure?" She pressed her other hand over their interlaced ones. "You really wouldn't mind if people saw us together?"

"I'd be proud as hell to have you on my arm."

And that was the truth of it.

"And you honestly have feelings for me?" The doubt was evident in her voice. She needed to hear it.

"If we weren't close on time, I'd pull this vehicle over and convince you. You wouldn't have any doubts, I promise."

She giggled.

And his heart did a little flip-flop.

He wanted to say more, to tell her how insanely crazy he was about her and for how long, but it didn't seem like the right time, particularly right before her important meeting.

That wasn't entirely the truth. He was afraid and wanted to delay it a little longer.

He wanted to see her face when he told her.

He gave her hand, still locked with his, a little squeeze. "Now that that's out of the way, do you know what you're going to say to Fran? Who is Fran, by the way?"

"She's the owner."

"Another female owner?"

"I know. Isn't it perfect? I'm so excited about it."

"And what's the plan?"

"I have no idea." She slumped in her seat.

"What do you want to say to her?"

"Just that I want to feature her wine, serving it exclusively as our local option at the café. I can use it in dishes and advertise it on social media so people who follow us know where they can get it." She ticked things off on her other fingers. "And fliers for the winery, to promote it. I'd ask her to do things to help promote the café at her winery too. Maybe she or her vintner could come do tastings at the café when she releases a new barrel or whatever they call it. Maybe she can come up with other ideas, too."

"Like a seasonal dinner you could cater with wine pairings."

"Ooh, I love that idea! But I'd have to close the café that night."

"The townspeople could drive to Liberty for dinner." He paused. "Or Maggie could run things for you."

"I might need her there with me." She bit her lip. "I'd have to think about it."

"It sounds like you know exactly what you want to talk to Fran about."

"Yeah, I guess so. It's just easier talking to you about it. It doesn't feel like a big business meeting where I have to sell the idea."

"I don't think you will. It's mutually beneficial. It's not like you're trying to get her to invest in your business."

"No, nothing like that."

"Then, you're not asking for much of her. You're offering her free advertising too, depending on how much she wants to get involved."

"That's a good point." She sat silently for a moment. "I'm really glad you came with me."

"Me too."

CHAPTER 17

"**A**re you sure this is the way?" Nell glanced over at Emiliano, who was walking beside her. His calm demeanor helped ground her. They followed a flagstone pathway from the parking lot to the tasting room. It was covered in moss and lined with perfectly rounded lavender bushes. The buds were just beginning to open, filling the air with their heady, herbal scent. A gentle rain drizzled on them from in between the canopy of trees.

"Yeah, I think that sign says 'office' on it." Emiliano pointed.

"I see it." Now that they were here, she was nervous again.

She wasn't Shelby. Could she do this? Her hand found his.

The unconscious action surprised her. It had to be because of their shared moment earlier and his reassurance that he had feelings for her.

When he said he would convince her of it, anticipation had sparked up in her like bubbles in her sourdough bread, alive and excited.

Emiliano gave her hand a small squeeze. "You've got this. Remember, what you're asking for is mutually beneficial."

"Right." It was the perspective she needed.

She walked up to the office door and went through to find a boy sitting behind the desk.

"Can I help you?" he asked politely. He couldn't have been more than ten or twelve.

"Yes, I have an appointment with Fran." It felt so formal.

"Oh, the chef!" He slid from the stool where he'd been reading a comic book and ran off through the entryway separating the room from the one beyond. His voice carried through the air. "Hang on a minute!"

Grinning at the cute kid, Nell shared her smile with Emiliano, only to find him frowning after the boy.

"Probably her son."
He nodded.

"Kinda like you at that age, helping out," she went on, filling the silence. She winked at him. "You were equally as cute."

She noticed a line appear between his brows.

"I know you're not a kid anymore." She squeezed his hand reassuringly. "I haven't felt that way in a while."

Emiliano flashed her a tight smile. "Thanks for that."

"Sorry for the wait," said a woman, coming around the corner. Her hair was a halo of long, beautiful steel-gray curls. "I'm Fran."

Releasing his hand, Nell stepped forward to shake hers. "Nell Wilder. And this is my friend Emiliano Gil."

She wasn't sure how to introduce him. They could figure that out later.

"Nice to meet you both. We can sit outside if you don't mind." Fran directed them back out the door. "We have a covered patio."

"Sounds good." Nell followed her out.

The woman led them to a large area outside French doors near the tasting room. Wrought-iron bistro tables with glass tops were scattered over the patio blocks. Wooden canopies were set up over the space, with light-gray canvases and string lights hung under them. It created a perfectly romantic mood.

"This is lovely."

"Thanks." Fran tilted her head to appreciate the ambiance. "I'm proud of what we've built here. You've got your own space, too, I hear."

"I have." Too often, Nell was focused on making enough sales and expanding her skills as a chef. She rarely stepped back to appreciate what she'd accomplished. "The Wild Café in Orca Cove is mine."

"It's the best food in the area." Emiliano gave her an encouraging smile.

"I've heard of it," Fran said. "Geoduck sashimi? And homemade everything?"

"I try to make as much as possible. Part of why I'm so successful, though, is the fresh ingredients I have access to. I have a market and marina right next door that buys directly from the local fisherfolk." Nell wanted to say Emiliano was an owner, but with his current issues with his dad, it felt better not to use the label. She settled on, "Emiliano and his dad run the place. I'm pretty lucky to have them so close."

"Looks like it." Fran's eyes crinkled in a friendly smile.

Nell turned to Emiliano, hoping her choice of words wasn't too touchy, but he just gave her a flat, courteous smile. She'd have to check in with him later.

"And you built it yourself?" Fran asked.

"Well." Nell shifted in her seat. She hadn't gotten used to talking about Gary with people who didn't know him. "My late husband and I did. We started with a little sandwich stand on the marina when I was eighteen and built up from there. He passed a little over a year ago."

"I'm sorry to hear that."

"Thanks. I have a lot of support from friends. I was always the cook, but Gary took care of the business. The most challenging part has been learning how to do that. Which is why I'm here." It was the best transition she could think of. "I'd like to establish relationships with local business and copromote."

"That sounds interesting. You have a good reputation on the peninsula. What did you have in mind?"

Nell went over her ideas with Fran, explaining different options depending on how much interest she had. The woman looked open to everything.

"So, it'd be mutually beneficial for both of us, and I'd exclusively list Mt. Olympus wines as the local feature.

I'll probably need to offer a California option and an international one, but most of our tourists are here for the experience and want to try our local menus. You'd get a lot of exposure."

"It sounds like a good collaboration." Fran was silent a moment, thinking over everything she'd said. "I'm not sure I can expand too much, though. I have a dependable team here, but it's just me and my son. I'm not sure I'm at a point where I could bring in servers and offer food, even if it's being catered in."

"I'm not necessarily suggesting bringing a regular full menu for you to serve. I don't know that I have the bandwidth, either, for that type of expansion. We had another proposal, though." Nell glanced at Emiliano. It had been his idea, not hers, but he was silent. He was probably trying to leave her to it, and she needed to do this herself. "If you're interested, I could do a seasonal wine-pairing dinner at the winery. I'd curate a special menu around your new releases."

Fran propped her elbow on the table in front of her and looked around the patio. "How many wait staff would we need for that?"

"It depends on how many seats we sell. We'd presell them to keep the cost of the dinner reasonable. Then I could really play with good ingredients." The idea excited Nell. It was surprising she'd never thought of doing a special prix fixe herself. Although it would be easier to do it in her own kitchens. "We could do it at the café, but the ambiance here is better suited for a wine pairing."

Fran nodded.

"I have some waiters I could bring, but I'd have to close the café that night if I did," Nell thought aloud.

"Would you be willing to do that?"

"I'm honestly not sure. I'd have to talk to my staff about it."

"Can I offer a suggestion?" Emiliano asked politely.

"Of course." Nell turned to him. She'd never intended for him to stay out of the conversation. Heck, Shelby would have run it if she'd have been there.

"If it's seasonal, you could have a special staff of VIP customers invited to help. They could have their own private tasting and meal afterwards that they wouldn't have to pay for. Or you could do it as a fundraiser and take volunteers."

"Both are solid ideas." Fran worried her bottom lip as she considered what they were offering.

It was probably overwhelming. It had taken Nell weeks to think through it all herself.

"This is a lot. I've given you several ideas I'm willing to do to feature Mt. Olympus wines. Why don't you take some time and think through what you'd like to do? Maybe come have dinner at the café in a few weeks, and we can figure out where to go from there?"

"That's a good idea."

"And make sure you bring that cute kid of yours. I've got a cookie with his name on it."

"He'd love that." Fran's eyes lit up with her smile, and she sat back in her seat. "What's next for you two? Do you have to rush back, or are you staying for a tasting?"

"We're going to have a tasting. I want to try the wines again, and I have someone covering the dinner shift and closing for me." Nell glanced at Emiliano. She was looking forward to celebrating her personal victory and talking more about what the future held for the two of them here in the beauty of the vineyard.

"Then, you have plenty of time. I'd appreciate your thoughts on our appetizers if you don't mind." Fran leaned in. "Honestly, I think they need work. If you have better ideas—maybe something we could get from your market, Emiliano, something shelf stable—I'd appreciate it. Right now, all we have is nuts, olives, and chocolates. None of which are terribly good."

"I'd be happy to."

"Thanks." Fran tilted her head. "I'm excited about this. I don't normally have anyone to toss ideas around with. I'm looking forward to working with you. You're really good at it."

"Really?" Nell asked, amazed.

"Definitely. Maybe this was just the nudge I needed to get out of my comfort zone."

"Well, thanks. I'm looking forward to it, too."

Fran stood. "Enjoy your tasting. It's a gift from me. I'll go let Marilyn know that it and the appetizers are on the house. It's a business expense."

"Thanks!" Nell stood and shook her hand.

"I hope you two have a nice evening." Fran left them alone at their table.

"Did you hear that?" Nell spun to Emiliano. "*I'm* helping *her*!"

"You did a great job." He smiled warmly at her.

"I was like Shelby, being all business lady. I was *doing things*!"

"You most certainly were. You should be very proud of yourself."

"I am! Thank you so much for your help."

"I didn't do much except listen."

"You're really good at that." She took his hand. "You've been so supportive."

"I'm glad for the opportunity." He squeezed her hand back. "And we get to enjoy a little evening off."

"I could get back." She worried her lip. "It took less time than I thought."

"It's your choice. We can do whatever you want."

Nell smiled, feeling a little rebellious. "Let's stay. Maggie's all geared up for tonight, and I'd hate to take that away from her. Besides, I need to taste out what I'll be working with. If you're okay with staying."

Emiliano nodded. "I'm up for the adventure."

"And we can talk more about this." Nell tugged at their hands, as her stomach gave a little flip-flop. "If that's alright."

Emiliano's eyes softened. "Nell, I'm up for any adventure with you."

The sentiment warmed her heart in a way she hadn't felt in a while, and she bit her lip.

"Fran said you were staying for a tasting?" said a waitress, approaching their table.

"Yes, please," Nell replied.

"I'll bring two tastings and the appetizers. Any allergies?"

"None for me." She didn't think Emiliano had any, and she had a decent list of the residents' illnesses, but she wasn't going to assume. "You?"

"None here."

"Great. I'll be right back." The waitress left them.

"So this is the place that supposedly has better pizzas?" Nell looked around the Liberty Tavern. It wasn't bad. A cozy little pub at the far end of town. Not the kind of place you'd expect to grab dinner at after a winery like Mt. Olympus, but it worked. And, boy, was she hungry. The wine had been delicious, but the appetizers left much to be desired.

"Not anymore! You sold me on those sourdough ones." Emiliano held his hands up in surrender. "Never let it be said that I can't change my mind."

"Should I get the pizza to see what the hype was all about?"

Emiliano leaned in and put his hand to the side of his face to keep their conversation private. "I have a confession to make. I always liked your pizza better. I just wanted you to make more of it to prove me wrong."

"You didn't!" Nell threw her napkin across the table. It fell gently and unsuccessfully between them.

He laughed, picking it up. "You seem to have dropped something."

Nell huffed and snatched her napkin back, tucking it on her lap like a cloth one and shaking out the menu. "I guess I can be a little competitive when it comes to food."

"You have every right to be. You're the best chef I've ever met." He crossed his arms on the tabletop and smiled warmly at her.

"Well, thank you." He made her feel special. She'd missed that. After perusing the options, she folded it shut. "The patty melt."

"You're getting the patty melt?" He cocked his head in surprise. "That's probably the least impressive thing on there."

"Don't underestimate a good messy sandwich." She winked at him. "I can do impressive. I want something comforting and delicious. You can't to go wrong with a sandwich fried in butter."

"Fair enough." He studied the menu for a moment before closing it as well. "The patty melt. I can't have you going into that all on your own. But I'm getting sautéed onions on mine."

"Ooh, that sounds good. Me too." Nell looked for the waitress, who made her way through the busy crowd to take their orders. "Do you have Guinness?"

"Just in a bottle."

"I'll take one, please."

"You're full of surprises tonight," Emiliano said to her, then to the waitress, he nodded. "I'll take one too."

Nell shrugged. "I used all my fancy taste buds on the wine and appetizers. I need something simple and tasty. Besides, the dry beer will balance the greasy sandwich."

"That's my girl." Emiliano chuckled, then stopped in the middle of the laugh, his tight eyes catching hers as though waiting for her response.

It was an unexpected term of endearment, and a delightful buzzing warmth traveled up the back of her neck. She smiled, hiding her face as Emiliano let out the breath he'd been holding. Maybe he was nervous about all this new stuff too.

"Thanks for all your help back there. And the company."

"It's my pleasure. And you did all the heavy lifting. I was just moral support. And a wine-tasting partner."

"That was a lot of fun. The wine was better than I remembered. Her new Field Blend was stellar."

"It was. We're lucky to be in such a good region for it."

"And I'm so excited she's going to come to the café. Her and her son." Nell thought about what she might serve them when they visited. She'd plan a fancy special that night. Emiliano had seemed odd around the boy. She didn't want to call him out on it, but it was almost like he hadn't liked the kid. That wasn't like him. "You seemed a little tense there, at the beginning. Everything o kay?"

He cleared his throat. "Yeah. It's just. Well, Pops and I had another argument today."

"Today?"

"Right before I left."

"Oh, no. I'm so sorry, Emiliano. Do we need to go so you can work things out?" Nell looked around the pub for their waitress.

"Definitely not." He waved her down. "Unfortunately, I don't know that it's going to be that easy. Besides, I wanted to come."

"Are you sure?"

"Very much so." He covered her hands on the table with his. "This is where I want to be."

"I'm so sorry you're going through all that with Hugo. I know that's got to be rough on you."

"It hasn't been easy."

"You've worked so much on your plans. He's not open to any of them?"

"Not a one. And I don't see that changing." He glanced up as the waitress brought their beers and set them down, lingering near him. Nell could see her looking him up and down before she turned and left their table.

She tugged at the front of her shirt, feeling self-conscious about how it didn't fit quite as well as the curve-hugging top the waitress wore. The slender, dark-haired waitress with big eyes and perfect skin was much closer to Emiliano's age.

"What will you do?" She tried to brush it off.

"I'm not sure yet."

She didn't like the sound of that. He might leave Orca Cove for a job in Seattle. Not that she'd want to hold him back. What would Gil's Market even be like without him there? The place had been so strange when he was away at school.

"But that doesn't matter now." He lifted his beer. "Cheers to your new business venture."

She clinked her glass to his and took a swig. It was bitter, dry, and perfect.

"You were impressive today."

"You really think so?"

"I always think so." Emiliano studied her face, then glanced at the table. "I have always thought so."

"That's sweet."

"It's true." He took her hand back in his. "You should know I've always had a thing for you, Nell. I don't want to scare you off, but I want you to know how I feel."

He'd said always. Like when they were kids? She frowned, thinking back. She hadn't realized he had a crush on her when he was younger. That part seemed kinda cute but, as he'd grown older, unlikely.

"I still have a difficult time believing you'd want me when you could be dating women like"—she gestured towards the waitress walking by—"her."

She'd seen him with cute younger girls like the jet-black haired beauty over the years. It had never bothered her before, and it felt weird to be jealous of it now. She had been with Gary. This whole thing was new territory, and she wasn't sure what was okay to feel.

"She doesn't hold a candle to you."

"But how?" Her words sounded like she was angling for a compliment even to her own ears, but that couldn't have been further from the truth. She didn't understand the appeal.

"You're beautiful, Nell. Do you really not see that?"

"Stop." She looked away, uncomfortable and unsure how to react. Was he being serious? She's seen herself in the mirror.

"Seriously. There's something about your face that's always been beautiful to me. It's kind and intelligent. And I love the way you drift off when you're creating dishes. Your eyes sparkle."

"That's so kind of you to say." Nell shifted in her seat. "But I'm not as thin as I once was. Younger women aren't as...soft."

"You mean your soft curves?" He made a pleased hum and looked up to the ceiling as though he was tasting delicious food. "That's all woman, and I think it's sexy as hell."

"Really?" She was starting to believe him.

"Nell." Emiliano zeroed in on her, and the rest of the room fell away. "You are the kindest, most supportive person I know. You always put stew on the menu in the fall for Conrad because it's his favorite. You deliver Mary's steak even though you don't do deliveries. You feed half the town and always put others before you. You're incredible."

Her stomach flip-flopped, and tears threatened to emerge. She didn't know anyone had noticed all those things. "I care about them."

"I know."

"Food is my love language."

"I know." The corners of his eyes crinkled with humor.

"That day you came by and I was making the cookies?" she started, wanting to be open with him as well. He'd shared way more than she had. "The rye ones with the sesame paste?"

"I remember. It was your birthday." The corner of his mouth curved up.

"It was the first time I saw you as a man." She swallowed loudly. "That probably doesn't sound flattering. I'm sorry. But it's true."

"Okay."

"I was so flustered. I thought I was having a hot flash." The words tumbled out before she thought them through.

He barked, covering it with a cough. "I shouldn't have laughed at that."

"It's okay. It's funny. Seriously, though. I was so caught up by how close you were and how good you smelled that I nearly dropped the batter."

"That would have been a shame." He grinned at her wolfishly, with one eyebrow flicking up.

"That's why I brought the cookies by later. I wanted to see if it was a fluke."

"And was it?"

She turned her hand under his, squeezing it. "You know it's not."

The breath Emiliano let out sounded shaky, and he closed his eyes for a brief moment. "I'm glad to hear it."

"But I thought you were considering leaving Orca Cove." It was what she'd been worried about.

He shook his head. "I've thought a lot about that. If I do leave the market—and it's starting to feel like I don't have a choice if I want to have something that's mine—I don't think I can just leave the cove. I have some other ideas. But they're way less interesting than this topic."

He winked at her, and she melted.

Their food arrived, and they separated to dig into their plates. She should have chosen something more ladylike to eat, but then again, the sandwich was everything she'd hoped for.

Relieved and a little overwhelmed by everything that had transpired today, she ordered another beer when the waitress came by.

"Do you want another one?" she asked Emiliano.

"I'd better not. I'm driving." He shook his head. "But, please, enjoy. You've earned the celebration."

It was nice, feeling taken care of. And she wanted him to kiss her like he said he would.

It made her feel like a teenager.

If she was being honest with herself, she'd admit she was building up the courage to ask him to.

Or to initiate it herself.

CHAPTER 18

The alarm on Emiliano's phone woke him the following morning. Flicking it to silent, he blinked, remembering where he was. Memories fell into place, and he glanced over at the sleeping form beside him.

Nell.

Her beautiful chestnut hair spread across her pillow, and it looked like a dream. He didn't know what he'd done right in life to get here, but here he was.

"Nell." He gently nudged her.

She purred like a kitten and stretched, then went completely still, her eyes flying open as she took in her surroundings.

"How're you feeling?"

"What happened?" She frowned and pursed her lips to think. "The tree."

By the time they left the tavern, Nell had finished two more Guinnesses. Which was fine. He'd planned on taking her safely home and dropping her off, but the wind had picked up, and a tree had fallen over Highway 101. Unless they wanted to drive all the way around the peninsula, they'd have to wait until it was removed.

The road crew had estimated three to four hours, so he'd called around to find the nicest hotel in Liberty.

"But why am I naked?" She squeezed her eyes shut. "Did we?"

"As much as I wanted to, no. I don't make a habit of sleeping with drunk women." Emiliano swung his legs over the side of the bed. He had stripped down to his boxer briefs and enjoyed the feeling of her eyes on him as he tugged his jeans on. "Although it was extremely challenging when you took your clothes off."

"Oh, no." She covered her face with her hands.

"Please, don't be embarrassed. It was the most beautiful thing I've seen in a long time. You're extraordinary."

She sat there, her eyes wide, but said nothing.

He pulled his shirt on, moving away from the bed to give her space. "I'll head downstairs for coffee. I think I saw a sign saying they had toothbrushes. Then we can grab something to eat on the way home."

It would also give her time to shower and get herself together.

"Wait!" She gripped the sheet to her chest. "What time is it?"

"Don't worry. I set the alarm early so we could make it back in time for you to open." He unplugged her phone from the extra cord he'd brought from his vehicle. "All charged."

"Thank you." The words stumbled out of her mouth. Now that she was sitting up, with the sheets clutched to her chest, her hair tumbled down around her shoulders. It was mussed in a slept-in way that made Emiliano want to walk over and take his clothes back off.

But she probably wasn't ready for that.

Instead, he handed her phone over and paused to drop a light kiss on her cheek on his way out.

Balancing coffees and a small bag, Emiliano knocked on the door. Nell answered it, her eyes not quite reaching his.

"Toothbrushes." He held the bag up. "And I found a couple of shirts at the gift shop downstairs. They have Mt. Olympus Winery on them, so we might actually wear them again."

"Thank you." She grabbed the toothbrush and headed to the bathroom. "I showered while you were out."

Nell came out a minute later, smoothing down the dark-purple T-shirt he'd bought her. "That feels so much better. I love this color."

"I know." He winked at her, touching her shoulder as he brushed by.

"Do you want to shower?"

"I washed last night." Emiliano walked into the bathroom and opened his toothbrush to clean his teeth.

"When I was passed out?"

He glanced through the door to see her sitting on the end of the bed, looking sad and embarrassed. After spitting, he rinsed his mouth and wiped his face on his towel. That was better. He pulled yesterday's shirt off over his head and put on the clean navy one he'd bought before returning. "You were celebrating. It happened."

"I'm sorry." She finally looked up from her lap. "I'm really, really sorry."

"You have nothing to be sorry for. I'm the luckiest guy here. Honest."

"Even though we…I…" She glanced back at the bed, then sprang to her feet and paced to the window like a gazelle dancing away.

"Nell?" Emiliano sat down next to where she'd gotten up from. "Please, don't make this a mistake. I don't want it to be a mistake."

She chewed on her bottom lip and looked around for something or nothing; he wasn't sure which. Then she nodded and slowly said, "Okay."

Standing, he went to her and took her hands in his. When she looked at him, her eyes traveling over his face, he said, "I'd really like to kiss you now."

"Okay," she repeated.

Leaning over, he pressed his lips to her soft ones slowly, taking his time, teasing hers in a sweet, minty dance. Nell sighed, the sound hitching high in her throat as she pressed against him.

Releasing her hands, he pulled her closer, feeling her arms weave around to his back. When his right hand traveled up to cup the back of her head, it dove into her soft, full hair. Something he'd wanted to touch pretty much his entire life.

It was the most satisfying, sensual act he'd ever done.

Tears sprung to his eyes.

Not wanting to rush things, he blinked them away and pulled back, pressing his forehead to hers. Nell breathed heavily, staring up at him, so close, her eyes glazed and unfocused.

He grinned at her. "Come on. Let's get some breakfast."

She blinked when he grabbed her hand and led them out.

"This coffee is kinda awful," Nell said, taking another sip from the drink he'd brought them.

"There's a coffee shop across the street." He took her cup and threw both of theirs in the nearby trashcan. "I bet they have breakfast sandwiches or something. Unless you'd like to find something else."

"That works. I don't normally eat a big meal this early."

After getting a burrito for himself and a scone for her, they took coffees to go and got back on the road.

"You look great with and without makeup," he said, finding himself staring at her buckling her seat belt.

She blushed, running a hand over her face. "I don't normally wear much."

"You don't need it."

She dropped her hand. "Thank you."

Getting his mind back on track, he pulled out of the lot and headed back onto Highway 101 and toward their hometown.

"When can I see you again?" Emiliano asked, reaching across the console for her hand. "I know today's Friday and the weekend starts, but do you think you'd have any time to get away before Monday?"

"I'll probably see you later today." She shot him a coy smile, then laughed, her fingers intertwining with his. "I should have some time. It might be a little late, though. If you're interested in coming to the live music tomorrow, we could hang out after."

Her voice stumbled on the word "hang out," as though she wasn't sure what to call it.

"I'd love to come for that." He relished the fact that she'd invited him over, even if she would be working the event.

He knew how busy she was on those nights. It was mainly the bar that was bustling, but the customers liked to see her out and about and catch up. It meant a lot to him that she wanted him there.

There was no question about it this time.

It was a date.

Their fingers played together, gently touching and exploring where they met on her lap.

Maybe things would work out, after all.

"What are you talking about?" Hugo's red face was stone cold.

He'd been trying to explain the situation to his dad, but he still wasn't listening.

"I'm leaving the shop, Pops." At this point, Emiliano wasn't even angry anymore. He was feeling resigned and a little sad, but he'd made his decision. "It's the best thing for both of us."

"How can you say that, Emil?" His dad clutched his fist against his chest. "I need you here. That's why you came back."

"It is." He dropped his head and reached a hand out to use the wall of their shared office for support. "But I want something of my own. I always thought of this place as ours since I could remember."

"Of course it is."

"It's not, Pops. You know it's not." He shook his head, pushing away from the wall. "You won't let me be a part of anything that matters. I can't even suggest anything without you dismissing it on the spot."

"You're always trying to change things!"

"You're afraid of change."

"Change isn't always good."

"It isn't always bad, either." Before his dad could retort, he held up a hand. "It doesn't matter. You're not willing to let me in on the business in any other capacity than as an employee. And that's okay. You built it. It's your choice. But so is mine in leaving. I need to find something of my own. Like you did."

He knew his dad couldn't argue with that. The stubborn Spaniard had been determined to make something of himself when he was younger.

"But it's always been just the two of us." His dad finally quieted.

"I know, Pops, but you'll figure it out. Besides, you won't have anyone trying to suggest doing things differently or wasting time on the computer. Things will just go your way."

It was a potshot, and he knew it, but he couldn't help himself. He didn't want to hurt his dad, but he needed him to understand why he was quitting.

It simply wasn't working.

"I'm not leaving Orca Cove. I'm just not going to be your employee anymore. Look, I think I have more to contribute in this world, and I don't want to waste that. I have to see what I can do."

Wordlessly, his dad nodded and turned back to his desk, dismissing him.

That was okay; they needed a break. And he had things to do.

It hurt to turn around and walk away from the only parent and the only job he'd ever known, but it was something he needed to do for himself.

Inside, he was battling feelings of being ungrateful and selfish, but for what his dad wanted, he could hire another assistant manager. Hell, he'd probably be happier that way.

Maybe they both would.

Stepping back out to the parking lot, he drew in a deep, centering breath. He hated the idea of not seeing Nell every day. And not working with Solomon and the other fisherfolk. Nerves tangled in his gut at the thought, enough that he nearly turned back around.

No, he'd find a way to do both. Besides, now that they were dating, he'd be able to see her more often, not just dance around the fact that he was in love with her.

His boots scuffed in the gravel as he rewound his words. Now that they were dating...

The words still didn't feel real.

His life was far from perfect, but he felt like he could get there. Well, maybe not perfect, but he believed he could build a satisfying one. He just needed a little help.

Flicking through his phone, he dialed Nick's number. The man picked up on the second ring.

"Emiliano. Everything okay?" He could hear a saw dying down through the phone.

"Yeah, everything's okay," he told the police-officer-turned-woodworker. "I was wondering if you and Willa were home. I'd like to swing by for a short visit. I had something I wanted to talk to you both about."

"O-kay." He drew the word out, obviously curious at the reason. Emiliano had never visited his house before. "We're here. Feel free to come by anytime."

"Thanks, I'm heading that way now."

"See you."

He pocketed his phone and got back into his Subaru, heading back out of town.

The couple lived just on the edge of Orca Cove, at the foot of the Olympic National Park. Pulling into the long drive, he looked up to admire the line of bigleaf maples that lined each side.

A modest cabin sat at the end of the gravel road, looking picturesque, nestled into the landscape, with tall firs hovering overhead like watchmen. Nick had recently rebuilt the place from the ground up after it was burned down by arson. With the help of Duke and a couple of townspeople doing utility work, it had gone up much faster than anyone would have guessed. And probably much sturdier, too.

Nick stood on his front porch with Willa, and the double doors to his shop, off to the side, were open. Wood and a saw were pulled out under the overhang to work in the warming spring air. Sawdust and inquisitiveness covered the man.

"Good morning." Nick tugged Willa close to him, wrapping his arm around her protectively.

"Everything's really okay, Nick." Emiliano shut his car door with a snap and walked up to greet them. "I wanted to talk business. Sorry if I worried you."

"Told you." Willa's eyes slid up to her boyfriend, who raised his shoulders. She gave him a peck on the cheek and turned to go in. "Come on in, then. Tea is on."

Following the pair, he sat at the square table in the middle of their dining room. It was open to the living room and kitchen, with windows all around them.

"Sorry to pull you away from work. I won't take up too much time."

"Don't be silly." Willa sat a steaming mug in front of him. "Herbal coffee."

There wasn't much Emiliano wasn't willing to try. Taking a light sip, he thought through the flavors as he did with Nell's food. It reminded him of the café au lait from New Orleans. "Chicory?"

Willa's face lit up with a smile, and she nodded. "And a few other things. It's good for your liver."

"Thanks."

"What's up?" Nick pulled a chair out across from him and sat.

Willa perched on a barstool at their kitchen counter.

"I'm starting an online business," Emiliano said. "For you, it's similar to the online website you're already selling on, but it's geared toward the locals. I'll have a delivery service set up for people within forty miles, and we'll organize shipping for anything beyond that. You could sign up for sales only with local delivery, only shipped service, or both. It'd be your choice."

"We already talked about this, Emiliano. I told you I'm in."

"It's not exactly the same thing." His lips pressed into a thin line. "This is my business. It won't be part of Gil's Market and Marina."

Nick and Willa exchanged a glance. It was one of those that close couples shared, passing information between themselves.

He cleared his throat and went on. "I understand if you're not interested. You already have an online selling platform. I can offer you a reduced sales fee for using my platform, and I'd take care of the shipping for you, so those would be the two benefits of using my site. You can still sell at Gil's and use my online local-delivery sales if you choose to. It doesn't have to limit your exposure. The site will help locals get your product without driving into the store. But it's honestly up to you. I support whatever decision you make."

He knew the words were tumbling out, but he wanted to make sure he was being clear.

"I see," Nick said.

"I'm not trying to pressure you into anything."

"We don't think you are." Willa walked over to him and laid a hand on his shoulder. She glanced back at her boyfriend, who said something to her nonverbally. "What's happened with Hugo?"

He should have led with it. He knew that. It had just seemed easier to stay on the topic of business.

"You know Pops doesn't like change." He chose his words carefully. "I want to invest my time in something I'm a part of. Something of my own."

Nick nodded slowly as he listened to what he said and what he didn't say. "Okay."

"Just like that?"

"Yeah." He leaned back in his chair and raised his mug to his lips. "I'd still like to sell at Gil's. The tourists buy a lot, and the locals are used to finding my stuff there."

"I think that's a smart decision. If you're interested in online nationwide sales, you can sell on both platforms, mine and what you're currently on. It'll just expand your reach, and you won't lose your customers who know where to find you."

"No need. I can just redirect them on my social media."

"You have social media?" Emiliano couldn't disguise the surprise in his voice. The man had moved here from Seattle to hide from a criminal organization. He was one of the most private people he knew.

Willa giggled.

"She posts everything for me." Nick indicated the curly-haired herbalist. "I wouldn't have a use for it otherwise. People like to see how things are made."

"*That's* why they watch your videos," Willa said dryly, cutting her eyes to him.

"What do you mean?" Nick frowned.

"Three-quarters of your followers are women," she said, pulling a leg up under her and sitting back on the stool.

"Oh." Nick frowned. "I didn't know that."

"It's okay, honey. I've included myself in some of the pictures. They know you're in a committed relationship."

"That's good." He sat forward and laced his fingers, addressing Emiliano. "So, what else do you need?"

"Need?"

"You're going to need delivery drivers, a vehicle, more crafters, and more space to store everything unless you have people drop off the sold items."

"Yeah. That's why I wanted to talk to you both."

"I'll sell products with local delivery, nothing more," Willa said with finality, and he wasn't going to argue with her.

"I appreciate that. I need more products to offer on the site." He glanced down at the mug in his hands. "But that's not all. I wanted to ask you about your place."

"My place?" She looked around the cabin. "What about it?"

"Not this place. I mean your downtown condo. You had a lease with Shelby, right?"

"That's right. She told me she'd let me out of it early if she could find someone else to rent it, but she hasn't yet."

"She's trying, right?" Nick teased her.

"Of course she is."

"I'm interested," Emiliano said. He wasn't sure if it'd be easier to sublease it from Willa or rent it outright from Shelby.

"I'll call her," Willa offered.

"I'd appreciate it."

It was a cute little condo and more space than he needed, but it would make the break between him and his dad easier if he had his own place.

And less embarrassing to have Nell over if he wasn't living with Hugo.

CHAPTER 19

Still nothing.

Nell cocked her head curiously. Typically, by this time of the day, she'd have seen Emiliano milling about outdoors, talking to the fisherfolk and boat owners.

Earlier that morning, she had sent Carlos over for haddock and produce for the night's menu. Even though they'd made it back early, she was behind on prep work.

Maybe she was hesitant to run into him again, but she preferred to chalk it up to being focused on work. She planned on texting him later to thank him again for taking care of her the night before. And setting the alarm so early. Not everyone understood the responsibility that came

with owning a business. He certainly did. He'd grown up i
n it.

She still felt bad about the situation he was in. She'd
never lived in her parents' shadow. They'd been more than
happy for her to get out on her own. As she made her way
back inside, she bumped into Maggie.

"Sorry." She grabbed her friend and favorite waitress's
shoulders to steady herself. Vaguely, she remembered the
excitement in the dining room before she walked out to
the back deck. "Hey, what was all the commotion about
earlier?"

"Conrad losing crops. He's worried we have locusts or
something."

"Locusts? Did he see them?"

"Not many. The other farmers are arguing with him
over it. Then one of the tourists, a biologist from the University of Washington, told him it was absurd. He'd have
more damage, and there would be indisputable evidence."
Maggie executed a perfect eye roll.

That was strange. And awful for Conrad. "Did he have
any pictures?"

"Yeah. He was showing them around to see if anyone
had any ideas. Honestly, it looked like the plants had disap-

peared. Or been eaten away." She winced. "The biologist told him it was probably deer."

"Conrad has a fence around his crops."

She nodded. "He told him that. A few other things too. Then he unfortunately told him he either needed to look at his fence's height, or it was rabbits. It was as simple as that."

"Oof. I bet that went over well."

"About as well as you'd imagine."

Farmers didn't take kindly to people questioning their practices.

"Sounds like things have settled down now." Nell headed to her office.

"You look distracted," Maggie said, interrupting her.

"No, I just have a lot in my head."

She tried to move around her, but Maggie stood her ground. At barely over five feet, the petite woman was surprisingly well adept at getting in her way.

"You've been distracted all morning." Maggie propped her fists on her hips, her arms akimbo. "When I got here, you'd barely started the menu. That's not like you. What's going on?"

"I..." Her voice died on her lips. It didn't feel right to lie to her friend. She'd been there for her through good times and bad ones. Really bad ones. "Emiliano went with me to the winery last night."

"Oh really!" Maggie stepped in closer, her body wiggling from side to side, as she pushed them both into her kitchen. "Tell me everything!"

"Well...we only got back about thirty minutes before you walked in this morning." She ran a hand self-consciously over her hair. It was still a little wet from her morning shower at the hotel.

When she got home, she'd run inside, dumped her things, and changed out of her jeans and undies for some cleaner ones. A quick swipe of mascara, and she was ready for the apron and clogs she normally cooked i n.

Maggie's mouth was hanging half open. "Are you serious?"

"Do I often exaggerate?"

"You're not Shelby, no." Maggie pushed her into the chair at the small table in her kitchen. "Now, you're really telling me everything."

"Oh, I didn't sleep with him or anything!" Nell exclaimed, realizing what Maggie thought. "I mean, I did. But at least he was dressed. Mostly."

"What?" Maggie screeched. "*He* was dressed? Does that mean *you* weren't?"

"I had a little too much to drink."

"And you took all of your clothes off?" Her eyes couldn't get any wider.

"Apparently."

"You don't remember?" Concern etched on her face. "Then, how do you know?"

"I remembered enough, eventually." Nell ran a hand over her face. The memory of ripping her shirt off and plastering herself to Emiliano would have traumatized her if she didn't also remember the struggle on his face when he sat her on the bed.

It didn't end there, though. She'd gotten back up and kissed him. He'd let her that time. Let her take his shirt off and explore his body with her hands until he pushed her away, telling her he wanted her. He wanted her like crazy, and he'd be more than happy to continue when they woke up if she was still game.

Heat rose in a flush. That was probably why he'd been so cautious with her that morning. She hadn't remembered until she got back to work.

"So, you're together now?" Maggie asked.

Her stomach twisted. "I think so? He's coming over tomorrow for the live music, and we're going to talk after. And we might have a date on Monday. It's all so new; I don't know what to think."

"Wow. I'm so happy for you!" Her friend grabbed her hand. "You don't look happy. Are you happy?"

"Yeah, I just... It still feels weird, you know? Gary still feels here, everywhere."

"Yeah, I know." Maggie patted her hand.

"Do you think you could keep this between us for right now? I need to figure out how to tell the crew."

"Of course."

"You don't feel like I'm betraying him, do you?"

"Oh, Nell. I really don't. Gary would want you to be happy."

She knew that. Deep down, she knew that. But emotions still tumbled around in her stomach like battery acid and concrete.

Her phone dinged.

"*Hi,*" it read. "*Did you have any trouble getting the café opened in time?*"

"It's him," Nell told Maggie, who winked at her and pointed to the door, announcing her exit.

"*No,*" she texted back. "*I got it opened just in the nick of time. Thanks again for that, by the way.*"

"*Of course.*"

"*I haven't seen you out and about today. All okay with you?*"

"*Yes. I've been busy today.*" There was a pause where dots danced on her screen, indicating he was texting. They stopped, disappeared, and started again. To her surprise, they stopped, disappeared, and started yet again. Maybe he was as nervous about their newness as she was. "*I do have something to tell you about. Show you, really. Will you still be able to get away tomorrow night?*"

"*After the band wraps up, yes.*"

"*Great.*"

"*I'm looking forward to it.*" Her stomach felt wobbly as though she was on a roller coaster, not knowing what was going to happen next. She hadn't permanently scared him away with her actions the night before, thank goodness.

"*Me too.*"

She grinned like a teenager at her phone. Then, thinking about his tanned chest, his lean, lightly muscled twenty-something tanned chest, she let out a long breath.

He'd said he wanted her.

Her insides went warm like half-baked brownies.

Getting up from the table, she walked to the cooler to let the cold air hit her. She blinked. She needed to get her libido under control before tomorrow night or else she'd be throwing herself at him again.

They were packing up.

Nell's heartbeat skyrocketed. She had a date. She glanced back out to the bar and noticed Emiliano still sat there, chatting with Duke and Nick. She'd only been out to say hi a few times, and her nerves were still getting the better of her.

"Hey." A voice behind her made her turn. It was the kid from the band.

"Hey, JD." She smiled. "Good set tonight."

They'd played their hearts out, and the customers had loved it. They were more excited about the music than she'd have ever imagined. It was like she'd unlocked a secret need of the cove.

"Thanks." He shifted back and forth on his Converse high tops. "I was just wondering if you'd thought any more about scheduling us further out. Or...like, maybe making it a paid gig? I mean, if you thought we were worth it."

A paid gig. One look at the bar showed it busier than normal. It was reaching full capacity, something that happened only during summer, and it was barely mid-spring.

"Um." She should talk to Shelby or Emiliano first.

Wait. Did she need to do that?

Turning to the young man, she looked him right in the eye. "Tell you what, JD. I can't guarantee we won't ever have another band at The Wild Café, but anytime you play here, you'll be compensated."

"Really?" His eyes lit up.

She nodded. "How about I think about what's fair, and I'll call you tomorrow to talk about it?"

"That'd be great, Nell." He pumped her hand up and down in an enthusiastic handshake. "Wait 'til I tell the band!"

He rushed off, his long blond hair and plaid flannel flying behind him like proud flags.

"Looks like you made his day." A warm voice slid like honey down her spine.

Emiliano stood behind her, and she was tempted to lean back into him. She wanted his arms around her. But with all the customers still settling their tabs, it felt unprofessional.

"I told JD it would be a paid gig." The words sounded so official and businesswoman-like. In some ways, Emiliano was responsible for that. He'd supported her and encouraged her every step of the way.

"Makes sense. Your bar should be looking pretty flush."

"It is." She was proud to know that, but she'd been getting more and more familiar with the online ledgers. A local bookkeeper had been helping with it over the past couple of years, after Gary found out he was sick. And Shelby helped explain things occasionally.

Absently, her hand found Emiliano's in the space between them, and his chocolate-colored irises, reflecting light from the string lights overhead, softened at her touch. His fingers intertwined with hers.

Nell gulped, seeing Duke and Nick were watching them and noticing their hands. Embarrassed at being caught flirting on the deck, she dropped his hand. "Did you enjoy the band?"

"Yeah." His eyes flicked down to their broken hand-hold. "They were even better tonight."

"I think so too." She spotted her friend picking up plates. "I need to help Maggie get cleaned up. We shouldn't be much longer. You okay to wait another fifteen or twenty minutes?"

"Sure. Do you need any help?"

"Nah, I won't take long." She rushed off.

Twenty-five minutes later, she found him sitting alone at the bar.

"Sorry it took so long." She stood close, wanting to touch him, but feeling self-conscious about it. "Maggie looked wiped out, so I sent her home and finished closing."

"No problem. Things come up." The smile he gave her didn't quite reach his eyes.

"Is everything okay?" She slid onto the stool beside him.

"Nell." He turned to face her. "Are you sure you're ready for this?"

"What? I..." For a flash, she thought maybe he wanted an out. But then she noticed the hurt look in his eyes. "Yes. I mean, if you are."

"Of course I am. I just—" He cut himself off and looked out over the water. "I noticed you pulled away when you saw people watching us earlier."

She blew out the breath she'd been holding. "Oh, that was because I didn't want to be seen fawning all over you by my customers."

"Is that all?"

"I mean, I haven't told the crew yet, but after Duke and Nick saw us, the cat's probably already out of the bag."

"And you're okay with that?" His eyes narrowed as they searched hers.

"Yes." She blushed. "If you are."

A slow grin spread across his face, and he leaned toward her. "Most definitely."

Sliding a hand up her jaw, he cupped the side of her face and laid a slow, melting kiss on her lips. She shuddered at the chill dancing down her spine.

"Come on." He gave her a final peck. "Let's take a walk in the moonlight."

"Okay." She turned off the patio heaters and grabbed her jacket, then pulled it on.

She followed him down the steps and onto the beach, the pebble rocks shifting underfoot. Thankfully, she'd taken time to change out of her clogs and into her tennis shoes.

The moon was nearly full overhead, and without thinking of it, she reached out and took his hand as the waves crashed on the shoreline, creating a romantic overture.

"This place is magical, isn't it?" she finally said.

"It really is." His eyes lit on hers, and not the waves.

"You said you wanted to tell me something." She'd been curious since he texted it.

"I did it." He squeezed her hand excitedly. "I talked to my dad yesterday. And I left to start my own business."

She froze in her steps. Did that mean he was leaving? "What are you going to do?"

"I'm still doing the website I told you about, but I'm doing it on my own. I figured I didn't need to be aligned with Gil's to do that."

"Will you still sell groceries?"

"Only as a delivery service."

"I guess you could sell even more products, then. Expand around the peninsula."

"That doesn't feel right." He resumed their walk, tugging her along, his hand firmly clenching hers. "At least not right now, it doesn't. I don't want to compete with Pops."

She admired his loyalty. "I understand."

"I figured you would." He glanced at her. "I already have a few people signed up to sell through my online platform."

"Platform?"

"The site," he explained. "Nick and Willa, both."

"Willa's selling online?" That was new and unlike her friend. It would also be problematic if too many people found out about her magical health potions.

"For local delivery only. She was clear about that."

"That sounds more like Willa. She wants to know her customers."

"She said something like that." He worried his bottom lip. "I also talked to Shelby today."

"You did?" That made all her friends in one day. Not that the town was large enough to make the fact overwhelmingly unusual. "What about?"

"I thought I should have a place to myself." He pulled her to a stop. "I didn't want to have you over for dinner, or whatever, at my dad's place."

Whatever. She could imagine what that meant. Something pleasant dropped into her stomach, like sun-warmed honey sliding to form a pool at the bottom.

"Oh," was all she could manage.

"I moved into Willa's old condo today." A grin split his face. He gestured up, off the beach, to the long row of buildings that overlooked the water. "It's the first place I've ever had completely on my own, apart from my dorm room, of course. Can I show you?"

"I mean, I've seen it before," she teased him. "But I'd love to see it again. With your things in it."

Laughing, they took off up the beach, rocks sliding underfoot.

He led her up the stairs onto the small back deck, and she ran her hand over the wooden handrail, still seeing Willa's herbs stacked along the edge. She'd spent many evenings here. He'd unlocked the sliding glass door, and they walked into the living room, where she toed off her tennis shoes out of habit.

Boxes lined the wall and a flat-screen TV hung above them. Willa hadn't had one in her living room, but it fit perfectly in that location. The kitchen looked the same, but without the glass jars full of herbs. A coffee pot and a towel were the only things out, but it still felt comfortable.

"Your kitchen isn't unpacked, but the TV is on the wall?" she teased him. "Your priorities are all wrong."

"Hey, I got all this boxed up and out of my old place. It was a busy day."

"Sounds like it."

A comfortable leather couch sat in the living room, but there was no table in the small dining room. Instead, he'd set a couple of crates upside down with a sheet of plywood on top of them.

"Nick." He pointed at the board.

"I'm glad you didn't leave town," she confessed.

He frowned. "I told you I wasn't going to."

"A lot's changed. I was worried."

"You shouldn't be worried about that." His hand drifted up her arm, and his thumb rubbed her shoulder. "Would you like a glass of wine?"

"Only one." She held up a finger, laughing. She didn't intend to mess up wherever this was heading, like she had in Liberty. "To toast your new place."

He moved into the kitchen, rifling through a box, then another, and finally produced two glasses and a bottle. "I need a corkscrew."

"Oh!" Reaching in her back pocket, Nell produced a bottle-opener-corkscrew combo. It always paid to be prepared in case the bartender was knee-deep in customers and she had to jump in. She held out a hand for the bottle. "Old habits die hard."

"You've worked all day. Let me."

She passed him the tool, and he made quick work of the cork before pouring the wine and handing her a glass.

It was nice being waited on.

"To a prosperous business." She held up her drink. "And many happy memories in your new place."

He clinked his glass to hers, holding her eyes with his as he took a sip.

Nell wandered into the living room, poking at the bookshelf in the corner. Novels by Neil Gaiman, R.A. Salvatore, and Terry Pratchett graced the shelves. "I didn't know you were a sci-fi, fantasy fan."

"There's a lot you don't know about me." He winked at her, following her exploration with interest.

The extra bedroom was overflowing with boxes, but his bathroom looked fairly set up.

"I'm going to use the extra room for storage right now. I might need it for things that are posted online. I haven't figured it out yet."

Finally, she poked into his bedroom.

A large bed with a thick, heavy frame sat against the far wall, next to the window overlooking the cove, and a dark navy pillow and blanket covered tit. The window was cracked open to let the cool breeze in. A dresser sat across from it, with boxes stacked in front of it.

He'd taken more time on his room instead of the kitchen. He'd need it if he planned on staying the night.

She suddenly realized they were alone in his place, and heat flared up her neck. And since she still had her hair in its ponytail, she knew it was visible. *Way to be obvious, Nell,* she chided herself.

Emiliano caught her gaze.

"I'm not expecting anything, Nell. I was just hoping for some more time with you." He shifted his body toward the living room. "We can sit there or out on the back deck with the wine."

But she didn't want to.

She'd missed out at the hotel and didn't want to again. She wanted this.

"Maybe I want it." The words came out in a whisper. She was barely able to keep the question out of the phrase, and she could feel her face flush further and her eyes widen with uncertainty as she found his.

He stood still. "Are you sure? I want you to be sure."

She hesitated, then took a large gulp from her glass before setting it down on the dresser. Her knees moved stiffly.

"Nell, we don't have to do this. There's no rush." He reached for her, catching her elbow in his hand.

"No." She looked up into his eyes. Just being near him sent her pulse off the scales. But she didn't know how to start things. She considered throwing herself at him, but that felt all sorts of wrong. "I want this. I just need to... I'd like to wash up first. Is that okay? It's been a long day."

"Of course."

Before she could change her mind, she unbuttoned her jeans and wriggled out of them, pulling her T-shirt over her head and dropping it on the floor before looking up at him. He stood like a statue, his chest rising and falling heavily.

"Are you coming?" she threw over her shoulder and headed to the bathroom. She'd barely caught his grin, but it bolstered her nerves.

He'd caught up to her by the time she had the water turned on. She noticed he'd stripped off his jeans and T-shirt, but had left his boxer briefs on as she had her bra and panties.

His lightly tanned skin looked kissed by the sun. The stretchy fabric of his underwear hugged his muscled physique, and her fingers itched to touch him, but her stomach was still in her throat.

Immediately, she wanted to cover herself. Why did bathroom lights make people look washed out, highlighting bulges and wrinkles? But not on Emiliano.

He stood there, patiently waiting for her, his eyes never straying from hers.

Steam built in the room. Glancing back at the water, she touched it and found it hot. As she adjusted it, she couldn't bring herself to strip completely nude in front of him. Not without the inhibition of alcohol. Was that a bad sign?

So she simply stepped in, underwear and all.

Without a word, he followed suit.

Leaning into the spray, she burrowed her face in it, hiding from what she wanted. Just for a moment. Lathering the soap he had on the shelf, she washed the day from her face, letting the water run down her back. She gathered her courage. She was older, but he wanted her; he'd told her enough times. Maybe she should just believe him. Maybe she wasn't as worn down as she t hought.

When she turned, she saw what she needed. His breathing was ragged, and his eyes were attempting to stay on hers. He was trying, but failing. And she noticed the bulge in his briefs soaked in water.

It filled her with encouragement, relief, and a little bit of power. She needed the confidence boost.

Reaching a hand behind her, she unsnapped her bra, turned around, and slid it down her arms, swinging it over the shower rod and looking over her shoulder. "Help me wash?"

He nodded wordlessly. Taking the soap, he ran his lathered hands over her skin, his fingertips tracing sensual lines down the center of her back. He stopped at her underwear as though it was a line she'd drawn. His hands moved up and over her shoulders and down her arms.

She turned, and he clutched her, locking eyes with her, and she nodded. He dropped his gaze to her chest then, as his own rose and fell faster. Lathering his hands again, he paused over her breasts, then taking them into his palms, he circled them. His thumbs flicked over her nipples, sending a jolt of white heat to her core, and she gasped.

His fingers trailed down her stomach, circling around her belly button and stopping at the waistband of her panties.

Pulling at her underwear, she slid them down. Heat lit like fire in his eyes, and she took the soap from him, quickly washing her underarms and between her legs. She wasn't ready for that.

"Your turn?" She stepped aside.

Emiliano blinked to clear his mind and moved under the stream, his hand reaching for the nob to cool the water, then he leaned into it. As it ran down his back, it travelled around his muscles in long rivulets. It was fascinating.

Nell reached out to touch him, but stopped. "May I?"

He looked back over his shoulder at her, his eyes dark with desire, and he nodded.

With the soap, she lathered her hands and let them explore his back. His skin was so soft and firm. Running her fingers down his sides, she leaned into him for a moment before turning him around and looking up at him, her nails tracing a slow, lazy pattern up his chest, learning his body.

He hooked his underwear, pulled them down, and dropped them behind her, in the tub.

Nell's eyes drifted down. She hadn't seen a naked man in such a long time. Soaping up her hands again, she slid them down the length of him, coating him in bubbly foam. Her fingers wrapped around him, cupping his balls and wiggling the soap around them.

Emiliano caught her hand, and her breath caught in her throat.

"I don't think I can handle that." He exhaled quickly and pulled back. He'd made quick work of finishing to clean and rinse, then turned off the shower.

The age-old pleasure of taking a man to his knees settled like a mantle over her shoulders. Not wanting to wait any longer, she stepped out of the shower and silently dried off, handing him his towel.

She knew what came next, and although she wanted it…

"Can I have a moment in the restroom?" she asked.

"Of course." He wrapped the towel around his waist and left her the room.

Emotion welled up within her. It was what she wanted, but it would also be the first time she'd let someone other than Gary touch her like that. It wasn't a small thing.

She buried her face in her hands and breathed. Standing, she opened the door and walked out to find the young man who'd made her heart beat again.

CHAPTER 20

Hearing footsteps behind him, Emiliano set down the phone he'd plugged in to charge and turned to face Nell. He still felt unsure about the whole thing. Deep down, he was worried she'd change her mind.

Her taking time in the bathroom to cool off and think through what they were doing was a good thing. If she didn't want to right now, it would be fine. They could still take their time with each other. He was more than okay with that. The flirting had been fun.

Nell leaned against the doorframe, watching him. She smiled and dropped the towel she'd been holding against her chest. Relief filled him. If she still wanted it, who was he to argue? It wasn't in the heat of passion, and she wasn't inebriated.

It was good enough for him.

Untucking the edge of his towel, he let it fall as he walked to her. Reaching for her, he took her in his arms gently, softly. The way she responded was nothing short of extraordinary. She lifted her face to him, and their lips met, hotter than before.

Their damp skin grew warm as the heat built between them. She was breathing heavily, but then again, so was h e.

He buried his hands into her hair, turning her head to kiss her neck. He tried to slow down, to calm the building excitement, but all he could hear was the thump of his heartbeat in his ears. That and the sound of her moan.

His fingertips ached to explore all her soft skin. He needed to get his hands on her. Walking forward, he backed her to the foot of the bed. Mid kiss, she climbed on, then broke free as she slid back across his bedspread. The look she shot him was pure feminine devilment. And, boy, did he love seeing it on her face.

He leaned over the soft mattress, crawling up to her. He could feel her eyes on his frame, her breath caught in her throat, and he knew she was taking pleasure in the view. It might be vain, but he was enjoying it. As he moved over her, he paused, nearly undone by the sight of her naked body underneath him. She wriggled in anticipation.

Shifting up onto her elbows, she caught his mouth with hers, and he bent into the kiss, giving her everything he could to show her how much she meant to him. Her knees wrapped around his hips, pulling him closer, but it was too soon. He wanted more. More time, more exploration.

Edging down, he nuzzled a breast, his hand spreading across her rib cage, feeling her breath rise and fall raggedly as he took her nipple into his mouth, licking the tip of it. She cried out and gripped his head with her hands. He drew back to taste her other one and then traced kisses along her collarbone and down the middle of her chest.

Nearing her center, he looked up at her. She panted, pulling him closer. It was the only encouragement he needed. Using his tongue to gently part her, he slid in and up. She moaned and wrapped her heels behind his back, pressing in as he lavished her until he couldn't hold back any longer.

Rising, he kissed her thighs and stomach and looked down at her. Her lips were swollen, and she was shaking with need. She was a vision.

"Please." Her fingers dug into his shoulder.

"Are you sure?"

"Of course, I'm sure." She raised an eyebrow at their naked, sweaty forms.

"That doesn't mean we have to."

"I'm well aware of that." She leaned up and glanced around his room. "Do you have protection?"

He dipped his head in confirmation, sliding from the bed and flipping the top of a box open across the room. He'd made sure he had some, not knowing when she'd be ready. He didn't want to be unprepared. Hopefully, that didn't make him an ass.

Gaze locked with her, he put it on and moved back over her. He waited a beat, in case she had any reservations and changed her mind, but she pulled him closer, and he slid home.

It felt like home.

It was overwhelming. The feel and smell of Nell wrapped around him was something he'd had wet dreams of as a kid. And as he grew older, they'd transformed, growing more adult and full of respect, but the want never changed.

He'd felt guilty about it, of course, especially since he respected Gary so much. So, he'd kept his distance out of preservation and admiration of their relationship.

Things had changed.

Here, moving over her, inside her, hearing her mewls of enjoyment, he felt like he was truly home for the first time.

He held back until he could hear her pleasure building, then he let go, let all his hopes and dreams spill out of him as he tumbled over.

What felt like a million years later, he rolled to the side, pulling her into the crook of his arm. She snuggled in close, wrapping her arm around him.

"I really needed that," she whispered.

He saw a tear drop from her eye and run down her cheek.

"You okay?" He wiped it away.

She nodded. "It's just been so long."

She nuzzled in closer, tucking her head.

Running his hand down her still-wet hair, he pulled her nearer to his chest. As they cooled from their lovemaking, their damp skin left a chill. Using his other arm, he dragged a blanket folded at the foot of the bed over them.

She dozed off for a while, and he stroked her back, enjoying having her in his bed, in his arms.

A little while later, she stirred, and her arm trailed over his chest, playing with the few hairs lining the center.

"I should go." Her voice was barely more than a whisper.

"You don't have to." He kissed the top of her head. "You could stay."

Please stay.

"I really shouldn't." She pulled away, sitting up, her hair falling over her shoulder. "I have to get up early."

He'd already set his alarm, just in case, but he wasn't going to try to talk her into it if she didn't want to.

"Tomorrow is brunch," she said in explanation. She made a special Sunday brunch menu that people waited all week for.

"Are you free Monday?" He didn't want to sound impatient, but he was. He had to know when he'd see her next. Hold her in his arms again.

"I think so." She smiled. "I told the crew I'd meet up with them at some point, but I'll text you, okay?"

"Of course."

She leaned into him and kissed him soundly. Her hand moved from his chest to his shoulder before pulling back. "I need to go before I talk myself out of it."

He'd be okay with that, but he respected her choice. Following her out of the bed, he wrapped the towel around his waist.

Then she disappeared out of the bedroom, returning with her soaking-wet bra and underwear. "I guess I'm going to go commando."

"I'll get a bag for those." He brushed past her, running a hand across her back, and rummaged in his bare kitchen for a plastic bag. Returning with it, he held it out for her.

"Thanks." She pulled her shirt over her head and straightened it over the jeans she'd already put on. "I left my jacket around here somewhere."

"I think it's on the couch," he said, leaving to find it. "It's going to be a little chilly. Do you need something warmer?"

"Nah, I'll be fine." She rose on tiptoe to kiss his lips.

"I'll walk you home."

He hadn't expected her to leave so quickly. He'd hoped to hold her longer, but if she was leaving, he needed to throw some clothes on.

"No need."

"Nell, it's getting late."

"It's only down the beach. What could go wrong?"

He raised his eyebrows, knowing they both remembered having criminals in their sleepy town just a few months back.

"But, seriously. I'll be fine." She tugged her jacket on. "I'll text you when I get in, okay?"

The thought of losing her to something stupid like a drunk driver or a deranged criminal did not sit well with him, but they'd barely got together. She was used to being on her own for a while now.

"Be careful, okay?"

"Okay." She pressed her lips to his once more and left via his back deck, the same way they'd entered.

Ignoring the cold, he stepped out. The cool, salt-water-misted wood felt rough underfoot. She waved, a wide, sloppy grin on her face that made his heart swell.

He stood there until he saw her in the lights of the parking lot he knew was just beyond her café. Feeling better, he went back inside and locked the door. Running a hand over his head, he sighed, plopping down on the one real piece of furniture in his living room. The leather enveloped him, inviting him to rest.

His phone pinged in the bedroom, and the corner of his mouth edged up in a smile. She was home safe.

Ignoring the call of the couch, he shoved himself to his feet and headed to the bathroom to brush his teeth and go to bed. He'd clean their wineglasses tomorrow.

Nell's toast rang in his head. His first night in his new place felt like it was setting the stage for a new phase of life.

Boy, was he ready to embrace it.

The sound of his phone jerked Emiliano awake. Only, it wasn't the alarm; it was a phone call.

"Nell?" He answered his cell, all at once worried about her.

"Emiliano, it's Conrad Brooks," the farmer's voice said.

In his half-asleep panic, he hadn't seen the name on his screen. Checking the time, he saw it was very early morning.

"What's wrong, Conrad?" The man wouldn't have called him this early if something wasn't wrong.

"It's not locusts. At least, I don't think it is."

"Locusts?"

"I thought it was locusts on the property, and that smug little scientist pissed me off, but he was right. There'd be more signs."

"Sorry, I'm not following you." Emiliano rubbed his eyes, blinked hard, and got out of bed. He needed coffee, and fast.

"I'm sorry if I woke you, but I need another damned camera," the man hissed out. He could hear him stomping around outside. "Better make it two."

"Two more cameras?" Emiliano asked. "What's happened?"

"I'm losing more crops," he growled out. "Whatever's getting in is sneaky."

"Definitely not a bear, then?"

"No, it couldn't be. We had some rain last week, and I still haven't seen any definable tracks. The place isn't fully protected. An animal could get over the fence or get in through a loose section, although I've been looking for anything not fully secure. But I should be able to catch some kind of activity on the camera. So I need more cameras. I must not be looking in the right place."

He'd only ordered an extra one before leaving, but he didn't think it had arrived yet. It was due any day.

Briefly, he considered telling him he didn't work for Gil's anymore and didn't have his shop live quite yet. But he couldn't leave the man hanging. Not with how stressed he was. "You got it."

"Can you see if you can put a rush in on them again? I'd pay extra."

He could ask Duke again. Mentally, he tried to figure out how he'd charge it through the store so his dad got his markup while still getting it done quickly through Duke. This was going to be more complicated than he'd have imagined.

"Sure, let me see what I can do."

"Thanks," Conrad huffed out and ended the call.

Emiliano stood in the center of his room—his own room—and settled back into himself long enough to revel in the realization that it was his first morning in his own place. He considered getting back into bed, but coffee was now calling him, so he pulled on a pair of gray pajama bottoms and made his way out to the kitchen.

Riffling through boxes, he finally found the coffee beans and his grinder. He carried it to the kitchen, plugged it in next to the coffeepot, and let it whir. Soon, the invigorating aroma filled the air.

Sighing in pleasure, he let the domestic motion lull him into contentment. Stealing a cup from the pot, he padded into the living room, slid open the sliding glass doors, and stepped out onto the cold planks to look over the cove. The cool air slid over his bare chest and back, but he didn't care.

He took a sip of the scalding-hot elixir. It was perfect.

He'd had a decent view from his loft above the garage, but this was so much closer. He could make out the orca pod on this side of the cove. Their dorsal fins cut through the water, causing long ripples to cascade across the calm surface. A nose popped up from the clear blue waves, and he had a good view of its black-and-white head. Its blunt nose dipped in and out of the sea.

They were incredible creatures. Lifting his mug in salute, he took another sip. The orca dipped its head under the water and back up, almost as though it was returning the salute.

He blinked. No way was the orca communicating with him, let alone nodding at him across the distance. Shaking his head, he went back inside. Apparently, he hadn't had enough coffee yet to function properly.

But he didn't need too much brain power to unpack. Sitting on the ground, he pulled a box closer to him and started taking things out.

After getting a few more kitchen items out and finishing another cup of coffee, he decided he'd done enough to make a quick breakfast and head out. He needed to talk to Duke early, in case he was headed out.

After frying up a quick pan of eggs and toast—all he had on hand at the moment—he got dressed and headed out.

Taking the back door, Emiliano walked along the beach to the marina, turning to smile warmly at The Wild Café sitting peacefully on the coastline. Nell would be up by now, but it was too early for the doors to be opened.

Stepping onto the dock, he followed the rope down to the boats. The smell of pine tar and crisp morning saltwater in the air erased any final dregs of sleep lingering in him.

He stopped at Duke's slip, looking at his large vessel bobbing in the waves. It was early. He was probably awake, but it might not be a good idea to jump on board and set him off. They were just entering a friend zone.

Rethinking his tactic, he pulled his phone out and called Duke, instead. The man answered on the second ring.

"Ugh, it's early."

Maybe not a morning person.

"Sorry, I wanted to catch you before you headed out for the day. In case you were making a run to Seattle."

"I am, but I'm not leaving for another hour or two. When I fully wake up."

Emiliano chuckled. "Late night?"

"You can count on it," came his groggy reply.

"Ah, okay. Well, I can talk to you later, then."

"Oh, hell. What do you need?" He could hear the man move around and the groans of a mattress.

"Two more game cams. Conrad's still having issues and not finding a solution."

"No problem. I'm going up to Victoria Island today, but I can swing by Seattle."

"Unless there's a shop on the island."

"It'll be cheaper in Seattle." Duke stopped talking for a moment, then added dryly, "You're here, aren't you?"

Feeling sheepish, he turned to gaze out over the cove, as if staring at his ship was too personal. The orcas were still there, looking back at him. One was closer than the others. It lifted its head and blinked, as though listening to his conversation.

That was weird.

What was weirder still was the scar on the orca's face. A memory tickled the back of Emiliano's brain. It was like he'd seen that scar before elsewhere, but he couldn't quite recall it.

"Yeah. I was going to stop in, but then thought better of it and called." Emiliano turned away from the orca, trying to focus on the conversation at hand.

"Smart move." Duke yawned. "I'll be out in a second. You can come on board and wait."

Emiliano repocketed his phone and gingerly stepped over the line Duke had stretched across the entry. Making his way down the stairs, he found a spot on the starboard side to watch the water while he waited. The orca was still there.

A few minutes later, Duke walked out, scratching his head. His hair was sticking up in the back, and he pawed at it, taming it and tucking the longer strands behind his e ars.

"You're up early." He walked over to a bench and plunked down on it.

"No earlier than normal." Emiliano shrugged. "Work to do."

"Little bird says you left Gil's." Duke placed one ankle over a knee and yawned widely.

"News travels fast." He dropped onto the bench across from Duke.

"So you don't exactly have work to do."

"I have a lot of planning."

"But that's not why you're up early, is it?" Duke narrowed his eyes.

It felt like he could see straight into Emiliano's soul.

"Um, well, actually, it was Conrad. He called a couple of hours ago, and I couldn't go back to sleep."

"Ah." Duke rubbed his eyes and blinked, still waking up. "Crazy farmer hours."

"That's not what you were asking, though, is it?" Emiliano decided to level with the man. He knew Duke had seen what passed between him and Nell the night before.

"Not really."

Emiliano pressed his lips together, deciding on what to say. "You know I care about her."

"I do."

"I only want the best for her. That's the truth. If that's not me, so be it."

"Okay."

"And I'm not telling you what happened last night. That's Nell's story to tell."

Duke nodded slowly. "You told me enough."

"I wasn't saying—" Emiliano began, but Duke caught him off.

"Hang on." He held his hands up. "I just mean that you told me what I needed to know. Thank you. She means a lot to us."

"She means a lot to me too. Everything."

"So how can I help your new business?" Duke stretched his arms across the bench and leaned his head back, taking in the sun, which had decided to grace them that morning.

"My business?" His mind whirred with possibilities. He hadn't even thought about it, but it made sense to work with the courier. He wasn't about to miss an opportunity like this. "I'd like to pay you to make the occasional pickup or delivery across the water. Like you're doing for Conrad. Maybe either way. If that sounds like something you'd be interested in."

"It's what I do."

He was elated. This meant he could deliver farther and faster. "I'll give you a good cut from the sale, or a flat fee, whichever you prefer."

"A flat fee works better."

"I'll come up with a proposal and add time or mileage depending on distance. I'll make it worth your while."

"I know you will. I wouldn't do it otherwise." The look he shot Emiliano was full of cocky satisfaction. Not in a mean way, but just as a fact. It also reminded him of Shelby.

He considered himself a self-assured guy, at least where looks were concerned, but Duke's level of confidence vastly outweighed his.

Before he could figure out how to respond, Duke's phone rang again.

"Ah, hell." The older man stretched to retrieve it from his back pocket. "Willa?"

Emiliano watched him listen to his friend then frown and stand up, looking back toward the shore. Something was definitely wrong.

"Does Nell know?" he asked Willa through the phone. "Okay, thanks for the heads up. I'll talk to her."

"What happened?" Emiliano asked Duke as soon as he hung up.

The courier pursed his lips, still staring at The Wild Café. "Mary's sick again."

"Mary Johnson?" He'd nearly had to stop himself from asking if it was Mary, Mary, Quite Contrary. They weren't kids anymore. "Is she okay?"

He shrugged. "Not sure yet. Willa's on it, though. I have faith in her."

"And Nell?" He didn't understand why Duke needed to tell her.

"She was Gary's great aunt or something."

Vaguely, he remembered that. It made sense Nell would want to know, but his body language said there was more.

"Duke, what is it?"

The taller man turned to him. "She's not the only one. Five in total. Three are being rushed to the Hood Canal Medical Center. They think it was something they ate."

"And they all ate at the café last night." Dread settled over Emiliano like a dank blanket.

Duke's head moved up and down in confirmation. "That's it."

"After last time, she's going to take this hard."

"She is."

If the townspeople hadn't already started the rumor mill that it was coming from the café, it wouldn't be long until everyone heard about it.

"She should hear it from people who care about her."

"I agree." Duke blew out a short exhalation. "Wanna go with me?"

Emiliano nodded. "Yeah."

She'd need all the support she could get.

CHAPTER 21

Sunlight filtered through the windows to settle on Nell's face. Her toes extended, and her arms went overhead in a big stretch that felt incredibly good. Her right foot drifted across the bed to find no one was there. Frowning, she reached out and found a cold blanket. Gary must have already gotten up to start the coffee.

She froze. Realization hit her like a blast of oven steam to the face. The reel of his passing away flitted through her mind on fast-forward.

She was alone.

Then, the night before lit up her mind like a hyper-saturated film. Emiliano's touches, his mouth, his body moving against hers. Their sounds as they'd moaned and delighted in each other. She wanted to hide her face. From what? She wasn't sure, but it felt taboo and wrong.

He was so different from Gary. Things had always been fun, light, and carefree with Gary. Emiliano was so much more serious. The sex had been more intense and focused.

Nell sat up in bed, trying to figure out what to feel. It was thrilling, but out of the norm and uncomfortable. That couldn't be good, could it? Getting out of bed, she quickly pulled the sheets and gray blanket up, her hands straightening them and making them as crisp and sorted as possible. Part of her wished it had been just like it was with Gary. Easy, relaxed, safe, how she'd remembered it fe eling.

But he wasn't Gary.

She remembered when Gary brought home the heavy charcoal blanket that lay on their bed. She'd wanted a big fuzzy one to curl up with on cold nights. He liked to bring it out to the living room to cover them both on movie nights so they could snuggle. She'd press her cold feet against his legs, and he'd tease her that he was married to a vampire. Her lips curled up at the memory. And when she'd pull away, he'd tug her back, wrapping her feet in his ever-warm hands until they were no longer icy.

"What am I doing?" she said aloud, hanging her head over the bed, hands digging into the soft fibers.

She shook her head, feeling ashamed for wanting more, wanting something different. Detached, she moved to dress, a tight knot swirling in her stomach.

Walking into her little upstairs kitchen, she vaguely noticed the coffeepot in the corner. She hadn't used it in some time. It made more sense to go to the main kitchen below. It was only her, after all.

"Don't take my job!" Gary used to swat her away, pretending to be offended. "It's one of the few I have."

Which they both knew was crazy. He'd spend the rest of the morning at their kitchen table, doing books and working through business contracts and costs while she was prepping for the day. Then, later, he'd come down for breakfast and a kiss and tell her what he was going to be off doing. Generally, some sort of work or repair on the café. He was the best handyman in town.

Things had been easier then. Luckily, she had Nick for that sort of thing now. And a few plumbers and electricians saved to her phone's contact list for when the occasional emergency arose.

She took the stairs down, her tennis shoes falling heavily on the wood planks.

Heading to her kitchen, her hand paused on the polished barn beam, like it did most mornings. She looked out over the dining room in the front, remembering how much work Gary had put into it. So many layers of polyurethane on the floors. So much sanding to the old shiplapped walls. He'd replicated it when they built the back dining room.

The heavy wooden beams lining the corners of the kitchen and restrooms separating the front and back dining rooms had been put up by Gary and Duke when they were adding to the place.

Her eyes glanced up where she knew the symbol had been carved. TLA. Gary had engraved the three letters, standing for True Love Always, and the heart that framed them on the beam next to her kitchen so she'd see it every day.

The first time she'd noticed it, she was royally pissed, thinking he'd messed up the beautiful wood with some sort of silly etching. He had an interesting sense of humor. It wasn't until she got a better look that she realized what he'd done for her. It was a daily reminder of how they'd gotten here and what this place meant to them.

He'd loved her so much. They were home for each other. They'd been young high-school sweethearts, finding love in each other, and had been certain they were soul mates. When her parents left town, they'd clung to each other even more, becoming each other's worlds. And their crew, their little makeshift family, Gary had helped put together.

He'd kept them connected, checking in on everyone like the dad of the group. No one felt alone when Gary was there.

Tears streamed down her face. How had she forgotten that? How could she sully their memory with someone else? Especially someone so different. Gary had put everything into this place to make a life for them.

Sliding down the wall, she sat heavily on the floor and cried into her hands. It felt so shameful that she'd tried to replace him. No one could ever fill his shoes. She missed Gary with every fiber of her being.

Sniffling, she eventually dragged herself off the floor, pushing one foot in front of the other, like she had done so many mornings before, trying to make herself keep going, if only to prevent The Wild Café, the symbol of their life, from going under.

"All you have to do is start brunch. That's all you have to do." She could still hear his voice play in her head. The single task was something she could focus on as she was forced to watch Gary's body fail him. He knew she needed t hat.

She started coffee first, then got ingredients out. Quiche would be good and an easy feature for Sunday. She sniffled again and pulled out morels, asparagus, and some smoked Gouda she'd picked up from a local cheesemaker on the peninsula. Maybe she should make a second one. She liked her sun-dried tomato, pesto, and pepperoni one too.

But it seemed like too much work today.

She wiped her eyes on her sleeve and tied her apron around her waist. First, she had to get the bacon and sausage out, plus eggs for avocado toast.

She needed to get a grip on herself. Carlos would be here soon to help prep. She should probably have him slice the smoked salmon. She didn't need all her customers going home depressed and weepy.

A knock sounded at the back door. Crap, Carlos was early. She hadn't gotten herself together yet. Sniffling heavily, she blew her nose and peeked at the small mirror she kept on her cabinet. Ugh, her eyes were red.

She'd have to tell him she was having a rough day. She hadn't had one in a while, but he wouldn't question it. He'd give her space.

Heading out to let him in, she stopped short. Emiliano and Duke stood at her back-deck door. She wasn't ready to see him yet, and his bright eyes died when they noted her body language and red eyes. He took a step back and glanced at Duke.

Making her feet move, she hung her head, unlocked the back door, and stepped aside so they could enter. She couldn't meet Emilano's gaze.

"What's wrong?" Duke asked.

"Nothing." She shrugged it off, taking another step away. "Just a rough morning."

She hoped he'd leave it at that.

"Did you talk to Willa?" Duke asked.

"Willa? No." She sniffed again, wiping her nose with the back of her hand. "Is something wrong with Willa?"

Duke frowned, looking from her to Emiliano. Her eyes flicked to the man whose bed she'd been in the night before. Whose body she'd enjoyed, although she'd promised herself to another man. A man who'd loved her fiercely, leaving her with a place of security when he passed. Shame filled her.

Emiliano's eyes were tight at the corners, and his shoulders tensed. She dropped her gaze to the clogs she'd changed into when she got to her kitchen.

"What's going on here?" Duke demanded, turning to Emiliano.

"Nothing." Nell grabbed Duke's arm. "It's just me. What's wrong with Willa?"

If she focused on that, she wouldn't see the hurt in Emiliano's eyes.

"It's not Willa." Duke didn't move. "It's Mary. She's sick."

"Mary?" Panic laced her chest. The older woman hadn't been close to anyone since Gary's mom, her cousin and only real friend, passed away. "Is she...okay?"

Duke shrugged. "I'm not really sure. Willa's with her, though."

"That's good." It was a big relief. Her friend could heal anybody. If only she'd been able to when Gary was still alive. It wasn't fair. Then again, they wouldn't have been in that water if it hadn't been for him. "She'll figure it out."

"Probably, but that's not all, Nell." Duke took her arms in his hands.

It wasn't a good sign. She heard her voice turn shaky as she asked, "What happened?"

"Several people fell sick last night."

Her stomach tightened again. She felt like she was going to throw up. "There's some bug passing around. Lots of people have been getting sick."

"Five more last night. And right after they ate here." Duke's jaw was set. It was serious.

"They..." She took a shaky breath in. "They think it's because of me, of the restaurant?"

The restaurant. She couldn't lose it. She pulled away and pressed her forehead against the smooth, worn wood of the barn beam. She could feel Gary's presence here.

A warm hand laid across her back. It was Duke. "It'll be okay, Nell."

"How will it be okay?" She sobbed. "I made everyone sick."

"Even if you did, you'll fix it."

"But what if I can't? What if I can't cook safely anymore?" It was her real fear. Cooking was her only real purpose in life.

"We'll figure it out. Later today. All of us together."

Nell nodded, turning around. "Let me know what time Willa can get away."

She'd be busy with the townspeople, doing whatever she could.

"Sure thing."

"I won't be cooking today anyway," she said bitterly.

"It's only temporary." Duke gave her shoulder a firm grip, forcing her to look at him.

"Sure." She only halfway believed it.

Emiliano stood on the back deck, having left them to talk.

When Duke walked out, his movements fast and focused, Nell hurried to follow. Emiliano didn't need Duke's anger at something he didn't do.

"What happened?" Duke stepped into Emiliano's space. "You need to tell me."

Emiliano looked at her, his lips pressed, then addressed Duke. "It's private."

"Duke." She got between them. "He didn't do anything wrong."

She gulped. He'd done nothing she didn't want at the time.

Duke's eyes narrowed, moving from her to him and back to her. "You two need to talk, then. Figure your shit out."

He turned and banged down the back steps, stalking into town, presumably to find Willa.

They were alone on her deck. Emiliano's back was tense, and she could feel him staring at her although she wasn't meeting his gaze.

"What happened?" he finally said, his voice soft with pain.

She hung her head. "I don't think I was ready."

"Dammit, Nell." He turned and paced to the edge of the deck. "You said you were. I told you we could take it slow."

"I know. I was wrong." She wrung her hands. "I'm so sorry."

He ran his fingers through his hair and stared up at the clouds. "So we take it slower. We go back to friends and see how it goes."

"I don't know, Emiliano." She shook her head as tears welled up. "I'm not sure I can do this. I had the love of my life. Maybe that's all we get."

Emiliano exhaled quickly. He turned and headed to the stairs, his feet heavy and fast.

"I'm so sorry," she called after him.

He paused at the top of the stairs. His voice was barely over a whisper. "Me too."

Then he was gone.

"How can you eat at a moment like this?" Maggie asked Shelby, frowning.

"Sorry?" Shelby looked around the group, sitting inside the rear dining room at The Wild Café. "It's good."

Her tall, dark-haired friend had raided her upstairs kitchen and found leftover scallop fettuccine with the pickled sea purslane Willa had brought up a couple of nights before.

Nell hadn't wanted to sit outside, in everyone's view. Her friends told her she didn't need to worry about it, but she knew what they were all thinking. Especially after the health inspector came by. She had looked pained to give her the slip of paper, but at least she hadn't tried to talk about it.

"Are you sure you should eat that?" Nell asked for the second time. She didn't want Shelby to get sick on top of everyone else.

"I'm telling you." Shelby raised her fork and used it to punctuate her words. "You didn't make anyone ill."

"People have been getting sick on and off for months," Nell argued. It was the only thing that made sense.

"People are always catching bugs," Maggie said encouragingly.

"True," Willa spoke up. "But not like this."

Maggie elbowed her herbalist friend.

"Sorry." Willa leaned forward to lay a hand on Nell's arm. "I'm just trying to figure out what caused it, so we can fix it."

"I know," Nell mumbled, feeling even worse than before.

"When did this new wave start?" Nick stood at the head of the table, a notebook in hand.

"From what I can tell, Monty got sick two days ago." Willa tilted her head, staring up at the ceiling in thought. "Then Beatrice and that new guy at the hardware store."

"Paul," Duke said.

"That's right."

"Do we know they all ate at the café?" Nick asked.

Nell winced. "Monty had the salmon chowder. Beatrice had the scallop pasta."

"This scallop pasta?" Shelby lifted her bowl.

Nell nodded.

Her friend swallowed and set the bowl down.

"And Paul had the lentil sloppy joes," Nell finished.

"That's not from the ocean," Nick said.

"I added purple laver to it." Nell laid her head on the table in front of her.

"Then, last night, Mary, Todd, and Izzy got sick," Willa went on. "Plus, Ryan, Adam, and Ned."

"Izzy too?" Shelby asked. She was friends with the eccentric boutique owner. Her store was close to Siren's Song Cabins.

"Yeah, but she's already feeling better," Willa told her. "I gave them both some echinacea tincture and a garlic oxymel."

"Were you using your powers when you cooked?" Duke asked.

"Only a little." Nell's voice was whiny even to her own ears. "But I've been using my happy playlist."

"If it's too happy, maybe they're having some sort of heart arrhythmia," Nick hypothesized.

"No, they're vomiting and have headaches," Willa said, filling them in on their symptoms.

"Could they be vomiting from an overdose of happy? Is that a thing?" Maggie asked.

"I don't think so." Willa shook her head. "That doesn't feel right."

"I've been careful," Nell said, even though she knew she hadn't been as careful as she was in the beginning. "Maybe I slipped."

"It's difficult not to use your powers when you're working on things," Willa said, coming to her aid. "Have you been feeling sick? Have you been depressed?"

Nell looked at her friend, her eyes still red-rimmed and sore from crying.

"Duh," Shelby said.

"No, not really." Nell shook her head. "Honestly, until this morning, I was doing pretty well."

"I thought you seemed happier." Maggie smiled.

Nell saw Duke stand at the edge of the crew, his arms crossed. She'd need to give him some kind of explanation.

"What about when you cook?" Nick resumed his questioning. "What's this happy playlist do for you?"

"I make sure I'm not in a bad mood when I cook anything from the sea. I make a point of it. I clear my mind and have a few artists on the list that are always there for a good mood, Michael Bublé, Queen, Stevie Nicks." Nell ticked them off her fingers.

"Some of Stevie Nicks' songs are kinda sorrowful," Maggie said. "Maybe when you were plating their food, one of those songs came on, and it only affected them."

"That's a good point." Nick raised his pen. "Wouldn't it have been a lot more people if it was the entire dish?"

Shelby's mouth turned down as she considered the bowl in front of her before picking it back up.

"Nell only makes a little at a time, especially with the seafood. It cooks way too fast," Maggie said.

Shelby sat the bowl back down and crossed one long leg over the other, propping her chin on her hands and pouting.

"But things like the lentils would have been done earlier," Nell said. "I had a large pan of them cooked and kept warm in the drawer."

"And only around twelve people had the lentils last night," Maggie pointed out.

"Wouldn't more people be sick?" Shelby asked, eyeing the bowl.

"More people *were* sick." Willa's eyes slid from Duke's to Nell's.

"What do you mean?" Nell sat up straight.

"Some said they had a little stomachache and didn't think much about it. It's tough to know what it was," Willa explained. "Are you sure you didn't get a stomach cramp or nauseous?"

Nell shook her head. "Not at all. I felt fine. I'm sure of it."

She'd been feeling great, actually. Not that it made her feel any better.

"Is there any commonality about those who didn't get as sick?" Nick asked his girlfriend.

"They're younger and healthier, so it could be stronger immune systems." She shrugged, then looked at Nell and lowered her voice. "They also don't eat at the café as often. Sorry, Nell. I have to think through everything."

"I understand." She slid down in her seat. It felt like her world was crumbling around her. How would she cook again? What would she do for work? She'd lose the café.

"Maybe we need to do another deep clean," Maggie suggested, her eyebrows pitched up in the center and down at the corners in the sweetest expression of concern.

"We've done that several times, Maggie." Nell patted her on the back. It wasn't her fault, either. "Besides, I'm not sure people will trust us again."

"Don't be silly," Shelby said. "It's probably bad fish or something. Maybe there's something in the water."

"That's a possibility." Duke unfolded his arms and strode closer. "Percy was on the dock a few days ago. It's not like I never see him, but he's never just come up and wanted to talk. Maybe he knows something and was poking around."

"Did he seem like that?" Nick asked.

Duke shrugged. "He's hard to read."

"We can ask him," Shelby offered.

"If he comes back to shore," Duke said.

"We could ask Solomon," Maggie's eyes lit up. Now that they'd discovered the fisherman had likely been gifted magic to talk to creatures that lived in and on the water, he was a connection to the Orca-man-shapeshifter Percy. "He would know, or he could send Roy to find Percy again. And Roy loves Nell now."

"Uh-oh," Nell said, putting her hands on either side of her face.

"What?" They all turned to her at once.

"I forgot to take Roy his treat this morning." Of all mornings to forget. What if the pelican was pissed at her now? Was that possible? She hadn't seen the bird flying around the back deck, but then again, they'd made a deal that he'd wait in the parking lot.

She got up and peered out the back windows of the café, not seeing the bird.

"Maybe he forgot too?" Maggie asked at her elbow.

"One can only hope."

"What happened?" Shelby cocked her head and narrowed her eyes, catching on to something being wrong.

"I had a rough morning," Nell said, attempting to blow her off, but she shared a glance with Duke, which Shelby caught.

"What about regular food?" Nick said suddenly. "Is anyone getting sick on non-seafood dishes?"

"No." Nell shook her head, then froze. "Wait. Mary didn't get the chowder last night. She just wanted her rib eye."

"Mary eats rib eye?" Shelby asked, impressed.

"Mary's got good taste." Duke gave her a half grin.

"What sides did she have?" Nick ignored the two and pressed forward.

"Lyonnaise potatoes and asparagus," Nell said.

"Not sea asparagus?" Nick asked.

Nell shook her head. That didn't make sense. Mary had gotten sicker than the rest of them.

"Did she get a cookie?"

"Yes, but it was just a rye chocolate-chip one. I didn't do the tahini-and-seaweed this time. I was going to ask Willa for more."

"Nell." Willa's eyes went large.

"What?" Her stomach dropped even though she didn't yet know what her friend was going to say.

"Don't you use sea salt on those cookies?"

"Well, yeah, but—" The words died in her throat. How could she be so dense? All of this was useless. It wasn't just seafood related, but nearly every single thing she'd made.

All the testing and care she'd taken, and she'd been infusing foods left and right.

Thinking back, she could remember times when her hands had burned, but she'd been zoned in on cooking and wrote it off as an aftereffect. She hadn't been worried about it because Willa said she had tried to charge her hands up with algae or a mix of valerian root or something. Much to her friend's dismay, it hadn't worked. Even with the energy still pulsing in her hands, she could only charge it if she added the distilled water to the plant as it grew.

"Shit," she whispered.

"But now, we know." Maggie tugged on her. "You can be more careful with salt too. Or you can get Himalayan salt instead."

Nell shot her a look that made her pull back. "Sorry, I'm not mad at you. And those salt pits might have been oceans at one time. It might still trigger the powers. I can't avoid the sea. I'd have to move to an area that didn't have seafood on the menu and double-check every single ingredient. And who knows if that'd even do it? I might be forgetting something else. Like the salt in canned or pickled vegetables or anchovy paste in Caesar dressing."

She hadn't even considered any of those other things, except maybe the anchovy paste. It felt hopeless.

"You make all that anyway, and you don't use canned vegetables." Maggie tried to argue with her, but even her positivity was fading.

"We'll think of something," Willa said.

"Maybe just take a little time off," Shelby suggested. "You can go through your kitchen and refamiliarize yourself with anything from the sea. Take it slow and carefully. Then, after everyone is well, you plan a reopening. You can work with the winery during their summer harvest. You'll get the tourists, at least. The locals will eventually come ba ck."

"That's a good idea, Nell." Maggie mustered up a smile and patted her on the back. "It'll work. I can help you."

Nell just nodded. It was sweet that her friends wanted to help so much, but she knew she'd never be able to afford to be closed until the summer hit full swing. It just wasn't possible.

CHAPTER 22

Emiliano stared at the ceiling of his new place. Then he glared at the half-opened boxes scattered throughout the living room from his position on the sofa. Throwing a hand over his forehead, he let out a long breath.

Why was unpacking so much more tedious than packing? He'd tried to make progress, but in his anger and frustration, he'd split them open and upended them on the ground. Now, his belongings sat scattered everywhere like his emotions.

What was wrong with him? Was he just unlovable?

He'd tried to take his time with Nell. Hell, he'd slowed them down on more than one occasion, afraid of being hurt again. And yet, it had all ended the same; another woman had found him unworthy.

Nell's words sat heavily on him, pinning him to the couch.

"Maybe that's all we get." Her voice resonated in his ears. The pain still thrummed through him as fresh as when he'd received the blow.

What if she was right? She'd already had her love. He, on the other hand, had always loved her. Would it always be unrequited? Was it doomed from the beginning?

Bitter, he kicked to his feet. It wasn't going to do any good, lying about. As of yesterday, he no longer had a job. If he didn't get his shit together, he would lose his new place and be forced to go back to his dad's, tail tucked between his legs. That wasn't going to happen. He'd get a job at the gas station before he'd do that. Or maybe on one of the fishing boats. He knew all the crews. At least one of them would take him on.

Walking outside to clear his head, he took off for the beach. Instead of going down to the marina, he went past it and headed out to the jetty. He didn't want to run into Nell or Duke now. Emiliano huffed at the change of things.

He felt like he'd always been chasing after them. After being accepted.

Been there, done that. Didn't last.

It figured.

He jumped across the boulders instead of taking the gravel pathway up and around to the head of seawall. They were slippery underfoot, but anger and resentment fueled him. He dared the gods of the sea to make him come crashing down. It would serve him right if he did, though.

Muddy tennis shoes and jeans, he made it to the top and stalked out farther onto the narrow strip of rocky land separating their little cove from the rest of the Hood Canal. It was the reason the water in the cove was so calm.

A couple of people, with their fishing rods cast on the canal side, raised their hands in greeting, but he pressed on. Crunching through the gravel, he neared the end of the walkway. A large black man stood there, peering out over the water. He was wearing cut-off shorts and a T-shirt again and was barefoot, even on the rocks.

Percy, wasn't it? Emiliano shook the curiosity from him. He wasn't in any condition to be making new friends. Giving him a brief nod, the bald man's eye caught his with interest. Emiliano's brain registered the thick silver scar that ran down his face, and his foot paused mid strike as memories tumbled around in his mind.

Images overlaid one another. The detail he'd seen on the dock. The view right now, head turned. Another, more unusual, picture flashed in his mind. The orca watching him from the cove that very morning while he was talking to Duke. The angle was different, the face was different, the species was different, but the shape was undeniably the same. It hooked from where it started at the corner of his eye straight down, then squiggled back and forth in a fierce zigzag and ran down the neck to disappear under the water or, in his case, the neck of his T-shirt with the arms cut off.

And from where he stood, he could see the scar cut across his rib cage and down his side.

Emiliano's eyes flashed to Percy's, full of questions and disbelief. The corner of the other man's mouth kicked up in humor, like when you saw someone figure out something obvious but completely new.

His dad had looked at him like that when Emiliano found out they had to pay property tax on the shop and their house.

"But you own it, Pops, don't you?" he could still hear himself asking his dad, not understanding why you'd have to pay for something you owned.

"There's this thing called taxes." His dad had clapped him on his back and guided him into the office, where he'd explained things.

"It's Percy, right?" He took a step closer, focusing on the curious man instead of the ache in his heart for his frayed relationship with his pops.

The stranger nodded, humor still on his face, but he stepped forward and dove into the sea.

Shocked, Emiliano ran to the edge of the jetty, stumbling on the boulders. He slid clumsily to the water's edge as waves crashed onto his jeans, soaking him from the waist down. It was colder than he'd thought it would be.

His eyes searched the white-crested waves, looking for any sign of Percy or the scarred orca he'd seen earlier. It didn't seem possible, and his heart stopped in his chest as he looked half amazed and half hopeful to stumble upon something so fantastical, so incredible.

Moments passed, stretching to a minute or two, as he crouched, peering past the rocky boulders lining the jetty. Nothing.

Finally, motion across the water much farther out drew his attention. A dorsal fin sliced through the surface. His mouth dropped open, and he fell back on his butt.

The orca slid through the waves, turned in a wide curve, and faced him. Emiliano could see the stark white scar from this distance. He froze, waiting to see what would happen next.

The animal bobbed in the water, watching him. Then, it winked and disappeared under the water. Emiliano's head whipped around, looking for some confirmation that he wasn't hallucinating.

It wasn't totally uncommon for people to dive into the chilly waves, but they were thrill seekers or cliff divers. Only, this wasn't a cliff, and Percy didn't look like your normal crazy tourist. In fact, he was looking less like a human at all.

The closest man was bent over, baiting another hook. The next couple, a few yards down, were in deep conversation over their equipment. It seemed no one had noticed anything.

Suddenly, the orca burst from the water, sending a tall spray several feet into the air before he curled and disappeared back under the surface.

"Look at that!" the nearest man said, pausing over his bait, finally taking note of his surroundings. He shook his head. "Incredible creatures."

"Yeah," Emiliano agreed, feeling the sensation return to his face. More incredible than he'd realized.

The orca glided through the cove towards another two farther out. Emiliano slid on the rocks, got his feet underneath him, and carefully made his way back to the rocky pathway.

"You alright, son?" the fisherman asked, noticing the mud and water on his jeans.

"Yeah." He nodded, wiping his hands down his pant legs. The man's concern reawakened the emotion toiling in his chest. "I'll be alright."

Deciding to honor the words, he drew air into his lungs and headed back to the shore.

Maybe Duke or Solomon could answer some of his questions.

With a new goal in mind, he turned to the marina and scanned for the masts on Duke's ship. Seeing them, he dropped his gaze to the people walking on and off the docks, surprised when he saw Duke's tall frame stalking toward him.

The courier's eyes narrowed in anger, and Emiliano frowned.

It had been hours since they left Nell's. At that point, he'd told them to figure their shit out. He didn't feel like he was being blamed for it.

Duke pulled up to him, his jaw clenched, and Emiliano met it, lifting his head to face the slightly taller man's gaze.

"What did you do?" Duke growled.

"What is Percy?" Emiliano shot back.

The corner of Duke's eyes ticked in a quick, short motion. "It doesn't matter."

"It matters."

"Nell first."

Emiliano nodded. "She wasn't ready."

"What do you mean she wasn't ready?"

Duke drew closer, the toes of his shoes nearly touching Emiliano's. Even though Emiliano wasn't as tall or as broad as the other man, he had more functional muscle. And he was pissed enough. He'd take him on, whether or not it was really his fault.

"Do you need a definition of the word? She wasn't ready."

"And still you tried?" The words were spat out, and a vein pulsed in his forehead.

"She said she was."

"You telling me you can't tell the difference?"

"Of course I can." His hands clenched into fists. He didn't have to explain himself to the long-haired outcast. "I had no idea."

"None?" he challenged.

"None. I was sure. I told her we could wait, not that it's any of your business."

Duke's eyebrows snapped together. "Had she been drinking?"

"Not even a full glass." His words were short and clipped. He was offended Duke would even suggest a thing like that. He wanted to defend himself, but he wasn't going to recount something as personal as what they had shared. No matter what it had meant to her. "Look, you'll have to talk to her if you want details."

"I want to hear it from you."

Emiliano bit back the words he wanted to say. Instead, he settled for the only thing he was willing to share. "It was her idea. And that's all I'm saying on the matter."

The expression on Duke's face shifted from anger to assessment. He could feel the man's eyes taking in every nuance.

"So, this morning?" he said finally.

"I was as surprised as you were." He could feel his nostrils flare in embarrassment.

"I see." Duke shifted to his heels and took a single step back. The silence stretched between them. "Damn."

Emiliano broke his gaze. "Yeah."

"I guess I should ask if you're alright, then."

Emiliano could see he was serious, and not just mocking him. For the second time that morning, emotions bubbled back to the surface. He'd be damned if he would be reduced to weeping in front of the wild and free guy he'd wished he could be growing up.

"It's been a shitty day." He cleared his throat and swallowed heavily.

"I can only imagine," Duke said quieter this time. "Look, what they had—"

"I know what they had," Emiliano cut over him. "I've been watching them all my life. I've been in love with her all my life."

It was something he'd never said to another person. Duke listened without saying a word.

"I wasn't trying to take anything away from that. I respect what they had. Gary was a hell of a guy, always nice to me." Now that Emiliano had someone to listen to him, it just spilled out. "I wanted to be patient, but not miss my chance. I would have waited another year or five if that's what it would have taken. I didn't care."

"Maybe that's what you have to do," Duke said.

"No." His voice sounded distant in his ears. "It's over now."

"You don't want her anymore?"

"I, uh," his voice faltered, but he pressed his emotions down into a pit in his stomach. "She made it clear she's had the love of her life. Anything else would be a sham."

"She said that?"

He shrugged. "About as much."

"Emiliano," Duke said. "Don't lose hope. Just give her time."

"It's not about that anymore." Emiliano shook his head, pain filling his heart so much he thought it would break. "I was afraid this would happen. She doesn't want me. I'm not going to sit around like a broken puppy and hope she throws me a second-best bone. I might not have a lot of pride when it comes to her, but I don't completely hate myself."

He turned to face the water, not wanting to look at Duke.

"I see," he said gently. "I guess that's it, then."

Emiliano nodded tightly.

"Then, maybe we should talk about Percy."

He'd nearly forgotten. Glad to have another topic to focus on, he gulped in brain-clearing air and addressed Duke. "What is he?"

"*What* is he?" Duke repeated, emphasizing the first word.

"Yes, what?"

Duke cocked his head and tucked his hands in his front jean pockets. "What do you think he is?"

Emiliano crossed his arms, trying to decide what to share. Duke obviously knew, so whatever he said wouldn't shock him. "A human-orca hybrid."

"Hybrid?" Duke's eyebrows shot up.

He lifted a shoulder. "Or whatever you want to call it."

The other man's mouth turned down. "I like that fine. Honestly, I've never thought to ask him to put a name to it."

"Or a shapeshifter."

"That's a running theory as well."

Then it dawned on him. If Duke knew about it, so did the rest of them. Suddenly, all the times he'd watched the five of them talk excitedly on the back deck of the café hit a little deeper. Six, now that Nick had joined them.

Nell had known and not shared it with him. It was another reminder that he'd thought they were closer than they were.

"The criminals from Seattle?" he asked.

"What about them?"

"Were they shifters too? Is Nick?" Questions stacked one on each other.

"Not that I'm aware of." The corner of Duke's mouth eased up. "He's the only one I've met."

"But there are others?"

"That's not my story to tell, man," Duke said. "But I think so."

He'd heard of things in the area, unexplainable things. The Olympic National Park was full of believers, people who trusted in or were looking for evidence of Sasquatch. It made him wonder if that was true as well.

"That's incredible."

"That's not the word I used when I found out." Duke huffed. "How did you figure it out?"

"The scar."

"That's a pretty strong connection from a scar."

"It's pretty recognizable."

"Maybe to some."

"I know everyone in town."

Duke nodded. "It's easier to notice what doesn't fit when it stands out."

"Exactly."

The older man appraised him, then clapped him on the arm. "You'll do just fine."

"What do you mean?" Emiliano asked, shocked.

"Just in general." A grin split the other man's face. "Don't think too hard on it. Just be you."

"O-kay."

Duke laughed. The sound felt jarring after their earlier conflict and resulting emotions. "Tell me more about this new business of yours. Did you figure out what my cut's going to be?"

Emiliano blinked in astonishment.

"If we're going to be in business together, we should talk money." Duke strolled along the water, looking back at him to join him.

"Business together?" He hurried to follow.

"Maybe I want to invest in it."

"Maybe I don't need an investor." He had savings he'd been building, thinking he'd eventually buy his own place on the water. That money would go to his business now. If things went well, he'd be able to start saving again eventually.

Duke chuckled. "It depends on how big you want to take this thing."

"I honestly don't know."

The courier raised his eyebrows. "Come on, man. Let's talk."

They walked along the shoreline, tossing ideas back and forth. He still wasn't sure he wanted to share his business, a fact that made him begrudgingly understand his dad a small, minuscule amount.

"Don't let me forget to give you Conrad's game cams," Duke said suddenly.

"You got them already?"

"Between the other drama happening on the cove, I had to make a flying trip—speed things up, so to speak—but I made it."

"I'm sure he'll appreciate it. He was pretty beside himself this morning."

"I would be too if I thought something was going on around The Aurelia without me knowing about it. She's my baby."

Duke cast a fond glance over his shoulder to see the large fishing vessel-turned-cargo ship bobbing and rubbing against the bumpers on the dock.

"Is Nell going to be okay with the café?" Emiliano asked quietly.

Duke stopped and turned to him, his lips pressed into a thin line. "She doesn't know it yet, but I think so. We just have to figure out what's causing all these sicknesses."

"Maybe it's not her." He tried to think rationally without getting emotionally involved. "Nell gets most of her food from Gil's. Maybe it's a salmonella outbreak."

"That's an idea we haven't considered."

"You thought it was her?" He was shocked they had let Nell believe she was following unhygienic practices. It was unthinkable.

"Not exactly." Duke didn't elaborate.

"I know she's been a little distant lately, but I don't think she'd miss something like that." An idea struck him. "We should ask Percy."

"That's who I was looking for when I stumbled onto you. Truthfully, it was both of you."

"He would know if there was an algae or something in the water that the Washington Fish and Wildlife Service haven't found out about yet." He focused on the shifter angle.

"Solomon might know as well. He's on the water here every day."

Solomon had been talking to Percy and Duke that day on the marina. "He knows about Percy too."

Duke nodded, watching him. "He does."

The fisherman with the pet pelican. Pet pelican. More thoughts clicked together. Could he?

"Is Roy a shifter too?" The idea flashed into his mind like a bright Edison bulb, illuminated from within.

"Not that I know of."

"Is he really communicating with him?" he wondered aloud.

Duke rocked back on his heels, considering him. "I know you hate hearing it, but again, that's not my story to tell."

It was enough confirmation, though. The realization stunned Emiliano. Solomon wasn't just spending too much time alone on his boat; he had actually been gifted with the ability to talk to Roy. Maybe it was all birds. Maybe it was all animals. He had so many questions.

"I could talk to Solomon," he offered.

Duke resumed walking. "Take it one step at a time, man. Conrad first, then check into recalls and salmonella cases. The others are looking for Solomon. I'll work on Percy, then catch up with you later."

Duke's pace quickened, and he veered away.

"Later."

He stood there, stunned. Not only had he had his heart broken this morning, but he'd discovered a fantastical human-animal shifter-hybrid existed, a fisherman could communicate with a pelican, and oddly enough, Duke and he were becoming friends.

It felt like one of his sci-fi books. Each thing was as surprising and strange as the last. Except in his story, happily ever after wasn't going to happen with the girl of his dreams.

Maybe he needed new dreams.

CHAPTER 23

"I can keep looking for Solomon if you want to go back home," Maggie offered.

Nell wasn't ready to go back and see the notice posted on her front door by the health inspector.

"Closed until further notice," it read, announcing to anyone who saw it that there was something wrong with her and her café. Something unsafe that was to be avoided.

She'd officially lost her ability to cook and serve food.

They could come back and reassess her kitchen, but it would take time. It would also take her confidence that it wasn't going to make more people sick. Confidence she didn't have.

Nell shook her head even though it felt pointless to pursue this lead. "No, I need to stay busy."

"Things will work out." Maggie nudged her.

Nell attempted a flat smile and nodded. Here, her friend slash waitress was trying to make her feel better, and she was getting affected by all of this too. "I'm sorry about everything."

"What do you mean?"

The two of them turned up another block. Solomon's boat was docked for the day, so they were hoping he was at home. He had a small house behind the post office, at the end of a side street.

"I mean, it's my business, but it's your job. And now, you're out of work, too."

"Temporarily." Maggie shot her one of her winning smiles.

Her stomach felt like she'd poured vinegar inside. She needed to figure out another path for the sweet waitress. Maybe she could find her an office job, somewhere she could help people. She was good at that.

In fact, she could help Hugo out now that Emiliano had left. It would be good for Hugo to have someone like Maggie there to encourage him. She wouldn't push him out of his comfort zone, and her bright, sunny disposition might soften his edges.

She'd be better suited for Emiliano too. The sour vinegar feeling in her stomach rose to her heart, tightening and pulling at it. She was younger and sweeter. She didn't have the U-Haul worth of baggage Nell was carrying around.

Her fingers tightened around the paper box she was holding.

"I think they're home." Maggie pointed to Solomon's roof, where Roy was perched.

"Oh, good." At least something was working out. "Hi, R oy."

She wiggled her fingers at the pelican, feeling silly. It hissed loudly and hopped across the roofline. Nell didn't know how to read Pelican, but it didn't look happy.

"Look what Nell has for you," Maggie called out.

"I'm sorry I missed this morning." She opened the box and set it down on the ground. She'd cleared out her shrimp. It wasn't going to get used, anyway. "Things got a little busy."

Roy flew off the gutter, diving toward the two women. Nell jumped back with a squeak. Wide wings spread out to catch a thermal current, and it hitched up, hovering in the air for a moment. Then, beating its wings, it slowly descended right over the shrimp. It hissed again.

The large pelican turned its head, gurgled, and used its beak to scoop the shrimp up. Lifting its head, it made a sawing motion, rocking back and forth before swallowing the small shellfish. It flapped its wings happily and hopped up and down. Then, letting out a lighter hiss and chatter, it turned to the opening door.

Solomon came out, scratching his bald head. "What's going on? Oh, good afternoon, girls."

"Hi, Solomon." Maggie waved. "Nell stopped by with a treat for Roy."

"So, he was saying. He says it's apology fish."

"I forgot to leave him a treat this morning," Nell said sheepishly.

"Looks like he forgives you," Solomon said. "He's nice that way. A little fish goes a long way with him."

Nell smiled thinly at the bird, then turned to Solomon. "We were also hoping to talk to you if you had a minute."

"Sure thing." He stepped farther out, onto the concrete porch in front of his house. It was just large enough for four plastic chairs. "Let's have a seat. Do you need a drink? I made some lemonade."

"That'd be lovely." Maggie's eyes lit up.

"You don't have to go to the trouble," Nell said at the same time.

But Solomon disappeared into his house. Coming back out a few minutes later, he handed each of them a tall glass and ushered them to the chairs. "Go on, take a load off."

They complied, and Nell took a long sip of the tangy-sweet drink. It tasted like fresh lemons. She wasn't sure if it was the sugar or the icy coldness of the drink, but it improved her mood and lifted her spirits, even if only a little bit.

"Thank you," she said honestly.

He smiled broadly, grabbed a hold of the armrests, and said, "So, what's going on?"

Maggie glanced over at Nell. "You've probably heard people are getting sick in town."

He nodded. "I've heard a little."

"Many of them ate at The Wild Café recently, before they got sick." Maggie reached out and put a hand on Nell's arm in support. "Of course, most everyone in town eats at the café. And most of them like seafood. We were wondering if you've heard from anyone, Roy maybe, about sick fish or something bad in the water?"

Solomon pushed his lips out and ran his tongue up and over his teeth. "Well, I can't recall anything like that, but he did tell me to put a fish back, saying it wasn't a good one. Now, I thought maybe he was planning on going back for it himself, but it could have been something else."

He turned to the pelican, who was still hopping around the tiny postage-stamp-sized yard. The bird was currently pecking at the empty paper box as though it would produce more shrimp.

"You hear anything about that, Roy?" Solomon asked.

Roy clicked and grunted, his head ticking this way and that.

"He said no." Solomon narrowed his eyes. "What about that fish?"

The bird repeated its actions, this time spreading its wings and dropping them.

"That's what I thought!" Solomon raised a finger. "You greedy pelican!"

A peel of laughter rose from him, and he slapped his knee.

"Does he know how to get a hold of Percy?" Nell asked. "Like, where he lives?"

Solomon looked at the bird and listened again before shaking his head. "He said he could give him a message that you're looking for him, though, when he sees him next."

"I'd really appreciate it," Nell said directly to the bird. Pointless or not, at least they'd know for sure. "I think I have some extra fish I can set out for you tomorrow morning."

Now, they just had to wait and hope Percy would come find them.

Finishing their drinks, the two women thanked Solomon and Roy and made their exit.

"What should we do now?" Maggie asked her.

"I honestly don't know." Nell looked up and down the street. She wasn't used to having this much time off with nothing to do. "Maybe we should check in on Willa. See how people are doing."

She'd be back at her house by now focused on creating herbal remedies, infused with a little sea magic, to heal the townspeople of Orca Cove.

"She might use a little help." Maggie nodded, turning onto the street she lived on. "We can take my car."

"Sounds good," Nell said, even though she wasn't sure she would be of any use. She couldn't touch anything she was making without infusing it with her own tainted magic.

Maybe if they got to talk to Percy, he would know how to strip her of the curse.

It was a short drive out to Willa and Nick's place, and they found her elbows-deep in a large wooden bowl of sea purslane. "Hey, ladies! Just give me a second. I'm almost done with this."

The other bowls on the counter were full of different herbs and liquids. Nell recognized peppermint, garlic, basil, oregano, and cilantro. The other two looked like roots and a green-stemmed herb that smelled peppery and metallic. "What are these?"

"Echinacea, dandelion root, and burdock root," Willa said without looking up.

They weren't ones she'd ever cooked with. "What are they good for?"

"Echinacea helps prevent sickness from spreading. The infected cells don't multiply. Dandelion root, to detox the liver and bladder. Burdock root, to cleanse heavy metals found in the blood, since we don't definitively know what's making people sick, and help support kidney function as it cleans things out." Willa washed her hands in the sink Nick had built into her countertop and dried them on a towel.

"How's Mary doing?" Nell asked. Everyone was important to her, but she felt an obligation to the older woman with her connection to Gary.

"She's not doing very well, but I'm hoping this will help speed things up." Willa clicked the electric tea kettle that sat on her counter on.

The weight in Nell's stomach felt heavier than ever. If she had only stopped when she realized her cooking was affecting people, Mary would be okay right now.

"Hey," Maggie said, noticing her reaction. "With Willa's gifts, Mary and everyone else will be feeling better in no time."

"I hope so," Nell mumbled.

"So, as far as I can tell, there are three main groups of illnesses, with one possible outlier," Nick said, strolling into the room. His eyes were focused on the notebook in his hands. Finally noticing the two new women when he glanced up, he said, "Oh, hi, ladies."

"Hi." Maggie raised a hand in greeting.

"Three groups?" Nell said.

"Yes." He bent back over the notebook to consult it. "If we include everyone over the past few weeks, there've been twenty people with just nausea, fifteen of them had vomiting, eight of them also have diarrhea. Six people had rashes ranging in seriousness but no other symptoms. Seventeen have coughs, increased asthmatic reactions, and some chest pain. Three people are experiencing some strange twitching or nerve pain. Forty-six in all."

"Nerve pain?" Nell asked. "How is that possible?"

She thought back over the last few weeks. Had she had nerve pain? She remembered some body aches, which could explain it, but nothing twitchy.

"Maybe it's unrelated." He looked back up from his notes. "But I wanted to keep track of it. Sometimes, details become more important as you gather additional facts."

She couldn't remember having any trouble breathing or rashes, but she certainly had been sick to her stomach. Heartsick, if she was being specific, but it felt similar, settling deep in her gut at times. In her chest too. Maybe that explained the chest pain?

"I can't remember anything that serious."

"See? Maybe it's something else," Maggie said brightly.

"Maybe. Or maybe it's multiple things." Willa poured boiling water over a pot of herbs and spices she'd combined.

Nell couldn't remember any rashes. Maybe a burn or two. Would that count? Everything else attached to the blasted magic was related to emotion. Her mind spun to connect the dots. "Where were the rashes?"

"Mainly on fingers and hands. I only cataloged six cases of that, though. With as many people as we have hiking out here, it could be a case of poison ivy or poison oak."

Nell studied her fingers. She'd burnt several over the past few weeks. "Or it could be that more than my emotions are being replicated in my customers."

Victims was more like it.

"An extension to your power?" Nick wondered.

Nell nodded.

"That doesn't make sense," Maggie objected. "Willa's power focuses on healing only."

"Her power amplifies the properties of plants from the sea," Nell clarified. "Maybe mine passes along my personal state of being onto plants and animals from the sea."

"I never thought about it." Willa's eyes unfocused, and she drifted off. "But maybe I could use fish byproducts too, things like omega fatty acids from salmon oil and amplify its ability to improve brain and heart health, plus its anti-inflammatory qualities."

"Or heal underwater creatures with no plants at all," Nick continued her line of thought.

"Exactly!" Willa clapped her hands. "I never thought of that."

"My powers might not be confined to emotion," Nell concluded.

"You also don't know it's not," Maggie argued. "Mine is limited to gathering and moving water around in the air. It's pretty simple."

"Yes, but you can also move the clouds and cause thunder," Nell pointed out.

"She can?" Nick asked, impressed.

"When I got upset the other day, it got cloudy and looked like it was going to rain." Maggie bit her lower lip. "There was a little thunder. But that happens naturally with reduced atmospheric pressure, based on the additional moisture in the air."

All three of them looked at her with amazement.

"What?" She backed up, holding her hands palms up. "I've been reading up on it."

"So, it could be anything." Nell threw her head back in defeat and stared at the ceiling in Willa's product room. "We might have no idea how it works."

And that felt even more overwhelming than before.

"I guess we don't, but hopefully, this helps those affected either way. Right now, that's the most important thing." Willa stirred her concoction. "This is almost ready. I just need to pour it into bottles and label them, then we can make the rounds."

"I can help deliver them," Maggie offered.

"I can't touch anything." Nell backed up a step, feeling helpless.

She was normally the one to take care of everyone. This was unfamiliar and uncomfortable.

"That's okay." Willa laid a hand on her arm. "You can go meet up with Shelby and Duke. Shelby only needed a few hours at work before she could break free again, and Duke was going to look for Percy. Maybe he's had a lead on that.

If you want to go meet up with them, the three of us will catch up with you at the café as soon as we deliver these."

Nell nodded.

"We'll get to the bottom of it," Willa went on. "We can also spend more time figuring out what your powers are."

"And we have documented facts." Nick tapped his books. "If we keep gathering evidence, it'll eventually become clear."

Nell believed that. She was just afraid it would all point to her.

CHAPTER 24

Emiliano stared at the fencing on Conrad Brooks' large property. The T-post had been knocked over, and a section was hanging loose. An animal could have gone over or under it.

This portion of fence was farther into the woods, lined heavily with trees on either side. It was no wonder it had taken him so long to find it.

"Now that I know how it's getting in, though, I'll catch it on camera for sure!" Conrad held up the two extra game cameras Emiliano had brought him. "Thanks for getting these so fast. I can't believe you were able to get them in a single day. Did you drive yourself?"

"No. Duke made a trip out today anyway and was able to pick them up."

"Well, shoot. That was a great idea. Your new delivery service is going to take off."

"I'm glad you think so." It was the last thing on his mind at the moment.

"I'm ready to sign up as soon as you get it up and running."

"Thank you, sir."

"I'm just anxious to catch the sucker on this bad boy." He shook the camera for good measure. "I don't have a clue what's going on."

"Me neither." Emiliano leaned in close to examine the fallen fence. "I don't see any fur on it."

"I didn't, either. Looked all over for evidence of it, but there's nothing to be found."

"Either way, it's big enough to have taken down the post."

"Exactly. And the ground's been too dry to capture any good tracks. There's some smudged depressions." He pointed to the dirt. "I had about considered wetting down the soil around the fence just to catch tracks, but it's a long fence line. Never thought I'd be wishing we were having more rain."

The two men laughed. Living in Washington State meant dealing with a higher-than-normal level of rainfall. It also meant lush crops. Emiliano never minded a nice, steady drizzle. It was kind of relaxing and romantic. Not that he'd ever really had anyone to share it with.

"The weird part is that the affected crops are down there quite a ways." He pointed down to a brown patch a hundred yards away. "These crops seem fine."

"That *is* strange."

"With any luck, I'll have my answer tomorrow." Conrad studied the fence. "I just need to repair this and find a good place to post a pole to mount it on."

"Sounds good. You let me know what you find." Emiliano shook his hand.

"What do I owe you?"

"How about I get back to you on that? I haven't figured out my billing system yet. I can send you an invoice in a few days?"

"Works for me."

It also gave him time to figure out if he could charge it through Gil's Market. Conrad would have gone through them if he hadn't helped him the time before. He also hadn't known he was working independently when he called.

It wasn't a lot of money, but it seemed like the right thing to do.

"Hey, Pops," Emiliano said, standing in the doorway of the office that had been theirs just two short days ago.

"Emil." His dad stood, surprised to see him. He ran a hand over his receding hairline and stepped away from his desk.

"Do you mind if I come in?" It felt strange to ask, but he also didn't want to assume.

His eyes flashed to his old desk, empty of his personal belongings but, otherwise, sitting there as if he'd never left.

"Of course." Hugo gestured to the chair still waiting at Emiliano's old desk.

Emiliano took a couple of steps in but didn't sit. It was no longer his desk, nor his chair. It felt wrong to pretend like everything was back to normal.

"You've probably heard that The Wild Café was shut down." He stuck with the facts instead.

"Well, yes." Hugo scratched his head. "I heard. Several people are sick."

"Anyone who knows Nell, knows how meticulous she is with cleanliness. I'm worried there's something else going on."

"Something else?"

"I went online and checked all the recall sites." It was something they regularly subscribed to, and it had taken him a while to sift through them all on his own. "I couldn't find anything that looked like anything we carried, though. And I checked with the Washington Fish and Wildlife Service. There haven't been any reported issues with water cleanliness. At least, not yet."

"Okay." His dad looked confused. "You're trying to find the source of the illness?"

Emiliano frowned. It occurred to him that his dad probably thought he was trying to come back, already giving up on his dreams.

"Yes, Pops. I'm trying to help Orca Cove." He was doing it for them, not Nell, he reminded himself. "I wanted to check with you and see if you've heard anything."

His dad shook his head. "I haven't."

"If it's not bad food, it could be the coolers." Emiliano looked out to the hallway. "I don't remember when the next calibration dates are, but I think they're coming up sometime soon. I could check the temperatures in the cases, if you don't mind, just to see if they look right."

"If I don't mind?" Hugo's eyes went wide. "You mean you think it's my fault?"

"I didn't say that." He shook his head. "I simply want to rule out anything I can. We need to get to the bottom of it."

"If it's the thermostats, it's my responsibility," Hugo said, raising his gaze. "I'll check them myself."

Emiliano knew that look. He wouldn't get him to sway on his decision. He had never been able to.

"Could you let me know what you find out?"

Hugo nodded. "Although you might be disappointed with the answer."

"There was one more thing I wanted to talk to you about." Emiliano ignored his dad's insinuation that Nell's food was making her guests sick. "Conrad called this morning."

"Yes?"

"He needed two more game cams."

"Needed?"

Again, the feeling of going around his dad passed through him like ice water over fish.

"It was another rush order. Something's been on his property, and he's losing crops. I was out on the marina this morning with Duke, and he offered to pick them up on a run today." He felt thirteen again, rushing to explain why he'd done something out of the ordinary and hoping his dad didn't mind the change. "I just dropped them off."

"I see."

"Anyway, he didn't know about my..." Words failed him, and he waved a hand around in the air. "My new business. He would have come to you. The sale should be through you."

"And what you paid Duke?"

"We are working on a fair price for cargo transport."

Hugo nodded and worked his mouth as though chewing on unsaid words. "Keep it."

"Are you sure?"

"It's yours," Hugo said with finality. His voice rang in the small double office. "Conrad called you, and you arranged the shipment and the delivery. It's yours."

"But, Pops, it doesn't feel right."

"Maybe you should consider why it doesn't."

"I don't think having my own business is wrong." Emiliano stood up straighter. "I just meant. I don't know, Pops. I don't want to take a sale from Gil's."

Hugo's eyebrows raised as though implying that's exactly what he was doing.

Frustrated and a little shamed, Emiliano turned to leave. If his dad didn't understand, he couldn't explain it to him. It wasn't like his father had stayed with *his* family. He didn't understand the feelings of blame that were being cast toward him.

"I've got to get back to things." He laid a hand on the doorway that now separated them. "Thanks for your help."

It wasn't what he'd been hoping for, but he knew his dad would do it if he said he would. He just hoped he'd do it quickly.

On his way out, he texted Duke to update him on Conrad and the recalls, and he hoped he had found Percy. Maybe the Orca-man knew what was going on with the food.

"Hey, Emiliano." Loris saw him on the sales floor. "Good to see you! When is your new site up?"

"Oh." He glanced back toward the offices he'd just left. "Probably not for a few more days. Maybe a couple of weeks, max."

"That's good." Her eyes widened. "The earlier, the better."

"Why's that?"

"Josh tore his ACL, and he's been laid up."

"I hadn't heard that."

"It happened a couple of days ago. He came home last night. I'm picking up groceries for him." She held up the list in her hand. "But I know he'd prefer to shop for himself. Doctors say he's to stay off it for six weeks."

"That's a long time." Emiliano hated that he'd missed out on the news. He'd been too wrapped up in his own agenda to find out about Josh.

"At least, your site will be up soon, and he can order what he wants." She set a few cans of tomatoes in her cart. "I'll still check on him, but it'll be easier for him. He was worried about putting me out. I think he limited his list so as to not stress me out."

Loris used air quotes over the last few words.

"That's why I think it's a good idea."

"I do too. Everyone's excited about it."

"Hey, Emiliano!" A woman to his right came over.

It was the candlemaker, dropping off more candles for Gil's to sell on their local-crafts shelves.

"Hi, Britt." Once again, he glanced back, expecting his dad to emerge.

The shop was busier than ever today. Probably because the café was closed. Everyone was stocking up on food if they had to cook for themselves. Nell's place was such a staple in town. He wondered how everyone would fare.

"I heard you're opening an online site," she said excitedly. "I've been wanting to try an online platform for crafts, but could never figure it out. I make candles, you know? I'm not good at online marketing."

"I've seen your social media posts. I think you're selling yourself short," he said, smiling at her encouragingly.

"Yes, but that's still a creative outlet. Marketing and ads and figuring out those online sales just isn't my thing." She shuddered. "I just want to make candles."

"That's why I'm doing it."

"It's a great idea. I'm so glad you are!" She shoved a jar in his hand. "I heard you got a new place. Take this as a housewarming gift."

"You don't have to do that." He stared down at the candle: Cypress Forest. It was his favorite.

"You love that one." She smiled at him with a coy expression.

"I do."

"Then, take it. And I want in on the online sales. It'll be so much easier."

Hearing a scrape behind him, Emiliano turned to see his dad standing in between the pickles and the canned green beans. He pursed his lips and walked out to the front of the store where the fresh fish and cash registers were.

"I think you'll want to keep some stocked here as well," Emiliano told her. "You'll miss out on foot traffic if you only sell online. I think you would lose sales. Remember how many you get from the summer tourists?"

"That's a good point. So, I can do both?"

"Of course. You can select to sell locally, with local delivery, or nationwide with shipping. Your choice," he explained. "I'll get worldwide shipping figured out eventually, but VAT taxes and tariffs are going to take more time."

"That's fine." She waved a hand. "It'll still increase my sales."

"It absolutely should. It'll broaden your reach for sure."

"How do I sign up?"

"I'll have an online submission process, but I can help out if you want."

"I'd love that." She smiled warmly at him. "Like I said, I'm not great with all that computer stuff."

"Hey, Emiliano!" Tommy rushed out of the back room, his apron still halfway on him. He hurried to tie it.

"Are you late, young man?" Loris chided her grandson.

"No, Grandma." Tommy wiped his hands down his front. "I saw Emiliano and wanted to catch him before he left. I'm only working the evening shift. Hugo asked if I could come in and close. He's giving me extra hours."

His extra hours.

"Are you hiring for drivers?" Tommy asked. "My friend Heath is looking for a job, and I told him you'd be great to work for. Sorry, I'd work for you, but I just got a raise."

"You should stay right where you're at," Emiliano told him. "You're doing a great job here."

"Thanks." Tommy beamed at him.

"And text me Heath's number. I don't think I have it. I didn't realize he had his driver's license."

"He's had it for almost two years now." Tommy laughed.

People weren't kidding when they said time moved faster the older you got. Emiliano could remember when Heath would come in with his mom and throw a tantrum for ice cream.

He had planned on doing some of the driving, but if people were this excited about a delivery service, he might need to get help earlier than he'd expected. It was scary, but like Duke had said, he had to decide how big he wanted this to be.

"He was wondering how many grocery stores he'd have to pick up from," Tommy asked. "The one in Liberty Village has a larger selection of ice cream. He was excited to pick his own groceries up during trips if he could."

"Just Gil's," Emiliano told him. "I don't mind him shopping for himself while he's on the job as long as he's paying for it and adjusts for the time, but we're limiting it to Gil's Market for now."

"But you'd get more sales if you work with several shops." Britt frowned.

"Maybe, but I'm supporting Orca Cove here," Emiliano explained. Besides, it was still his family's business, whether or not his dad believed it.

Checking his phone, he didn't see an answer from Duke. Pushing through the glass doors of the market, he turned sideways to step around a group of hunters decked out in camo and scanned the docks for The Aurelia.

The large vessel was still out there, at the end, standing out, tall and proud amongst the pleasure crafts and smaller sailboats. He was probably on board, then.

CHAPTER 25

"Hey, Duke." Nell pounded on the steel door to his helm, the access to his living quarters below deck.

Frowning, she pulled out her phone and texted him. No update. Moving away from the door, she walked across the wooden planked flooring to see if he was elsewhere on the dock.

Still no sign of the ship's captain.

Wandering around, she made her way over to the metal edge of the boat's high sides, leaned against it, and sighed. The days were getting longer, and the sun had just begun to set. The moon stood high and proud over the water at the end of the cove.

It had been a long day. A long and emotional one, at that. Not only had she realized she'd totally miscalculated her magical abilities and the presence of sea ingredients, but she'd deeply hurt Emiliano. And even though the former fact directly affected her livelihood, her heart ached more for the latter.

Oh, and she'd made dozens of Orca Cove residents sick. There was that, too.

She searched the water for the orcas, but there were none today. Seagulls soared high overhead, their cries sounding shrill against the quiet lap of the waves on the ship's hull.

It began to rain, a gentle salty drizzle that misted onto her face and dampened the long-sleeved T-shirt she wore. But Nell didn't move to the single bench that sat under the cabin's overhang. The rain matched her mood: sad and quiet.

"Duke." A voice rose above the sea and creaky dock.

Nell spun and saw Emiliano standing at the side of the boat. The rope blocking the entry to the deck was the only thing between them. That and miles of heartache.

She caught his concerned expression before he saw her. His jaw set and his face closed off from emotion the moment his eyes landed on her.

"What's wrong?" she asked.

"Nothing." His answer was short and clipped.

She deserved that.

"He's not here," she said, pushing away from her position, but only to take a single step toward him.

He didn't move.

"Hey, man." Duke's head appeared on the dock. He was decked out in a wet suit and was carrying flippers.

The two men hand-slapped and fist-bumped before Duke noticed her on his boat.

"Hey, Nell." He lifted a hand.

"Gone snorkeling?" Shelby's voice announced her arrival. "I know I had to work, Duke, but geez. You could have tried to do *something* other than just have a good time."

Stepping over the rope, Shelby hopped down the steps and plopped down on the only dry bench on the deck.

Duke's attention ping-ponged between Nell and Emiliano.

"What? No comment?" Shelby crossed her arms, disappointed by the lack of banter. She sat up straighter. "Did I miss something?"

"No luck with Percy." Duke unhooked the rope and clambered down the steps onto his boat.

Nell's eyes slid to Emiliano, then she turned her back to the younger man still standing on the dock and widened them to silently remind Duke the former shopkeeper was still in their presence.

"He knows." The man dropped his gear with a thud near his cabin.

Nell spun to Emiliano, who just shrugged, his expression flat.

"Any luck?" Duke asked him as he waved him on board.

He shook his head and hopped down the steps onto the deck, but he stopped just off the stairs, keeping a distance from the rest of the crew. "I didn't find any recalls or reports with the Fish and Wildlife. Pops is checking the thermometers."

"You asked Hugo to help?" Nell was amazed. She knew how tenuous things were between them right now. It couldn't have been easy to go back so soon.

"The townspeople are sick. I'm trying to help figure out what's going on." His words came out bland and disinterested, but Nell knew he was hurting.

There was no way Duke had told him about the magic, though. He wouldn't do that, would he? She couldn't figure out how he knew about the shifter, though.

"How do you know about Percy?" Shelby sat up straight, finally catching on to what was going on.

"I figured it out," Emiliano said.

"How?" The words came out of Nell's mouth faster than she could stop them.

"I have eyes," he replied. "I notice more than you think."

"Did you have any luck with Solomon?" Duke asked Nell, pushing through the heaviness in the proverbial room.

"Um." Nell glanced at Emiliano again, unsure what she could say. "I found him and Roy at his house."

"Did either of them know anything about issues with the water quality or ailing fish?" Emiliano asked. "Just because Washington Fish and Wildlife didn't know anything yet doesn't mean there isn't a problem."

"No, neither of them did." Nell looked at Duke again in amazement. He knew about Roy, too? She went for it. "Roy is going to try to get a message to Percy."

Duke nodded. "That's good. I had no luck finding him, but hopefully, he'll hear and make his way to us."

"I got nothin'." Shelby stretched her legs out in front of her as though getting sun, even though it was nighttime, drizzling, and she was under an overhang.

"How'd your meeting go?" Duke asked Shelby.

"Fine. I may be picking up another plot of land or two from this investor I've been talking to. It'd be mutually beneficial, the best kind of deal."

"You aren't going into business with him, are you?" Duke asked, surprised.

"Probably not. You know I don't play well with others, especially in business."

Duke walked over to an outside fridge, opened it, and pulled out two beer bottles. He raised his head toward Emiliano. "Want one?"

"Nah, I gotta get back." His eyes flashed to Nell's, then away quickly. "To finish unpacking."

"The place working out for you?" Shelby asked, wiggling her fingers for the extra beer.

"Yeah," he said, looking at his feet. "Thanks for letting me rent it."

"Thanks for paying my mortgage." She smiled sweetly at Emiliano, who laughed in response.

"I finally found you guys," Willa said from the dock, taking the steps down to meet them. Nick and Maggie were with her. "We looked at the café, but no lights were on."

Duke lifted his beer, asking the three newcomers if they wanted one.

Nick and Maggie nodded. Willa shook her head. She didn't drink often. Opening the fridge, he pulled two more long necks out and handed them over.

"How's Mary?" Nell asked.

"Not much change yet, but we made the rounds. Hopefully, they'll all be doing better tomorrow." Willa sat down next to Shelby. "Sorry it took so long. Even with the three of us, it took a while to deliver everyt-hing."

"I have more time tomorrow," Shelby said. "I can help. I could probably even help mix or bottle them, or whatever it is you do after you do your thing."

Nell peeked at Emiliano, but he didn't react to her reference to magic.

Willa nodded. "I can handle the herbs. The delivery is the most time-consuming, but I'll want notes on how everyone is doing."

"Easy. I'm an excellent notetaker." Shelby took a pull from her beer. "When and where do we need to meet up?"

"How about the café at eight?" Willa suggested.

"Probably shouldn't go there." Nell bit her lip. "You don't want people to think it came from there and is tainted somehow."

Willa nodded. "Then, we meet here?"

"I have to get up at eight?" Duke sighed.

"And have coffee for the rest of us." Shelby held up a finger.

"Fine." He leaned against the doorway of his cabin. "But I won't be happy about it."

Nell wasn't sure if she should join them. There wasn't much she could do. She couldn't even make them coffee. At this point, it was too big of a risk. "Maybe I'll meet you here afterward?"

"That works." Willa gave her an encouraging smile. "With more people, we should be done in a couple of hours."

Nell nodded. At least, she could find out how everyone was. Hopefully, they were doing better, and they could start figuring out how to put all this behind them. And then, she had a lot to think about in her own life.

"I can help deliver," Emiliano offered. He had been standing just outside their group, watching the dynamics. "If you could use an extra hand."

"Apparently, we're all getting up early," Duke said, lifting his beer. "Don't be late."

"I'll be here." He inclined his head and turned to go.

"Emiliano." Nell stopped him before he could leave. She felt like she had to say something. "Thank you for helping out."

"Why wouldn't I? People are sick. What else would I do?"

"You're right. Of course, you are," she admitted.

He had always taken care of the town's residents. It was a quality they both shared. Before, he'd said he liked that she understood the need.

It wasn't necessarily about her, but in a way, with her business, it still was.

"Thanks, all the same," she said.

He dipped his head and left Duke's boat.

They all watched him walk down the dock.

Nell gripped the edge of the bench where Shelby and Willa sat, holding herself back from hurrying after Emiliano and apologizing again. To try and make things right between them. They'd had such an easy friendship and business relationship, and it had been really fun working with him.

But she'd screwed that up, too.

"What did you do to him?" Shelby broke the silence.

Nell glanced at Duke, who gave her a pointed look and then motioned with his head to the fridge, and the beer inside, in question.

She shook her head, not because she didn't want one, but after the day she'd had, she didn't think she could stop at one. And that didn't seem like a healthy way to deal with her stress. She'd intentionally stayed away from numbing her pain when she lost Gary—not to say she hadn't slipped a time or two, but she was intent not to lean on alcohol to handle life. She'd seen too many people lose their businesses that way.

It seemed she had already done that all on her own, though.

And here Emiliano was running around town, facing his dad, all to try and find the cause of the sickness when it was probably all her.

She was reconsidering the beer.

"You slept with him, didn't you?" Shelby said, watching her carefully.

"What?" Nell's pulse quickened.

"I've gotta say, I'm surprised."

Nell's mouth opened, then shut. "I don't know what to say. I guess I'm sorry." She frowned. It felt like a betrayal to Gary. To their friends.

"Doesn't sound like it's me you need to apologize to."

Her eyes followed Emiliano's shadowed figure crossing the beach at dusk.

Dragging her clothes on, Nell tried to make herself presentable enough to meet the crew after they'd finished their deliveries as planned. It had been a rough night, tossing and turning, dreaming of Emiliano, Gary, and the sick townspeople.

It was worse, knowing Emiliano would be with her friends.

She wasn't upset he was helping. It was just like him to lend a hand. But it was difficult to face him again after she'd been so irresponsible with him.

She dragged a hairbrush through her hair, cursing at it when it puffed up from the static. She pulled it back more aggressively than necessary into a tight ponytail and secured it. She might not be cooking today, but she felt more prepared having it together.

It might be the only part of her together, but right now, she'd take the win.

Catching sight of herself in the mirror, she paused for a moment to consider how she looked to Emiliano. He'd called her gorgeous. She ran a hand over her midsection. Not muscly and trim, but not awful either. Gary had always loved her shape. Tears sprung to her eyes as she processed emotions from the past and present. It was too much.

Shaking it off, she pulled a warm cardigan on, more for the comfort than for the chill in the air, and pounded down the steps of her café to meet Emiliano and the crew.

"Monty is better today, but is still experiencing some diarrhea," Emiliano reported, catching sight of Nell descending onto Duke's deck. His eyes followed her from his position on a bench, coffee cup in hand.

Nick was taking notes on his notepad. He, Duke, and Maggie were sprawled out on the benches. Now that the sky was clear, they had full use of all of them, not just the one under the overhang.

Duke stepped into the cabin and filled a mug for Nell, then brought it to her.

"Good morning. Willa and Shelby should be back soon." He gave her an encouraging wink. "Sleep well?"

"Not really." She took the cup and closed her eyes, breathing in the aroma of the dark, roasted bean. It smelled like life and tasted even better. Other than the cup Emiliano had bought her at the coffee shop in Liberty Village, it was the first time someone else had fixed a drink for her since Gary.

"Me neither. These fools demanded coffee at eight a.m.," he told her.

"Thank you," she mouthed to him for ignoring the fact that she had been unable to help deliver Willa's potions.

He dipped his head, swinging out to Emiliano. "You had Paulie, too, right?"

"Right," Emiliano said. "Paulie isn't any better, at least by his report. But he's always pretty grumpy."

"True." Duke sat back down.

"Maggie," Nick called out. "How were your deliveries?"She dutifully listed off several people and their status. Most were doing better already. It was a relief.

Willa and Shelby joined them a few minutes into her updates.

"What's wrong?" Nell asked, not liking the atypical frown on Willa's face.

"Well, almost everyone is doing better." Her friends pressed her lips together. "But there are several new cases today."

"New cases?" Nell said loudly. "How's that possible?"

Willa shrugged. "Something is still making them sick."

"Who?" Nick asked.

"According to Loris and Chief Warner, we have nine new people with nausea and vomiting and three more with coughs," Willa said. "That's what took us longer. I wanted to get all the details. I'll need to make more tonic for everyone after we're done here."

Nick made notes in his notebook.

"What about Mary?" Nell asked, clutching her cup of coffee. "How's she doing?"

Willa's eyes cast down for a moment, then went back to her. "She's not doing well, Nell. I suggested she check into the hospital."

"But your"—she paused before she said the word potions—"tonic is good for her."

"Yes, and she's doing a little better with it, but they can check her fluid levels and monitor her heart."

Nell's head swam. She couldn't lose anyone else.

"What did Mary say?" she asked, hoping the cantankerous woman agreed if Willa thought it was best.

"She doesn't like it, obviously. She hates hospitals and said she'd prefer having me as a nurse," Willa said. "I explained to her that I'm not a medically certified personnel and that they could take better care of her than me. She disagreed, unfortunately. But Loris was with her. I think she's going to convince her to go."

"Does she need a ride?"

"Loris said she would take her if she could get her to go."

Nell felt helpless.

"So, what's causing the new cases?" Nick asked out loud. "The fish?"

"I heard back from Pops this morning." Emiliano pulled out his phone to reference a text. "The thermostats were calibrated six months ago. I thought it had been longer. And he checked their temps manually. Everything looks fine."

He put his phone away and continued. "The only other possible thing at Gil's would be if the fisherfolk left the fish out too long or if the people on the floor didn't get them iced well enough. Both are things we look out for—*Pops looks out for*—but it's always a possibility. Either way, he said the health department was coming by. There's a good chance they're going to close the place down as well. Everyone got food from the market yesterday."

"But they have no proof of what's going on," Nell said, shocked.

"They didn't with the café, either," he argued. "All they need to see is one thing they can lean on. You had specific cases tied to people eating there. If they find even one cooler with a quarter of an inch less ice than they want, they'll shut it down."

"That's not fair." Nell was appalled that Hugo would lose business because of her mess. The town would have nowhere to go for food, other than the gas station, unless they wanted to drive to Liberty Village.

"They're trying to keep people safe. Besides, who knows?" Emiliano shrugged. "Maybe it is something at the market. If they can get it to stop, it'll be easier to figure out. People's health comes first."

"What's your guess, then?" Nick asked him. "Gut reaction?" "The water," Emiliano said calmly. "My best guess is there's something going on that Fish and Wildlife doesn't know about yet."

"I trust your gut." Nick raised his pen. "Can we get it tested?"

"It'd be easier if Percy came by." Duke raised his head to search the waves. "He'd likely know right away."

"Wait." Nell couldn't stop the whirl of thoughts on full speed in her head. "You mean it's not me?"

The thought of it nearly drove her to her knees. Could it actually be possible?

"Why would it be you?" Emiliano asked, confused. "You know you keep a clean kitchen. Hell, you scrubbed that place from top to bottom when the first people got sick. You could eat off your floors."

Nell felt like her heart was going to stop. Hope bubbled gently like a soft boil inside her, afraid to be too excited.

Maybe it wasn't her.

"Ew, but who would want to?" Shelby asked, taking the attention from her.

Emiliano frowned but didn't say anything.

"You rang?" a husky voice called out from the docks.

Everyone turned to see Percy's tall, broad form standing wide-legged on the wooden planks.

"Percy!" Nell hurried over to him. She'd never officially talked to the man, but she'd seen him on the docks after Duke and Willa told her about him.

"A little birdy told me you were looking for me?" He casually glanced around Duke's boat but didn't board it.

"People are getting sick." Duke strolled over. "We were hoping you knew something about it."

"I've heard," Percy replied.

"Is there something wrong with the water?" Emiliano asked. "Are fish getting sick?"

"Some are." Percy crossed his arms, his thick, bulging biceps apparent in his sleeveless shirt. "But I don't think it's what you're looking for. It's some sort of groundwater runoff. Unfortunately, not that rare, and not enough to be causing people to get sick."

Nell's heart fell. Not that she wanted fish to get sick, but she had hoped they could pinpoint and fix the issue.

"Could it be something else?" Percy's eyebrows went up, looking directly at her and Willa.

Her friend shook her head. "The café has been closed for a couple of days, and we got new cases today."

"I don't know what it is, but I don't think it's the fish," Percy said.

Nick bent over his notebook, scribbling on its pages.

Sighing, Duke turned back to his cabin. "Want a cup of coffee?"

"Nah," Percy shook his head. "I've got to get going if that's all you needed."

"It's all I wanted to ask," Duke said.

Percy nodded and turned to go.

Nell ran for the steps, hurrying up them to catch Percy before he got too far, her feet slipping on a stair tread in her rush. When she met him on the swaying dock, she spoke quietly so no one else could hear their conversation. "I had a question."

The mysterious man turned around, not appearing to be in any sort of hurry, and took note of her, eyeing her up and down. "I will answer if I can."

Her hands twisted in the ends of her cardigan. "Is there any way to get rid of it?"

"I told Duke I didn't know why people were getting sick. I have no reason to lie."

"No." She glanced back behind her. Everyone's eyes were on them. "I mean the magic."

"Oh." Percy's eyebrows drew together, and he studied her curiously. "You want to get rid of it?"

"I'm a chef, you see. It's how I make my living."

"Wouldn't that help you out?"

"Not if I'm making people sick."

"It sounds like it's not you." He canted his head, looking confused. "Unless you're still feeding those getting sick."

"I'm not. But it's such a risk, you know?"

Percy looked out over the water, his eyes drifting to the jetty where Willa and Duke first saw the luminous creature under the sea. No one really knew what it was, but she knew Willa liked to think it was a mermaid.

"The magic is a gift. It's not meant to harm."

"It's not much of a gift if I can't make a living from cooking for people."

"Are you trying to make them sick?" He raised his eyebrows.

"Of course not!" she exclaimed, stepping back.

"Then, why are you worried?" Humor traced lines over his face. He made it sound so simple.

"I don't know how it works. Do you?"

"Not the particulars. You'll have to figure that out by yourself, but if you're not trying to cause harm or illness, you should be safe. It sounds like your friends know this."

"They do, but I'm worried. I don't know if it's worth it. Worth the risk."

"Is it worth giving up something like this?" he asked her seriously.

"If I can be sure I won't hurt others, yes." Of that, she was certain.

"And if you can help others?"

She thought about it for a moment. "I don't know. I guess if I was sure I could use it for good, maybe that would be a positive."

He nodded.

"It can be taken away, then?" she asked.

"Honestly, I don't know," he said. "It's why we were worried when the powers extended to you all that night. We didn't know what kind of people you were or what you would do with them."

"That's why you've been keeping an eye on us," she said, suddenly understanding why they'd had more orcas than ever before in the cove.

He dipped his head.

She sighed. It didn't feel like she was any closer to figuring things out, and it seemed she was stuck with her powers. Even though she still didn't know if they were a curse or a gift.

"It looks like you've got people to help you get through this." He indicated those gathered on Duke's boat with his head. "Just keep doing what you're doing."

"But nothing's working," she exclaimed, feeling helpless. She spread her hands out wide. "More and more people are getting affected by whatever it is."

"Then, it's a good thing you've got a healer on hand." A grin split his face, and he winked at her.

Nell watched as Percy calmly walked off to the end of the dock and disappeared beneath the water below.

CHAPTER 26

Every ounce of Emiliano's energy was being used to not focus on Nell and Percy's animated discussion on the docks. He was failing epically.

"Do you want more coffee?" Duke asked him.

"Huh?" he asked, physically tearing himself away from watching the two. He shifted his body to face the courier, focusing solely on him. "Oh, sure, yes. Coffee is good."

Duke's face broke into a grin. "Coffee *is* good."

"What should we do next?" Emiliano asked no one in particular.

The smile gracing Duke's face fell flat, and he took in a long breath. "We keep doing what we're doing. Nick is documenting everything. Willa is healing her little heart out. We'll deliver and keep an eye on everyone."

It would seem he and Duke weren't that different, after all. They were both trying to take care of the people of the town, just in their own ways.

It felt nice to be included. More than he'd have thought.

His cell phone buzzed in his pocket.

"Hello?"

"It's like they knew where I put them," Conrad's voice came through his phone.

"What?" Emiliano blinked, switching gears. "The cameras?"

He mouthed a thank you to Duke when he handed him a fresh cup of steaming coffee.

"Yeah." He could hear the ting of chain link. "Another area of fence is busted down, farther into the woods."

"Any tracks?" He moved away from the rest of the crew to hear Conrad better. "Any trace of fur?"

"Not that I can see. It's almost like the animal knew where I set them. Maybe it was the light? There's a red dot on them when they're on."

"I wouldn't think so." Emiliano was starting to wonder if it was something else.

"I guess I should have tried wetting the area down. I thought, with the rain we had last night, it would help, but we didn't get as much as I had expected," Conrad said. "I'm sorry, Emiliano. I probably shouldn't have called to bother you about this. It's not like there's anything you c an do."

"I told you to keep me in the loop, Conrad. I'm glad you did."

"It's just so frustrating. I'm not getting much sleep. And a whole other section of crops that I thought was going to pull through looks like it's done for."

"Do they still look trampled on?" Emiliano asked.

"Some, but not most of them. I think they are just dying off. Maybe I'm crazy. Maybe it's some parasite I've missed. I don't know. Maybe I need to test the soil.""It's not a bad idea," Emiliano agreed. But why was the fence getting knocked over? "Conrad, any chance it's not an animal?"

"Whaddya mean? Like a person?" he asked, surprised. "Why would someone want to come in and kill my crops?"

"What about a competitor?"

"You know there's barely enough farms to keep the locals and tourists stocked, especially with Gil's and The Wild Café purchasing produce. Course, I'll see a small hit from the last few days. There won't be much of a delivery needed this coming weekend."

Of course he would. This illness was affecting everyone.

"Maybe leave the fence the way it is and try setting up a camera out of sight. Hide it somewhere."

"I don't see why someone would do this."

"What would it hurt?"

"It could be inviting the wildlife into the field." Conrad huffed. "But I suppose one night wouldn't hurt anything. Besides, I could use the extra sleep. I just don't have a lot of energy today."

"You sure you're feeling okay? Something's been going around.""It's probably just a passing bug. It wouldn't be the first I've experienced. I'll take a little rest this afternoon and be right as rain tomorrow."

"Good idea." Emiliano made a mental note to check on the man the following day. He had been one of the first to be ill. Maybe he was getting sick again. Hanging up, he turned to Duke. "I think Conrad's not feeling well."

"Should Willa add him to her list for tonics?"

"I'm not sure he's ready to take them." Emiliano considered. "We could try."

"I'll stop by his place later and leave a bottle," Willa offered. "If he doesn't take it, that's his choice."

Everyone's attention shifted to Nell, who had finally rejoined them from her conversation with the orca-man. Hybrid. Shifter. Emiliano really needed to figure out what to call him.

"Everything okay?" Duke asked.

Nell dipped her head in a short confirmation, but no one believed her. "I wanted to ask more questions. I'm worried about everyone getting sick.""What do we do next?" Shelby asked.

"I make more tonic." Willa shrugged.

"How often does everyone need to take it?" Emiliano asked.

"Three times a day is ideal," she said. "I made extra this morning, but with the new cases, we'll need more. I have to go back home and restock."

Nick stood and started stacking baskets. "I'll go over these notes and see if I can make any sort of connection to what they're eating and what they're experiencing." His finger tapped against the wicker in his hands. "There's a pattern here, but I can't quite put my finger on it. When do you all want to meet back up?"

"What time should we deliver?" Shelby asked.

"Two o'clock would work," Willa suggested. "I can make a nighttime tonic to help them sleep as well. We can deliver both at the time. I'll just go ahead and make some extras to pass around."

"Good idea. We could leave some with Chief Warner too," Nick suggested. "He might hear of more cases."

"I think I'll stop by Mary's and check on her," Duke said. "Hopefully, she'll be at the hospital."

"Do you mind if I join you?" Nell asked.

"Not at all." Duke nodded.

Everyone gathered their things.

"Nell," Emiliano said, stopping her. Something was still bothering him. "Why would it be you?""What do you mean, why is it me?" She shook her head.

"The illness. You're meticulous. Why'd you think it was you?" He had a hard time believing it, but had she done something careless that she was embarrassed of?

"Oh." Her gaze dropped, then she looked at the rest of her friends, who were in various stages of leaving.

"What is it you know that I don't?" he asked.

Duke was hovering nearby, and Emiliano could see in his peripheral vision that he was giving her a look, but he didn't care. He was focused on Nell. She was keeping something else from him, and he was tired of secrets.

"It's affecting our town. Don't I have a right to know?"

"You're right." She lifted her gaze to meet his and bit her lip, but went on, nonetheless. "You know about Percy and Solomon."

"Well..." He nearly argued with her. He didn't know everything about Solomon, but he knew the fisherman could talk to animals.

"Months ago"—she glanced over at Duke, who inclined his head, then she began talking and didn't stop—"we were all in the water. It was crazy, but it was for Gary, you know? He thought it was fun to jump in the sea once a year. You probably already knew that. And we thought it would be a way to honor him. It was Willa's idea, actually. We didn't hang out as much. It took a toll on all of us."

He had noticed and had hoped they would fix things between themselves. Gary's death had been hard on all of them, not just Nell.

She took a breath and gave him a soft smile before continuing. "There was a storm that night, the same storm Nick was also in, but that's another story for another day. The crazy thing was that when we were in the water—Solomon too, we've found out—Percy's friend, or something like that, was in there too. Lightning hit the surface, and ever since, strange things have been happening."

Emiliano frowned. He was struggling to keep up with her download of information. It was a lot all at once, so he focused on one thing at a time. "Strange things. Like Solomon talking to animals?"

"Sea animals only," she clarified. "But he wasn't the only one."

"You mean Percy's ability to shift?"

"No." She shook her head. "I think he was already like that. I think that's just how he is. He's magical. I think whatever else is in there—Willa thinks it's a mermaid—got hit and *her* magic spilled out into the water and onto us. At least, that's what I've gathered from the bits we've been able to eke out of Percy, or what Duke's found out."

"Onto all of you? Are you saying you can *all* talk to animals? Sea animals?" he clarified. "How does this have anything to do with making people sick?"

His mind was reeling.

"No." She touched his arm, but then dropped her hand and blinked at it. "I didn't think I got a power, but then later, I realized my emotions were being transferred into the food I was cooking. Or at least, that's what I thought was happening."

It was like the bolt of lightning hit him as well. She had been affecting people with her cooking these past months, and here he was, running around, trying to figure out what was going on. He'd stood up for her, argued with his dad that she couldn't be behind the sickness, and it could have been her all along.

Not only that, but his emotions had been more scattered than normal as well. Could that have been her, too?

"Did you play with my feelings?" he asked harshly.

"I don't know." Tears sprang to her eyes. "I thought I did. I thought that cookie I gave you was why you asked me out at your and your dad's place."

"Paella night."

She nodded.

"Why would the cookie make me do that?"

"I was thinking about you." Her eyes cut to the side. "Like that."

Suddenly, it made sense. He hadn't been wrong. She had been flirting with him.

"That's why you ran out that night."

"And tried to figure out what was going on."

He remembered her get-together with her friends after she'd left him so suddenly.

"I thought I spelled you into wanting me," she went on. "I tried to figure out what I had done and how to cook safely."

"It's why you closed the shop." Pieces just kept clicking together.

"I didn't reopen until I had it under control. Or at least, I thought I had. But people kept getting sick."

"So, you don't really know?" he questioned her. He knew it wasn't nice, but she hadn't been honest with him and had tried to have a relationship anyway.

"Tried" being a very loose word.

"I guess not." Her voice sounded shaky. "But today gave me hope. Maybe it's not me, after all."

"But you don't really know," he repeated himself. "They could have leftovers or something."

"Not everyone, not all those who are getting sick."

"Maybe it's spreading." He was being an ass, and he knew it. But he couldn't get past the idea that she had kept him in the dark this long.

And she'd found him lacking.

"I don't think it is." Her words came out in a whisper. "Percy doesn't think it is. But even he doesn't know exactly how it all works."

Emiliano nodded, stepping back and away from Nell, and stuffed his hands deep into his windbreaker. Bitterness filled him, and if he stayed any longer, he'd take it out on her more than he already had.

"I hope it all works out." He'd meant it as an olive branch, to soothe some of the pain and hopelessness he'd showered on her, but it came out more like sarcasm. Wincing at his words, he pushed off on the balls of his feet.

Then he brushed by Duke, who looked at him with an expression of disappointment.

Get in line, he thought.

"But we need groceries," Loris argued with the health inspector who was taping an ordinance to the window of Gil's Market and Marina. "Where are we supposed to go?"

"Liberty Village has a grocery store," the health inspector said. "Look, I don't like this any more than you do, but I have to close it down. Until we can figure out what's going on in Orca Cove, we have to take every precaution."

It hurt Hugo to see that blasted paper on his clean window, but there was nothing he could do about it. He couldn't even summon the courage to say anything encouraging to the townsfolk.

"Patricia's right," Chief Warner spoke up, trying to calm the crowd gathered in front of the store. "Hopefully, things will be back to normal in a few days. Until then, you can make the drive out to Liberty Village if you need something."

An older man in the back spoke up. "Some of us don't drive."

"It's too bad Emiliano's delivery service isn't in place yet," Britt, the candlemaker, said. "Maybe he can speed things up."

It felt like a blow to Hugo's ego. It was the very thing he'd been against. They didn't realize what hazards change could cause. It trickled out like waves, affecting more than they'd ever know.

But he knew.

And Emiliano's service would bring in groceries from all over. They'd never figure out the source of the food poisoning.

"Emiliano's not delivering from Liberty Village," Loris said, shaking her head. "That won't do any good."

"What do you mean?" Hugo asked. "He's delivering groceries and things from all over."

"No." She frowned. "It's for local stuff only, but making it available to people all over the peninsula if artisans want it. Or even nationwide, he said. But he said he wasn't taking business from Gil's Market."

Hugo's face felt ice cold. He'd thought his son would expand to other towns to offer more variety after he left. It only made sense from a business perspective.

It seemed as though he'd assumed a few too many things about the boy.

"I can make a trip, but I have to go soon," Loris went on. "I need to get back to check on Mary."

"Did you get her to go to the hospital?" he asked.

"Yes, but just barely. I don't want to leave her too long. She complained the whole trip there and during check-in, even though she barely had the strength."

"I'll go," Hugo said suddenly. "Everyone, give me your lists, and I'll make the trip to Liberty Village."

"Are you sure?" Loris asked.

"Yes." He nodded. "You go be with Mary."

CHAPTER 27

"I told you, I don't need that medicine." Mary's bottom jaw jutted out decisively. "You can take it away."

"Miss Johnson, the doctor recommends it to help you rest." The nurse set the container of pills on the tray next to her bed and slid it closer. Then he turned to Nell and Duke, who were in the room. "Maybe you could get her to take them?"

"What is it?" Nell asked.

"It's just Tylenol," he answered. "But it could help her feel better."

They had hooked her up to an IV for additional fluids and were monitoring her vitals, but she was refusing to take anything else.

"Willa's medicine makes me feel great after I take it," Mary said smugly. "And it's natural. You can't come close to recreating anything that clean."

With a little help from magic, Nell thought, but kept to herself.

"Willa isn't a certified medical professional," the nurse argued.

"She's a certified herbalist."

"It's not the same thing."

"Then, why do I feel better when she brings me her tonic?"

"What's in this tonic again?" he turned to ask Nell and Duke.

"It's just herbs. I've seen her make it," Nell said.

The nurse raised his hands in surrender. "If you can get me a list of the ingredients, I'll take it to the doctor to make sure it doesn't have any contraindications to anything we're doing. We can at least put it in her chart."

"Good idea, because I'm going to continue taking it." Mary made a short, sharp exhalation and smoothed the blankets covering her lap. Her gray, shoulder-length hair had been brushed smooth as always, with not a hair out of p lace.

"Tylenol probably wouldn't hurt you, Mary." Duke stifled a grin. He'd always been fond of the woman, cantankerous or not.

"Why would I take something I don't need, young man?" She turned her face to him and raised her eyebrows. "Just because it won't hurt me isn't enough reason to put it in my body."

"I can't argue with that logic," Duke said.

"I'll get a list from Willa," Nell promised.

"How're you doing, Mary?" Loris burst into the room. She zeroed in on the nurse. "Is she doing okay?"

"Apart from refusing to take her medicine and follow any typical medical orders, she's doing just fine." The nurse huffed, heading out. "I'll be at the desk if you need anything."

"The doctor knows what he's doing," Loris pressed Mary.

"We already tried that," Nell filled her in. "I'm getting a list of ingredients for Willa's tonic for her chart."

"Willa helped me when no one else could," Mary said. "Why would I do anything different?"

"We should get back," Duke said to Nell. "Willa will have the next batch ready to deliver soon, and I need to meet with her."

"I can stay with Mary."

"I don't need a babysitter," Mary said to both Loris and Nell.

Loris plopped down in the chair beside Mary's bed and pulled her knitting from her bag. "Well, I have to get this shawl done, so I might as well sit here."

"Let us know if anything changes," Nell said to Loris and waved to Mary. "I hope you feel better soon."

"I'm sure I will," Mary said, eyeing Loris in the chair. "As soon as Willa gets me better and out of here."

Nell and Duke walked out of the room and found the elevator. She pushed the button.

"Mary's still Mary," Nell shook her head. "At least, she's feeling like herself."

"Mary's great." He grinned.

The elevator opened, and they got in it.

Duke turned to her as soon as the doors closed. "Do you want to talk about it?"

"About what?" She frowned. "Oh, the Percy thing? I wanted to see if there was a way to remove my powers. Get back to normal, so to speak."

He raised an eyebrow. "You still think it's you?"

"Maybe not, but there's so much I don't know about it. I'm just worried about hurting people."

"Do you really think that's going to happen?"

"I honestly don't know. And I'm scared."

"I know." Her friend put a hand on her shoulder. "Thanks for telling me. I wasn't asking about your conversation with Percy, though."

"Oh? Oh, that." Stepping back, she leaned her head against the polished stainless steel. "I hate that I hurt him. I shouldn't have done that."

"Shouldn't have done what? Been with him? Loved him?"

She straightened quickly. "I don't love him. How could I? I'm still in love with Gary."

Duke waited quietly.

"I mean, it would be so disloyal if I loved someone so unlike him. Almost like I hadn't really wanted Gary, after all. I can't do that."

"Would it?"

"Of course," she mumbled.

"You told him about your powers."

"Just about mine. It was only right. He's spending so much time and energy trying to find out the source of whatever's making the town sick. He went to his dad, even with the tension between them. It wasn't right, holding that back from him."

"You felt safe sharing it, though."

"Emiliano's a good man. That was never the issue."

The elevator dinged, and they walked through the hospital lobby and to Duke's old pickup truck. He opened her door for her.

"Then, what is the issue?" He stood at her door.

"It doesn't feel right." Nell stared straight ahead. He wouldn't understand.

"It felt right enough at one point."

Heat spread across the back of her neck. "I thought it would be okay, but I don't anymore. I don't think I can do it."

"Date someone else?"

She nodded. "Or maybe just him. I don't really know."

"Because you have feelings for him?"

She spun to face him, uncomfortable with what he said. "Of course not. Like I said, that would be impossible. It would dishonor our marriage."

"You said 'til death do you part."

"I'm not dead."

"Exactly." His brow wrinkled. "Do you think Gary would have wanted you to shut down?"

"No." Nell pulled the truck door shut, ending the conversation. But Gary wouldn't want what was going on between her and Emiliano. The thought of him seeing them together filled her stomach with acid.

Duke got into the driver's side and drove them back to the marina without saying another word.

The crew had begun to disperse from the docks, and Willa handed a basket to Duke when he approached. "The list is inside. There are some for this afternoon and some for tonight. They're marked. And there are extras in case you find any new cases."

Duke took the wicker handle and headed off.

"Emiliano already left," Willa told her.

Nell realized she had been searching the area, looking for a sign of him. She brought her attention back to Willa and Shelby, who were the only two left.

"You could cook us dinner," Willa offered. "I think we could all use a home-cooked meal."

"I'm not supposed to," she said bitterly.

"You can in your personal kitchen."

"It hardly has enough equipment." She had a couple of hot plates and a countertop convection oven. Not enough to cook for the crew.

"You could use my kitchen," she offered.

"Isn't it risky?"

"Nell, this isn't you."

"But if people keep getting sick, if you got sick, people will think it's me."

"Aren't you being a little selfish?" Shelby said unkindly. She was rarely unkind. Sarcastic and sometimes rude, but rarely ever unkind. "You can't help deliver; it's the least you can do."

Nell couldn't disagree, but she was still too scared. Until she knew for sure what it was, she couldn't bring herself to cook for others.

"What's going on?" Willa's eyes softened on Shelby.

"What the hell's wrong with you?" Shelby turned the full force of her frustration onto Nell. "You get a second chance at love, and you spit in its face? You know how few of us even get one?"

Nell froze in place, blinking. "You're right, but I had mine. I had Gary. How could I ask for more than that?"

"You're not." Shelby's hands went up in the air. "That's why it's so messed up. You're not asking, and it's still there, staring you in the face, and you refuse to accept it."

"And you'd do the same?" Nell came to life, her fears and frustrations igniting a second wind in her. "If Keane came back?"

She knew it was a low blow, but she struck it anyway. Keane and Shelby had been as close as her and Gary once. But that was high school, and a lot of time had passed since then. He'd left the month after graduation with only a note saying he needed to find his purpose. His parents had told a tearful Shelby that he had moved in with a cousin in New York City and wanted a little time away from Orca Cove. They hadn't seen him since. He hadn't even come home for Gary's funeral.

"That's different."

"How's it different?"

"It wasn't true love. Not for him." Her face twisted. "Or he wouldn't have left."

Shelby spun on her heel and took off, her basket abandoned at Willa's feet.

"I'll take it to her." Willa bent to pick it up. "Are you okay?"

"I will be." Nell put a hand to her face, trying to calm the tears threatening to spill over. "I think I just need to stay in tonight. I'm so sorry."

"It's okay, Nell." Willa leaned forward to wrap her free arm around her friend. "Take your time to feel what you need to feel and do what you need to do. It's not an easy thing, what you're going through. You take care of yourself, but call me if you need anything. We're meeting up again to share notes on Duke's boat later tonight. All of us except Emiliano. He said he had some things to do but would call Nick later to report on everyone. So, if you decide to stop by there, feel free. Or I can stop by your place. Whatever. Just let me know."

"Okay, thanks." But she knew she wouldn't be setting foot outside her house tonight. She wanted to take a long, hot shower, pull on comfy clothes, and curl up on the couch underneath their thick gray blanket. And probably cry herself to sleep.

If she couldn't wrap herself up in Gary, it was the next best thing.

Three hours later, Nell shoved an empty tub of ice cream farther away on the coffee table. Her stomach cramped from all the sugar, but it still was nowhere near as bad as the ache in her heart. It was different from when she'd lost Gary, though. This felt more like betrayal, not like the fresh pain of losing half of herself.

Part of her expected to see him come around the corner and accuse her of her traitorous actions. The other part of her wanted to see him so badly that she didn't care if he was angry with her. Toying with her phone, she called the only other person she could.

"Hello, Nell?" Chuck, Gary's dad, answered the phone.

Just hearing his voice soothed her soul. He sounded so much like his son.

"Hi, Chuck." Her voice was thick.

"Everything okay, honey?"

The endearment brought tears to her eyes. "Yeah, I'm just having a rough day."

"Do you want to talk about it?" She could hear him sitting down.

"Not particularly." She laughed. "I just wanted to hear your voice."

Chuck's understanding rumbled with a reassuring sound. "What do you want to talk about, then?"

"What have you been up to lately?"

"Actually, that's something I planned on talking to you about," he said.

"You did? What's that?"

"I started seeing someone."

Nell nearly dropped her phone. She couldn't imagine Chuck with anyone other than Jean, Gary's mom. All she could manage was a squeaky, "Really?"

Jean had passed a couple of years before Gary. It had crushed Chuck when Gary passed. A month ago, she'd have been happy for him, but now that she knew how challenging it was to actually move on, she was more shocked than anything.

"I'm sorry if you don't approve." He cleared his throat. "But I've thought long and hard about it. It's difficult being alone, and I'm ready to try again."

"I'm not upset with you, Chuck. I'm just surprised."

"You and me both. I didn't expect it at all, but who am I to turn down a second chance at happiness?"

It made sense, but it was so much more difficult in reality.

"I'm so happy for you, then."

"Nell," he began carefully. "You do know you are allowed to do the same, don't you? When you're ready?"

Her throat thickened again, and she felt her eyes fill with tears. "I'm not sure I can."

"I understand. Give it time, kiddo."

Feeling a little better, she hung up.

It was still early, but her exhausted emotions and mind needed rest. She'd tried to doze off earlier, but couldn't sleep. Too many thoughts were rolling through her brain.

Gathering her blanket around herself, she padded to the kitchen, opened her freezer, and took a small container from the back. Popping it open, she sat it on the counter and looked at it.

The final piece of Relaxed Rockfish. She wondered if she would ever be able to get back to that state of mind to make more. Maybe Willa could create something like that if she couldn't get up the energy.

She watched it bubble in her convection oven. It wouldn't taste very good after being frozen, but she wasn't eating it for the flavor. Removing it with her oven mitts, she squeezed a lemon wedge over it and poked at it with a fork.

Taking it back to her spot on the couch, she studied it. She was taking the easy way out, but she was aware. She needed the break. Tasting a bite, she was surprised it wasn't as bad as she'd expected and finished it quickly.

It didn't take long for the shroud of calm to settle over her shoulders. It was such a relief that she would have cried if she didn't feel totally chill about the whole thing.

She still missed Gary, but in a detached way. It wasn't wholly pleasant.

Curious and caught up in thoughts she hadn't let herself think about in a while, she went to her bedroom and pulled a box from the bottom of her closet, sitting on the floor of the small space to look through it. A handful of Gary's things still hung above her; she hadn't been able to give everything away. Her fingers reached up to touch his favorite dark-green plaid shirt. She could still smell his presence.

Flipping the lid of the box open, she riffled through it. It had odds and ends she'd saved over the years, memories, hopes, and dreams. She picked up a plastic drink mixer from her twenty-first birthday. A smile played on her lips. Gary had taken her to a bar a few towns over. They'd already been married for two years, but it was their first time going to a bar.

"Did you remember your license?" he'd asked excitedly.

"Of course I did." She'd produced it from her oversized purse. "See!"

And then they'd both laughed when the waitress didn't even ask to see it.

Her fingers found a stack of pictures she'd taken over the years. Dreams, really.

She turned them over to flip through them. There was a photo of a small speedboat in the marina. At one time, she'd thought it would be fun to own one and go zipping about in the Sound. And a cute little cottage that stood overlooking the cove. It wasn't large, but it had such a great view and was only a block from the marina. It had been terribly expensive when it was for sale, and they'd probably never have been able to afford it.

She'd hidden the pictures away so Gary wouldn't feel bad about it. He hated not being able to give her things she wanted. It was easier to dream in private. But dream, she still did. She couldn't throw them out.

It wasn't that she needed them. She was happy with their little life. It was more than most people ever dreamt of having. They'd had their own business, and she made her own hours, long though they were. And they had a cute little place above the kitchen that made it all easy.

But still, she liked looking at them. She could be happy and still have dreams.

It occurred to her that she had felt guilty for wanting them. Not now, of course, but normally. They weren't things that mattered much to Gary, or at least, she had never thought they did. He never talked much about his d reams.

Nell wondered what he'd fantasized about. He'd been so focused on her and the business, she'd never considered he might have had some of his own.

She knew Emiliano's dreams. He wanted his own busi-ness, something he'd built himself. And he was doing it.

She was glad for it. She liked that they might be able to grow their businesses together. She'd hoped Emiliano's service would deliver food from the restaurant as well. Maybe not outside Orca Cove—it wouldn't be fresh and warm—but for residents like Mary. It would be a great expansion for the café.

Why hadn't she thought of that before?

Was it because she'd been clouded in emotion between her late husband and the man she had growing feelings for? Now that she was thinking rationally, it was because she was scared. It was fine in the beginning, but Duke was right. Once her feelings became involved and she'd started falling for him, she worried it was wrong.

It had seemed okay to date someone, but not to share her heart. That just seemed silly now. Maybe because she was enjoying something so different, she was worried it looked like she'd preferred it over Gary all along?

Did it have to be cut and dry? She didn't know.

Things hadn't always been perfect for them. Maybe that's what she was afraid of exposing.

Her fingers found the engagement ring he'd bought her. It had a high crown holding up a small stone. She hadn't cared that it was small—that had never bothered her—but it was the height and the nooks and crannies all over the ring's filigree edges that were an issue.

She held it up close to her face, inspecting the swirling sides. It was beautiful, but it would get filled with dough and ingredients every time she baked.

She hated wearing it, taking it off every time she cooked in the kitchen. It wasn't that big of a deal when she was just making sandwiches at her little stand on the marina, but she'd already been working on figuring out how to make bread. Failing miserably for a long time, but still. She'd been trying. And when they opened their first version of the café and she was mixing cookies and making bread regularly, she'd often forget it on the counter.

Eventually, she'd put it back in its box and stuffed it into this little shoebox for safekeeping. At least by then, she had her slim gold band. He'd argued she should have something fancier, but she didn't want anything different. It was simple and easy to clean. It now sat in the case with the engagement ring.

He'd proposed on the marina; it was where they were the happiest, watching the boats go by. It was also why she'd chosen this spot to set up her stand. She got all the traffic from the fisherfolk and the customers from Gil's Market.

Hugo had always been okay with her selling there. He said as long as she bought most of her ingredients at the market, he'd always support her business. Besides, he had no intention of opening a café, so it made good business sense. She could still hear his voice. Her younger self felt like he was giving her a gift.

Gary had looked so handsome on their wedding day. They were on the marina, with the docks in the background. Duke and Keane had stood with him, and Willa and Shelby with her. That was before Maggie rolled into t own.

And then after he was diagnosed with leukemia, they'd only had nine short months. The amount of time it took to create a life. And he was gone.

They'd talked about a baby, but he was too worried about her. It would have been nearly impossible if she had been a single mom running a restaurant.

Replacing everything where she'd found it, she pushed the box back in its spot and, rising to her feet, went to bed. She stretched out over Gary's side, trying to find his scent in the pillow. It was no longer there. Rolling onto her side, she wiggled back, just like she used to when he'd been there.

She imagined him beside her, his body lining up perfectly with hers. His arms would come around her, pulling her close, his nose burying in her hair. She sighed happily, content to be lying with the memory of him.

"I'm sorry I picked the wrong ring," he murmured into her hair.

"You didn't pick the wrong one. I loved it." She pulled his imaginary arms around her tighter.

"I don't think you can get any closer." His chest vibrated with a chuckle as his thumb stroked her arm. "I should have known you'd prefer something simpler."

"I'm a chef. Diamond rings are unnecessary."

"There was a lot I didn't do right by you."

"You're crazy. You were perfect."

"We weren't perfect. We were messy and did the best we could."

"Doesn't that make it kinda perfect?"

"For me, it was."

"For me, it was too." She could practically smell Gary's warm, woodsy scent, and she breathed in deeply. "What did you dream about?"

"Me? I dreamed of taking care of everyone. Of our happy little found family. Of making everyone feel as safe and

loved as my parents did for Duke. I've never been so proud of them."

"He needed that."

Gary's family had been the surrogate parents their wild friend needed.

"You'd be so proud of him now."

"I am proud of him. I'm proud of all of you."

"I've made so many mistakes." Even with the Relaxed Rockfish, she felt tears fall from her eyes. They weren't as heartbroken and achy as before, but still, they fell.

Gary's arms tightened around her. "Mistakes make you human. I wouldn't have you any other way."

"But I..." Her mind went to Emiliano. The kisses they'd shared, the touches.

"You mean Emiliano." His voice in her mind was flat.

"Yes." She breathed, and tears fell again. "I wasn't trying to ruin your memory. I wasn't trying to replace you."

"I never thought you were." He stroked her skin and laid kisses on her shoulder.

Their differences flashed in her mind. Emiliano made her feel safe too. Even though his smell was different, his kisses were different, and his lovemaking was so intense it had made her toes curl. "It's all different."

"It is."

"That doesn't make it better."

"It doesn't make it worse."

"I don't think I can do this." The tears were falling faster now, soaking her pillow.

"I think you can. I think you need to. I love your passion and joy, and I hate the thought of you sitting in sorrow. It was part of the reason I didn't want to leave you with a child. It would have made it so much harder for you to start again." She felt his hand come up to her face and wipe the flowing tears away. *"Maybe our marriage wasn't perfect. Maybe different isn't bad. Maybe each relationship is messy and beautiful in its own way. Happiness and love are to be fought for."*

"I've been trying to fight for ours. Don't you see?"

"You're trying to fight against yours and his." His voice softened. *"You don't have to."*

"Don't I?"

"You don't." His hands cupped her cheek. *"Nell Fitzgibbons-Wilder. I give you my permission to be happy. To find love with whoever brings you joy."*

Tears continued to fall, and he pulled her in tighter than before.

"I love you, Gary James Wilder."

"I love you too, my Nell." He kissed her shoulder, and then he was gone.

CHAPTER 28

Emiliano jerked awake. Someone was knocking at his door. It was still dawn, and the sun was just rising above the water's edge. Pink-and-peach hues hovered in the air like blush on the clouds.

It had taken him ages to fall asleep, and it felt like he'd only gotten a few hours.

Dragging himself upright, he groped around for his pajama bottoms and pulled them on, hopping as he walked to the living room. He ran a hand over his face, letting out a loud yawn before turning on the light and blinking under its brightness. He saw a figure at his sliding glass door.

Nell.

She stood there, fresh as a flower, her rich brunette hair flowing around her face, rosy with a flush. And she was smiling.

Confused, he walked over, not bothering to grab a T-shirt or flannel. Flicking the lock, he slid the door open.

Maybe they found out what was causing everyone to be sick.

"Everything okay?" he asked tentatively.

"Yes." Her eyes settled on his chest, then moved back to his face. "Can I come in?"

"Sure." He looked behind him. His living room didn't look any better than it had the day before. "I don't think anyone's meeting up until later. Did something happen?"

"No." Her hands twisted in front of her. "I just wanted to talk."

"Give me a minute, okay?" He wasn't sure he was in the mood for what she had to say, but he wasn't spending another second talking to her without brushing his teeth first.

She nodded, following him in. He left her and went to the restroom, relieved himself, and freshened up.

He was still tired, but less crunchy-feeling from sleep.

Taking a look in his mirror, he braced his hands on the sink's edge. It didn't feel so long ago that he'd stood like this, gathering enough courage to talk to Nell. Now, she stood in his living room, waiting for him.

Things were different.

He found her sitting on his couch, staring at his belongings strewn around the room. She stood when he entered.

"Do you want coffee?" His manners outweighed the hurt in his heart.

"If you're making some." She smiled briefly. "That'd be nice."

Relieved to have something to keep his hands busy, he moved into his kitchen, grinding beans and filling water. He turned and leaned against his counter, keeping the distance between them.

"I'm so sorry, Emiliano," she began.

"What for?" He could feel his emotions shut down to protect himself. "For keeping me in the dark or for stringing me along?"

She exhaled, and her body deflated. "For all of it."

He nodded.

"I should have been more careful. I should have ensured I was ready before…" Her eyes flicked to the other room. "Before things went too far."

"I probably should have followed my instincts and slowed things down too," he said quietly.

"This wasn't your fault." She came over to him, her face tight with worry. "And I was wrong. I was so wrong."

His teeth set together. He didn't like being a mistake.

"You're so different from Gary." Her fingers curled around the counter edge near her. "I thought it somehow meant I didn't want what I had with Gary. Like he was never who I really wanted. I don't know if that makes sense; it sounds silly now that I know… It sounds silly now."

"I see." He wasn't sure where she was going with this.

"What I'm trying to say is I was wrong. I didn't mean to hurt you. You've been nothing but kind and wonderful." Her hand lifted from the counter and then dropped again.

"You were wrong?" Was she saying what he thought she was saying?

"So wrong." She left her spot at the counter and came closer. They were only a foot or two apart. "I was scared. Do you think you could give me a second chance?"

"A second chance?" The air left his lungs completely, and it took him a moment to recover. "To do what? Leave again? Decide I'm not enough? I might be young, Nell, but I'm not just some puppy to run after you, starving for any attention you might give me."

"I can understand how you would feel that way. I really do. But that's not how I think of you. I'm not trying to play games here."

"You aren't?" He took a step closer, feeling his chest rising and falling heavily. "You were very clear. You said you had your love. You said you believed you only get one. There's nothing left in you for it again."

"I was wrong."

"I've loved you for as long as I can remember. You were kind to me when everyone teased me for not having a mom. Do you remember that?"

"I, uh." She shook her head. "Not really."

They'd both been kids at the time. She'd been in high school and he, in elementary school, but he could remember it as clearly as if it were yesterday.

"I tried to be patient. I didn't want to rush you. I was too afraid that if I did, you'd bolt. I'd lose the only chance I'd ever get. I'd fall completely for someone who might not yet love me." He shook his head, wincing at how weak he sounded. "I don't think I can go through that again, Nell."

Closing his eyes, Emiliano turned from her. He was afraid, if he didn't, he'd pull her in his arms and kiss her blindly. Then, when she left again—and she would—he'd be more heartbroken than ever. He didn't think he could recover from it.

"I didn't know," she whispered. "I had no idea."

"Well, now, you do." He stared at the wall ahead of him and didn't turn around.

"I don't want to hurt you again, but I don't know if I can guarantee it'll be forever. We'd have to try, but I'm willing to give it a shot. I'm willing to fight for happiness."

He finally turned and studied her. "I'm not sure that's good enough for me anymore."

He didn't think he could put his heart on the line again. She'd already stomped on it once.

In self-preservation, he backed out of the kitchen and walked out of his house, barefoot and bare-chested, leaving the woman of his dreams and a fresh pot of coffee behind.

Thirty minutes later and half frozen, Emiliano came upon a group of teenagers searching for shells on the beach. They stared at him, in nothing but plaid pajama bottoms, and giggled. One blushed.

He could barely feel his toes.

Turning around, he looked to the other end of the cove and his new apartment. His resolve was slipping.

Had he just made the biggest mistake of his life?

He took a faltering breath, not knowing what he was doing anymore. He was alone. He'd left his dad. He'd lost and almost got back the woman he loved. Was he an idiot?

The pain he'd felt when she told him she'd made a mistake cut through him again. He needed more time to think. He probably shouldn't have dismissed her so quickly, though. The hurt on her face was etched in his mind's eye. This was all so complicated.

When he made it back to his apartment and climbed the stairs, he hoped she'd waited. But it was empty.

He poured a cup of the still-hot coffee and took a long sip, wishing it would warm the icy depths of his heart, but disappointment still sat there, immovable and frozen.

Taking his drink with him, he showered and went into his room to dress. If he hurried, he could still meet up with everyone and find out how the townspeople were.

He could help deliver more of Willa's tonic. At least, that was something he knew he could do right.

After pulling a three-quarter fleece over his head, he picked up his phone and noticed a string of missed texts.

"*Nick's found something,*" Duke's message read. "*Brooks Farms. Heading there now.*"

Emiliano shoved his feet into his boots and hurried out as quickly as he could.

Conrad's front door was open when he arrived. The rest of Nell's crew was there already, and an ambulance pulled in behind his SUV.

Following the responders through the door, he found Duke and Willa crouched over Conrad's prone form on the floor. Seeing the team arrive, they moved out of the way.

Nell stood with Shelby to one side. Her body tensed when she looked up and recognized him.

"What happened?" he asked, going over to Duke even though his heart screamed at him to go to Nell.

"Nick put the pieces together. Brooks Farms was the common denominator, not the café or Gil's," Duke said.

"I was focused on the three different groups, trying to find similarities within each: with the people, what they were doing and what they weren't doing. And I was getting too hung up on seafood, since it's so common. But until I put them back together again, I didn't notice the source."

"They were all eating produce from Brooks Farms?" Emiliano asked. "But we've eaten Conrad's food too."

Nick nodded. "That's why it threw me off. It was only specific vegetables. Once I connected the dots, I called everyone right away."

"I should have come back to check on him last night." Emiliano watched the ambulance team load Conrad on a gurney and carry him out of the house. He had planned to.

At that moment, Chief Warner walked in, heading straight to Nick. "What is it?"

"Some kind of food poisoning, but I haven't figured out the cause. It's not normal contaminated food," Nick filled him in.

It was too much of a coincidence. It had to be related to whatever was killing his plants.

"Something's been tampering with his fields," Emiliano told the chief. "I got him some game cams to catch what it was."

"Show me." Chief Warner went outside, and everyone followed.

Emiliano led them to the section Conrad had shown him just a couple of days before. The fence was still down, but there weren't any visible tracks. Maybe he hadn't felt well enough to soak it. Or maybe it'd dried before whatever it was came through.

"I suggested he leave the fencing down this time. When he fixed it earlier, whatever was coming through found a different spot."

Chief Warner studied the area. "Where are the cameras?"

Emiliano searched for them. He'd suggested Conrad try to hide one, so he didn't see it at first, but eventually, he found it, tucked under a wheelbarrow. "There it is."

Kneeling, the police chief pulled the SD card from the camera. "Does anyone have an SD-card reader?"

"I do in my car," Emiliano said. He kept his laptop with him most of the time.

"Let's check it out."

Everyone waited while he got his laptop, inserted the card, and set it on the hood of a tractor Conrad had left in this section of the field. He pulled up the images.

They weren't the highest quality, but the pair of dark-blue coveralls passing in front of the camera were impossible to miss. They didn't look like denim or canvas, like a farmer might wear, but were instead made of a Tyvek material.

"That's not Conrad," Emiliano said unnecessarily.

The camera wasn't angled high enough to see the person's face, but the figure was much slimmer, at least from what was visible in the video feed. Fabric was covering their shoes as well. Even if they had left tracks, Conrad might not have noticed them. He had been looking for animals.

"Any idea who that is?" Nick asked.

"Not that I can tell." He angled his laptop screen so the others could see it. Everyone shook their heads.

"You think this is causing the bug that's going around?" the chief asked Nick.

"I do." He nodded.

Chief Warner turned to survey the crops. Several sections of the field were brown or burnt away, but other areas looked healthy. "Why would anyone try to make people sick? What would their motivation be?"

"No clue, but Conrad seemed to think whatever it was came through practically every night," Emiliano said.

"We could do a stakeout," Nick offered.

"If we set up the camera in a better area, we can catch whoever it is on film," Emiliano said.

The chief nodded. "I'll post a car down the street, but we wait to see if the camera gets a better shot. Meanwhile, Ronnie, take some samples of both the healthy and sick plants. We won't get the results back quickly, but they can get started."

"Yes, chief." The officer pulled gloves on and went to collect evidence.

"Meanwhile, everyone out. We don't want to call any more attention to the area." The chief turned to the group that had gathered close and shooed them away. "I'll let you know when we find something."

"Chief," Nick said. "We can help.""Not if they catch sight of you and take off." He shook his head. "The camera is a safer bet. If we don't get him on the game cam, we can try another way. Emiliano, help me get it set up better."

Nick backed up and turned to Duke.

Emiliano went to help the chief. "There're three. If we set them up to surround the downed fence, we should be able to get a good shot."

Working to attach a camera under the tractor and another in a different spot under the wheelbarrow, Emiliano found a third place outside the field. He secured it in the branches of a Douglas fir.

"Thanks, son." The chief patted him on the back. "I'll let you know what we find out."

Wishing he could do more, he found Duke and Nick back near their cars. They were deep in conversation.

"My Subaru is less conspicuous," Emiliano said. There was no way the two men weren't planning on holding a stakeout, and gray Subarus were about as common as rain in the state.

Duke lifted his head, considering the offer. "He's right."

"We could leave one of our trucks farther down the road." Nick studied Emiliano.

"But then we won't be able to leave quickly if needed," Duke said.

"True." Nick nodded, getting on board. "We'll meet at your place at eight."

"But what about Chief Warner?" Emiliano asked. "How do we avoid him?"

"Chief said not to let them catch sight of us." He grinned mischievously. "He knows he won't keep us out of the area. He was just warning us to stay hidden."

The three broke apart, with Duke and Nick heading back to the rest of the crew.

"Are you helping deliver tonics?" Willa asked. "I brought them."

"Yes." Emiliano saw Nell watching him from Duke's truck. He wanted to go talk to her, but wasn't sure he should. "I'll take a basket."

He could do more good delivering than anything else at the moment.

"Continue to take notes," Willa advised. "Just because they found the source doesn't mean we can back down now. I might need to adjust things if people aren't improving."

They hadn't had many new cases the day before, and everyone who had taken her tonics was recovering remarkably fast.

Most of them, anyway.

What if Willa's herbalism was more than just herbs? Nell had only shared what had passed to her in the water, but Willa, Shelby, Duke, and Maggie were all with her that night.

Their gifts didn't seem to be as potentially life-threatening as Nell believed hers to be. He hoped they'd share when they were ready.

Today's findings confirmed that Nell had been wrong to blame herself, and he wanted to reassure her. To celebrate with her.

"I'm heading to the hospital to bring one for Mary and another for Conrad," Willa said, pulling his attention from Nell. She pushed a basket into Emiliano's hands. "The lists are inside. Let me know how they're doing."

"You got it." Casting one more glance in Nell's direction, he left to do what he could.

CHAPTER 29

"What should we do now?" Maggie asked Nell.

"You have potions to deliver." Nell nodded at the basket in her friend's lap, then turned her blinker on to head back into town.

Seeing Emiliano had been tough. Not only had he turned her down when she asked for a second chance, but he'd looked tortured when he arrived at Brooks farms. Tortured and angry.

"I hate leaving you all alone to sit by yourself," Maggie said.

"I'm fine." She attempted a reassuring smile.

She'd gotten permission, in a fashion, from Gary. It was what her heart had needed, and she had come to terms with her feelings for Emiliano. At least, that weight on her heart had lightened. She still needed to fix things with him, even if it didn't mean he gave her a second chance.

He was in pain, and it was her fault.

She hadn't realized the man was in love with her. The feeling was both sobering and thrilling. She had so many reasons to have hope.

"I have things I need to do," she announced. The swirl of ideas and plans spiraled up in her. "I can't reopen yet. I have to call the health inspector back and review the new illnesses to show it's not me."

"If they catch whoever's messing with Conrad's crops, that'll take care of it."

"Exactly, but Chief Warner doesn't want that spread around yet. Whoever's behind it could hide evidence, and they could lose their advantage. But"—a satisfied smile spread across Nell's face, one of the first real smiles she'd shared in days—"it's not me."

"I told you it wasn't you." Maggie rocked her head, happy with herself.

"I know you did. You never stopped believing in me. I'm sorry I doubted myself so much."

"You've been in a rough patch."

"For too long." She glanced at her friend. "I'm going to change that.""Really?" Maggie's eyes brightened.

"Really."

"So, whatcha gonna do first?"

"First?" Nell turned into the parking lot for The Wild Café. "I'm going to plan my reopening."

"I can help!"

"After you deliver those bottles and report back to Willa," Nell instructed. "They're our first priority. Then, we can plan."

"I'll handle the social media launch."

It was a turning point.

Finally, things felt like they were coming around.

If only she could say the same thing about the situation with Emiliano.

Several hours later, Nell and Maggie had cleaned the entire place from top to bottom, including her upstairs apartment. She had scheduled a meeting with the health department for the following day, crossing her fingers that they'd catch the true guilty party that morning. If not, she'd still put whatever she could into action.

Nell called Barnaby, Carlos, and her other staff, checking in on them and letting them know she'd update them as soon as she had a date when they could reopen. Barnaby had enjoyed his days off, taking a short vacation to Victoria Island, but even he sounded restless to get back to work.

She'd made a list of things she wanted to do. She'd called Fran to invite her to the reopening. The winemaker had heard about her misfortune. Once she'd listened to her carefully worded explanation, she was more than happy to help. She would sample her new menu, and they'd discuss business.

Going through her cooler, Nell removed all traces of produce from Brooks Farms. He had cattle as well, but she didn't have any of his beef on hand at the moment. Reviewing the prepped foods or sauces in her freezer, she found a few she had to toss.

She'd need new stock.

Taking her other list, she told Maggie she'd be back and headed out to Gil's Market. Knocking on the door, she gave it a try and found it unlocked. She hadn't been sure he'd be there, but since she'd never known the older man to sit around at home, even on his days off, she figured this was the better bet.

"Hello?" she called out in the darkened market.

"I'm sorry, but we're closed," Hugo's voice came from the offices in the back before he poked his head out. "Oh. Hi, Nell. Everything okay?"

"Mostly," she said honestly. "And we've got some planning to do."

She explained what they'd found out at Brooks Farms and that it should be coming to a close soon. She left out Emiliano's involvement. He'd be worried, and she knew the three men would keep an eye out on each other. Most importantly, he needed to prepare for re-opening as well.

"Make sure you check for any pre-mixed salads or frozen soups," she recommended. Gil's carried a few of her frozen meals to sell.

"Oh, I hadn't even considered that." He scratched his balding head.

"I've been thinking about its possible effects longer than you have." She'd honestly thought it was her for so long; she'd been narrowing down food items and ingredients for weeks.

He nodded. "I'm just glad we'll be able to put all this behind us."

"Me too."

There was a knock at the door.

"Delivery time," he explained.

"What's that?"

Hugo told her he'd been making trips to Liberty Village for groceries for the town.

"They don't buy from Brooks Farms, do they?"

"Not that I know of," he said, considering. "But I'll check the produce before I hand any of it out."

"I'll get a message to Conrad for a list of everyone he's selling to. We need to stop the spread."

"Good idea."

Nell followed him out the front door. He kept the groceries at his place because of the health inspector's ban. He couldn't run anything through the market itself, but as a fellow townsperson, he could pick things up for his friends.

"Thanks for doing this," Loris said, taking her bag of groceries from Hugo. "I need to restock Mary's place before she gets home."

"I'm always happy to help out," Hugo replied with a smile.

"You're a lifesaver, Hugo!" Paul told him, taking his bag. "I've been taking care of Jana and the kids all day. If you hadn't picked these up, I'm not sure how I could have gotten food for dinner."

The smile on Hugo's face faltered as he moved on to the next person. "This one's for you, Izzy."

In the back of the parking lot, Nell saw her friends arrive. It looked like Willa was back with the afternoon-and-evening potion run. She touched Hugo's arm. "I'm headed out, but let me know if you need help with the health inspector. I can lend a hand cleaning if you need it."

"I'll be fine, but thank you, Nell," he said sincerely. "It was the good news I needed."

Understanding the pain in his eyes, she turned to him and gave him a big hug. When she pulled back, he had tears in his eyes.

"What was that for?"

"I needed it." She gave him a wink and headed over to her friends. "How're Mary and Conrad doing?"

"Mary's starting to turn the corner," Willa said, unloading Nick's truck. "Although she's running those nurses ragged. They'd be better if they just left her alone, but they all want to check in on her."

"She's complaining about her roommate. She had her cell phone out and was playing videos all afternoon," Nick told her.

"Not anymore," Willa said. "They moved her to her own room."

"That's good. And Conrad?"

Willa frowned. "I don't know how we didn't catch his symptoms sooner. He's not doing so well."

"He didn't tell anyone how badly he was feeling."

"No, he's not one to complain."

"Did you give him the tonic?" Nell asked.

"I did, but the doctor advised against it. I think he's a little sore that Mary keeps touting my virtue over his medical experience. And Conrad doesn't know me like Mary does." Willa looked up at Nick, concern evident on her face.

"You did everything you could." He pulled her close.

"Can we sneak it into his juice or something?" Nell asked.

"That doesn't feel right," Willa said. "Shouldn't it be his choice?"

"But he doesn't know the whole story," Nell said. In her peripheral vision, she noticed Emiliano's silhouette making his way through the crowd.

"If he's not doing better when we go back tonight and he's still refusing to take it, we can talk about other measures." Willa leaned against the truck bed.

"You'd think the nurses would notice how well Mary's doing," Nick said.

"It's not how they do things," Willa explained calmly. "You can't fight a lifetime of information."

"It's wrong," he said.

"Not for them." She laid a hand on his arm. "We have to respect their choices. Not everyone feels as we do. All we can do is focus on what we can control. Offer what we can and help where we're able."

"I'm able," Nell realized. It hadn't occurred to her earlier. "Unless you think people won't want to take it from m e."

"I think they'll be happy for the delivery." Willa handed her a basket. "Nearly everyone is doing better."

"Except Conrad," Nell said.

"What's going on with Conrad?" Emiliano approached them with a frown, his attention on Willa and Nick.

"He's following the doctor's orders, which don't include my tonic," Willa filled him in.

"What do we do?"

"I'll see how he's doing this afternoon when I go back, and if I need to, I'll nudge him again."

"But it'll help him," he argued.

"It's his decision, Emiliano." Willa smiled warmly at him. "We let him make his own choices."

A woman made her way through the crowd of people in front of Gil's with her arm raised. "Emiliano, hi."

He turned. "Hi, Britt."

"You were going to call," she playfully scolded.

Jealousy flared through Nell at the young blonde, so obviously taken with Emiliano. He wasn't hers, she reminded herself, no matter how she felt.

"I've been pretty busy, sorry." He looked around. When he found Nell watching him, he rocked back on his heels. "Wednesday or Thursday should be better."

"I can always stop by if that makes it easier," she offered. "You're down on the beach, now, right?"

"Yeah, I don't know if I'll be home, though." He glanced down. "It might be best if you call first."

"Just let me know, then." She leaned in close. "You have my number."

Emiliano glanced at Nell, looking like he wasn't sure what to do.

He didn't owe her anything. She'd messed up. If he wanted to take the pretty blonde up on her offer, he was more than free to.

"I'll give you a call." He pulled back from Britt.

She said something too low for Nell to hear, but it made him laugh and her heart sink further.

It occurred to her that Emiliano must have felt like that a lot with Gary. Reminders of their life were all over her house, restaurant, and in generally anything they talked about.

It's not like she was going to erase all memories of Gary, but it made her understand him a little better. When they'd started to become serious, he got a new place, never suggesting taking her back to hers.

Maybe he was hesitant to be with her in the home she'd made with another man.

She imagined how things would have gone if they had been at her place. She'd probably have had her breakdown much sooner. Maybe right in the middle of things between them.

It would have been much worse.

She hadn't thought through things half as well as she believed she had. She was in a better place now, but was it too late?

Emiliano glanced around the parking lot. "What're they all doing?"

"Hugo ran to Liberty Village to pick up things for the residents," Britt told him.

A deep furrow settled between his brows. "Did he, really?"

He broke away from the woman, who didn't look happy with his exit. With a last glance at Nell, he made a beeline for his father.

She heard his voice ring over the crowd. "What's all this?"

"Your dad offered to drive to get groceries for me," Loris explained, but he didn't look very satisfied with her explanation. "I told him it was a shame your delivery service wasn't up yet."

"I suppose it is." Emiliano's lips pressed together, and he watched his father, waiting for him to respond.

"They needed groceries." Hugo lifted his shoulders. "I had to help."

Emiliano's hands twitched at his sides. "It's a good thing you were here, then."

Nell watched him disappear into the crowd, heading out to the shoreline. For the second time that day, she had to fight the urge to run after him.

CHAPTER 30

"Did you see something?" Duke peered through the back seat of Emiliano's Subaru. "It's too dark to see anything back here."

"Nothing yet." Nick sighed. "No one is going to come this early."

They'd been sitting in the blackness for an hour and a half. Their coffee had gone cold, and Duke had eaten all the chips he brought to share. Emiliano wasn't hungry, but sitting here, with nothing to do, made him feel munchy. Maybe it was just the stress of the day.

In the last twenty-four hours, he'd turned Nell down, a fact that still didn't make sense in his brain, and found out his pops was doing exactly what he himself wanted to do.

But for the townspeople, his dad would do it. Of course. He hadn't been open to it for his own son.

He was bitter, and he didn't like the feeling.

"We should go wait in the trees behind the field," Duke suggested, fidgeting in the back seat.

"If we do that now, we could expose ourselves. It's better if we wait until we see signs of someone," Nick said. "Just relax. We could be waiting for hours."

Emiliano stretched in his seat, leaning forward to relieve the pressure on his back.

"You just wait, kid," Nick said. "When you hit your thirties, it gets even worse."

"I'm not that young," Emiliano said quickly. "I'll be thirty in a couple of years."

Nick chuckled.

"What are you, thirty-four?"

"Thirty-six," Nick replied.

The feeling of inadequacy settled on Emiliano's shoulders again.

"Hey, I didn't mean anything by it." Nick elbowed him. "I wish I was still in my twenties. Course, it wasn't an easy time of life."

"In Seattle?" Emiliano asked. Nick had never told him about his days at the police department.

The ex-cop nodded and filled his lungs. "I was in deep, trying to get rid of this guy."

"Larry Dupree," Emiliano filled in. He'd been in the news, and Dupree's men had come to Orca Cove, looking for Nick.

"Yeah, Dupree. We worked that case for years." Nick's voice sounded farther away. "Life was different back then. I hadn't met Willa."

A dream of a smile danced on the man's face.

"Is that why you left?" Emiliano asked.

"I got tired of it all. Tired of the crime and just taking one bad person off the streets for another to surface. I know someone's gotta do it, but I realized it didn't have to be me. We were working on evidence to take him down, my partner and I. But I wanted to get out anyway. Jimmy was able to find it while I made a safe place to hide it."

Emiliano knew Dupree's men had taken his friend out in the process. "I'm glad he's behind bars now."

"At the cost of Jimmy's life."

Duke clapped Nick's shoulder, giving it a squeeze from the back seat.

"He's not hurting anyone else now."

The ex-cop shook himself out of his slip into the past.

"Do you see that?" Emiliano squinted into the dark night where he thought he saw a flash of light in the woods.

The other two men went silent as they peered through the shadows.

"There it is," Duke said.

A beam bounced around the field.

"That has to be him. Or her," Nick corrected himself. He flicked the automatic door light off. "Open your doors quietly. Don't shut them. Stay close to the ground."

They followed his orders, filing out of the vehicle. They met at the tail end of the SUV, crouched.

The beam bounced around more, then stopped.

"Are you ready?" Nick asked.

Duke nodded. Emiliano had never done anything like this before, but he was willing to follow the two men.

Staying close to the ground, Nick hurried across the other side of the field, leading them toward the woods. Duke and Emiliano followed closely behind.

They gathered together near a stand of firs, watching the shadowy silhouette move through the field. The downed fence was just on the other side.

"I don't see anyone else." Duke had his back pressed against a wide tree trunk, searching the darkness.

The figure was wearing the Tyvek coverall and carried a large duffle bag. They set it down next to a row of plants and crouched beside it.

"I'm going in," Nick told them.

"I'll stay here and watch for company," Duke said.

"What should I do?" Emiliano asked, feeling unnecessary.

"Come on." Nick motioned with his head. "Circle around them. If they try to run, cut them off."

He nodded.

Nick pulled a flashlight from where he'd had it clipped to his belt and moved into the field, walking low and fast. Emiliano hurried to follow, swinging wide around the tractor to get behind the figure.

Then Nick flicked the light on, shining it at the intruder.

"Freeze." His voice was clear and commanding in the silent night.

The figure dropped its bag and then bolted to the left, away from Emiliano.

Emiliano lunged ahead. There was a fence between the intruder and the end of the field. It was unlikely they would be able to go over it, but he wasn't going to risk it. Not if it could put an end to whatever was going on in town. The café and the market could reopen, and he could try to salvage whatever was left of his business and delivery idea.

Gaining speed, he leaped forward, toppling the Tyvek-covered body. He heard a grunt and landed on the ground surprisingly harder than he'd imagined.

Arms and legs swung out, and something smashed his face. Not wanting to be shown up by the two older men, who were obviously more seasoned in this type of event, Emiliano bore down on the body, grasping to keep them contained.

The trespasser kicked out, and a foot smashed into his kidneys. Emiliano groaned and tightened his hold. Getting his arms closer together, he locked his hands over his wrists and held on for dear life. His legs were fighting for stability with the ground, but as they rolled, they ended up wrapping around the figure.

"You need a hand?" Nick asked calmly from above him.

Emiliano looked up, still struggling to hold the bucking body. "A little help would be good, thanks."

Nick chuckled and pressed a knee into the person's back, pinning him to the ground. He produced a zip tie and bound their hands behind their back. Reaching for the hood, he pulled it back to reveal a young, snarling man.

"I'm going to have you arrested." The words came out of the secured culprit's mouth with distaste.

"You are, huh?" Nick asked.

Duke walked into the field. "If that didn't shake out a partner, nothing will. He's alone."

"I have rights." The stranger slammed his arms and legs into the ground, trying to buck free from the ties.

"You certainly do," Nick agreed. "But I'm not the one to read them to you."

"Emiliano, if you haven't completely used up your tank of twenty-year-old energy, could you call the chief?"

He realized the ex-cop was teasing him and that he'd probably been a little too assertive with his takedown, considering the man's lack of exit or team, but he couldn't wipe the smile from his face. It was stuck there, for the time being, even if he looked like a beaming teenager.

"Sure thing." He stood, dusted off the dirt from his palms, and found his phone in his back pocket. His hands were shaking with adrenaline as he dialed the number.

"Did you get them?" Chief Warner answered on the first ring.

"Yeah," Emiliano huffed, trying to catch his breath. "He's ready for you."

The chief clicked off the phone.

"I guess they're on their way." Emiliano stared at the body on the ground, still demanding for his lawyer.

"Nice job." Duke clapped him on his back.

In no time at all, Warner and his team were on site, taking notes and going through the man's bag while flashing lights bounced off the ground.

"State your name," Chief Warner ordered.

Ronnie slid cuffs over the zip ties on the man's wrists and pulled him to his feet.

"Joe Perry, and I want my lawyer." The man stumbled on the uneven dirt.

"That's fine, Joe Perry, but you're still going to answer for all the people you've hurt."

"Science sometimes requires sacrifice." Joe puffed out his chest. "Once I get funding for my research, they'll cover my legal bills."

"They?" Chief Warner asked.

A smug smile spread over Joe's face. "The farmers."

"The farmers won't want anything to do with you, son." The chief crossed his arms. "You're making people sick."

"Not anymore. I isolated the gene. It's stable now."

"What in the blue blazes are you talking about?"

"Not that you'd notice, but this field over here is perfect." He angled his head behind him.

They all peered behind the man. The patch looked healthy, but nothing stood out.

"Idiots." He rolled his eyes. "There's no evidence of any insect bites. They're completely leaving it alone."

"Are you telling me you made everyone in my town sick to develop a chemical to get rid of bugs?" Chief Warner grabbed the front of the young man's Tyvek overalls.

"You have no idea how much money this is worth. I'll make millions."

"You're an idiot."

"I'm a scientist!"

"What is it?" Nick asked, crowding the man from the other side. "Several people are still sick. If you tell us what it is, the doctors can treat them better."

The man shrugged. "It's a type of glyphosate."

"Glyphosate is already in use," Duke said. "And it's getting phased out in many countries. It's only a matter of time before it's banned in the States too. No one will pay for that."

"I said it's a *type* of glyphosate." Joe sneered. "But where most glyphosates only kill the growing weed, they don't stop any seeds from germinating. This variation is an organophosphate, also a highly effective insecticide, so it binds readily with my tweaked version. Organophosphate attacks the neuromuscular junctions and causes the eventual paralysis of invertebrates. It's a one-stop shop for all your agricultural needs."

"And what does it do to humans?" Emiliano thought of Conrad not taking Willa's tonic. What would happen to him if he didn't get the chemical out of his system?

"The new version isn't toxic to humans. It took me a while to play around with it, but it's relatively safe now."

"Relatively safe?" Nick's eyes bugged open. "What do you consider safe?"

"Money talks." Joe huffed. "People will pay for it even with a safety concern. They always have. Just need to wear gloves. And probably let it off-gas for a while before consuming."

"Sounds great," Duke said sarcastically.

Chief Warner shoved Joe forward, leading him to the waiting cop car.

"At least, it doesn't work like a carbamate," Joe said, bending to sit in the seat. "That stuff is highly toxic to fish."

Emiliano swung around to look at Duke, who was shaking his head.

"All that knowledge, and he's still as dumb as a box of rocks," Nick said.

"Knowledge doesn't equal common sense." Chief Warner huffed and slammed the door shut on the scientist, who was still spouting off facts. "I want you all to go home and shower. Throw your clothes in the washing machine. Who knows what this stuff does on contact."

"I need to call the hospital," Nick said.

"I'll call them," Warner offered. "You get home."

"Thanks, Chief."

"You sure you don't want a job?"

"No, sir, but thanks for the offer." Nick backed a few steps. The three of them stood by to watch Ronnie drive off with the evil scientist.

"I'm getting too old for this." Warner walked away, mumbling about how Orca Cove used to be a quiet little town.

"Conrad's going to have a long road ahead of him to clear his land of that stuff. It's experimental. Who knows how long it'll take to effectively get rid of it." Nick shook his head, watching the chief direct the other officers around the field to remove the game cameras' SD cards, tag Joe Perry's bag, and take additional evidence from the ground and surrounding plants.

"The EPA's going to be all over this area," Duke said. "I hope the evidence gets buried deep after the case."

"Why's that?" Emiliano asked.

"I'd hate to see the insecticide companies getting a hold of the chemical makeup. They might try to recreate it."

"Maybe it's best that his equipment was lost." Warner stuffed the duffle bag in a trash bag before addressing Nick. "Let me know if the hospital needs more information on what they're treating. We might be able to locate it if needed."

Nick inclined his head. "You got it, Chief."

Emiliano had barely finished drying off from his shower when he heard a knock at his door. It hadn't been as long of a night as it could have been, but he was already feeling exhausted by the emotional roller coaster of the day. Pulling on his pajama bottoms and a T-shirt, he silently hoped it wasn't Britt.

It had been flattering to have the candlemaker flirt with him. And satisfying to see Nell jealous, but he felt bad for not being clearer with the blonde. He'd dated women like her before, sweet, young, and a little wild. She was nice enough, but not really his type.

Opening the door, he found his dad standing on the other side. He was worrying the bill of his ballcap, curving it to fit even though the hat had been stuck in that position for over five years now.

"Pops?" Emiliano said, surprised.

"Can I come in?" His dad's foot hovered over the ground, as though hesitant about gaining entry.

"Of course." He stood to the side to let his pops come in and shut the door behind him. "What's going on?"

"Emil," Hugo began, reaching out a hand to touch his son's face. "You're all right."

"Yeah, it's just a scratch, Pops." Emiliano flexed the corner of his eyebrow that had been split open during his struggle with the mad scientist.

"I had to come see." Concern filled his dad's eyes. "I was out when Chief Warner came back. He told me all about it. You helped them take down a criminal."

News traveled fast in the small town.

"I didn't do that much."

"That's not what Larry said. He said you helped Nick and Duke secure him until they got there."

A trickle of pride wound around Emiliano's heart. He'd never had the opportunity to help like that. Normally, he was limited to providing for the people. It felt good.

It felt even better to see the pride in his dad's eyes. It wasn't something he witnessed often.

He cleared his throat. "But what are you doing up at this hour?"

Hugo shrugged. "I wasn't able to sleep."

That was unlike his dad. Most nights, he fell asleep in front of the TV after working nonstop all day. "Something wrong?"

Hugo turned to look around Emiliano's place. He'd stacked a handful of napkins on top of the container of coffee beans. He should have taken more time to tidy up that morning.

"Do you know that when my grandmother passed, my parents and I had already moved out of Olympia?" his pops said suddenly.

"No, I thought that's why you left." His grandparents had immigrated to Seattle from Spain and settled in the suburb.

"Actually, my father wanted to open a shop, but he didn't have much. So he found a little, abandoned gas station and turned it into a convenience store in Shelton. It was the closest he could afford to Olympia, and he wanted to make something of himself."

Hugo was barely twenty when his dad passed away from a heart attack. They didn't have any life insurance and had had to sell the shop to pay for his funeral. But Emiliano knew this story well. Where was he going with this?

"When Grandmother passed, she no longer had family nearby." Hugo turned to walk into his dining room. "It took them four days to find her."

He hadn't known that. "That's awful."

Hugo nodded, then turned to him suddenly. "You were right."

"Excuse me?" Emiliano blinked.

"I was worried about people in town getting forgotten. Especially those who are older, have more trouble getting around, or keep to themselves. Your delivery service would have kept them even further from society." He spread his hands out on Emiliano's makeshift plywood table. "Where we couldn't check on them and make sure they're okay. I wanted to be there for them in the way no one was there for my grandmother."

When his dad turned back to him, his eyes were shiny with memories.

"I wouldn't have let that happen, Pops."

"I know you wouldn't, Emil." He patted him on the cheek, his expression soft. It was how he'd looked at him as a young boy. "You're talking to Heath about driving for you. He's a good kid."

"He is. I'll do some deliveries too."

"Until you're so busy you need to be managing every-thing."

"Hopefully." That had been the plan. But he'd never let it get to the point where his delivery team wasn't keeping an eye on everyone. It wouldn't be just a drop-off on their stoop. This was their community, after all, and he cared about it.

"It will happen, son. I know it. And if I learned anything these past couple of days, it's that a lot of people would benefit from a delivery option. And it would expand our reach."

"It would." That was the entire reason he wanted to do it. It felt like something the town needed.

Hugo moved away from him again. "I'm also not so good with change."

"That one, I knew," he teased his dad, trying to lighten the mood.

Hugo raised his eyebrow and gave him the same direct look he'd given him when he was young and broke some-thing. Emiliano's smile dropped.

"Change hasn't always been kind to me. My father struggled with that shop. He'd barely been able to keep the lights on and food on the table. He was desperate to find something that worked, and when he did, we weren't to change it. Things change anyway, of course, but if he was pulling a profit, we couldn't afford to lose it."

"But Gil's Market and Marina is very profitable. I don't think there's a chance of it failing at this point."

"You never know what's going to happen, son. Things change, people change. There are no guarantees.""I highly doubt people will stop coming to shop at Gil's. It's the only market in town."

"For now." Hugo raised a finger. "If you expand to other towns, who's to say they won't do the same?""People already go to Liberty Village. I doubt that will change simply because they can get it delivered to their door. They'd be paying a service fee for delivery."

"I know. I've been holding on too tightly to things the way they are. I've been afraid to let go of the past." His dad sat gingerly on the crate he'd placed next to the table. "After your mother left, I've been worried of the day you'd leave, too."

Emiliano's heart stopped in his chest. His dad never talked about his mom. She hadn't wanted anything to do with him and had left him with his dad shortly after he was born.

"She always liked new and shiny things." A ghost of a smile played on his lips. "I was worried about affording the lifestyle she wanted. Eventually, she got tired of it and moved on. She liked change. It was her idea to buy the old marina."

That had been a good one, at least. But he didn't speak for fear his dad wouldn't continue.

"It nearly drove us under," Hugo went on. "You were a baby, and it cost a lot more to fix the old docks than we'd anticipated. They were falling apart. I sold the car and remortgaged the shop, and eventually, we started to right the ship, but it took years."

"I had no idea."

"Nor should you have, son. I wanted you to be able to go to college and to have something when I passed. Who knows when that would be? And I didn't want to leave you in debt when I left. You'd have options to do what you wanted."

It made so much more sense now. Emiliano felt awful he'd ever complained to his dad. He'd always worked so hard and often missed crucial events in his life, but it was only because he was afraid of leaving him with nothing.

"I'm so sorry I didn't pay more attention."

"Oh, don't be silly." Hugo waved him off. "I've been treading water for so long that I forgot to lift my head to see where I am. I missed so much."

"It's okay, Pops. You took care of me and gave me the entire town as a family."

Hugo grinned. "That's what I always wanted for you. A big family, so you can all keep an eye out for each other. Like you and Nick and Duke did tonight."

Emiliano shuffled his feet. He liked that idea, but they were too tight with Nell, and he would never really be one of them without being around her all the time. That would be too much on his heart.

"I'd like you to come back to the market," Hugo continued. "As an owner with equal partnership and equal weight on decisions."

"Is that a good idea? I can do my thing and still be connected to Gil's."

"No, you belong there with me," Hugo said. "I was too single-focused, trying to leave you the best legacy I could. I was trying to teach you to make good decisions and be safe. But look where it's gotten me. I pushed you away."

"I'm right here. I'm not going anywhere."

"Well, I want you in the store with me." Hugo pushed to his feet. "The office is too quiet without you. The market doesn't mean anything to me if I don't have you in my life to share it with."

Emiliano swallowed the lump in his throat and met his dad halfway. They hugged tightly.

"I love you, son, and I'm so proud of you." Tears streamed down Hugo's face. "Would you come back?"

"Of course I will, Pops." Emiliano's face was as tear-streaked as his father's. "I love you, too."

They hugged for a moment before Hugo pulled away. He sniffled and patted his taller son on the back. "You just have to explain one thing to me."

"What's that?" Emiliano wiped his eyes on his sleeve.

"Have I taught you nothing? This place is a mess!" Hugo said the words with emotion and shook his hands around the dining room.

Emiliano barked out a laugh and pulled his dad back in for a second hug. Hugo snickered at himself, and soon, both men were laughing heartily, glad for the break in the tension.

Recovering, Emiliano handed half the stack of napkins to his dad and used the rest to blow his nose and wipe his face off.

He felt better than he had in days.

"I should let you get to sleep, son," Hugo said, wiping his face as well. "We're going to have to get started early if we're going to reopen tomorrow."

"We have to go through everything," Emiliano said. "I'm not sure we'll be able to open so soon. Maybe the day after."

Hugo shook his head. "It's already done. Didn't Nell tell you?"

"Tell me what?" He frowned.

"She came by earlier today to let me know what was happening. We both had to clear our stocks of Brooks Farms produce."

He hadn't even thought to fill his pops in on it. It was a scary realization. His dad could have gotten sick from eating something from the market.

"I'm so sorry I didn't come to see you myself."

"You were mad at me."

"That's no excuse."

"It doesn't matter now."

But it did to him. And Nell had come through for his dad. The crack in his heart widened.

"What's wrong?"

"Nell and I are..." He stopped, unsure what to say. "I thought we could be together, but she wasn't over Gary."

"I see."

"Apparently, she is now, though."

"So?"

"But what if she's not?"

"What if she is?"

"You don't understand. I love her, Pops."

"I know, son."

"You do?" he said surprised. He'd had no idea.

Hugo grinned widely at him. "Of course I know. You go in the bathroom to comb your hair and wash up every time you see her crossing the lot and spend twenty minutes in there if you're stopping by the café."

"Then, you understand. What if she decides it's too soon again? What if she doesn't love me the way I love her?" He dropped his eyes. "What if she can't handle it and leaves?"

"You mean like your mother?" Hugo asked.

"Yeah." Emiliano's voice was quiet and distant. "What if that happens?"

"Watching you grow into a young, thoughtful, intelligent man, I've seen a part of myself reflected in you I wish I'd noticed earlier. I shouldn't have been so afraid to take chances and live life. I'm not doing that anymore. I don't want to leave this world behind while only living on the sidelines, preparing for disaster. I want to enjoy it. My dad never got to do that."

"You can now." He wanted that for his pops.

"You're right. And so can you. Don't be the thing that holds you back, son." Hugo gripped Emiliano's hands tightly in his own, one set fine-lined and one soft and supple. "You're afraid of getting hurt."

"I am."

"But that's living. I forgot what that was like." He gave Emiliano's hand a firm squeeze. "What if she doesn't leave? What if she decides to stay?"

The crack in Emiliano's heart burst open, letting emotion bubble to the surface. His breath shuddered.

"Go get her, son."

Nodding blindly, Emiliano walked out the back door and out onto the beach. For the second time that day, he found himself barefoot on the hard pebbles.

CHAPTER 31

Nell took a sip from her glass of wine. She pulled a foot up and propped it on the seat underneath her, tugging her knee tight to her chest. She wasn't able to sleep, knowing Emiliano, Duke, and Nick were out in the field. And even after Duke had texted to let her know everyone was okay and the man behind all the recent illnesses was behind bars, a few blocks away, she felt unsettled.

The moon hovered reassuringly over the cove, illuminating the waves in her view from the back deck. She'd found a cozy spot in the corner around the bar to watch the sea. Dorsal fins were cutting through the surface on the far end of the cove, and she felt a little better knowing they were out there.

She had thought Emiliano might come around, regardless of what he'd said when he was upset. That maybe he just needed time. But seeing him in the parking lot, with Britt flirting with him, had caused her insecurities to come flooding back. Nell was still older than him, far older than Britt, and much less fit than the young lady. How could she compete with that?

There was no way she and her baggage wouldn't become stale after a while, no matter what he'd said about his feelings for her.

A shadow passed across the shoreline, and she turned to follow it, squinting in the moonlight. It was too far away to make out the figure. Whoever it was came in her direction, turning onto the parking lot. She froze. It was late, way too late to have someone this close to her house.

Just when she'd decided to duck back inside and lock the door, she heard footsteps on the stairs to her deck. Heavy footfalls took the steps, and Nell hid farther down behind the wall of the bar.

The figure approached her sliding glass doors. This close, she could make out Emiliano's gait and his thickness of chest. He was barefoot and was wearing his pajamas. Shocked, all words caught in her throat as she watched him raise his hand to knock on the door. He paused, dropped it, and spun on his foot, heading back from where he'd come.

She frowned. Just when she considered calling out to him, he stopped suddenly and tapped his heel, rocking his foot indecisively. Then he glanced over his shoulder at the door and stalked back, more determined.

She should say something. She knew that. But he looked at war with himself, and she wasn't sure she should interfere.

His hand dropped once more, and his shoulders sagged. But instead of spinning on his bare foot this time, he rested his forehead against the glass.

He looked dejected and exhausted.

She couldn't stay quiet any longer.

"Emiliano." She said his name quietly so as not to startle him.

His back tensed, and he placed the palms of his hands on the glass, slowly turning to glance behind him.

His eyes looked red and haunted, and she shot to her feet.

"Are you okay?"

"I didn't see you there." He dropped his gaze to the deck. "I was worried I would wake you."

"I couldn't sleep."

"That's going around." He sniffed. "I'm sorry it's so late."

"That's okay." Moving forward, she saw a dark line marking his eyebrow. "Did you get hurt?"

His eyes flicked up and to the side. "Oh, yeah. I got head-butted."

"By the scientist?"

He nodded. "Duke let you know what happened?"

"Yes."

"Ah." He glanced back to the exit, and she wondered if he was going to bolt again, but he stayed where he was. His eyes finally landed on hers. "I was scared."

"Tonight?"

He shook his head. "This morning."

Hope bloomed like a perfectly laminated croissant in her chest. "So was I. Many times. For so many reasons."

He took two small steps forward, his chest rising and falling. "It's just that I'm already so madly in love with you. I have been for a long time. I was worried it wouldn't be the same for you, and how would I handle it if it wasn't?"

"Emiliano." She raised a hand to reassure him.

"No." He stopped her. "Let me say this first. You should know where I'm coming from. I probably held on too tightly to you for the wrong reasons."

Her body went still. Maybe she'd been wrong.

"I had a mad crush on you when I was younger, that's for certain, but after you and Gary got together and I got over being mad at him for taking you away from me like the teenager I was, I was amazed by how supportive and loyal you always were with him. No matter what hair-brained scheme he came up with or what wild idea he had, you backed it. You let him be flawed and make mistakes. He could be himself, and you had his back." His brow drew together, and he gave his head a little shake. "I didn't have a lot of examples of that in my life at the time."

"It's not like there weren't happily married people in the cove," she said, trying to understand. She wasn't the only female he'd ever seen stick around with a man.

"But none of them were you, Nell. I saw you, the object of my teenage fantasies, with Gary, and well, that's all I ever wanted. It was the most desirable thing I'd ever seen."

She took a step back. "I don't understand. I'm not the same person with you. We are...different with each other.

What I have with you is different than what I had with Gary. It's not like a plug-and-play relationship."

It was something she had barely just realized. And it was a good way to honor what she'd had with her late husband.

"I know that." He raised his hands suddenly. "I'm not trying to say I wanted to be with you just because I thought I could take his place and have the same relationship he had with you."

"Then, what are you saying?"

"That maybe, when I was a teenager, it might have been true. It was more of an infatuation." He bit his lip. "I'm sorry to say that. I hate saying it, but it's true. But things changed between us. I grew up, you grew up. We became f riends."

"And now?"

He closed the gap between them by one more step, still leaving several feet to go. "I always respected you. I loved working with you and watching you create menus in your head. You drift far away to some place where I think you're actually seeing and tasting the food. And you're so kind. You hired Maggie when she needed a job. Hell, you'd do anything for the people in this town."

"So would you."

"Yes, that's true. It's something we share." He drew in a long breath. "I just want you to know that, even though what I once felt for you might have been infatuation and not based on who you really are, what I feel for you today is absolutely real. I'm not infatuated anymore, Nell. I'm completely, one hundred percent in love with you. And when you turned away from me before, saying you weren't ready after all, I was so afraid. I was afraid I would fall harder in love and be hurt again and again."

"You were afraid of being abandoned, like you with your mother." The light finally clicked in her brain. "You saw me as someone safe."

"It's true, but please, don't think that's still the case." He laughed nervously, rubbing his hands against his tortured face. "That's not what I'm trying to say. I'm messing everything up here. It's how I originally saw you, like some perfect female. I was attracted to you like a moth to a flame, but what I feel now for you is based in reality."

"Are you sure?"

He took another step closer. "Yes, because when you came to me this morning, I could bear to see the pain in your eyes. I tried to fight it for self-preservation, but it's impossible. Nell, I'd do anything for you, regardless of what you feel for me. I just want you to be happy. And if that means we take it slow or that things don't work, then I'm okay with that. I love you anyway. And I'm willing to take the chance."

"Even if it ends badly?" She was falling for him, but she didn't want to hurt him. There was no guarantee that things would work out between them. Relationships weren't easy.

"Even if." He finally reached her, taking her hands in his. "I think we were both holding ourselves back. But neither of our issues really had to do with each other."

"I was so scared of losing someone I cared about again." The tightness in her stomach bore down again at the thought of it. It had been so hard, losing Gary. Almost too hard. "And it was one thing to think about dating, but another thing altogether to think about having real feelings for someone. I guess I didn't expect that, as silly as it sounds."

"I was so scared of losing the chance with you that I was afraid at the first blush of rejection. I don't want to live in fear. I'm ready to put mine aside. It's not worth not having you in my life."

It's what she wanted. She could see a future with Emiliano, the young shopkeeper from next door. It seemed crazy and unlikely, but her heart was already attaching itself to him in a scary and exhilarating way.

"Will you give me a second chance?" he asked.

She jumped. "Yes."

Emiliano closed his eyes, his head tilting forward. When he finally opened them, they were wet with unshed tears. "Thank you."

"Thank you." She smiled up at him and lifted herself onto her toes to kiss him. A soft, tentative kiss filled with tender emotion.

He pulled her closer, sliding one hand up underneath her hair and the other around her lower back. The kiss deepened until her head spun.

She pulled away, her heart and brain in overload. "It's crazy how much I want you, Emiliano. It still scares me. You scare me."

"You scare the hell out of me, Nell Wilder." He held out a hand to her, and she took it. "Let's be scared together."

"Let's go inside. It's getting cold out here." She pulled him after her, through the door, locking it behind them.

She could recover her glass in the morning. "And you can tell me why you're barefoot and in pajamas."

"That's a longer story, but let's just say I had a visitor tonight."

"A visitor?"

"My dad." A smile graced his full lips. "Things are going to be okay between us."

"I'm so glad."

"Me too."

"But why are you barefoot?" She still didn't understand.

"He reminded me to not be afraid to take a chance. I couldn't wait another minute."

"I'm glad you didn't." Another thread of tension that had been holding tight inside her relaxed. She was so proud Hugo had been the one to go and talk to him. Emiliano needed that.

She opened the door leading to the staircase of her apartment but heard him stop when his foot fell on the bottom stair. "Nell. Are you sure this is a good idea? I don't mean us. I mean, would you rather go back to my place?"

Turning, she saw his eyes held fast to the barn beam behind him, the one with the heart carved in it. The reminder of Gary's memory decorated the very walls of the building.

"Are you uncomfortable here?"

"No, I thought maybe you would be." His fingers found hers. "I want to be where you are."

She squeezed his hand. "Then, we're going up. And don't worry about Gary; he's given his blessing."

"What?" he said, not understanding.

Leading him through the stairwell to her small apartment, she turned to him. "I was struggling with moving on, so I had a conversation with him." "I see," he said, but she could tell he didn't.

"I know it was probably more a conversation I had with a part of myself that knows him completely, but it felt real, Emiliano. It put me at peace."

"Then, it doesn't matter what it was. It was real for you."

"Exactly. It helped me work through my doubts and fears."

Emiliano looked around her little home. "I've never been up here before."

Nell scanned the place. She hadn't appreciated it in a long while. It had been a painful memory lately. He took note of the decorations on the walls, little reminders of the life she'd built with Gary.

"It's not fancy, but it's home. And it has a great view."

The emotion she now felt was pride. It was still painful, but because of the love they'd shared. Because it had been real and true and good.

"Did Gary build all of this?" Emiliano asked, running a hand over the walls.

"Yes. I don't know if you remember, but the place was the old office for the marina. The roof was barely holding on. Instead of rebuilding it, we built up. And then, eventually, expanded the first floor out back." She pointed to the windows next to the little kitchen. "We were going to have a large deck out there or add to the living area. It depended on cost and timing."

"You still could."

"Yes, once things with the café stabilize, but it's not important at the moment. I still have to figure out the reopening."

"I'm sure you'll make it a splash." He smiled warmly.

"Thanks. I have some good ideas." And she'd figured them out all on her own.

Walking him through the living room, she gave him the fifteen-second tour of the rest of the house, ending at her room.

"The bedroom isn't large, but the closets make up for it. Gary built them so I could hang everything up. I don't really have a lot of fancy things, but it's so efficient for space."

The room itself only had a dresser, some floating shelves on the sides of the bed, and a bench at the foot of it. A small low dresser sat underneath the windows facing town. That was it. It was all she needed.

It was getting late, but she wasn't tired.

"Are you really sure about this?" His eyes searched hers, which were caught up in the nostalgia.

She gave him a reassuring smile. "I really am."

Taking his hand, she pulled him close. She hadn't realized she was also worried about how he felt being in Gary's old space, but at her tug, he filled the gap between them immediately, wrapping his arms around her. He held her as though she were made of gold.

Nell turned her face up to his. "Thank you for coming back tonight."

"I couldn't wait until tomorrow. I was worried you'd change your mind."

Rising on her toes, she kissed his lips. Those lips she'd been dreaming about for months. "That would be tough to do. You're a difficult man to ignore."

"You're impossible to ignore." He bent down and kissed her again, deepening it.

Want and desire spiraled down through her, circling tightly at her core. Her hands dipped lower, tightening on his round butt and pulling him close. He made an approving sound, his hands tightening around her as well while she slid her hands up his back to delight in the smooth muscles under his shirt.

She stepped back, watching his confused face at her breaking away from him.

"Off." She ordered him with her finger to remove his shirt. "I want to touch you. I want to see you. If that's okay."

"It's more than okay." He whipped his shirt over his head and dropped it on the floor.

She'd gotten to see him, to touch him, once before, but it still wasn't enough. Her fingers found the flesh of his chest. His skin was soft and velvety, pulled taut over his full pecs. She didn't feel embarrassed this time. In no rush, she pressed and stroked, running her hands down his front, over his bumpy abs, and hooked her fingers around the elastic waist of his plaid pajama bottoms.

He wasn't wearing any underwear. Her eyes flew to his, and he grinned wolfishly. "I told you I was in a rush. I didn't take time to change."

Nell bit her lip under his attention, her insides going liquid. It would be so easy to escalate things, but she wanted to take it slow and enjoy the feel of him. Walking around behind him, she let her hand trail over his delicious skin.

Feeling brave, she pressed her lips to his shoulder blade, causing him to shiver. She flicked out a tongue to taste him and kissed down his back. Her hands ran down his arms and sides, and his breathing grew ragged.

Walking back around him, she saw his mouth was open and his eyes glazed over. Her hands went back to his stomach, sliding down, but this time, she took his pj's with them. He stepped out of them.

Nell caught his glance and went to her knees. His eyes darkened like a fire lit them from behind. It was her turn. Taking him in her hand, she explored him with her tongue, eventually wrapping her mouth over him. He was clean and firm, and she delighted in the sensation. Her nails dug into his firm butt.

He moaned, his fingers diving into her hair, his hips pressing forward. "Nell."

She looked up at him, and his tortured eyes pushed her need.

He stumbled back. "I need you, Nell. I don't want it to end this quickly."

She stood up, and his fingers tugged at her shirt, pulling it up over her head. His mouth found hers, desperately crushing it, devouring it with white-hot heat.

They both fumbled at her jeans, dragging them down until she stepped back to finally rid herself of them. She pushed him onto the bed, and he flipped her underneath him, covering her with his body, pressing into her. He kissed her wildly.

His hands roamed all over her skin, pulling, tugging, kneading at her skin. She moaned at the building sensations between them. "I need you too."

His fingers slipped between her legs, finding the burning flames. He stoked them, sending her arching into the mattress, and she whimpered, her nails digging into his chest. But he held her mouth with his, drinking in her cries until she pulled away, gasping for breath and blindly reaching for the basket on the shelf beside her bed.

Her fingers shook on the foil square. He took it for her and rolled it on. Poised over her, he hesitated.

"Please, Emiliano. Please." Her toes curled with need, and her knees pulled him closer.

Leaning over her once more, he took her mouth and entered her. She cried out, her heels pressing into his butt. Then they moved faster, each panting and touching and moaning. It felt like the tight ball inside her couldn't get any more wound with desire. It built and hardened, and she bore down on it, begging for her sweet relief.

Finally, in a blinding explosion, her nerves crashed to the shore. They hit so deeply she could feel the aftershocks rippling from where they were joined. He cried out soon after, following her over the edge. He stiffened, holding her tightly.

They stayed like that for moments, tight in each other's grip, until their breaths evened out.

The look he gave her held so much hope and adoration that her heart cracked further. It ached. Not like a wound bleeding painfully, but more like a surge so large that it didn't fit its previous shell.

Tears fell in streams down the sides of her face.

"Oh, Nell. Sweetheart. Are you okay?" His hands cradled her face.

"Yes." She tried to smile through the tears, her hands pulling him close. "I'm just happy. That's all. Very, very happy with you."

"Oh, thank goodness." His head fell to her chest, holding her tight for a moment, before he kissed the skin between her breasts.

He rolled to his side and pulled her close. She wrapped a leg over his, getting as near as she could to him. His hands ran up and down her back, causing goosebumps to spring u p.

They kissed and snuggled in, holding each other until they fell asleep.

CHAPTER 32

"We have another order for the rockfish." Maggie burst into the kitchen and slid the new slips onto her tension strip. "And two more to go. Heath will be here in ten to pick them up."

"Got it." Nell scanned the details, her hands moving of their own accord to toss butter into the hot skillet. She wiped her forehead with the back of her arm. She'd signed up for Emiliano's delivery service, and people were loving the convenience. If this took off like she suspected, she would have to hire more help. "Is Fran here yet?"

"She just arrived. She brought her son. He's adorable."

"He's probably already half in love with you," Nell teased her friend. The kids always loved the small blonde.

"Nah, that's your department." Maggie danced back to avoid the towel whip Nell snapped in her direction, howling with laughter.

"Emiliano's not a kid anymore."

"Not even close." Maggie smiled broadly.

Their reopening was a success so far. Fran chose that day to visit, anxious to see what she would come up with. The special of the day was pecan-encrusted rockfish with a beurre-blanc sauce, rice pilaf, and garlicky green beans, with dried cranberries, almond slivers, and orange zest.

And she was debuting a new line of desserts that she'd worked with Willa on. The Immunity Ice Cream with echinacea, rose hips, and mint. Willa had added a few other herbs of choice for a strong immune system. The Happy Hazelnut Cake was infused with uplifting herbs and sea salt. Bliss Bars. She'd left those just the way they were: dark-chocolate bars swirled with tahini and topped with smoked seaweed. Chocolate spoke for itself. Finally, Relax Rosemary Shortbread with chamomile and cranberries.

The desserts were a good way to promote Willa's herbal remedies, not that she needed it after the way she'd helped the town recover. It also made it easier for Nell to sneak a few of her emotion powers into her dinners. Willa's herbal background made it a little less fantastical.

Based on Duke's suggestion, except for the Immunity Ice Cream, Willa had simply provided the herbs, not infused them with her magical intentions. She let Nell do that. They didn't know what would happen if they double-dosed people.

She also had plans to make Giggle Gooey Butter Cake, but they'd just be for her and the crew. It probably wasn't too good of an idea to have anything that obvious on the menu. Now that everyone in town was on the mend, customers had come back in droves. Quite a few of them had ordered the Immunity Ice Cream, just to be safe. Nell planned on serving it any time a bug went through town.

Who didn't like fresh, tangy, mint ice cream, anyway?

"Is the crowd dying down at all yet?" Nell asked Maggie, who was taking pictures of her for her social media account.

"It's starting to. By the time Fran's done eating, you'll have time to sit with her and talk business."

"Perfect." It was what she was hoping for, but with the turnout, she'd been worried.

"And I can take over for a little while after that." Maggie poked her with a finger. "You hired extra help tonight. It'll be fine."

"You're right. It will be." Nell enjoyed the look of surprise on Maggie's face as she pushed two salads into her hands. "Now, get back out there and deliver this to table nine."

Maggie shut her mouth. "Aye, aye, boss."

Nell smiled, pleased with herself. The last few days had passed like a dream. She'd been busy with plans during the day while Emiliano worked to get Gil's Market and Marina up and running online. Boat owners were even able to pay for their docking fees online. Hugo and he were still arguing over the details, volleying back and forth, declaring why each other's ideas wouldn't work until one would bend and they found a compromise.

They would figure it out.

In the evenings, they were still discovering each other. She wasn't ready to share him with her friends just yet. Every night, she'd either go to his place or he'd come to hers, where they ripped each other's clothes off before they could talk about the day. That always came after, lying naked, wrapped in each other's arms.

Once they were able to get a handle on that, she'd have everyone over. Maybe in a few weeks.

Or months. She grinned again.

Finishing a handful more orders, she looked up to see no new slips on the bar. Washing her hands, she took her apron off and wandered out onto the floor to say hi to several couples.

Maggie made a beeline for her. "Fran just finished. Take your time. I've got the kitchen."

"Thanks." Nell approached her table. "Okay if I join you two?"

The winemaker nodded happily, extending a hand. "Of course. I've been dying for you to get out here and tell you how delicious this food is. You remember Albert."

"Hi, Albert," Nell said to the young boy sitting next to his mom. He was drawing in a notebook. "Looks like you've got an artist in the family."

Fran nodded, her gray curls bobbing. "He loves to draw."

"I'm glad you enjoyed everything." Nell sat down.

"It was wonderful." Fran's eyes rolled to the ceiling. "That rockfish. I'm going to have dreams about it."

"Thanks for giving me a chance after the health-department fiasco."

"That wasn't your fault. I'm so glad they caught the guy."

"Me too." Pride filled her that it was Emiliano and her friends who put a stop to it.

"I'd be honored if you featured Mt. Olympus Cellar wines at The Wild Café." Fran inclined her head. "We're releasing new ones next month. If you're up for it, we could do it here and pair the wines with a four-course meal. I can do the regular pick-up party at a later date. Maybe you could do some small plates for that as well."

Nell's heart soared. "That would be perfect! I'll get started on the menu right away."

"I'll send over some bottles for inspiration."

"I can't wait."

"I was also thinking about some prepared charcuterie platters. And maybe some other finger foods."

"Let me see what I can come up with." Nell tapped on her chin. "I also know a local woodworker who makes beautiful charcuterie boards. If you were interested in it, I'm sure he'd give you a discount for a larger order. I could prepare the contents, and you'd just need someone to transfer it to the board for serving."

"That's a great idea!" Fran leaned forward. "Wooden boards would look so classy to deliver it to the guests, and everyone loves the local-artist touch." She extended her hand across the table and continued, "I think we're going to have a happy business partnership."

"Me, too." Nell shook her hand. "Can I interest either of you in some Happy Hazelnut Cake?"

Fran looked at Albert, who was smiling all the way to his eyes and nodded his head excitedly. She laughed. "I think that's a yes."

Nell stood, her chair scraping on the floor. "I'll bring them right out. And dinner is on me."

"Are you sure?"

"Absolutely."

Elated, Nell walked back to her kitchen, where she saw Gary's barn beam standing at the entrance, between the two dining rooms full of happy customers. He'd always known they'd fill the place. Her heart gave a sweet pang.

Gary was proud of her. She knew that with as much certainty as she knew how to make bread.

Maggie brushed past her, stopping when she reached her.

"Nell." The waitress laid a hand on her arm, her eyes flicking around the room. "You better tone it down. The place is vibrating."

She spun to see everyone laughing and carrying on. The energy was palpable, and she stifled a giggle with her hand.

"Oops."

Maggie shook her head and propped her fists on her waist. "Try to rein it in."

"No promises." She winked, disappearing into her kitchen.

"Solomon's out getting razor clams." Emiliano popped his head into the doorway of her kitchen. He'd seen the man out on the sandy part of the beach in the twilight with his clamming gun. It was the best time of day for it. "Want any?"

"Ooh!" He could see her fade off, considering the possibilities. "I could put them on the menu tomorrow."

"You can." He walked over to her and touched her jaw gently. She lifted her face to his, laying a kiss on her lips. "Let me know how many you want."

"I'll take two buckets if you can spare them."

"You know he'll get more than that, besides"—he shrugged—"others will be out, too. It's the season. We'll still have some on ice for the locals."

"Okay," she said, mollified. Then her eyes brightened. "They're ready. You've got to try this."

Spinning, she grabbed a towel and removed a hot pan from her oven.

They smelled heavenly. Dark-chocolate cookies studded with chocolate flakes. A clean, herbal scent filled the air along with the deep, heavy cocoa.

"Mint?" He sniffed the bubbling cookies.

"And a touch of espresso powder. And sea salt." Using her spatula, she slid a few off the tray and onto her cooling rack.

"Sea salt?" He raised an eyebrow, knowing it meant they'd all be in a good mood by the end of the night.

"Of course." She rolled her eyes, then winked playfully at him. "You can't have chocolate without sea salt."

"Or seaweed, apparently," he pointed out.

"True." She smiled.

He snagged a hot cookie from the rack, passing it from hand to hand. He'd stuffed it in his mouth, moaning around the melty chocolatey goodness. The mint was strong, but so was the bitterness from the chocolate. It was a punch of flavor, with just enough sugar to make him want to dive back in for another. "Oh, man, that's good."

"Careful." She swatted him. "They're hot."

"Not as hot as you." He planted a kiss on her mouth.

She smiled up at him, kissing him once more. He lingered, extending it.

She pulled away, peering up at him. One of her hands played with the V in his button-up shirt. "Are you nervous about tonight?"

Emiliano's heart gave a heavy thump. "No."

She raised an eyebrow.

"Maybe a little." He looked away. The last few weeks had been amazing. For the past week or so, they'd just stayed at her place. He still hadn't gotten around to unpacking, and at this point, it didn't seem to make sense anymore.

Tonight would be his first time for dinner with the crew.

He'd seen them all since they officially got together, but it wasn't the same thing as being invited to dinner with them. That was inner-circle stuff.

"You don't have to be. They're going to love you as much as I do." She froze, her eyes flying to his.

He didn't speak. Couldn't speak.

"I should have told you earlier, but I was feeling nervous about it." Her hands clenched his shirt. "I know you've confessed your feelings quite openly, and I'm grateful for it, but...it was still difficult to say them back. I wanted to be sure."

"And you are?" His chest felt constricted. He wanted it so much.

She nodded, tears welling up in her eyes.

He felt moisture slid down his cheeks, and he peppered her face with minty kisses.

"Oh, thank goodness." He held her head to his chest, cradling it like the gift she was to his life. "Thank you so much."

"For loving you?" She bent back to look up at him.

"Yes. For loving me back."

"You make it easy to love you. Me, not so much."

"That's not true. We just had to get out of our own ways, respectively." "I'm glad we were able to." She pulled him tight.

"Me, too." He stroked her hair and pressed a kiss onto the crown of her head. "I'm glad you were able to find room in your heart for me."

"I'm not sure I did." Nell glanced at him, and he brushed aside a stray hair, tucking it behind her ear. "I think my heart expanded. I can't explain it any other way. Gary's always going to be there."

"I understand that." He really did. And he'd made peace with it. He'd always respected the man. He just hoped the rest of Gary's friends would feel the same way.

"But you are there, too, now." Tears fell from her eyes at that, and he wanted to kiss them away.

"Does it still hurt?" His hands ran up and down her back, trying to soften it.

"It's a little of both. It hurts, but it also feels good that it hurts. Does that make any sense?"

"I'm not sure."

"It's like a perfectly baked croissant; it takes your breath away. You don't want to ruin it by eating it, but if you don't enjoy it, it's wasted."

"I'm not one hundred percent sure I can relate to your analogy."

"It hurts because it was beautiful. I got to have what so few people get."

"I'm so glad you had that."

He meant it with his whole heart, even though it was about another man. It was complicated, but it was true.

"I'm going to honor that memory and let it hurt sometimes. I want to delight in the beautiful pain of it. Because I got to experience it."

His arms tightened, holding her close through another round of tears. To be treasured by a woman capable of that kind of care was the biggest honor in the world. This, from a man who'd felt unlovable for a good chunk of his life.

"And I get to have it again. Somehow, I was seen worthy to find love again."

He cupped her cheek and kissed her tears. His heart filled, feeling fuller than it had in years. "You are so very worthy. I'm honored that you chose me to share that beautiful, boundless heart with."

Shelby hit the door open, interrupting their beautiful moment. "He's here!" She skidded to a halt, her face forming a perfect "O." "Sorry, I'm just gonna..."

She backed out, eyes wide.

Emiliano and Nell laughed through their tears.

"You can come back," Emiliano hollered, letting Nell go. If he didn't, he'd be dragging her upstairs to kiss her senseless. Instead, he wiped his eyes and sniffled away his tears.

Shelby's head poked through the door, her eyes shut tightly. "Are you sure?"

"Yes." Nell grabbed her arm and pulled her through. "And who's here?"

"Nick!" Shelby exclaimed.

"Oh, already?" Nell jumped up and clapped her hands together in delight. "My wood-fired pizza oven."

"Are you sure you want to try it for the first time with everyone?" Emiliano asked Nell, but his eyes were on Shelby. "You don't want to test it out first?"

"Oh, yeah." Nell's face fell. "That might have been a good idea."

Shelby's mouth turned upside down, the sides curling downward, deep and menacing. "And here I thought I liked you."

Emiliano laughed.

Nell raced out to the back deck.

He took a moment to look around the kitchen. Nell's kitchen, but also Gary's home. And now, she'd made a place for him in it. Taking his time, he followed and stopped by the barn beam, looking up at the heart Gary'd carved for her. His palm sat on the wood, feeling the hands her late husband had touched the wood with, had sanded i t with.

"Thank you," he said. "I'll take care of her. I promise."

Nodding, he turned to follow the two women, but stopped short. Duke stood watching him. He'd obviously heard him talking to his old friend. Emiliano wasn't sure how the older man would take his message. It was persona-l.

Duke blinked and coughed, then he nodded.

"I know you will." He walked over and clapped Emiliano on his back. "Come on, man. We're needed out back. And we've a few things to tell you."

CHAPTER 33

"Are you sure it's not too early to tell them about me moving in?" Emiliano handed Nell the largest platter for the seafood pasta. It had been four weeks since they officially accepted him as their own, and Willa, Duke, Maggie, and Shelby had shared about the powers they'd received the night of the storm.

Nell couldn't have asked for it to have gone better, even if Emiliano was endlessly fascinated with Maggie's powers.

"Come on. You've been living here for over a month now."

"True, but I've unpacked my things in there." His eyes went to the floor above them. "And we packed some of Gary's things up."

"We did." She nodded, stopping to lay a hand on his chest. "It was time. They'll be okay with it. You really only have to worry about Shelby."

"Why's that?"

"She'll lose her rent." Nell flashed a smile back to him, carrying the platter out the door. "It'll have to go back on the market."

"Nah, I would have paid out the rest of my year. I signed a contract." Emiliano followed her out, carrying the two bowls of salads she'd already gotten ready. "But it's a moot point now. I have it figured out."

"What do you mean?" Nell asked.

"An old friend is going to take over the rent. And we can get serious about what we want to do here if you're ready."

They'd talked about expanding the upstairs apartment. Nell had thought they'd have a year to figure it out.

"Or we can look around. I know you like that house up on the hill."

"What house?" He couldn't possibly know.

"The house you used to talk about in high school." He set the bowls on the tables outside. "I think it's up for sale again."

"You mean Bea's old place?"

He nodded.

Her mouth dropped open. She could actually have it if she wanted to. Oddly, it didn't mean as much to her as it had when she was young. But maybe it did to him. To have a home without the ghost of Gary hanging around.

"Would you prefer to have a place of our own?"

"It doesn't matter to me." He took her in his arms. "I love being close to the market and able to check in on Pops."

"Argue with him, more like it." She smiled up at him.

He shrugged. "It's good for him. Besides, he's actually making his own changes now."

"Really?"

"Yeah. He's considering adding another row of docks to the marina. And he wanted to talk to you about an outdoor stand with premade sandwiches for people just coming through for gas."

Her eyebrows rose.

"But don't tell him I told you. He wanted to ask you himself," he went on. "I thought it was best to prep you first."

"Do you think it's a bad idea?"

"No, I just wasn't sure if you had the scope for it right now, with the summer season settling in. The café's been slammed most days. You've been exhausted several nights this week."

He dropped his mouth to her neck, nibbling at her skin. She giggled and tried to pull away, but he held her close, tickling her with kisses.

"I'm sorry. Maybe we'll get upstairs earlier tonight."

"You don't ever have to be sorry." He frowned. "I just worry about you. Anyway, I want you to make your own decision. Don't feel pressured on the stand idea."

It was a fair point. She'd always focused so much on anything financially advantageous that it was hard to consider saying no. "Let me think on it. If I can find that extra person, I might be able to swing it."

"That's fair. Just be clear with Pops. He can be very stubborn."

"I know. It's where you get it from," she teased him.

He went back after her neck, and she danced away, almost avoiding his grip.

"Do you guys ever stop?" Shelby appeared on the deck steps, rolling her eyes, but she was smiling. "And is the wine open? I had a helluva week."

"I brought some." Duke appeared behind her. "Hurry on up, and I'll get it opened."

"I didn't bring anything," Nick said, filing in with Willa and Maggie close behind.

"You brought me a wood-fired pizza oven last month. You've filled your quota for at least three years," Nell told him.

"But you paid for it." Nick frowned.

"It doesn't matter. You underpriced it, and you know it. Besides, it's absolutely perfect on the corner of the deck." Nell turned to admire the beautiful brick structure with a wood cabinet beneath it. He'd worked copper into the doors and even made her wooden pizza peels to slide them i n.

Nick dropped his gaze, uncomfortable with the praise. "It's okay."

They gathered around the table of food, and Duke poured glasses all around. Even Willa took one.

"We're celebrating tonight." Nell lifted her drink.

"Why's that?" Shelby asked.

Rain splattered onto the table.

"I'll take care of that." Maggie wiggled her fingers dramatically. She already knew about Emiliano moving his things in. She'd been around all week. So she concentrated on the clouds over them and pushed her hands out. "I think that'll work."

Emiliano stared into the darkening sky. "That's so freaking cool."

"What's your news?" Willa asked. She was smiling smugly, as though she already knew.

"Emiliano's moved in, for good," Nell told them.

Duke raised his glass.

"Good for you," Nick said, reaching over to clap Emiliano's shoulder. "It's nice having you around."

"Thanks." Emiliano blushed. It was too cute. "You can have your plywood back."

Nick waved it off. "If you don't need it."

"Don't really have room for it, but thanks."

Nick studied the roofline. "You could expand it if you wanted to. I could help."

Emiliano's hand found hers under the table, and he squeezed it. "We're still figuring out what to do."

The smile didn't leave Willa's face.

"What is it?" Nell asked her.

Her friend shared a look with Nick, and he shrugged.

"Well, I don't want to take away from your celebration, but we had something to share, too," Willa said.

"Holy cow, look at that ring!" Shelby pointed, noticing the glint on Willa's finger.

It wasn't large. A small green solitaire sat surrounded by white gold branches.

"Congratulations!" Nell jumped from her seat to gather her friend in her arms. Maggie and Shelby joined her in a four-way hug between the women.

"That's so you, Willa," Maggie said, admiring it. "I love it."

"I do, too." Willa beamed.

"We need to toast that." Emiliano raised his glass.

"To Nick and Willa." Duke lifted his drink high. "I'm glad she has you, man. You're a good match for our little Flower Child."

"Thanks, Duke," Willa said, smiling at her friend.

Nell took her seat next to Emiliano and pressed into him. "Isn't that wonderful?"

"It is." He wrapped an arm around her shoulders.

"I think we should build on. I want to stay here."

"I like that idea." His thumb rubbed circles on her skin, and he leaned in. "We haven't talked about it, but how do you feel about kids?"

Nell's eyes flew open, and she turned in his arms, heart fluttering in her chest. "Kids?"

"Just thinking about how many bedrooms we might need." He winked. "When you're ready."

She'd kind of assumed she wouldn't have any, that it wasn't in the cards for her, but she had a whole new future stretching out in front of her.

The rest of the crew was talking to Shelby about her week, not being privy to her conversation with Emiliano.

"It's the second time this month those pipes have broken," Shelby said, digging into the pasta. "This time, I had to hire someone."

"It's probably because you fixed them last time," Duke teased her.

Shelby shot him a death stare, but he only laughed.

"It's because the pipes are old. I need to think seriously if I want to rebuild all of them or start over on another plot of land."

"The land you're looking at buying to expand?" Maggie asked.

"Yeah, I can't decide if I want to do an expansion or something different like a few larger cabins."

"That's a good idea. We don't have any shortage of tourists," Nick said. "Let me know if you need help with any of it."

"You can count on it." Shelby crossed her legs. "I just gotta talk to the county about permits, and I need to get a perc test done. Charles already had one done, but he didn't file it, so I'll have to get it done again. He said it came through clean, though. It's ready to be built on."

"This Charles is the guy you've been meeting with, right?" Nell asked. Shelby didn't typically talk about any of her business meetings by name.

Shelby nodded.

"Are you dating him?" Maggie asked incredulously.

The dark-haired woman coughed and took a long pull from her wineglass. "No, why would you think that?"

Maggie slid a sideways look at Nell.

"What?" Shelby said, voice higher pitched than before.

"You just seem very excited about this opportunity with him." Willa smiled. "That's not a bad thing."

Shelby humphed. "We'll see. Men are too much work."

"One of these days, you'll find someone who will make you eat those words," Duke told the love-scorned woman. "It'll be fun to watch."

"So you say." She pursed her lips in response. "I can't wait until *you* fall for someone!"

Duke went quiet. "I'm a loner, you're not."

"Ha." Shelby scooped up a mouthful of pasta. "No offense, Willa and Nell. You guys found good ones, ones that are crazy in love with you, ones that'll stick around." Realizing everyone had fallen silent, she winced. "Seriously, I didn't mean to kill the mood. I'm so rry."

"It's okay," Nell told her. "We just want to see you happy too."

"I am happy. I make my own decisions, and no one tells me what to do." Shelby took another sip of wine and then looked around the group. "I just did it again. C rap."

"I wasn't ready for a real relationship until I met Willa. I get it," Nick said.

"Still." Shelby tried for a smile. "Love won for you guys. That's awesome. And I'm so glad you got your second chance at love."

She was trying, but it was obvious she was still sore after Keane left her. Nell wondered if she'd ever trust another man.

Shelby's eyes caught on a figure on the beach. "Who's that?"

"It's probably Solomon out clamming." Nell turned to look. The man was down near Emiliano's old place. "No, he's too tall. Maybe a tourist."

"Oh, no, that's Keane." Emiliano popped a shrimp in his mouth, chewing happily. "That's what I was trying to tell you. I found a renter."

The blood drained from Shelby's face.

"Did I do something wrong?" he asked, leaning in.

"Um." Nell struggled with the right words to say.

"Is that not okay?" He glanced from person to person. "You guys used to all be friends."

"He didn't exactly leave on good terms." Nell's eyes cut to Shelby, and Emiliano's widened, understanding what she was implying.

The woman still hadn't uttered a word.

"Shelby." Willa got her attention. "Maybe this is a good thing."

"Maybe he's here to make things right," Nell said. "You can get a second chance at love, too. You just have to be open to it."

Her bitter friend shot to her feet. "Keane is a lot of things: arrogant jerk, butt-faced miscreant. You take your pick, but he's no idiot. If he thinks he's going to waltz in here and pick up where he left off, he's got another thing coming."

With that, she stormed off the deck, making a beeline straight for him.

Thank you so much for your support. I hope you enjoyed Willa and Nick's story as much as I did. I've had Willa's story in my heart for a long time and am thrilled to finally being able to give life to it.

If you liked it, the nicest thing you can do is leave me a good review on Amazon, Bookbub, Goodreads, or wherever you review books.

Connect with me online:

Website: **jenflanaganbooks.com**

Follow me on Amazon

Facebook: **@jenflanaganbooks**

Instagram: **@jenflanagan_author**

Bookbub: **@jen_flanagan**

Join my reader group on Facebook: **Flanagan's Fanatics**

Please visit my website and subscribe to my newsletter at **jenflanaganbooks.com** for upcoming books, events, and free content.

About the Author

Jen Flanagan is a #1 Amazon best-selling author of enchanting magical romance and cozy mysteries, set in the mystical Olympic Peninsula. Her stories weave adventure, intriguing locations, and a touch of magic into tales of love and mystery, featuring richly drawn characters. A lover of travel, history, and culture, Jen offers readers a delightful escape into worlds where magic feels real.

Author of the Orca Cove and Detective Malone series, she also writes non-fiction as Willa Daniels. When not writing, she enjoys culinary magic, surrounded by good food, friends, coffee, and her beloved pups.

Connect with her at her website, Facebook group, or newsletter:

jenflanaganbooks.com

WHAT'S NEXT?

Looking for more Orca Cove? Can't wait to find out what happens next? Shelby has a lot of anger over Keane leaving her when they were younger. You know what they say about a woman scorned. It's a doozy! Turn the page for the first chapter of **Star Crossed!**

If I've piqued your interest in herbalism, look up **An Introduction to Herbalism,** by none other than Willa Daniels, my non-fiction penname. I've got several more non-fiction books in the works as part of The Natural Path series.

If mystery is more your thing, check out **The Detective Malone Series**, a non-paranormal, cozy detective mystery series.

Star Crossed

Chapter 1

Fury descended upon Keane Lennox like a hurricane. The onslaught of words directed his way whipped around him, filling his entire being with awe as would a raging storm or being thrown by thunderous waves. Shelby stood in front of him, her chest rising and falling with rage. But he knew her. He saw the pain in the pinpoints of her eyes. Those beautiful green eyes. It broke his heart.

But he'd broken hers first.

He was powerless to do anything but revel in her presence. After all this time.

He hadn't seen her, really seen her, for years. He hadn't seen her face, hadn't smelled her spicy citrus scent, hadn't felt her toned muscles gliding under her soft skin. He'd gone away to chase a dream, and after being away too long, he hadn't had the courage to come home to those he had abandoned.

Fifteen years was a long time.

Her face had thinned out from her youth, but the freckle just outside her eyebrow was still there. Her hair was still a dark, rich chestnut, and he wondered if she'd cut it recently. The ends hovered over her shoulders, thick, shiny, and straight. An object of perfection and poise.

All except those eyes. There was nothing proper about her eyes. Green as the grass, her slanted eyes sparked with electricity as though competing with the stars in the night sky above them. Even when they weren't lit with anger, they sparkled with humor, sass, and the promise of mischief. She was as he remembered her, and yet different. Pain and pleasure flooded his heart.

Her fists clenched as another shower of words flowed from her perfectly formed lips, her cheeks burning with a rosy hue. She was power defined.

It was glorious.

A smile twitched at his mouth. He struggled to contain his reaction. She stopped mid-sentence, her eyes narrowing.

"Well?" she demanded.

"It's good to see you, Greene." He released the smile he'd been holding back, knowing he looked like a schoolboy enamored by his crush. Crush? Hell, she was the love of his life.

Shelby's face dropped for a second, a wave of emotion passing over it. Her foot slid back several inches. Then her chin set, and she let out a guttural, frustrated cry.

This time, color rose to ring those beautiful eyes, pinched in pain. Damn, he hated that he had hurt her. If he could change anything, it would be that. But before he could say anything, she wheeled on the ball of her foot and stamped off, her shoulders tight and her back rigid.

Keane lurched forward, taking a few steps across the pebble beach to follow her retreat into the darkness. He froze. No, not yet. She was too angry. There was no talking to Shelby when she was like that. He'd wait until she had gotten used to the fact that he was back before attempting to talk to her. Tonight, it would be raw. She'd probably drown herself in ice cream and fall asleep in a sugar coma.

Keane watched her full retreat, unable to break his gaze from her after so long only holding her in his memory. His eyes followed her figure, illuminated by the parking lot light between the Wild Café and Gil's Market and Marina, to a car in the lot. Headlights passed him as she headed east of town, where he knew her cabins sat on a four-acre lot.

She'd only continued to thrive after he left, not that it surprised him.

Duke's ship sat out at the end of the marina from where she'd come. He knew from his parents that his old friend was still single. Duke was too wild to settle down, at least the Duke he remembered was. But that didn't mean Shelby hadn't found someone to fill the hole he'd left.

She had every right to be pissed at him. He shouldn't have left as he had. He didn't regret his decision, sadly enough, only how he'd done it. He should have talked to her first, explained why he had to go. He'd been so young and had made so many mistakes.

Keane wondered if Nell was on board the ship. Tension laced his heart again. He owed her an apology as well. He hadn't been here for her or for her late husband, his other best friend, when he passed the year before. He'd only found out about it after he returned from a

six-month-long art exhibit tour in Europe. He'd been too l
ate.

He didn't deserve to grieve with his old crew if he
couldn't even be here to say goodbye to his friend.

Tearing his eyes off the gleaming hull bobbing in the
dark waves, he saw an orca fin cut through the water.

Man, he missed the cove. He itched to find a surfboard
and get back into the sea, even if it was just to use it as
a paddleboard. He'd have to drive it up to the Strait of
Juan de Fuca or to the Pacific coast if he wanted to do real
surfing.

Or do what he used to in high school and head to Puget
Sound for some tug surfing. The thought of it lifted his
spirits.

The lights were still on in Shelby's apartment, the one
she owned that he was now renting. He trudged through
the loose rocks to the back deck and reentered. He'd run
into Emiliano a couple of days ago when he arrived in town
with no place to stay. The fit, younger man recently moved
out and offered to lease it to him, assuming he was doing
Shelby a favor by finding a new renter.

The shop owner's kid had grown up and filled out.
And from the sound of it, Nell had somehow found love

again with him. It was a bit of a shock, thinking Nell and Gary could be anything but Nell and Gary, but then again, Keane and Shelby had once been the same. It was hard to imagine anything different. Back then.

He had something to offer her now. He'd never had the courage to ask his parents if Shelby found someone, but if she had, he wouldn't pursue her. He wouldn't take that away from her. Wouldn't ask her to.

As hard as it would be, he wouldn't be able to stay and watch her with another man. Logically, he knew she'd had to have dated since him. Hell, he'd dated over the years, in between thinking he'd never make it or while convinced she'd moved on. If she'd found love, he'd make things right with Nell, catch up with Duke, and find another place to call home. Maybe closer to New York or Los Angeles. Europe or Belize didn't sound bad either. Anything but seeing Shelby smile into some other man's eyes.

And if she hadn't found someone... Well, he'd move hell or high water to get her back.

Shelby Greene slammed through her front door, finally allowing the sob to escape her throat. Tears flowed freely down her face. She locked the door and leaned against it, as if the wood barrier would keep her safe from all the memories pouring out of her heart. As if it would keep her from running back to him, only to be hurt again.

She pressed her forehead against the thick cedar. The solid wood would never betray her. It would never abandon her. She had worked hard for her little cabin, the last in a row of ten that she owned and operated as Siren's Song Cabins at the edge of town. She'd done it by herself. She'd needed his support to build up her business when she was a teenager, barely an adult, but no longer. She gathered her own strength from no one but herself now.

Sniffing, she pushed away from the door, her hand wiping her cheeks dry. Her spine straightened, and she raised her chin. Nope. Not her. She didn't need anyone anymore.

Opening her freezer, she got out a half-full container of Mint Moose Tracks ice cream. She grabbed her largest spoon, plunked down on her soft leather couch, and toed off her Chelsea boots. Settling into the fluffy pillows, she stuffed her face with the minty, chocolatey goodness.

Ice cream made everything better.

A buzzing in her pocket indicated one of her friends was trying to check in on her. It would be Willa. Nope. She didn't want to talk. Not now.

Tomorrow, she'd put on a brave face and leave it behind her. Today, she was going to nurse her wounds.

How was she going to do that with Keane Lennox in Orca Cove? Keane freaking Lennox! Another loaded spoonful popped into her mouth. Mmm. Sugar was good.

Was he here to stay? She shoveled another mouthful in to tamp down the seed of hope threatening to sprout. If she'd mattered to him, he wouldn't have left in the first place. Another mouthful. Not going there.

Her phone chirped. A message this time. She debated ignoring it, but knowing Willa, she would just stop by unannounced. That would be okay if she wanted to shovel ice cream into her face as well—the two had done that when Willa hit a rough patch—but she'd want to talk.

Checking her phone, she found two texts. One from Willa, as expected. "Are you okay? I can come over."

"I'm fine. Just need space," Shelby replied.

"I can bring ice cream."

That earned her a snort. The wild child was learning. "Got some. All good."

There was no way the herbalist wouldn't want to talk about it. She didn't know when to let a person work through their emotions. Not everything needed to be talked through.

"Talk tomorrow?" Willa texted.

She sent a thumbs-up emoji. Not likely.

The other message was from Emiliano. It simply said. "Sorry. I didn't know."

"I figured," she texted back.

A few seconds later, another line appeared. "I can tell him to find another place."

She considered it, but decided it wasn't worth losing the money. Cash was king, after all. And the now-famous painter could afford it.

"Nah, New York money is as good as Washington money."

She was definitely increasing the rent.

Emiliano had leased his place, having rented it from her before officially moving in with Nell. Correction, it was her place. The shop owner couldn't have realized what that would mean to her. She had bought it for her and Keane to start their adult life together after selling the record collection she'd driven to Spokane to pick up. With that and the entirety of what she'd put into her Roth IRA, against her advisor's urging.

She wasn't able to stay in the cute waterfront apartment after he'd left. Too many memories. It had prompted her purchase of the dilapidated cabin at the edge of town, though. And the submission of her business proposal to the bank. Back when they did that sort of thing. She'd pulled every string, gotten every reference letter she could possibly get, even joined the city council as the youngest member in history, but she'd done it. And they'd granted her the money to build Siren's Song Cabins.

A smile at the memory slid across her milky, icy lips. She'd paid it off in ten years. It was only four cabins back then. She'd stayed in the rundown cabin until the first one was up. She'd fixed up the original one and converted it into a registration office. The rent from the perfect little waterfront apartment paid for her mortgage payments and what conservative amount she allowed herself to live on.

It had taken her three more years to build the remaining units. Yep, she'd done fine without him. She didn't need him, after all. Scraping the bottom of the container, she slurped up the sweet, mint milk cream.

Exhaustion pulled at her. Either that or the amount of sugar she had consumed. Either way, she pushed the now-empty container onto her live-edge coffee table and settled into the corner of the couch. Keane's face floated into her mind, his eyes crinkled in the corners while he laughed. His wind-swept, nearly black hair tucked behind his ears like the surfer boy he was. Washington surfer boys looked different from California ones. Instead of sun-tanned skin and bleach-blonde hair, it was all about staying warm and having the courage to jump into icy water. Teenager Keane had practically lived in his wetsuit.

His hair was longer now; she remembered the man she had verbally assaulted on the beach. He'd worn it pulled back into a bun. Freaking man-bun. She rolled her eyes, even though she couldn't say it didn't flatter him.

He felt different now. More mature. Less devil-may-care.

Shelby squeezed her eyes shut to kill the images of him, but it didn't help. She tried to get angry again, but she couldn't. Sleep tugged, and even though she was fighting it, all she could do was think about Keane.

<u>**Jen Flanagan Fiction Books**</u>
Orca Cove Series:
Saltwater Cures

Uncharted Waters

Star Crossed

Red Skies (coming 2026)

Rogue Wave (coming 2026)

Books in the Detective Malone Series:
Bad Company

Here I Go Again

Under Pressure

<u>**Willa Daniels Non-Fiction Books**</u>
Stand-alone books:
The Art of Living Seasonally

The Natural Path Series:
An Introduction to Herbalism

An Introduction to Soap Making

An Introduction to Sourdough (coming 2025)

Home and Cleaning Solutions (coming 2026)

Body and Skincare Solutions (coming 2027)

9 781961 501027